RUDE ASTRONAUTS

Other Books by Allen Steele

Orbital Decay (1989)
Clarke County, Space (1990)
Lunar Descent (1991)
Labyrinth of Night (1992)
The Jericho Iteration (forthcoming)

RUDE ASTRONAUTS

Real and Imagined Stories

by

ALLEN STEELE

✳ ✳ ✳

Old Earth Books
Baltimore, Maryland

First U.S. edition.

Library of Congress Cataloging-in-Publication Data

Steele, Allen M.
Rude Astronauts : real and imagined stories / by Allen Steele.
p. cm.
ISBN 1-882968-00-X (alk. paper), — ISBN 1-882968-01-8 (pbk. : alk. paper)
1. Science fiction, American.   I. Title
PS3569.T338425R83   1993
813'.54--dc20   93-16413
                  CIP

Old Earth Books, P.O. Box 19951, Baltimore, Maryland 21211, USA.

For Ken Moore

ACKNOWLEDGEMENTS

Nothing gets written in a vacuum, especially not a collection of short stories. There are quite a few people who need to be thanked for helping, either directly or indirectly, to get these stories published. Although it's tempting to categorize them, I'd just as soon list them alphabetically and let the reader try to figure out who did what.

Aiding and abetting in the creation of <u>Rude Astronauts</u> were: Russell Banks, Deborah Beale, Gregory Benford, Michael C. Bingham, Mary-Rita Blute, Edward Bryant, Ginjer Buchanan, Dan Caldwell, Gardner Dozois, Art Dula, Rick Dunning, Donald and Genevieve Edwards, Harlan Ellison, Loren Ghiglione, Martin H. Greenberg, Frank and Joyce Jacobs, Bob Jennings, Steven Jones-d'Agostino, Dan Kaplan, Terry and Linda Kepner, James Patrick Kelly, Bob Liddil, Martha Millard, Ken Moore, Dorothy Mosokowski, Richard Phelps, the late Joel Oppenheimer, Ian Ralph, Frank M. Robinson, Paul "Tiny" Stacy, my mother Damaris Steele and sisters Elizabeth and Rachel, Michael Swanwick, Michael J. Walsh, Michael Warshaw, and Sheila Williams.

List of Illustrations

All interior photographs from the National Aeronautics and Space Administration, courtesy of the National Archives and Records Administration.

Back cover author photograph courtesy of Mark W. Tiedemann.

TABLE OF CONTENTS

INTRODUCTION:

WEIRD SCENES FROM THE BEACH PARTY

Not long ago, in the dim half-light of an early morning in Missouri, I awoke from a dead sleep with a scene captured from whatever movie I had been dreaming before the first light of dawn stirred me.

It was of a beach somewhere in Florida—perhaps in Sanibel or on Captiva Island, two of my favorite winter hangouts, although more likely it was Cocoa Beach on Cape Canaveral, where I've set so many of my stories—and there was a bunch of astronauts having a party. Old-school NASA astronauts, like the Gemini and Apollo pilots; they've got flat-top haircuts and are wearing aviator-style Ray-Bans and baggy madras-print swim trunks, and they're standing around a beer keg that has been stuck in the sand, drinking warm Budweiser out of Dixie cups printed with Disney characters.

They're drunk and obnoxious, these Right Stuff guys: slapping each other around, making lewd comments to bikini-clad girls who hurriedly walk past them, dropping their shorts to piss in the surf, dancing to rock music crashing out of a ghetto blaster, throwing up, throwing down...a bunch of grown men behaving like frat boys on spring break. For no particular reason, there's a spacesuit helmet lying in the sand next to the beer keg. I think they're using it as a trash can for their Dixie cups.

And underneath this scene, subscripted as if it were the caption for a Gary Larson cartoon, was a single line which I read just before I woke up: *rude astronauts*.

A godawful vision, undoubtedly inspired by a hangover and the stress of finishing a novel—unlike writers who have trouble starting a book, my personal turmoil always comes when I'm writing the final chapters—and yet funny as hell, in its own black-hearted way. I stayed awake just long enough to jot down the two key words on the notepad I keep next to the bed for just such occasions, then I fell back asleep, instinctively knowing that it was going to be the title of something.

And, boy howdy, look what happened: it's the title of my first collection of short stories.

This is the definitive edition of <u>Rude Astronauts</u>. A mass-market version of this collection appeared in England shortly before the Old Earth Books edition saw print, but for various reasons I consider this American limited edition, published during Balticon 27 on the advent of my first Guest of Honor appearance at a major science fiction convention, as the real McCoy.

The stories in this book were written within a relatively short period of time—late 1987 to early 1991—and all but three were concocted while I lived in Rindge, New Hampshire. Literary critics (at least in the SF field, because I rarely see it done elsewhere) often try to second-guess the writer's influences. They usually get it wrong, because there's no way they can be inside a writer's head at the moment of creation, but it doesn't stop them from trying anyway. My guess is that they do this because it gives them the chance to drop the names of other authors they've read, thereby demonstrating that they were reading science fiction before last month. That's okay, I reckon; it's more wholesome than masturbation, and if it keeps them from playing in the streets, I suppose their mothers are grateful for their rainy-day hobby.

I seek inspiration, though, less from books than from real-life settings. The little town of Rindge, for instance, was the major influence upon three of these stories. The log cabin which my wife and I rented for two years is faithfully described in both "Walking on the Moon" and "John Harper Wilson". During that time, my dog Zack and I walked a half-mile down a dirt road to check the windows and doors of an old sporting lodge on the shore of Lake Monomonac; that lodge appears in "Goddard's People".

"Live from the Mars Hotel" was my first published short story. Although most of it takes place on Mars, which I can't claim to have visited except in my imagination, its country music-scene background is derived from my years in my hometown of Nashville, Tennessee. I've often wondered how different things might have been if I had learned how to pick guitar strings instead of peck typewriter keys; this story comes largely from my fascination with music, be it country, rock, blues, or jazz.

On Merritt Island off Cape Canaveral not far from the south gate of the John F. Kennedy Space Center, is a bar whose exterior resembles the principal setting of "Free Beer and the William Casey Society",

Introduction

"The Return of Weird Frank", and "Sugar's Blues", the stories which comprise a trilogy in this collection. I've never set foot in this nameless bar, but the memory of spotting it from Route 3 sparked these stories. The interior is based upon the Blue Plate, a good bar in Holden, Massachusetts, whose atmosphere is nowhere near as hostile as Diamondback Jack's; the ambiance was derived from a biker/hippie/redneck beer joint which used to exist on the outskirts of Nashville before it was closed down by the cops.

Harry Hapgood's triple-decker apartment in "Hapgood's Hoax" once belonged to a friend of mine who lived in Somerville, Massachusetts; most of the other New England locations described in this story exist in reality. Likewise, the ski area at Mt. Wachusett which is the setting of "Winter Scenes of the Cold War" is accurately depicted; I got caught on its cross-country trails during a nor'easter, and this story is the direct result of that experience. The cityscape of Worcester, Massachusetts in the 1940s which figures in "Goddard's People" is drawn from contemporary observation and historical research, and the Okefenokee National Wildlife Refuge in southern Georgia depicted in "Trembling Earth" is not greatly dissimilar to the swamp and parkland which exist there today.

Not all the stories in this book are set in places I have visited.

When I was a kid, I wanted to be an astronaut when I grew up. Unfortunately, a minor handicap stood in the way of my childhood ambition: the partial color-blindness I inherited from my grandfather. When I was in the fourth grade, I discovered that Air Force and Navy regulations prohibited color-blind people from being trained as pilots. No aviation experience, no chance at getting picked for the NASA astronaut corps; sorry, kiddo, but that's the way it is.

Many years later, I tried again to become an astronaut, this time in 1985 when I applied for NASA's Journalist-in-Space Project. I was among three hundred reporters who attempted to sleaze their way onto the ultimate press junket, a ride into orbit aboard a space shuttle, but I didn't even make it past the first cut before the program was abandoned in early 1986, following the *Challenger* disaster.

So I opted for the easy way to space. I became a science fiction writer.

The first five stories in this collection are part of the near-future history I've been developing over the past several years and which has been featured in my novels. The short-fiction segments of this future history are completely reprinted here, with two exceptions: a short story,

"Ride to Live, Live to Ride", which was extracted from my first novel, <u>Orbital Decay</u>, and a novella, "Red Planet Blues", later rewritten and revised to become the first part of my fourth novel, *Labyrinth of Night*. The remaining stories—"Walking on the Moon", the beforementioned Diamondback Jack trilogy, and "Live from the Mars Hotel"—are part of this chronology.

A librarian who collects statistics on this sort of thing recently asked me for the name of my series. "Ralph", I said and started to walk away; when he didn't get the joke, I came back and let him know that I wasn't formally calling my series anything, except when I sometimes referred to it as "near-space" in homage to Larry Niven's "Known Space" stories. My buddy Bob Liddil likes to call it "Steele's Universe", so maybe that's another opinion, but I'd just as soon call it Ralph, Herb, Duke, or whatever. The Billy-Bob Universe. Who cares?

Readers have also asked whether this future history was preconceived and charted out in advance, using the methodology Robert Heinlein perfected in the 1940s. As much as I've been tempted to say that this is so, the fact of the matter is that I've been making the whole thing up as I go along. <u>Orbital Decay</u>, the first installment in the chronology, was originally intended to be a standalone novel, yet for better or worse this near-future history has become an obsession; ten years after I began work on <u>Orbital Decay</u>, I've continued to write about the near-term colonization of space.

It's all been done piecemeal, one story or novel at a time, with no prearranged outline or blueprint. Although I've tried to keep each tale self-contained, I make references to characters and events in other stories; over time, a loosely related chronology has emerged, although I skip back and forth in the timeline as I write the books and stories. So, while there are characters, institutions and occurrences repetitively mentioned here and there, there is no grand scheme.

Frankly, it's been more interesting for me to write it this way. All I've done is try to keep the thing consistent; sorry, but there's no chronological chart that will make things easier to understand, and I'm loath to create one anyway. However, if you're just dying to know, the five stories in <u>Rude Astronauts</u> which are part of "Ralph" or "near-space" or "Steele's Universe" or whatever the hell you want to call it take place between the events described in <u>Orbital Decay</u> and my third novel, <u>Lunar Descent</u>.

Likewise, "Goddard's People" and "John Harper Wilson" are two stories in a series which concerns an alternate-history of space exploration. Here, I was inspired by the non-fiction books Willy Ley and Chesley Bonestell wrote for Viking Press in the 1950's, the grand old visions of space travel immortalized in works like <u>Across the Space Frontier</u>, <u>The Conquest of Space</u>, <u>The Conquest of the Moon</u> and <u>The Exploration of Mars</u>. No formal name for this sequence either—let's call it "alternate-space" or "Chesley" and be done with it.

Will there be more stories or novels in either series? Probably. Or maybe not. We'll keep you posted.

Also included in this volume are a few non-fiction pieces. Most were written during the mid-'80s when I was a staff writer and investigative reporter for *Worcester Magazine*, a weekly alternative newspaper in Worcester, Massachusetts. The paper featured a back-page, shared-author column called "On the Road" (shades of Jack Kerouac); my greatest pleasure during that back-breaking, stressed-out, underpaid and overworked two-year tenure at *Worcester Magazine* was writing journalistic essays for this section of the paper.

Why? Believe me, if you spent each day covering random violence, environmental destruction, teenage suicide, AIDS, and last Tuesday night's city council meeting, you'd want to write about the subjects covered in these columns, even when they were as grim as the *Challenger* disaster. I'm quite proud of these columns; since some pertained to scientific or science fictional topics, I've included a few of them in this collection. Portrait of a yet-unpublished SF writer as media scum.

After I quit *Worcester Magazine* and went freelance, I often wrote for a now-defunct city slick which was also published in Worcester. One of the short stories in this collection, "Winter Scenes of the Cold War", was originally published in *Worcester Monthly*; so was the feature-length non-fiction piece about SETI research, which has been restored to its original title, "LGM" In fact, it was the research behind "LGM" which led directly to *Labyrinth of Night*.

There is a seldom-acknowledged yet nonetheless distinct relationship between journalism and science fiction. Many SF writers, including Ben Bova, Frank Herbert, Robert Silverberg, Clifford Simak, Harlan Ellison, Gardner Dozois, Bruce Sterling, Gene Wolfe, William Tenn, G. Harry Stine, Daniel Hatch and A.J. Austin, among others have functioned at one time or another as journalists and have rarely-mentioned bodies of non-fiction behind them which, one might think from the fact of their omission, the field has treated as skeletons in the closet.

True, some of these skeletons are best left in the closet. I'd rather not discuss the article I once freelanced for a supermarket tabloid, even if it was the easiest $800 I ever made in my life; nor is the article about snowmobiles I hacked out for a business rag in Vermont for fifty bucks worth more than a passing mention. Yet the connection between journalism and science fiction remains one of the genre's best-kept secrets, and I wonder why that is, despite the current atmosphere of media-bashing. I value my own experience as a reporter; the years I spent on the streets as a reporter were far more valuable than all the creative writing workshops and lit classes I attended while in college.

This is what it all comes down to in my stories: a ceaseless friction between real life and the imagination, an uneasy symbiosis between the fictional and the factual. Many people prefer stories about talking dragons and galactic empires; they are discomfited by any close association between the fantastic and the real. "If I want this kind of thing", they say, "I'll read a newspaper"...but you'd be surprised how many of them don't read newspapers, simply because they don't want to be reminded how weird or wonderful their own world has become.

Yet one of the many functions of science fiction is to hold up a warped mirror to our present reality, distorting the image so that reality is seen in a different way. Science fiction, in this sense, isn't as much about the future as it is about the present.

Events sweep past us so quickly that we barely have time to assimilate the changes. When I wrote "Live from the Mars Hotel" in 1987, for instance, vinyl LPs and singles were still the preferred format of most music buyers and even radio stations, and the CD was still a novelty many people, including myself, thought was a passing fad. Five years later, you can't find vinyl singles in a retail music store, except as—ahem—a fad item.

Likewise, several stories in this book make reference to the USSR, reflecting a time when the Soviet Union still represented a real or imagined threat to the West. Much has been written elsewhere about how the collapse of Soviet communism affected fiction writers; all I can plead in my defense is that I, too, thought the Iron Curtain would stay up much longer. Although I was tempted to revise these stories to reflect present-day political realities, I decided instead to let things stand as they were. These references represent a different time, different politics, a different world—even if that world is now less than a half-decade behind us and its remembrance now brings a sour taste to everyone's mouth—which should not be forgotten.

In one sense, we're all rude astronauts, getting ripped on a strange beach near the edge of space and time.

Your guess is as good as mine as to how the future will be. A few years from now, swamps in southern Georgia may indeed be roamed by genetically recreated dinosaurs; on the other hand, the Okefenokee could be soon populated by clones of Ronald Reagan, George Bush, and Dan Quayle. Stories about near-future space colonization are currently considered to be unfashionably optimistic; a reviewer for a British SF magazine once spent most of her time mocking the cover blurb of one of my novels for invoking the "dream" of space exploration, leaving me to wonder if she reads newspapers, for anything I've written about space may seem as quaint and old-fashioned as Arthur C. Clarke's projection that communication satellites would be placed in orbit sometime shortly before the end of the 20th century.

There are two great lessons which science fiction teaches us, each contradicting the other one. Anticipate the best, prepare for the worst; that's the most obvious lesson. Yet the second is more subtle, although it is the exact opposite: when you expect the worst to happen, things will likely become much better than you believed they would be. It's the old philosophical test. Is the glass half empty or half full? What does this random ink blot mean to you?

And what did you dream about last night?

It's midnight. I've got a six-pack of ice-cold beer in the refrigerator and a pack of cigarettes. There's nothing on the tube worth watching except an old *Dr. Who* episode we've all seen a dozen times. Everything around us looks dull and stupid...

But just past this horizon, over on the next block, I can hear one hell of a blowout going on. Liquor, loud music, lewd women...might be worth checking out.

Let's go.

The party's just getting started. Want a beer?

—The Rocket Farm,
St. Louis, Missouri
January 31, 1993

PART ONE
NEAR SPACE

ON THE ROAD: EULOGY

In the end, for everyone, there was the image which was replayed endlessly, both in TV news film-clips and as a memory, like an afterimage ghostly printed on the retina of the mind's eye: a fireball, a great blossom of smoke shot through with yellow and crimson, followed by two forking trails of solid-rocket boosters and tiny contrails of debris falling toward the ocean below. The image was played over and over, both on television and in the individual imaginations of those who were stunned by the occurrence. Everyone affected by that image has given it a label: the day the space shuttle *Challenger* blew up.

A few hours after it happened, I was having a cigarette in the company's lunchroom when I had a sudden, vivid recollection. The year before, I had been a news correspondent in Washington, D.C., writing for a couple of daily papers in Missouri and Vermont. Because I had always been a fan of the space program, I managed to talk the editors of those papers into letting me cover a space shuttle launch from Cape Canaveral. In this instance it was Mission 51-D on the shuttle *Discovery*, the one famous for sending Sen. Jake Garn into orbit. Two days before the launch, however, I had watched the shuttle *Challenger* being rolled from its hangar in the Orbiter Processing Facility to the mammoth Vehicle Assembly Building.

It was pushed out backwards by a tractor on that morning in April while a dozen or so photographers snapped pictures from the roadside nearby. It was a routine event, overshadowed by the upcoming launch of the *Discovery*, and the early morning hour in which the roll-out occurred accounted for the scarcity of reporters at hand, but for those of us who were there, it was a stirring moment. *Challenger* still bore the marks of its last mission; its re-entry tiles looked worn, its overall color was off-white, but it was still a majestic space vehicle. You couldn't help but be awed by its beauty, its grace. Another orange tractor hooked up to its forward landing gear and began to pull it slowly toward the VAB a couple of hundred feet away, and as it was towed at a walking pace toward the massive building where it would be mated with its external fuel tank and solid-propellant boosters, I strode alongside it for awhile. I remember feeling a thrill when its right wing tip passed over my head, and thinking: this is a creature which has gone into space, felt starlight on its skin...this is what it feels like to be so close to a piece of history. It was a moment which I would not have forgotten even if it had not been later marred by horror and sudden death.

Many months later, on the afternoon after the fireball, that moment would come back to me even as I tried to pull together a localized account of the disaster's impact on the community. Few people seemed to be in their offices when I called. In a strange moment, I found myself on the phone with Worcester mayor John Anderson—a young reporter and the top city official conversing— with both of us shocked, saying to each other, "Oh, my God, what happened?" I remember walking through the Galleria at Worcester Center, noting that the usual midday crowd had thinned, and those who were there looked as if each had been given news of a sudden death in their families. On the Park Avenue bus going home from work, riders either poured over evening newspaper accounts of the event or stared out the windows. There were not even the usual paranoid glances at the passengers on either side, or the socially-acceptable distant gazes into nothingness. Everyone had something on their minds that night, and it was not hard to see that behind the thoughtful eyes gazing at the passing streetlights was the image of a supersonic fireball arching over the Atlantic. New England, the United States, the world mourned its passage, along with the deaths of six NASA astronauts and a New Hampshire schoolteacher. The extent of the shock was enough to reach even a hardened city like Worcester, which was not the hometown of any member of the crew.

In the long run, perhaps this is what makes us worthy, as a species, of reaching out beyond our own planet. We can empathize with the deaths of those whom we've never personally known. We can dream of going places even though we, as individuals, may never, ever go there ourselves. Perhaps this is how we've come to the point of building spaceships instead of squatting in mud huts by firelight. We've learned how to reach out with our hearts and minds, and we've learned how to hurt in an existential way from the deaths of others. Our town felt part of that pain.

It hurts, but it's better than feeling like you've had nothing to lose.

WALKING ON THE MOON

Over the next couple of decades, the three of them would get together once every few years, usually with their families for an afternoon or an evening. Once they had moved away from the Cape, all three had relocated to different parts of the country, so their reunions were normally arranged during vacations. They would spend a few hours in each other's company, eating, drinking, telling funny stories, trading business tips, admiring each other's wives and children, sometimes reminiscing about the glory days. They rarely, however, talked about walking on the Moon.

A year after Roy and Irene moved to rural New Hampshire following Roy's early retirement from Citicorp, Roy put out phone calls to Dick and Howard, inviting them to come up next Fourth of July for a barbecue. Both men agreed, naturally. It had been a little over two years since the last time they had seen each other during a ceremony in Washington, DC, at the National Air and Space Museum, not really a get-together for them since they had been surrounded, and kept apart, by NASA brass, congressmen, various dignitaries and reporters. Roy figured that it was time for another, more private reunion.

Howie and Beth were living in Syracuse, New York, so New Hampshire was only a half-day drive away. Howie wasn't teaching any classes during the university's summer semester, so he simply had to pack Beth, the twins Jackson and Veronica, and their outdoor gear into the Bronco; the stop at Roy's lakeside cabin would be on their way to a camping trip in the White Mountains.

Dick was a different story. Although he had long since retired from the Air Force, he was still working for NASA as a civilian consultant at the Johnson Space Center, so he had to fly all the way up from Houston. Roy had to mince around the subject of family while talking on the phone with Dick. Word on the grapevine was that Dick's home life had gone to hell lately; Grace, his wife of twenty-four years, had just divorced him, and Richard Jr. had been last seen hitchiking around the country, coasting from one Grateful Dead concert to the next.

Trouble at home had always made Dick irritable, and Roy had half-expected his former teammate to turn down the invitation, but to his surprise Dick eagerly agreed to come up for the weekend. He caught an American flight out of Houston, connected in New York with a commuter flight to New Hampshire, and arrived at the tiny Manchester municipal airport on the morning of July 4. His rented Ford Escort pulled into Roy's unpaved driveway only fifteen minutes before the arrival of the Happy Howie clan.

There were the usual joyous, yet vaguely uncomfortable, first minutes of greeting each other again. The three men embraced, laughed, pounded each other's backs, then stood back and mumbled at each other while noticing the changes—receding hairlines, touches of grey, thicker stomachs, new mustache and beard on Dick's face, old mustache missing from Roy's, Howie's slight limp from when he had busted his leg last November on his ice-covered front walk. Meanwhile Irene and Beth, old rivals from their days in the Astronauts' Wives Club, were carefully sizing each other up after quick hugs of their own: Irene noticing the deep crow's-feet around Beth's eyes, Beth deciding that Irene was definitely getting lumpy. Howie's twins didn't pay a bit of attention to any of this, of course; Roy's friendly old collie, Max, came bounding out of the woods to meet them, and soon Jack and Ronnie were chasing the dog down to the lakeshore.

Another summer afternoon, another barbecue. They all changed into their swimsuits and went down to the dock to swim and admire Roy's second-hand Chriscraft cabin cruiser which he was gradually restoring. Roy, Dick, and Howie attempted to play softball with Jackson and Veronica, giving up when Howie popped a fly ball into the dense woods behind the house, losing it so thoroughly that even Max couldn't find it. By this time, Irene had started the charcoal in the grill on the backyard deck while Beth had fixed the salad, so Roy put the steaks on the grill and opened the case of Coors he had tucked in the refrigerator.

They ate on the deck while across the still twilight waters of the lake local teenagers shot off bottle rockets and firecracker strings. When dinner was over, Irene and Beth cleared the table and carried the remains into the kitchen. Max lay down on the deck and gnawed at a T-bone Howie had tossed his way. Jackson found the carved-wood Saturn V model in the living wood and tried to take it out into the front yard before Roy stopped him and gently removed the prized model from the child's grasp; the kids found their toys in the Bronco and ran back down to the dock with the dog.

Wives gossiping in the kitchen—thank God, they had finally learned to get along with each other after all these years—kids torturing the dog, the sun setting behind the distant hills, Roy, Dick, and Howie sat together on the deck, chugging beer. As the photosensor switched on the backyard lights, their talk finally turned to space.

As usual, the grapevine stuff came first, stories about what other ex-astronauts were doing. Glenn was making another re-election run in the Senate; no doubt his constituents in Ohio would let him keep his seat ("But, Christ, you'd think he would have switched parties by now."). Collins was publishing another book ("He knows how to write, but if he wants another bestseller, he'd better do fiction like that Tom Clancy guy.") Armstrong was maintaining a low profile again after his stint on the Rogers Commission ("You gotta admire the guy. He could have opened shopping centers for the rest of his life."), and Bean was solidifying his reputation as a fine artist ("He ain't no Rembrandt, but his stuff sure is pretty.").

Then there were the old yarns about themselves, retold countless times, always worth hearing again: the time when Dick had been chewed out for doing low-altitude aerobatics over the Cape in his T-38 trainer; when Howie had let a urine sample "slip" out of his hands to splatter all over a flight doctor's penny loafers; when Roy, flying a Gulfstream over Merritt Island just before the Apollo 14 launch to check the weather conditions, had buzzed a Soviet spy trawler operating just outside the ten-mile coastal limit. There were other stories they all knew—like when Howie had played "Moon River" on a Jew's-harp while in lunar orbit, just to annoy CapCom—but these weren't brought up. Stories about being up there meant, eventually, that they would talk about walking on the Moon.

Yet there are subjects which cannot be ignored for long. As night settled on the New England countryside, an alabaster crescent began to rise over the distant shoreline, tinting the lake with silver beams. The three men gradually fell silent and gazed at the Moon, each absorbed with their own thoughts. Through the cabin's open windows they could hear the unintelligible voices of Irene and Beth from the living room, just under the electronic beep-boop-beep of the kids playing a computer game on Roy's MacIntosh. The collection of dead beer bottles had grown around them and Roy was beginning to wish he had picked up a second case the day before, while the stores had been open, when Dick committed a heresy.

"Don't you sometimes wish you were back there?" he said.

Happy Howie looked at him with his habitual deadpan expression. "Back where?" he asked. "Oh, you mean Cincinnati...no, no, I never really wanted to go back. Why?"

"I don't mean your home town. I mean..." Dick tipped his beer bottle toward the Moon. "Don't you find yourself thinking about that sometimes?"

"Oh, that. Sure. I love beer. Can't get enough of it."

Roy chuckled. Dick glared at Howie. "You know what I'm talking about. The Moon. It's been more than twenty years now. Don't you...y'know...ever wish you could go back?"

"Jesus, Dick." Howard sighed. "Y'know, once each term, I get a kid in my office at the university, some sophomore from the campus paper who thinks he's made the biggest discovery...one of the engineering profs used to be a real, live astronaut, he once walked on the Moon. This kid sits there wide-eyed, just like one of the newshounds who used to hang around the Cape, and he always asks me in this solemn voice..."

Roy picked it up, from long familiarity with the same tired question. "'Don't you wish you could go back to the Mooooooooooon?'"

All three of them laughed; post-flight press conferences had made them all irreverent about the press. "And I look across my desk at this future Pulitzer winner," Howard continued, "and I say, 'Hell no, now ask me another question!'"

"And they always get flustered after that," snickered Roy, "because that's usually their best shot." He shook his head. "I don't miss talking to reporters, not one bit."

"Amen, brother," Howie said.

Dick took a swig from his beer and settled his feet on the deck's railing. "Well, I'm no news hack, and I want a straight answer from you guys. Do you ever wish you could go back to the Moon?"

Howie balanced his beer on his stomach and stared into the foamed amber glass. "Straight answer, huh?" he said slowly, and paused to think it over. "Yes. No. What day of the week is it? Monday? Okay, the answer's yes. Tomorrow's Tuesday, so the answer then is going to be no."

Dick blew out his cheeks. "What kind of swabbie answer is that?" Howie was a former Navy man. "Are you trying to tell me you never thought about it?"

"Of course, I've thought about it," Howie replied. "Jeez, I wanted to go back the minute the capsule splashed down. Even after going without water for two days and living in the same underwear for a week, I wanted to go back that minute. Going up was the greatest thrill of my life."

He sloshed the bear around in the bottle, laughed and nodded his head. "When Spiro Agnew said the next goal was going to Mars, I was all set to sign up. Just back from the Moon, and I was ready to volunteer for the Mars shot in 1976. I'd make my name bigger than Neil's. Gimme more, gimme more."

"Uh-huh. So what happened?"

Howie coughed, grew sober. "You know what happened. The program went into the friggin' toilet. Proxmire, Mondale, even damn Nixon...they got their wish. By the time the shuttle got things moving again, I was over the hill."

"You know what can happen if you think about it too much," Roy said. "I mean, look at Buzz. He had a lot of problems after he got back and it took him a long while to get over it."

Howie nodded vigorously, pointing his finger at Roy. "That's exactly what I mean. It's kinda depressing, if you let it get to you. Besides...hell, when you're over the hill, there ain't no turning back."

But Dick shook his head. "Bullshit. Young's gone up in the shuttle, and we were with him back during Gemini. You're no more over the hill than he is."

"Yeah, well..." Howie picked up his beer. "Space is a young man's game, my friend, and I'm not young anymore."

"No pun intended, of course," Roy intoned.

"No pun intended, of course," Howie replied, and the three of them chuckled. "Sure, I think about it sometimes. I look at that picture of myself I have on my wall, standing there on the Moon. I look at it when I'm swamped with term papers from the kids. I think, 'Man, I'd give my right nut to be there again, right now.'" He shrugged. "Then reality sets in. I'm a college teacher. I fly a desk now. I wouldn't know what to do with a LEM if my life depended on it again."

"Hmmm." Dick was quiet for a moment, then he looked over at Roy. "What about you, Eject?"

Roy grinned from ear to ear. "Been a long time since anyone's called me that." He picked up his empty bottle. "Anyone want a refill?"

He started to get up, but as if summoned by marital telepathy, the back door opened and Irene walked out, carrying three cold bottles of beer. The three of them looked at her in surprise, and Roy snapped his fingers as she walked up the steps to the deck. Irene gave each man a bottle, bowed from the waist like a harem girl, then faked a swat at Roy's head before walking back down to the cabin. Roy waited until the back door shut again. "My girl," he murmured.

"She's a good woman," Dick said. There was an unmistakable twinge of sadness and envy in his voice. Roy felt sorry for him. Grace had been with him since he was a teenager hot-rodding F-101's over Edwards Air Force Base, had stuck with him through the Gemini and Apollo years, done the brave-wife-at-home bit for the TV crews when her husband had piloted a LEM to the airless grey surface of the Moon, given him a son...and then, after all those years, split in the middle of the night with a New Age meditation instructor named Hernando. Hell of a note.

Roy sipped his beer, let the cool liquid slide down his throat. "Howie's got his story, I've got mine," he said. "When I left the bank, there was a going-away party in the office on my last day. You know the routine...big tinsel banner on the wall saying, 'So long, Roy', the secretaries giving you kisses, the champagne, the gold watch and the speech from the CEO, the whole schtick. Well, then, the guy who's been promoted to my job...practically a kid, your typical Harvard MBA, a yuppie who had just moved over from Paine Webber...glides over to talk with me."

"Probably looked like Al," Howie said.

"Yeah," Roy said, but without laughing. "But without Shep's qualities. Smug. Shit-eating grin. He's got my job, ha ha ha. But, y'know, I give him the time and he says the usual stuff about trying to fit into my shoes and carrying the torch..."

Roy took a breath, put his bottle down on the deck. "Then he tries to get funny with the script. He's grinning at me, and he suddenly says, 'So, Eject...'"

Dick took a breath. "How'd he know that name?"

"Probably from the Wolfe book, I dunno..."

"Goddamn Wolfe. Bastard started that Right Stuff shit and we'll never hear the end of it." Dick took a hit from his beer. "Nobody has the right to call you Eject unless they were there when it happened."

Roy had once punched out of an X-15 during a flight when its main egine had failed after it was dropped from a B-52. The plane had been lost and Roy had nearly washed out of NASA; the accident had eventually been overlooked when the Apollo team was selected, but the nickname always stuck. "Never mind. So this guys says, 'So, Eject, what's next?' I started to say something about buying this place here, but he doesn't copy me. He keeps right on talking and..."

Roy stopped, looked off the deck, over the stone chimney of his cabin, at the Moon. A fingernail shaving in the sky; a place where he had once stood. "Well, he says, 'So...are you heading for the Moon again? If we can open a branch there, let me know.'"

He picked up his beer, but only let it cool his hands. "One look in his face, and I knew it was all a joke to him. People walking on the Moon was a funny stunt we had pulled a long time ago. A human cannonball trick in the circus. I could see what he thought of me. Moon Man."

Nobody laughed. Dick and Howard looked at him for awhile, and Roy studied his front lawn. It had rained the day before last, it needed mowing again, the honeysuckle bush next to the driveway had to be trimmed...

Damn, why did it hurt so much?

"Was he old enough to remember?" Howie asked. Roy nodded, and Howie shook his head. "He was probably one of the ones who bitched when the Lucy show was pre-empted for live coverage of our shot." He sipped his beer. "Am I the only one who doesn't miss the silly bitch?"

"I wanted to slug him," Roy said softly. "Not because of me. Because of his attitude about everything we had done."

The three of them were quiet for a little while, reflecting. Tree frogs and crickets communicated with the night. Suddenly, across the lake, a skyrocket went off. It shot in a sputtering gunpowder arc over the lake, snapping and shrieking over the distant yells of the teenagers on the far shore, then detonated in a red and violet umbrella. They heard the front screen door open and slam close, saw Ronnie and Jack running out onto the front lawn to watch. After a few minutes another skyrocket went up, but it fizzled out and disappeared over the waters. "Ahhhhhhhhhh," moaned the kids.

"Happy Fourth of July," Roy said. He picked up his Coors and toasted his friends. Howie and Dick picked up their beers, tapped bottle against bottle, and they slugged down the brew.

"I love the Fourth of July," Howie said.

"You haven't answered my question," Dick said to Roy. "If you could go back to the Moon...?"

"Would I?" Roy watched another skyrocket launch over the lake. This one was more successful; it exploded in a yellow fire-blossom. He looked back at Dick. "I can't, so why do you want to know?"

Dick contemplated the lake for a moment. "You can go back," he said finally. "America's going back up there."

"Oh," replied Howie casually. "Tomorrow, or next week?"

"Probably in another ten years," Dick replied drily. "We could feasibly get one or two people there by '01, but if we take that approach it'll be a quick-and-dirty job again, and nobody wants to do that. The prime objective is to establish a permanent manned presence in the first decade of the next century, so the thinking is to send a major expedition."

Roy nodded sagely, absently chipping at the label on his beer bottle with his thumbnail. "Yeah, I've heard that NASA's taken a new interest in the Moon. I'll always second the motion, but I'm telling you, it's going to be the same song and dance with Congress. They won't fund it, and without the bucks we're just telling science fiction stories."

Dick smiled; he leaned back in his chair and cupped the back of his head in his hands. "It's not science fiction, Roy. It's going to happen. And we won't have to worry about Congress, either."

He was so self-assured that Roy's attention was caught. He stared at his former teammate. "You're not bullshitting me, are you?" Dick's smile grew broader, and he shook his head.

"Is this coming out of Johnson?"

Dick slowly shook his head again.

"Is it serious?"

Dick nodded.

"Why?" asked Howie.

"Why not?" replied Dick.

"C'mon. If it's serious, there's got to be a better reason than that. Congress..."

"Screw Congress," Dick said softly. "It's coming out of one of the privates. All we need is use of NASA facilities at the Cape. When the proposal is formalized and made public, Congress will go along with it. So will the White House, and so will the public. It'll be an offer they can't refuse."

"So what's the reason?" Roy prodded.

Dick looked back at him. "Sorry, Eject, I can't tell you that. At least not right now. It's insider info, and since the SEC's been getting tough lately, I shouldn't even be telling you this much. This is strictly between the three of us, okay?"

"So why are you telling us anything?" Roy asked.

"We're going to need experienced people. Guys who have been up there already. If it's going to succeed, it'll be important that we use the resources we've already developed, so we won't be starting over from scratch. We've got to get old Apollo vets back in the loop, and that means guys like you."

"So that means..." Howie began.

"What it means is, if you guys want to go back to the Moon, you can do it now." Roy started to speak, but Dick held up his hand. "Don't tell me again that you're over the hill, either. This isn't Apollo all over. Age isn't that important anymore, the medical requirements aren't nearly as tough. As long as you're in reasonably good shape and the docs know you won't drop dead during lift-off, you can go. Even that bum leg of yours won't rule you out, Howie."

"What about you?" asked Roy.

Dick's smile became a grin. "I'm already signed up. When the first expedition is picked, I'm on the A-list. As good as getting a reserved seat. We won't be sending just three men, either." He paused. "I want you guys along. Besides the fact that you're my buddies, I know I can depend on you not to screw up. Say the word, and you're on the list. I'm on the inside track for this."

The three of them were quiet for a few minutes, gazing at each other. Finally Dick broke the silence. "You're not old yet, fellas. Roy, you're in retirement only as long as you want to putter around with your boat. Howie, you're an ex-astronaut only as long as you want to grade papers and give interviews to the college paper. I'm not promising a fountain of youth, but if you want some of your youth back again, it's there for the taking. I know you're both settled down and it's hard to uproot. It's been easy for me only because Grace is gone and Richard's on his own. There'll be sacrifices for each of you, that's for damn sure. I can't even guarantee that you'll go. There's always the chance that you'll be working in the background, that you'll be sitting on the ground when we light up the candle."

Dick pointed at the crescent high above the trees. "But if it works out, you can be up there again. On the Moon."

He paused. "So what do you say?"

Howie and Roy were silent for a few more moments, then Howie slowly shook his head. "No, no...I'm sorry, but I can't do it again." He shrugged. "It's something that I did when I was twenty years younger, but that's all over now. I like being a teacher. I'll give any advice or consultation that the company wants, but...well, I'd rather just sit this one out, thanks anyway."

Dick closed his eyes, nodded his head. "No problem, bud. I can understand where you're coming from. I don't blame you one bit." He opened his eyes again and looked at Roy. "Okay, Eject, what about you?"

Roy had been looking away: at the cabin, the lake, the quiet forest around them. The summer heat lay over him like a comforting blanket; the night was gentle, broken only by crickets and frogs and distant fireworks. Through the kitchen window he glimpsed Irene, reaching into a cabinet to fetch a Milk Bone for Max, still talking to Beth.

"I'm going to have to think about it," he said slowly. "Can I have a little time for that?"

Dick nodded his head. "Sure. No problem, as long as you don't take too long. The snowball's already rolling."

"Hmmm. I bet it is." He remembered the frantic years of the Gemini and Apollo days, when no one was sure what the Soviets were doing, whether a Russian cosmonaut would be the first man on the Moon. That snowball rolled very fast, then; major decisions were being made virtually overnight. "I'll give you a call in the next week," he said. "I need to talk it over with Irene and...sorta put things together in my own mind."

Dick nodded again. "Sure. That's fine with me."

Roy let out his breath and gazed up again at the Moon. "You know," he said, "I resent you for this, sort of."

Dick blinked, looking surprised. "How come?"

"I've come to appreciate getting old," Roy said. "Retirement has its pleasures. It means you've finally grown up. I thought I had outgrown the Moon, but maybe there's still that kid in me." He hesitated. "I don't care what you say, Dick, but it's a choice between growing old and becoming young again. It's a helluva choice to make."

"At least you get a choice," Dick said.

Roy grinned and cocked his head. "Yeah, that's true." He studied the beer bottle again. "But sometimes, though, you'd rather wish you didn't know you had one."

None of them said anything after that. They killed their beers and listened to the night. A few minutes later the back door opened and the two women walked out to the deck. It was the usual signal that it was time for the party to end. Beth found Ronnie and Jack asleep on the front lawn, having dozed off during the fireworks, guarded by Max; she picked up Veronica and Howie lifted Jackson and, without waking them, loaded them into the back seat of the Bronco. They could get to the National Forest campground in Pinkham Notch in a couple of hours; Dick was reserved at the Holiday Inn in Manchester.

They had long since learned to make departures short and sweet; the three men didn't like mushy scenes. Handshakes and hugs, promises to call and write, then both cars were pulling out of the driveway and heading for the highway. Roy caught a meaningful final glance from Dick before his rental car disappeared from sight.

Roy and Irene cleaned up the deck and the kitchen, turned off the lights, put Max out for the night. In their pajamas, they lay in bed for a short while, Irene reading the latest Book-of-the-Month Club thriller, Roy staring at last week's issue of *Time*. A brief article in the international section said that the Russians had set another longevity record for a cosmonaut on their space station--nothing really new.

Irene finished a chapter, marked her place with a paper bookmark, and Roy dropped his magazine on the floor. She leaned over and kissed him goodnight, then Roy reached up and turned off the light. But while his wife rolled over and went to sleep, Roy lay awake and stared at the ceiling for a long, long time.

Remembering the last time he had gone walking on the Moon.

FREE BEER AND
THE WILLIAM CASEY SOCIETY

Cowboy Bob told me this story one slow Wednesday night while we were hunched over the bar in Diamondback Jack's, so I can't make a strong case for its veracity. If you drink and hang around in barrooms, you should know that half the stories you hear are outright lies, and the other half are at least slightly exaggerated. And one would have to be more than a little gullible to completely believe a former beamjack named Cowboy Bob. Gullible, stoned, or both.

If it weren't for the events which happened after Bob told me about the Bill Casey Society and the Free Beer Conspiracy on Skycan, I wouldn't be bothering to pass this yarn along. I'm a respectable journalist; I don't trade in hearsay. But maybe there's a moral in this story. If not a moral, then at least a warning.

Diamondback Jack's is a hole-in-the-wall beer joint on Merritt Island, Cape Canaveral, about two miles down Route 3 from the Kennedy Space Center. It's a dive for space grunts, which means that it's not the sort of place to take the kids. In fact, tourists, space groupies, execs from the space companies, NASA honchos, and most media people are unwelcome in Jack's. Not that the place is all that attractive; windowless, weatherbeaten pine walls, oil-spattered and littered sand parking lot, busted plastic beer sign, clusters of Harley-Davidsons and GM pickup trucks parked outside. It looks like the sort of northern Florida redneck joint where you can get a cold stare for requesting a vodka collins instead of a Budweiser, or get hit over the head with a pool cue for fouling someone else's shot. Appearances aren't deceiving, either. You're better off drinking in the fern bars down on Cocoa Beach.

But if you can survive a few consecutive nights in Jack's without being punched out or thrown out, you're on the way to joining the regulars: professional spacers whose lives revolve around the Cape and the space business. Shuttle pilots, launch pad crews, firing room techs, spacecraft mechanics, flight software writers, cargo loaders, moondogs, the Vacuum Suckers, and beamjacks.

Inside, Diamondback Jack's is all space. On the walls are framed photos and holos of Mark I, II, and III shuttles lifting off, of beamjacks tethered to sections of powersats, moondogs building the mass driver at Descartes Station, Big Dummy HLVs coasting into orbit, Olympus Station revolving like a huge wheel in geostationary orbit above a crescent Earth. The bulletin board near the door is pinned with job openings and torn-out articles from *Aviation Week*. Behind the long oak-top bar, along with the varnished and mounted skin of the rattlesnake that Jack Baker claims to have killed while fishing in the Everglades ("Sumbitch crawled into my boat and I kilt it with my shotgun. Blew the bastard's head clean off."), are snapshots of spacers past and present, dead and alive, unknown and infamous: Tiny Prozini, Joe Mama, Lisa Barnhart, Virgin Bruce Neiman, Dog-Boy and Dog-Girl, Monk Walker, Mike Webb, Eddie the Gentle Goon, Sandy Fey. There's a picture of Jack Baker, as a skinny kid, standing with Robert A. Heinlein, taken at a science fiction convention many years ago. And there's a picture of Cowboy Bob, wearing a hardsuit with his helmet off, sneering at the camera. He's wearing his trademark Stetson in that picture.

I think that Bob was born with that tan felt Stetson on his head. I don't think it could be removed without surgery. Maybe he's got a pointed head underneath. With his white beard, wrinkled eyes, and bad teeth, though, he was no singing cowpoke or last noble horseman. Bob was a space grunt. Once he told me he couldn't stand horses.

When I knew him, Cowboy Bob was one of those hard-up, unemployed cases who were regular fixtures in Jack's, pissing away the money they had made years ago as beamjacks on the powersat project. Jack was one of those semi-skilled young turks who had signed on with Skycorp and spent two tough years in orbit on Olympus Station—Skycan, as the vets knew the giant orbital base. They went because the pay was good, or for the adventure, or because they were wanted back home by the law, the IRS, or their former spouses. The ones who survived the experience and didn't screw up came home to small fortunes in accumulated back pay and bonuses. Those guys bought restaurants or small businesses, or just bought condos on the Cape and were lazy for the rest of their lives.

Some other vets, though, screwed up and lost much of their pay to fines and penalties. Those guys came back with not much more money in the bank than they had before they left. Most of these grunts left the industry. The ones who stayed, for the most part, tried to find ground jobs on the Cape, or went overseas to work for the Europeans or the Japanese. A handful of diehards tried to get another space job.

Cowboy Bob, the former Utah goat roper who couldn't stand horses, was one of those in the last category. Skycorp wouldn't rehire him, though; nor would Uchu-Hiko or Arianespace. So he took small jobs for the little companies which did short-term subcontract work for NASA or the Big Three. But I don't think he ever left Earth again after he finished his contract on Skycan; his jobs were always on the ground. I always figured that was because of his drinking problem.

So Bob spent his nights in Diamondback Jack's, swilling beer, talking shop with the techs and other unemployed space grunts, making sour-breathed passes at the college cuties who slummed in Jack's during spring break, keeping his feelers out for job leads, shooting the bull with anyone who would buy the next round. That's how he told me the story, that Wednesday night when the place was dead, about the Skycan beer scam.

He was already drunk when I sat down next to him at the bar. I signaled to Jack to bring me a Bud, and the first thing Bob said to me was the sort of thing one would expect from an inebriated wreck. Cocking his head toward the door, he asked, "You just came in, didn't ya, Al?"

I nodded.

"Did you see any cars parked out there?" he asked.

"Sure, Bob. Yours. Mine. Jack's. Whose car are you looking for?"

He cast me a look suggesting that I had become stupid since the last time he had seen me. "Brown Toyota-GM Cutlass. One or two men sitting inside." He paused, and added, "William Casey Society sticker on the rear window. Remember what I told you last Saturday?"

I shook my head as Jack pushed a tallneck in front of me. "I wasn't here last Saturday, Bob."

(Of course, I didn't say where I had been last Saturday. There's nothing wrong with attending a routine press conference at KSC, unless you're a patron at Jack's. Spacers and reporters have an acrimonious relationship going back to the days when Project

Apollo press pool reporters gave NASA a new definition—Never A Straight Answer. Jack used to keep a bag of Morton's salt underneath the counter for the novice journalists who wandered into the bar looking for sources, to dump on their heads as soon as they pulled out their notebooks "so the bloodsucking leeches will wither up and die." My presence was tolerated only because I was lowkey about my profession and because I never brought my work into Jack's. So the less said about my stringer work for the *Times*, the better.)

"Huh," Bob said, wearing the vaguely puzzled expression of a heavy drinker facing short-term memory lapses. "Maybe I didn't tell you about it." He looked towards the door again. "Well, is there a car like that out there?"

"I didn't see one. But I don't think I'd recognize a Casey Society sticker if I saw one."

Now Cowboy Bob had my curiosity worked up. Perhaps that was his intent all along; get me involved in a conversation and cage drinks off me all night. I decided to play along. It was a slow, humid summer night, and I was in the mood for a tall tale.

I got Jack to bring Cowboy Bob another Miller's and I pulled out my cigarettes. Bob took a long hit off his beer, tilted the frayed rim of his hat back a half inch, and leaned a little closer to me. "Did I ever tell you about how we got 444 cases of beer up to Skycan? Well..."

Ten years ago (Cowboy Bob told me) his crew was doing the final work on SPS-1, the first large-scale solar power satellite to be built by Skycorp. Almost five years and the labor of nearly three hundred men and women had gone into the project, not to mention over $10 billion in corporate investments and government loans. The result was the 21st century equivalent to the Golden Gate Bridge, a landmark achievement in space construction. All that remained to be done before the beginning of the low-power tests was the final installment of the microwave dish antennas at both ends of the thirteen-mile span of the powersat.

"So we were pretty proud of what we had done there," Bob recalled. "There would be other powersats, of course, but this was the first big one, and we were the crew that was putting on the finishing touches. That called for some kind of celebration, right? So one night a few guys from the second shift got together in one of the rec rooms and started talking about what we wanted to do. As it turned out, everyone wanted a beer bust."

The problem with that, of course, was that both Skycorp and NASA had stringent regulations against alcoholic beverages in space being made available to space work crews. The rules were tightly enforced; NASA inspectors searched all outbound orbital and lunar crews for booze, and Skycorp's security cops on Olympus Station had already found and torn out two stills aboard the space station. Skycorp had tried to compromise with the beamjacks' thirst by providing in the rec rooms non-alcoholic near-beer—a weak, watery brew which tasted like chilled boar whizz.

"That just wasn't good enough," Bob said. "I mean, we'd been gagging on that stuff for the past eighteen months. We wanted real beer. Budweiser, Miller's, Busch, Rolling Rock, Black Label...anything!"

He hefted his latest bottle of beer to show what real beer looked like. "At this point, y'know, nobody gave a damn about Skycorp's rules. The job was done, our money was in the bank. Once the last array of cells was laid down and the antennas were installed, we'd all be shipped home and it would be the end of a long tour of duty. So we were willing to take some risks, break some regs. Who cared? We were entitled to a good blowout, man."

Getting beer onto Skycan entailed a smuggling operation, of course. In the past, Skycan workers had managed to bribe KSC ground crews into packing off-limits personal items into the orbital transfer vehicles which resupplied Olympus Station on a weekly basis. A network of reliable connections at the Cape, therefore, was already in place. But the stuff which had been stashed into the OTVs before they were loaded into the cargo bays of the shuttles—tape players, cassettes, comic books, Monopoly games, and even the occasional fifth of whisky or vodka—had taken up little room in the OTVs and could be easily hidden from NASA inspectors. The more the conspiring beamjacks thought about it, the more they realized that, in order to get enough beer into space for a proper party, this operation demanded smuggling an unprecedented volume of contraband into orbit.

"Dog-Boy pulled out a calculator and figured it out," Bob continued. "A Mark II shuttle's OTV had a cargo capacity of 65,000 pounds, which translated to about a thousand gallons, water or beer. That was about 444 cases of twelve-ounce cans."

He paused and gazed at his empty bottle; I gave Jack the high sign to bring us another round. It looked as if I were going to have to pump a thousand gallons of beer into Cowboy Bob to get the story, which was probably what Bob wanted me to do. But the yarn was getting good and I wasn't about to start being cheap. Jack silently put another round in front of us—he had already deprived Bob of the keys to his Jeep—and the former beamjack continued his story.

"Of course, Dog-Boy made that calculation just to give us an idea of what could be done. 'Of course that's absurd,' he said. But once he told us it could be done..." He laughed, shaking his head.

"You only had about a hundred people up there," I said. "Ten gallons of beer for every crew member was a little overkill, don't you think?"

"You're missing the point, Al!" Bob slapped his hands down on the bartop. "It wasn't a matter of whether everyone had a six-pack or a hundred gallons. We had just gotten through building a nineteen square mile structure in space. There was nothing we couldn't do! We were the best space construction crew there had ever been! So it was...it was like..."

"A matter of pride."

"Hell, yeah! It wasn't having the beer that mattered. It was getting the beer, that was the point. The challenge was the thing." He shrugged and picked up his beer. "So what the fuck? We decided to do it."

So the handful of beamjacks involved in the discussion—Bob, Dog-Boy and Dog-Girl, Eddie the Gentle Goon, Suffering Fred, a few others—got to work in plotting the Free Beer conspiracy, as it came to be called. There were quite a few obstacles which had to be crossed, the largest of which was circumnavigating NASA and Skycorp. But the obstacle which they didn't foresee was the William Casey Society, personified aboard Skycan by one Leonard Gibson, sometimes known as Lenny the Red.

The William Casey Society, of course, was the extreme right-wing group which had taken up in the new century where the fanatics of the 20th century—the John Birch Society, the LaRouchians, the American Nazi Party—had left off. Named after an old CIA chief who had died during one of those White House scandals 'way back when, the Bill Casey Society had become the cause of choice for disenfranchised Communist-haters of every stripe, from conspiracy mavens to shellshocked vets of Gulf War II to survivalists disappointed that a global thermonuclear war had not occurred. Fueled by a distrust of the new cooperation between the United States and the Soviet Union—particularly in space, as typified by the joint exploration of Mars—and led by a minor presidential candidate named George White, the Caseyites compensated for a lack of political clout with fervor, paranoia, and a few well-placed connections.

Space industrialization had become a favorite target of the Bill Casey Society—in particular, Skycorp's powersat project. It was George White's contention that the building of SPS-1 was the first stage in a Communist-backed secret operation to control the world. Skycorp was being backed by the Soviet Union, White claimed, and the SPS networks were being established not for use as orbital power stations but as microwave beam weapons. Once three powersats were established over the United States and two were built in geostationary orbit above Great Britain and Japan, Soviet moles in Skycorp and NASA would take control of the SPS system, turn the microwave transmitters against American, British, and Japanese armed forces—namely, hypersonic bombers and submarines—and fry them, thus paving the way for Soviet global conquest.

Never mind that SPS microwave beams, designed to relay energy from space to ground-based rectennas with as little environmental damage as possible, barely had the power to blister the paint job on a bomber or a sub. Never mind that the Soviets were building their own SPS system in orbit above the USSR, or that the Kremlin had better fish to fry—so to speak—than whacky schemes for global domination. But this kind of paralogia always finds an audience, and it keeps the tax-free contributions rolling in.

The Caseyites, to their credit, realized that the SPS construction crews on Olympus Station—the latest generation of high risk, blue-collar, All American hardhats—were unlikely to be Communist sympathizers, but were guilty only of ignorance. This was obviously the soft belly of the Commie plot. So the Caseyites went so far as to plant their own agent on Skycan, picking a member from their ranks to go to work on Olympus Station in an effort to convince the beamjacks that there was a plot afoot and to convert them to the Caseyite cause.

That person was Leonard Gibson, a thin and somewhat wild-eyed former arc welder for Martin Marietta, who managed to get a job as a beamjack on Skycan.

"We already had Lenny's number by this time, of course," Bob said, "and we tended to leave him alone."

"What do you mean, you had his number?"

Bob sipped his beer. "He came aboard Skycan, from day one, passing out Caseyite leaflets, trying to make converts out of his bunkmates, claiming that certain members of the command crew were Russian sleepers. Lenny used to get into these brain-damaged rants in the rec room about how we were all Commie dupes, that sort of thing. He even insisted on changing his bunk assignment regularly, saying that he was being bugged or something."

I shrugged. "There were a lot of weird cases on Skycan. He should have fit right in."

Bob shook his head. "Yeah, but not hostile weird like that. Even Virgin Bruce wasn't that twisted. Even the religious fanatics got the hint to shut up. Lenny the Red thought he was on a vital mission to save the world." He grinned. "We used to have some fun with him, like the time Suffering Fred casually pulled out a copy of <u>Das Kapital</u> in the rec room and started reading it aloud. Blew Lenny's mind. That's one thing about fanatics, Al. No sense of humor whatsoever."

So Lenny the Red found himself ostracized. That made the situation even worse. Now Lenny Gibson began to suspect that the situation was even worse than George White had predicted; somehow, most of the Skycan beamjacks had been brainwashed, had become willing Commie dupes. How else could he explain this complete rejection of his claims?

So Lenny the Red changed tactics. Instead of seeking converts, he began to make careful observations of the behavior of his fellow beamjacks, watchful for indications that a conspiracy was afoot. Lenny the preacher became Lenny the spy, the guy who sat quietly in the corner, listening, watching, waiting.

"And sending coded messages," Bob added. "The communications officers who worked in Command, y'know, handled the phone calls which crewmembers made to the folks back home. They sometimes listened in for kicks, and they used to tell us about these bizarre calls Lenny would make to some number in Baltimore. 'Tell Aunt Jane to water the begonias. Repeat, tell Aunt Jane to water the begonias. The moon is red. How is Uncle George?'" Cowboy Bob chuckled "God knows what that shit meant, but it was obviously reports to the Casey Society."

"You didn't get bothered by this?"

"Naw. He was basically harmless." Bob paused and sighed, his eyes rolling up toward the ceiling. "Until he caught the rumors about the Free Beer Conspiracy, though."

"Let me guess..."

"Right. Commie plot."

There was little which could be kept secret for long aboard Olympus Station. The space station was enormous, but it was only so large; rumors and hearsay tended to spread quickly among the hundred-plus men and women living in the big wheel, sometimes but not always missing the attention of the security team or the station supervisor. In this instance, word seeped out that something special was being sent up to celebrate the completion of SPS-l. Yet only a small handful of people knew the details. If Phil Bigthorn, the US federal marshal who headed station security, or Hank Luton, the station supervisor, had known what was going on, the jig would have been up; but apparently they didn't, so the conspiracy continued to build itself.

Eddie the Gentle Goon managed to make covert contact with one of the usual sources for goodies at the Cape, a cargo loader who for years had fattened his bank account by smuggling personal-request items into the OTVs bound for Skycan. (Cowboy Bob wouldn't tell me his name, saying that the same person was still working for Skycan at KSC.) The cargo loader was willing to take the risk, which was considerable, but he also put a large fee on the job—fifty grand up front, overhead costs included. Eddie dickered with him and managed to get the price down to $30,000 through a combination of sweet talk and menace for which the Goon was renowned, and authorized a transfer of thirty grand from Eddie's bank account to the loader's. The price was still steep, but the co-conspirators grudgingly agreed to reimburse the Goon for the expense.

The date for delivery of 444 cases of beer was to be on or before April 15, the day that final work on SPS-1 was scheduled to be completed. Dog-Boy and Dog-Girl, who had both worked previously as ground crew at the Cape, worked out the rough framework of the plan. They figured that, once the beer was packed into an OTV and the transfer vehicle was loaded into a shuttle's cargo bay in the KSC Shuttle Processing Center, it would be smooth sailing. Under standard procedures, the OTV would not be reopened for inspection once the shuttle was mated with its flyback booster and moved to the launch pad. Once the shuttle reached orbit, the flight crew would routinely deploy the OTV from the cargo bay and fire its engine, sending it towards Olympus Station as if it were any other resupply mission.

So the hard part was to get all that beer into an OTV, a difficulty compounded by NASA regulations forbidding all alcoholic beverages at Kennedy Space Center. There was no way a beer truck could simply drive past the checkpoints and offload over four hundred cases of beer at the SPC. Not without attracting the wrath of KSCs security cops, infamous for their lack of humor.

Eddie relayed these concerns to the bribed cargo loader at the Cape. The cargo loader's reply, in effect, was: don't sweat the details, we've got it covered. Eddie was also asked if he and his buddies wanted a hundred pounds of beer nuts, cheap.

The cargo loader did his job well. First, he purchased 444 cases from a liquor wholesaler in Titusville, apparently explaining that he was planning a little get-together for a few friends. The wholesaler, not asking too many difficult questions, delivered the beer to the loader's house in Cocoa Beach, where the cases were stacked in his garage.

Then the cargo loader approached a few touchable cronies who also worked at KSC and, bribing them for $500 each, managed to enlist their help. He was careful to select Skycorp employees who worked at the SPC, were less than completely honest, and who owned pickup trucks. He found four guys who met that description.

"The big hangup," Bob continued, "was getting an OTV. The cargo manifests for the weekly shuttle flights were scheduled well in advance and were pretty tight at that point. With SPS-1 soon going on-line, the low-orbit factory stations wanted to stock up their supplies. This guy wouldn't and couldn't bump any life-critical cargo, and he couldn't slide any military or scientific pallets off the board without attracting a lot of attention. So for awhile there we were stuck. We had the beer, we had the plan, and we had the people, but we didn't have the OTV."

"The Mark III shuttle was in operation then," I pointed out. "It could have gone direct to Skycan, and you wouldn't need to use OTVs at all."

Bob shook his head. "The *Columbia II* and the *Shepard* were big-ticket birds then. Too high-profile for smuggling stuff, and their cargo bays could be opened anytime, even if you could get something bumped from their cargo manifests. We had to use a Mark II like the *Ley* or the *Sally Ride,* which were doing milk runs with no big fanfare. But, y'know, they had LEO ceilings, which meant we had to find an OTV.

"Anyway, Dog-Boy came up with the solution, but Fred and I did the actual engineering. Three OTVs were permanently docked at Skycan, mainly used to ferry stuff over to the construction shack. Fred and I, when nobody was looking, climbed into one of the things, accessed the guidance computer, and plugged in some new co-ordinates that Dog-Boy figured out. Next time the OTV was sent out to the shack, the engine misfired." Grinning, Cowboy Bob sipped his beer. "It ended up in an elliptic polar orbit over the Moon. It was a real bitch to retrieve the thing."

"Oh, ho. Convenient little accident..."

"Exactly. Hank Luton had to request a new OTV for Skycan, since we were running three shifts to get SPS-1 finished on schedule and we needed three OTVs to get the job done. Skycorp was pissed, but they managed to get NASA to bump a science payload back a couple of weeks so we could be sent a new OTV. We got lucky. It was manifested for the *Willy Ley,* with launch scheduled for April 12, right on the money."

"Hmmm. KSC doesn't send up empty OTVs, so something must have been bumped from the manifest anyway."

"Toilet paper, logbooks, frozen food, screwdriver heads, shit like that. Funny how easy it is to misplace that stuff in the warehouse, y'know."

While the Free Beer conspirators were taking care of the OTV problem, though, another annoying hassle came to their attention, one much closer at hand: Lenny the Red, who had taken to spying on them.

"It wasn't hard to figure out that Lenny was keeping tabs on us," Bob said. "I guess he thought he was James Bond, but he was about as subtle as an elephant fart. Fred and the Goon and I would be in the rec room, right? Maybe not even talking about this thing. And here he'd come down the ladder, kinda sauntering across the compartment to sit down real close to us, but being careful not to look our way so we wouldn't notice him. Whistling, for Christ's sake..."

"Inconspicuous behavior."

Cowboy Bob sneered. "Nothing about Lenny was inconspicuous. It didn't take a genius to see that he knew something was going on. At first we thought it was funny, 'cause if the Bill Casey Society thought smuggling beer into space was subversive..."

He shook his head in disgust and polished off his latest beer. "Anyway, they were definitely dumb to rely on a flathead like Lenny for intelligence, and that was the scary part."

As it turned out, the Caseyites did not know that beer was being smuggled into space. Instead, the Society was once again gnawing on a favorite old bone of the right-wing fringe which had been lying around since the Soviets had launched Sputnik in 1957, that the USSR was preparing to place nuclear warheads in orbit in preparation for a sneak attack on the US from space. Apparently the group had discarded one Commie plot for another. In any case, the Society had informed Lenny to be alert for such a scheme, if there were indeed an active Communist element infiltrating Olympus Station.

So naturally Lenny Gibson, America's vigilante in space, had discovered just such a plot. There were signs that a nuke would be ferried into orbit aboard an OTV, to be launched by the shuttle *Willy Ley* on April 12.

"Whoa, wait a minute," I said. "How did you know what he was thinking?"

"Remember those coded messages he was sending to Baltimore? Lenny would write them down first in plain English, then rewrite them into code on the same page. Once he memorized the coded message, he would tear up the page and dump the scraps into the toilet in his bunkhouse. But the moron forgot to flush the pot one day."

"So you found the scraps and put the uncoded message together."

Cowboy Bob nodded, grinning. "Plus he talked in his sleep sometimes. Some secret agent, right?"

"Right." I decided to take Bob's story with a few more grains of salt. The yarn was getting a little implausible. But I wasn't ready to call it total bullshit yet. "So now you knew that Lenny thought you guys were smuggling a bomb up there."

"Yeah. Even though it was funny as hell, it did present another problem. If the Caseyites took Lenny's reports seriously, they might decide to tip off somebody, like the FBI or NASA. Of course the feds might not take 'em seriously, but on the other hand NASA might not take any chances, and might make sure that security at the Shuttle Processing Center was tighter that week. So Lenny was becoming a pain the ass and we had to take care of him."

Pitching Lenny out the nearest airlock was briefly considered, but dismissed because nobody wanted to take a murder rap, although the idea was tempting. They also discussed tying him up and stuffing him into a suit locker for a few days, but the drawback was that he might be missed from his workshift. The conspirators thought about simply letting Gibson know what was going on, letting him in on the plan so that he would be aware that beer, not bombs, was the contraband inside the OTV scheduled to arrive on the 12th; yet a paranoid like Lenny would probably not believe the truth. Even if he did, it was always possible that he would twist it around so that the beer was being laced with mind-altering drugs by those evil Russians.

"Dog-Girl, bless her, came up with the answer," Bob continued. "Pretty simple, actually. Lenny had to maintain contact with his pals in Baltimore to do any real harm, right? This meant he had to use the phone. Orbit-to-Earth phone calls were rationed items, and you were only allowed to use up so many minutes a month. So we managed to get the communications officers to adjust the phone logs in the computer just a weensy bit so that, suddenly, Lenny was overdrawn on his phone rations for April. No more phone calls, no more messages to Aunt Jane and Uncle George. No secret messages, no word of a Commie plot."

"Nice going," I said. "But that just took care of the Caseyites leaking word to NASA. What about Lenny himself?"

"You're getting ahead of me, Al. I'll get to that. Hey, Jack! Another round here?"

Around this time a few more of the regulars were wandering into Diamondback Jack's; some were loitering around the bar watching a baseball game on TV, and a pool game was getting started at the table on the other side of the room. Bob was getting blitzed on the beers I was buying him and I was catching up, so I barely noticed the guy who had elbowed up to the bar a few feet behind Bob. He didn't look familiar, but that was the only impression I had of him. He seemed not to be paying attention to us and Bob didn't notice him; the next time I happened to look his way, he was gone. I didn't think about him again until later.

Two days before the *Willy Ley* made its April 12 milk run, the cargo loader whom Eddie the Goon had bribed, with the help of the four other loaders he paid off, quickly placed 444 cases of beer into OTV OL-3643. THe load-in took place during the first shift at the SPC, in the wee hours of the morning of April 10.

For the past week the cargo loaders had been smuggling the beer, a few cases a time, through the KSC security gates, hidden under camper caps in the backs of their trucks. The graveyard shift at the Cape was more easy-going than other shifts at the launch center; the shift supervisors tended to huddle over coffee in the cafeteria, so the loaders apparently had no trouble stashing the beer into the OTV. By the time the SPC's shift supervisor finished his early-morning coffee break, the OTV was sealed and was being trucked out to Pad 40 to be loaded into the *Ley's* cargo bay. The shift supervisor routinely checked off OL-3643 as ready to fly, not bothering to check inside.

Eddie the Goon received a telegram from his enterprising friends later that day, innocuously informing him that the party supplies were on the way. Goony grin plastered across his face, Eddie told Bob and the other principal people involved in the scam, and they put the next phase into motion by spreading word along the station grapevine: something wonderful was arriving by OTV at the docking module on April 11, at the beginning of the second shift, and a few volunteers were needed at the Docks to get it hauled from the station's hub down to the rim modules.

"You didn't tell them what was coming?" I asked.

Bob belched and shook his head. "Naw. We wanted it to be a surprise. We also didn't want Hank to find out. But we got enough guys to say they'd be there. Everybody knew it was something good."

As anticipated, Lenny the Red got the word through the grapevine. He had realized by now that his messages weren't getting through to Paranoid Central—all part of the Commie plot, of course—so he interpreted the subterfuge as the hatching of the conspiracy. Right idea, wrong conspiracy. To the quiet satisfaction of Cowboy Bob and company, Lenny began to get jumpy. He even switched his bunk assignment again.

"We knew that Dick Tracy would be at the Docks when our OTV arrived, of course," Bob said. "He was planning on something, though we didn't know what. There weren't any guns on Skycan that we knew of, but maybe he had managed to sneak one up in case he had to assassinate some Commies. Maybe he was planning to defuse the nuke all by himself, I dunno. But we just made sure that he was covered when he got there."

He reached for a cigarette and almost knocked over his beer without noticing. Jack threw us a look of warning which Bob didn't catch either. He was ripped. "So when the day came, at 1100 hours about, there were ten, fifteen guys crowded into the Docks when the OTV hard-docked with Skycan. Eddie and Fred and me and a couple of the other 'jacks were kinda casually floating around Lenny while Chang pressurized the airlock and undogged the hatch, so I got to see Lenny's face when the thing was opened up."

Cowboy Bob coughed loudly, and then began to laugh. "Jesus! Was he pissed! He was staring with this look on his face when Dog-Boy got the covers and ropes off and started pushing one case after another out into the Docks."

Bob drunkenly hobbled off his bar stool. "Man! One case after another! Fred screaming 'Free beer! Free beer!' And all the guys howling, cracking up, grabbing the cases. Someone opened a can—and you can imagine how shook up that stuff was, after sitting through a rocket launch—and beer started spewing all over the place, making these big yellow bubbles that flew all around, splattering everywhere, and more guys started appearing, hauling the cases out of the Docks, down the ladders through the spokes to the rim. A fucking riot, Al...and in the middle of all this, Lenny, mouth working like a fish, can't believe what's going on, shouts..."

Bob shot his arm out wide and yelled, getting the attention of everyone in the bar: "'This is un-American! Where's the goddamn bomb?'"

"Hey, Cowboy!" Jack snarled from the other end of the bar. "Cool it or I'll cut you off!"

Bob was doubled over the bar, cracking up and breathless with the memory of the scene. He got control of himself after a few moments. Clambering back on his stool and reaching for his beer, he said, "And that's when we dropped the blanket over him."

Jack Baker gave us one last round of beers and then shut us both off, after first making me walk a straight line to see if I were halfway capable of driving both Bob and myself home. While Cowboy Bob sucked down his last beer he finished the story.

Once Bob, Eddie, and Fred had grabbed Lenny in the blanket and trussed him with nylon cords, they shoved him into an empty suit locker in the Docks and locked it shut. By then the party was beginning to roll down into the rim modules; most of the second-shift beamjacks were logging in sick, and the third shift was looking for excuses. Once it became obvious that a surprise party was in progress and that trying to shut it down would only incite general mutiny, Hank Luton grudgingly called the day off, halting construction work for the next twenty-four hours before heading down to the rim himself. He later told the honchos at Skycorp and NASA that a spread of stomach virus had caused the stop-work. No big deal, in the long run; the party only delayed the low-power tests by a day.

Sometime during the celebration, Bob and Eddie and Dog-Girl slipped to the Docks, hauling behind them two garbage bags filled with empty beer cans. Dog-Girl had already sneaked into the vacant medical bay and swiped one of Doc Felapolous' sedative guns. The three of them opened the suit locker and Dog-Girl tranked Lenny with a shot to the neck, and once Lenny was in a stupor they untied him and stuffed him into a hardsuit, making certain that he had two full airtanks in his life-support pack.

"We then threw him in the OTV, emptied the bags in there so that there were dozens of empty cans floating around with him, and closed the hatch." Bob said. "Dog-Girl and the Goon reset the nav computer so it would rendezvous with Columbus Station in LEO, and then we fired the sunnuvabitch back to Earth. Never saw him again."

"That was all?" I asked.

Bob, smiling and slumped over the bar, looked at me and shook his head slowly. "Well...not quite. See, I taped a note on the back of Lenny's suit, where he couldn't see it or take it off. It said, 'To the Bill Casey Society...take your drunk stool pigeon and shove him!' I didn't sign it, but I think Lenny let 'em know who the author was, and I don't think they appreciated my sense of humor."

Neither did Skycorp, which was how Cowboy Bob lost his contract bonus and got nailed with a couple of fines with deflated his payroll. He ended up on the "unhirable" list with the major space companies as a result of the Free Beer Conspiracy. When the hammer inevitably came down, he alone took the pounding.

"But y'know what, Al?" he said as I half-carried him towards the door. "I don't give a shit. Y'gotta have a sense of humor. Flatheads like the Casey jerks...they don't have a sense of humor, goddamn fanatics. Following me, telling me I gotta keep my mouth shut. I pissed on them from a considerable height, and I'd do it again if I could..."

Bob threw up in the bushes behind the bar, then passed out in the shotgun seat of my car after mumbling directions to his house. I concentrated on keeping my vision straight as I carefully drove down Route 3 towards Cocoa Beach. It was a quarter pass midnight when I drove over the Banana River causeway onto Route A1A, cruising through the beachfront commercial strip of Cocoa Beach. The night was black as space, wet and humid like the inside of a dog's mouth, neon-glittering like the old visions of the high frontier.

A couple of units, a pump and a ladder, from the Cocoa Beach Fire Department screamed passed us in the left lane as I passed the old Satellite Motel. Bob, snoring in the depths of his drunken sleep, paid no attention, nor did I until we passed the commercial zone and headed into the residential part of town. Then the stranger, the guy who had lingered in Jack's near Bob and I while he was telling me the story, oddly came to mind, for no particular reason. Remembering him, I also recalled something Bob had told me about Lenny Gibson, how he used to hang around in the Skycan rec room, attempting to eavesdrop on conversations. I began to feel uneasy. For no particular reason.

As I turned the corner onto the residential street where Bob told me he lived, I spotted the fire trucks again, parked in the street in front of a small white Florida-style stucco house, practically identical to all the other white stucco houses lining the road. The house was ablaze with fire shooting through a collapsing roof and the firemen directing streams of water through broken front windows, while people stood around beyond the piles of hoses, watching the blaze. I slowed to a stop behind the trucks and shook Bob awake.

"Hey, Bob," I said. "One of your neighbors has his house on fire."

Bob's eyes cracked open, and he stared through the windshield at the burning house. He didn't say anything for a few moments, just stared.

"It *is* one of your neighbor's, isn't it?" I asked, feeling an unseasonal chill.

Cowboy Bob didn't look at me, nor did he laugh, but his mouth twisted into a sad, angry sort of smile. "What did I tell you?" he whispered at last. "Fanatics. No goddamn sense of humor."

True story.

THE RETURN OF WEIRD FRANK

This is a warning, the only one you'll get, so don't take it lightly: this is a truly bizarre and ugly story. In all probability it is a lie since it was told to me second-hand in a seedy Florida barroom, the last place one should ever expect to hear the truth about anything; if it isn't a lie, then human affairs are even more depraved than you may have imagined.

If you're searching for a nice, soothing yarn which will make you sleep easier tonight, snug and secure in the knowledge that people are essentially decent and that, even in the frontier of space, there are certain codes of human behavior by which all men and women abide, then it is strongly suggested that you skip this story. This tale is a rabid dog with a mouthful of foam and an attitude.

This is the story of Weird Frank and the terrible things which were done to his stinking corpse, and if you're not ready for some unsettling weirdness, it's time to go away before things get messy.

You have been warned.

By sheer coincidence, it was on a Halloween night when I first noticed the photo of Weird Frank on the wall behind the bar at Diamondback Jack's. I wasn't thinking of ghosts, zombies, or the so-called things which go bump in the night. In fact, I had even forgotten that it was Halloween. It was a dull evening and I had dropped by the roadhouse to have a couple of beers before heading home to my place in Cocoa Beach.

Diamondback Jack's is a scruffy little beer joint located on Route 3 on Merritt Island, about two miles down the highway from the west gate of Kennedy Space Center. It is very much a blue-collar kind of place, and not even a nice one at that; don't seek it out unless you know how to handle yourself in a fight with a mean drunk who has murder on his mind because you happened to bump into his cue while he was laying up a two-corner shot on the pool table. The ambiance is Late American Redneck: sticky floors, battered cheap furniture, bad lighting, and a juke box filled mainly with country-western CDs. No windows, a sand parking lot splattered with oil, vomit and piss, and a men's room in which you don't want to spend much time. The varnished hide of a four-foot rattler is mounted above the bar; it either came from the hide of a snake which the owner, Jack Baker, claimed to have killed while on a fishing trip in the Everglades, or from one of the regulars who bounced a check on him.

Diamondback Jack's is a hangout for space pros, the men and women at the Cape who do the hands-on dirty work of the high frontier: shuttle jocks, pad rats, cargo dips, software weenies, firing room honchos, Vacuum Suckers, itinerant beamjacks and moondogs who hang out there between off-Earth jobs—and it shows. Framed photos of space scenes are on all the walls: shuttle liftoffs, shots of the lunar base at Descartes, the big wheel of Olympus Station under construction, the assembly of the first SPS powersat. Behind the long oak bar where the owner, Jack Baker, holds court every night are more pictures: vets of the final frontier, living and dead, famous and infamous. Some of the faces belong to regular customers; most, though, are legends, if only among the fraternity of pros. No one else knows their names.

I thought I was familiar with each face on the wall, but that night, for the first time, I spotted a picture which I had simply never noticed before. Jack had rearranged the bottles behind the bar, so the tall-necked vodka bottles were in a different place and no longer blocked this particular photo. I was bored, and while sitting on the bar stool and absently scanning the pictures, I happened to notice this one.

The man in the photo had dark, curly hair and a greasy handlebar mustache; he looked like the sort of person you might imagine making obscene phone calls to a Catholic convent. He was wearing a Skycorp jumpsuit with the sleeves cut off, grinning at the camera while throttling a rubber chicken in his hairy hands. Fairly unremarkable, compared to some of the other pictures on the wall, except that someone had taped a handwritten caption to the bottom of the frame. I stood up on the rungs of my stool, leaned over the bartop, and squinted at the caption. It read:

THE RETURN OF WEIRD FRANK

FRANK MCDOWELL — THE GREATEST CORPSE WHO EVER LIVED.

Who can ignore a line like that?

"Hey, Jack," I called out. "Who was Frank McDowell?"

Jack Baker was sitting at the opposite end of the bar, suffering through a newspaper crossword puzzle. He looked up, followed my gaze to the photograph, then sighed and closed his eyes. "Never mind," he said.

"I'm serious," I insisted. "Who was Frank McDowell, and why was he the greatest corpse who ever lived?"

Jack glared at me, then laid down his pencil and walked over to my end of the bar, pulling a fresh Budweiser out of the cooler on the way. "This one's on the house if you drop the question," he said as he placed the beer in front of me.

It was tempting, but the worst way to shake a journalist's curiosity is to attempt bribing him. "I'll pay for the beer, thanks. I just want to know..."

"Yeah, right." He gave me a long, hard stare, saying nothing for a few moments. "This doesn't end up in your paper, does it?" he asked quietly.

That was a serious question, potentially endangering my good standing in the bar. In my case, being in bad standing at Diamondback Jack's possibly meant being dragged out back and having the shit kicked out of me for no good reason at all. There are a number of different people who are not welcome in the bar: top NASA officials, executives for the major space companies, union reps, tourists, space groupies, children...and journalists. Especially journalists. Reporters are perceived around the Cape as having screwed the space pros since the Project Mercury days. Gators, leeches, and rattlesnakes are held in higher regard on the Space Coast than the press; at least their behavior is excusable because of their nature, and none of them has ever pushed a camera or a live mike into the faces of a family who has just watched a shuttle blow up nine miles downrange from the pad. With only one exception, none were tolerated in Diamondback Jack's.

I was the exception. I was the only writer allowed on the premises, and this was because I never opened my notebook or turned on my recorder in the bar, or repeated anything that I had heard or seen in my freelance articles for the *Times*. For this reason,

Jack served me and the other regulars didn't beat me up in the parking lot on general principles.

My status was hard-won, and I was careful never to abuse the privilege. "I promise," I said solemnly. "Just tell me what..."

I shrugged and pointed to the photo with the mysterious caption. Jack gave me one more look of warning—"fuck with me and I'll ram an ice-scoop down your throat"—then he raised a hand and whistled. "Hey, Marty! C'mere! Al wants to know something."

There was a heavy-set guy with long, dirty blond hair shooting pool by himself at the other side of the room. I had seen him in the bar before, but had never met him. He put down his cue, walked over and elbowed up against the bar next to me. Jack introduced us: his name was Marty—last names seldom matter in Diamondback Jack's—and he had been a beamjack on Olympus Station back in '22 and '23, the years when SPS-3 was being built. Marty looked tough as a whore; when he reached for his beer, I noticed that he had the letters H-A-T-E tattooed across the thick knuckles of his right hand. But he was willing to talk as long as I bought the suds.

Jack put another round in front of us, then returned to his crossword puzzle. "What do you want to know?" Marty asked.

"The picture," I replied, pointing again to the photo of Frank McDowell. "What's with the caption on that picture? 'The Greatest...'"

"'The Greatest Corpse Who Ever Lived,'" Marty finished, nodding his head. "Uh-huh. I wrote that."

"What's it mean?"

Marty smiled and looked down at the scratched bartop, idly tracing his finger around the wet ring left by a bottle. "Do you know it's Halloween?"

"It is? I forgot...yeah, I guess so. Why?"

He laughed and picked up his beer. "Are you in the mood for a Halloween story?" He took a sip and peered at me over the neck of his bottle. "I mean, a true story? None of this shit about the Hook, stuff like that?"

"Sure. Why not?"

"Right." He looked at the picture on the wall for a moment. "Okay...so long as you don't say I didn't warn you."

THE RETURN OF WEIRD FRANK

When Marty had been employed by Skycorp in 2022 as one of the high-orbit construction workers who were building the first powersats, there had been another beamjack aboard Olympus Station named Frank McDowell. It's a well-known fact that many of the men and women who worked as beamjacks aboard Skycan were deranged. Sanity was not a necessary prerequisite for working in space, at least not with the private American space companies. The big buffalo went to work in space, and only the toughest and craziest of the herd were hired for the obligatory one-year contracts on Olympus. Weird Frank, though, was one of the most fucked of a fucked-up crowd.

Weird Frank was a practical joker without a decent sense of humor. He was the type of person who is compelled to play pranks, but doesn't have a good handle on what is funny and what is not. Weird Frank liked to put fresh turds in people's bunks or line the crotch of their hardsuits with Ben-Gay. Weird Frank would find out that someone had a dead sister, then would tell another guy that the poor girl had a great body and he should ask about getting a date once they got back to Earth. Weird Frank, while some guy was floating next to him in the EVA ready-room, suiting up for work on the next shift, would surreptitiously drain his air supply from his life-support pack; when that person got out on tether, he would find that he only had about ten minutes of oxygen in the tank, just enough time to get into an emergency airlock. Weird Frank would borrow your water squeezebulb during a break and spit down the tube, then crack up when you put it to your mouth: "Heeeeey, Phil! I just spit in your water..."

"Weird Frank was a sick kinda dude," Marty said. "I don't know why we put up with him as long as we did."

"So why did you?" I asked.

Marty swigged his beer. "He was a nice guy somehow. He got under your skin, sure, but nothing he did was much worse than any of the weird bullshit anyone else did up there. And there wasn't anything really malicious about what he did ... it was just the way he did it. Every now and then someone would grab him by the neck and get ready to pound the fuck out of him, and his eyes would go wide and he'd put up his hands. 'Hey, man, I didn't mean it, I swear!'"

I nodded. I knew a jerk like Weird Frank, during my teenage exile to a boarding school in Tennessee. That guy, though, was too large to be pounded and his daddy was too wealthy for the school to afford to expel him, which explained how he got away with his pranks. After twenty years, though, I would still like to get him alone in a dark alley. "Nobody ever got serious with him?"

"Not really. Frank wanted to be a pal, that's all. He just didn't know what a good joke was...except when he told one accidentally, then we all laughed." He shrugged. "But that wasn't very often. The guy was a freak. We were looking for some way to get him off Skycan when he got killed." Something in my chest went cold. "Marty," I asked tentatively, "did somebody...?"

He shook his head. "Uh-uh. Nothing like that. We only were trying to find a way to get his contract cancelled. What happened was an accident, believe me."

In March, 2022, a wicked series of solar flares occurred on the surface of the Sun. Solar flares are extremely difficult, if not impossible, to predict. The only way astronomers can tell that they're coming is by gauging the eleven-year cycle of increased sunspot activity and watching for an increase in solar luminosity preceding a major flux...a dicey proposition at best, considering that these flares occur with the swift, random violence of a serial killer deciding it was time to take to the streets again.

The protons were potentially lethal to the work crews on the powersats, since they were on EVA outside the shielded environments of Olympus Station or the construction shack, Vulcan Station. On the other hand, everyone had to play things very close. The construction schedule for SPS-3 was such that Skycorp couldn't order an indefinite stop-work just because someone thought a solar flare might occur soon. Crying wolf could result in several days of labor being lost for nothing, and even the beamjacks didn't want to sit around in the bunkhouse modules, wasting time for little reason. Not when their bonuses depended upon completing each stage of construction on time. So flare alerts were done at the last minute, when it was absolutely certain that serious storms were kicking up on the Sun's corona and that everyone had better dive for cover. In general, there was a nine-minute leeway between the time the flares reached lethal proportions and time their radiation reached Earth orbit. When the alerts happened, beamjacks on EVA abandoned whatever they were doing, untethered from the powersat and split for the Vulcan Station, mucho pronto.

On the day that a flare alert was called, Weird Frank was on EVA, but not on the powersat, where he could have seen everyone heading for shelter in the construction shack. He was outside Olympus Station, performing one of the routine jobs that, once each week, someone draws from the duty roster: "hole patrol," checking the outer hulls of the rim modules for micrometeorite damage and filling the little holes with "Silly Putty", the goop used to repair small punctures. When the alert was called, Frank McDowell apparently did not hear, nor did he respond.

"Why didn't he hear the alert?" I asked.

Marty finished his beer, belched and signaled Jack to bring us another round. "The stupid sumbitch had stuck a micro-CD in his chest unit, where you usually put talk-through tutorials for new guys. He had put in Led Zeppelin and cranked it to the max, so he couldn't hear anything coming over his comlink. When Command was trying to warn him to get inside, all he was hearing was Led Zep. Drowned out everything else." He shrugged. "Can't knock his taste, though. Led Zep was classic shit for spacewalking..."

"But he never got inside?"

"Oh, he finally got in. Not until the CD ended, though, or until he started feeling dizzy. They had been yelling for him to get inside for ten minutes after the storm hit us before he cycled through the hub airlock and told Dave Chang he felt sick. Then he collapsed, right there in the Docks. Chang got his suit off and called Doc Felapolous, but by the time Doc got up there, Frank was comatose. The radiation had gone right through his suit. Bone marrow, lymph glands, guts and nuts..."

Marty winced and snapped his fingers. "Boom. He was a dead man before he even got to the airlock. The only good thing was that he was unconscious when he kicked off. Poor bastard died hard. It's a shitty way to go."

"Hmmm." I took another hit off my beer and gazed at the photo of Weird Frank, grinning and strangling a rubber bird. "That's it?"

Marty chuckled morosely and looked at the picture himself. "Nope. That was just the beginning. Weird Frank wasn't about to let go that easy. The fucker couldn't leave without playing another practical joke."

"But he was dead...."

"That's what I said." Marty took another chug from his beer, oblivious to his own rhyme. "The problem was, we couldn't get rid of the body."

In the old science fiction movies, the cliche was that the dearly departed was given a burial in space, much like the traditional burial at sea practiced by sailors, except that in the films the shroud-wrapped corpse was ejected from the spacecraft, presumably to float through the cosmos forever. Stirring music, bagpipes, grim comrades, Matthew 7 read by the captain...yeah, you know the bit.

The truth, however, is that nobody is ever buried in space. For one thing, the families and friends of the deceased usually want to bury them at home. For another, NASA pathologists back at the Cape perform autopsies as standard operating procedure, at least to settle life insurance requirements, not to mention making sure the space companies aren't overlooking government regulations. Besides, the way people die out there is still a seldom-documented aspect of space medicine, since it doesn't occur all that often. Every stiff is an education, you might say; the more you learn from one chap's demise, the more it may help to save the next guy who knocks on heaven's door.

Because people do get killed in space, though, there are a number of contingency plans. Black, heavy-duty plastic body bags were stowed in Skycan's sickbay; once Frank was pronounced dead, Doc Felapolous zipped his corpse into one of them. Yet it was more difficult than usual to inter Frank's body until it could be returned to Earth.

Standard practice, albeit seldom mentioned beyond the pages of the NASA manual, dictates that the body-bagged corpse should be taken outside the pressure vessel and tied to the outer hull with cables. When people had died before on Olympus Station, their bodies were lashed to the station's hub to await pickup by the next OTV to dock with Skycan. The stiffs were then taken down-orbit to Freedom Station where they were loaded into a shuttle for the last leg of their final journey to Earth.

In Frank McDowell's case, however, this couldn't be done. The solar flares which had killed him were still raging, and were likely to continue for several days. Anyone attempting an EVA to tie the body to the station hub would have suffered the same fate Weird Frank had met. To make matters worse, all OTV flights to geosynchronous orbit were halted until the storm was over, since solar flares tended to screw up their inertial guidance systems and cause them to head for the Moon and points beyond. A retrieval of the corpse any time soon was out of the question, and even to load Frank's body into one of Skycan's own OTVs was inadvisable, since the hub airlock was the least shielded of the station's modules.

"So you were stuck with a dead body," I said. "What did you do with him?" Marty belched into his fist. "'Scuse me. Doc took the only option that was available. He had one of the big refrigerators in the galley emptied out and the racks removed, and we stored him in there."

"Oh, jeez! The cooks must have loved that."

"They weren't crazy about it, no, but Doc made sure all the food was removed so that there wasn't a chance of contamination." He absently picked at the label on his beer bottle. "It wasn't a bad idea, considering the circumstances. At least then no one had to look at him. The fridge had a temperature of 37 degrees Fahrenheit, so Frank remained...well, fresh."

"Fresh meat. Sure."

"Yeah, right. Anyway, he was put in an upright position and sealed in a black body bag. Doc hung a 'Do Not Disturb' sign on the door, so..."

I started to laugh. Marty gave me a dubious look. "If you think that's funny," he said, "you're gonna love the rest."

Death didn't occur often aboard Skycan, but when it did there was tradition to be observed, even when the deceased was a geek like Frank McDowell. His passage from the mortal coil was marked by an Irish wake in the rec room.

This is swell for scholars and saints, but by then there were already signs that Weird Frank was not going to be honored in a manner befitting scholars and saints. At dinnertime, someone had altered the chalkboard menu in the mess module to announce that tonight's entrees would include Soup du Frank, Frankloaf, and Frank-eyed peas, with Frozen Frank Pudding for dessert...and it didn't help that the real main course was liver. But it was not until the wake that everyone's true feelings emerged in regards to their fallen comrade.

There was plenty of beer to go around, since Skycorp had finally relaxed its in-orbit alcohol standards after the smuggling incident with the Free Beer conspiracy. For this mournful occasion, one of the weekends-only kegs was released from storage; since no one was working any EVA shifts because of the flare and wasn't likely to do so within the next couple of days, almost everyone took the opportunity to get loaded.

During the first couple of rounds, most people were sincerely regretful about Weird Frank's death: "Christ, man, what a way to buy the farm." By the third round, though, many former victims of Frank's bad practical jokes were recalling their experiences ("Hey, remember the story he told about your sister?") and the rest were expressing the opinion that it was better that Frank's number had been called instead of their own ("I was supposed to be on hole patrol tomorrow, d'ya'know that?"). By the fourth round, a few folks were quietly saying that the asshole deserved it ("Like, y'know, you get what's coming to you in this life, right?") and by the sixth, the opinion was unanimous ("Fuck him and good riddance").

"That was when Frank made his first appearance," Marty said.

"Let me guess," I said. "A picture fell from the wall, or a cup mysteriously moved from one side of a table to another." I couldn't help it. Marty had promised me a Halloween story, and I had heard enough ghost stories from allegedly reliable sources to think I recognized a punchline when it was coming. Okay, here comes another bullshit yarn about the Haunted Space Station...

"No, no," he replied. "I mean, *Frank* returned."

"Yeah. You looked up and saw him sitting in a chair. He was surrounded by this strange glow and..."

"When nobody was looking," Marty said calmly, "Russ the Bus and Horny Harry had sneaked over to the mess deck, found the fridge where Doc had stashed the body, and carried Frank back to the party."

"...come again?"

He smiled and took another swig from his beer. "I didn't even see it happen. I was over at the holotable watching the Lakers game when I heard some commotion behind me. I didn't pay any attention, but I had just gotten through telling somebody about the time Weird Frank had reset my suit comlink so that I was picking up Russian crosstalk when Russ tapped me on the shoulder. 'Hey, Marty, why doncha tell Frank what you thought about his shit?' I turned around to tell the Bus to get lost..."

Marty grinned and shrugged. "And there was this body bag leaned up against the wall next to the hatch ladder. Frank."

"Jesus Christ," I murmured.

"No, it was Frank..."

"That's pretty ill..."

Marty's head cocked back and forth. "Actually, it was pretty funny at the time," he said, completely blasé about the notion. "We were all bombed, of course, and Frank wasn't high on anyone's list of best-loved dead people."

"But still..."

"Hey, the party was for him, so what the fuck? Anyway, everybody got their chance to come around and give Frank their last regards or whatever."

"That's sick!"

"Looky. The Russians put Lenin's stiff in a glass case for almost a whole century. That was a national symbol for them." Marty smiled and tipped his bottle toward me. "I mean, there's worse ways to be remembered. If anything, showing up for his own wake was the best practical joke Frank ever pulled."

I started to say that Weird Frank hadn't led the Russian communist revolution, as a practical joke or otherwise, but Marty sipped his beer and went on.

"The bag was kept zipped up, because nobody wanted to really look at him, but the thought that Weird Frank had made it to his own wake...well, you had to be there. It was funny."

The humor was lost on Doc Felapolous when he stopped by the rec room a few minutes later to see how the wake was going. Skycan's chief physician went berserk when he discovered that the body had been stolen from the refrigerator. After chewing out everyone in sight, he picked two crewmen at random to carry Frank's body back to the galley, and Felapolous sealed the hatch with his keycard so no one else would try the same thing again.

That should have been the end of it. It wasn't.

While Marty visited the men's room, I got Jack to bring us another round and a shot of tequila for myself; this was beginning to look like a story best taken with raw liquor. Marty continued his tale when he got back from the head.

"You couldn't keep the mess deck locked at all times because everyone had most of the keycard codes for everything else," he went on. "Even though Doc had encrypted the hatchlock, it wasn't hard for Horny Harry to figure out that, in a hurry, Doc might use the numbers 4-15-3 on the keypad...which spells D-O-C in alphanumeric. So it was easy for someone to get in there to steal the body from the fridge."

I nodded. There was no real need to ask why a normally sane person would resort to body-snatching for kicks. It was well known that life on Olympus Station was monotonous: sleep, eat, work, and not much else. People often compared the wild nightlife in Skycan to that of Deadhorse, Alaska. The guys who signed contracts with Skycorp to work for one or two years on the powersats didn't do so to meet girls or to visit thrilling countries. They went up to make big fast money in a gritty, dangerous job, not to conquer the universe. Nonetheless, time tended to drag on Skycan, and bored people often do weird things to keep themselves amused. Skycan was a place where the circle jerk could easily be recognized as a team sport by the Olympics Committee. In this instance, the crew didn't even have their jobs to keep themselves occupied. The flare had forced a construction shutdown for several days; it was too dangerous to leave Olympus Station. So what do you do, after Monopoly becomes monotonous and you've watched all the old movies in the rec room several times?

Well, when there's the dead body of a practical joker no one particularly liked...

"The Bus got it next, which was appropriate since he was the one who had the idea of springing Frank from the fridge in the first place." Marty grinned and shook his head. "He was in the rec room playing poker when someone behind him slipped and fell against him with a cup of coffee. Accidentally, of course."

"Of course."

"So that meant he had to go back to his bunk in Module 28 to get a clean shirt, right? He opened his locker and...boom, Frank falls out!"

"Terrific. Amazingly humorous."

Marty snickered. "Four or five of us were waiting up on the catwalk outside the module. We thought he would scream his head off, but there was just this long silence. Then he climbs up the ladder, sticks his head through the hatch, and said, 'Very goddamn funny.'"

"Hmm. Kind of anti-climactic." I sipped my beer as a thought occurred to me. "By the way, shouldn't Frank have been getting a little whiffy, shall we say?"

Marty shook his head. "Naw. For one thing, we were keeping him in the body-bag. And he was in the fridge between appearances, so he was staying...fresh, y'know? Rigor mortis had set in, though, so we couldn't bend his arms or legs without breaking 'em. One of the guys in the Weird Frank Fan Club..."

"The what?"

"That's what we started calling ourselves. The Bus, Harry, myself, a few other guys. Anyway, one of us, Gene, had been an intern with an Army medic unit in Nicaragua before he signed up with Skycorp, so he knew something about the care and feeding of corpses. As long as Frank was kept on ice between his guest appearances and they were kept pretty brief, we didn't have to worry much about decomposition."

Marty took another hit from his beer. "In any case, the stunt with Russ's locker had been a little unsatisfactory, so we had to come up with something better. Something Frank would have appreciated. After thinking about it for awhile, we came up with it. For his next mission, though, Frank had to come out of the bag."

Later that same day, the fan club raided the fridge again and smuggled Frank to the data processing center in Module Six. Lonnie, the data processing chief, had often complained about the daily updates he had to make to Skycorp's Operations Center in Huntsville. The verbal status reports sometimes took more than a half-hour and were boring reiterations of everything which was already on the data downlink, and Lonnie was never certain if he were being heard by a human or just another AI mainframe. That afternoon, with Lonnie's blessing, the Weird Frank Fan Club put the system to a test; they unzipped Weird Frank from his body bag, propped him in a seat facing the camera, and while Lonnie crouched below the camera with a mike and hard-copy of his update, they called Huntsville SOC.

"And y'know what?" Marty asked. "Nobody down there noticed. They had a dead man on their screens for twenty fucking minutes and no one in Huntsville even mentioned that his lips didn't move or his eyes were shut. Lonnie had a hard time keeping from cracking up. As for us..." He shrugged. "Well, it just confirmed that the front office people were even more dead from the neck up than Frank. But it wasn't much fun."

"So?" It was all beginning to sound just a bit juvenile. "What were you expecting?"

Marty looked at me askance. "When you were a kid, didn't you ever put a rubber rat in your mother's bed just to watch her scream? Something like that. We wanted to see someone loose their shit, but good. I mean, hauling a dead person around ain't fun unless someone pays attention."

"I get what you mean." I knew the general idea, although the most I had ever done with it was sending a roadkilled squirrel to an editor who had stiffed me on a check. I played with my empty bottle, holding the narrow neck between my thumb and forefinger and rolling the wide bottom back and forth across the bartop. "Did you ever....?"

"Uh-huh. But by then, we had taken the joke a little too far."

Weird Frank fell out of two more lockers and made another visit to the rec room, but the joke was quickly becoming stale. Then somebody—Marty would not tell me who, but the disturbed twinkle in his eyes gave me a strong hint—came up with the ultimate gag.

"The Sex Monster was a beamjack who had been up there for seven months," Marty explained, "and had already frightened half the guys in the station. She was the horniest woman in Skycan..."

"That should have made her popular," I said drily. It was no secret that most men who worked on the station went through involuntary celibacy...blueballs is the operative term. Skycan was a small, closed environment, and the company frowned on sexual congress in space ("insurance problems" was the catch-all phrase, as it was for almost everything else which was fun). So if a male got attracted to any given female among the crew, she was probably either happily married or formally engaged to some dork on the ground. And, even if a guy got lucky by finding a good woman who didn't care about her fiance in Great Falls tonight and was ready for a little sleazy sex, there was damn little privacy for making whoopie. Unless, of course, you didn't mind being interrupted by the comments of half a dozen spectators standing right outside your bunk, many of whom had placed bets upon who would achieve orgasm first.

But the Sex Monster was a different case altogether; she was the subject of nobody's wet dream. She was six-four, weighed close to two hundred pounds, and had arms and legs like a gold medal Iron Man Triathalon runner; those who had seen her in the buff said that she resembled a sumo wrestler. This was a woman who practiced sex as a form of unarmed combat, a bull-nympho who could probably take on the entire starting lineup of the San Francisco 49ers and leave them in traction until the Superbowl. The Marquis de Sade would have hidden in a closet.

The Sex Monster had a temper, her sex drive was insatiable, and the combination spelled terror for every man in Olympus Station. A dozen guys would be in the rec room watching TV when a pair of heavy boots would coming clomping down the stairs and a deep, not-at-all feminine voice would howl...

"I wanna get fucked!"

And every man would hold his breath and stand still like a rabbit...

"I said, I wanna get FUCKED!"

Then the entire room would be squirming uncomfortably, cowering against the bulkheads, and faking chest-colds until she had selected today's lover and dragged him, whimpering pitifully, up the ladder back to her lair in Module 34, a bunkhouse which all the other women who had shared had abandoned rather than witness any more of her depravity. God forgive the putz who couldn't get it up for her.

"But Frank didn't have that problem," Marty said with an evil giggle.

The Fan Club noticed that Weird Frank's corpse had undergone a strange, morbidly funny change. In the cold confines of the refrigerator, propped up in a vertical position, all his blood had gradually drained down to the lower half of his body, a phenomenon not unknown to morticians. This had produced for Frank a formidable erection that would have put a porn-movie star to shame, a permanent hard-on which simply could not go limp. The stiff was stiff, one could say.

The opportunity was too good to miss.

By now I was shaking my head. "Oh, no," I was saying. "Don't tell me you did. Please don't tell me you did. Please don't tell me you did..."

"Yes," he said softly, "we did." Marty took a long draw from his beer. "When the Monster returned to her bunk after her shift, there was a man waiting for her in bed. And, needless to say, the lights were out..."

"God, that's vile...!"

"We were waiting outside the hatch, but we couldn't hear anything for the first couple of minutes. I think she might have actually started to go down on him when she noticed that he was rather cold and unresponsive..." The leer on his face was hideous. "Mainly cold."

"You're EVIL!" I yelled. I started to grab the neck of my beer bottle, preparing to bash in his skull. Baker, who had been listening from the other end of the bar, made a grab for the Louisville Slugger he kept under the cash register for salesmen and lawyers; judging from the look on his face, though, he might have been getting ready to help me.

Marty went on relentlessly, oblivious to both of us. "Then, all of a sudden, there was a screech you could hear halfway across the station. Pure fucking terror..."

"I can't blame her..."

"Then we heard her scream again. This time, she was nothing except pissed off, because she had been in the rec room during Frank's wake. 'Goddammitattohell,' she yelled, 'I'm sick of this fucking shit!' We jumped back from the hatch and suddenly the Monster comes up the ladder, hauling Frank behind her, wrapped in a blanket."

Wearing only a bathrobe and with a homicidal look in her eyes which made even the Bus scurry away, the Sex Monster hauled the body up the ladder. As every one dove for cover behind each other, she began dragging the swathed corpse down the upward-curving central passageway. It was understandable why she was less than respectful to the condition of the body, but it didn't make the situation less macabre. A couple of Frank's mortified fingers broke loose and lay on the green industrial carpet in her wake.

"She headed straight for Module 30, the waste reclamation center, screaming obscenities all the way," Marty continued. "We didn't know what was she was planning until she opened the hatch and started to shove Frank down, and even then there was nothing we could do about it. I mean, she had completely flipped...!"

The station's main airlocks were in the hub, but there was a small, exit-only airlock in Module 30 which was used by the life-support engineers for the disposal of solid waste which could not be recycled. Before anyone could stop the Sex Monster, she had shoved Weird Frank into the tube, slammed the hatch closed, and hit the jettison button.

She didn't even bother to decompress the airlock first; Frank went in one end of the tube and was shot out of Skycan through the other. There was no reading from Matthew.

"And that was the last you saw of Weird Frank," I finished.

Marty shook his head; the grin had disappeared from his face. "No," he said slowly, "it was not."

The main reason why dead astronauts are not given burials in space has to do with physics: if they were simply let loose from an airlock, without sufficient forward motion, their bodies would establish their own miniature orbits around the spacecraft or station. But, in the case of the Sex Monster ejecting Weird Frank from Skycan, two different things happened. She had not bothered to decompress the airlock, thus the sudden opening of the outer hatch blew the corpse completely clear of the station.

Frank's remains went into their own eccentric orbit, all right...but in a geosynchronous orbit around Earth, not around either Skycan or Vulcan Station.

"Once we realized what had happened," Marty continued, "someone ran up to the command center and explained things to one of the traffic control officers. We thought that, if we could pinpoint Frank's location on radar, we could send out a work pod to retrieve him from space."

He leveled his hands in a shrug. "But the TRAFCO couldn't find anything on his screen, so we figured that, just maybe, the station's rotation had been such that Module 30 was pointed toward Earth and..."

"Frank's trajectory would take him to burnup in the upper atmosphere," I finished. "Okay. Reasonable assumption. What did you do about it?"

Marty shrugged and picked up the fresh beer which Jack Baker had placed in front of him. "Nothing, really. What was done, was done. Doc Felapolous was pissed off and we lost a week's salary in company fines when Skycorp got the story out from him, but Doc explained to Frank's relatives that we had opted for burial in space..."

"They didn't know better?"

"Naw, they didn't know better...and how would you explain it if you wanted to tell the truth? Anyway, we figured that was the end of it. The next day the flares died and the alert ended, so we all went back to work on SPS-3."

And that still was not the end of the grim affair.

Two days later, during the second work-shift on the powersat, a beamjack who was welding trusses at the far end of the platform was informed by the foreman in Vulcan's command center that a mass of small objects was headed in his direction. This was unusual, but not unlikely; space junk tended to float through the construction zone from time to time. It only meant that anyone on EVA had to take cover until it passed, then a robot sweeper would be sent out to gather up the garbage before it posed a hazard to anyone else.

"I was on tether on the other side of the powersat," Marty explained, "and even though I was hearing everything over the crosstalk channel, I wasn't really paying much attention. So here was this poor slob, who had taken cover within the trusswork and waiting for what he thought was old third-stage rocket debris or some lost bolts from the Russian powersat, something like that, to pass by...and suddenly we all hear him gagging and screaming, 'Frank! Frank! Frank...!'"

I shook my head. "I don't understand. If they were small objects, then how could they be Frank's body...?"

Then it hit me, and the last few beers I had enjoyed began to roil in my stomach. It had been Weird Frank's body, all right...but it had no longer been in one piece.

Take a dead body. Allow it to attain rigor mortis, put it in a refrigerator and freeze it until it becomes so stiff that, if you were to drag it down a corridor its fingers would begin to fall off like a leper's extremities, then brutally eject it from an airlock at a velocity akin to that of a Kansas tornado at ground-zero...

And take a guess what happens.

If you haven't had even the *urge* to barf by now, you're qualified to be either an undertaker or a politician. Or a journalist.

"Yeah," he said, and sniggered. "Funny as hell, ain't it?"

Marty told the last bit as he polished off his beer and made ready to drive home. A sweeper had collected the remains of the corpse in its net, then the guidance system was reconfigured to take it for a long trajectory through the inner solar system to the Sun itself. Nobody on Skycan wanted to be the one who removed the net from the robot's maw...and, considering all the terrible things which had already been done to Weird Frank, it was fitting that his final fate should be incineration by that which had killed him, the Sun itself.

"And that was the end of it, I guess." I played with an empty beer bottle as the former beamjack shrugged into his denim jacket. I couldn't look at his face.

"That's it." He pulled on his jacket with its Harley-Davidson eagle-patch on the back and the breast-pocket button which read FUCK EVERYONE, swigged down the last of his Budweiser, and stared back at me for a moment. "You must think I'm a real asshole, don't you?" he asked abruptly.

THE RETURN OF WEIRD FRANK

I imagined his right hand, with the word HATE tattooed across the knuckles, curling into a fist and slamming into my jaw. I didn't give a shit. "Yeah," I said, looking up to squarely meet his gaze, "I think you're a real asshole."

His right hand didn't become a fist; it leisurely went into the front pocket of his jeans, covering the four-letter word on the knuckles. "Then you haven't gotten the point of that whole story," he said, "or why I wrote those words under the picture."

"No, man, I don't get it. Where's the fucking joke?"

"Looky here, then. Frank was a guy without a good sense of humor who tried to make people laugh. He could have sat buck-nekkid in the rec room and wacked off with a copy of *TV Guide* and nobody would have laughed at him..."

"So? What's the point?"

Marty grinned. "And then he died, and by doing so he became funny. Maybe you can say that death improved his character. Maybe it made him a better man."

Hands in his pockets, he rocked drunkenly back on his feet. "I dunno. But nobody would have remembered him unless his body hadn't fallen out of lockers or went to his own wake or any of that shit. And I'm glad I helped him realize his potential, I really am. I'm fucking proud of it."

He shrugged again. "If that makes me an asshole, great. But you're an even bigger asshole if you don't get the joke. Sometimes death or a good joke are the only things which give a man's life some kinda meaning, and that's why Weird Frank was the greatest corpse who ever lived. Y'know what I mean?"

He didn't wait for my answer, even if he had expected one from me. Marty gave my arm a slap and walked past me to the door. A minute later I heard the rev of his Harley's engine; then the bike roared out of the parking lot and down the highway, mowing down Route 3, headed for Route A1A and Cocoa Beach. An ugly brute on the road, looking for another loser's corpse to transform into a better man...

Jack Baker put down his pencil and crossword puzzle, fetched me another beer, and silently placed it in front of me on the bar. I barely noticed; I was looking at the picture on the wall of Weird Frank, strangling that stupid rubber chicken. After awhile, I began to laugh to myself, a chuckle which sounded like a death-rattle from beyond the grave.

It's a joke, son. Don't you get it?

SUGAR'S BLUES

This is the third story I've written about Diamondback Jack's, and it will also be the last. I've told you about the Free Beer conspiracy and Weird Frank's corpse; these were tales which were first relayed to me by others in that greasy bar on Route Three on Merritt Island, just down the road from the Kennedy Space Center. Now I have one more story to tell.

Diamondback Jack's is no more. It's gone. The joint burned to the ground last week, taking with it the pool table, the jukebox, the booze, and all the pictures of living and dead spacers which had been framed, tacked, and taped on the wall behind the bar. The last and best of the hangouts for the pros of the Cape is gone, leaving behind only a ugly heap of busted glass and blackened rubble. Only the Budweiser sign in the parking lot was unscathed by the fire, but since it was broken long ago by some drunk fool, it's nothing to get nostalgic about; if anything, it's a fitting tombstone to a broken promise.

My broken promise.

When I went back there for the last time yesterday, Jack Baker was clambering through the debris, trying to locate anything salvageable in what had once been his court and kingdom. Maybe he was trying to find the varnished rattlesnake skin which had been the bar's namesake. I don't know, because I didn't have a chance to talk to him. As soon as my car pulled into the lot, he recognized it; the half-melted whisky bottle shattering on the hood of my Datsun informed me that I wasn't welcome round here no more, if I ever had been in the first place. I put it in reverse and got out of there in a hurry. The last I saw of Jack was in my rear mirror; he was standing atop the wreckage, silently glaring at me as I sped back down the highway.

Jack is not an inherently violent man, but I know that, if he had been able to find the sawed-off shotgun he kept beneath the counter for the occasional stick-up attempt, he would have gladly pointed it in my direction. He might have even squeezed the trigger and blown me straight to hell. I can't even say that I would have blamed him.

He asked me not to report the story; under the old ground-rules, I usually respected his request. This time, though, I betrayed his trust. In my rush to clear the names of three good men, I forgot our gentlemen's agreement, and it's for that single reason that no one drinks at Diamondback Jack's anymore. Yet, as they always say in the journalism business, the public has a right to know. Memorize that phrase: it's one of the great all-purpose cop-outs of all time. Sorry I ran over your dog, totalled your car, destroyed your career, fucked your sister and gave her a virus, but hey, don't blame me because The Public Has A Right To Know. Says it right here in the First Amendment.

Telling the truth is a dangerous game, but it's the only one I've got. I can't rebuild Jack's bar with some words on paper, but I can tell you why, the next time you go down to Merritt Island, there's an empty gravel lot where a bar once stood.

It started with a fistfight.

Offhand, I can think of several good ways to spend a Saturday night on the Cape. Midnight bass-fishing on the Banana River, sitting on the beach in Jetty Park and watching a cargo freighter lift off from the Cape, enjoying the pig-out special at Fat Boy's Barbecue in Cocoa Beach...or, as in this instance, going down to Diamondback Jack's to hoist a few beers and catch one of the local rockabilly bands Jack Baker used to hire for weekend gigs.

One of the bad ways is to receive a bloody nose during a bar brawl, but that's what I get for drinking at Diamondback Jack's.

I didn't witness the beginning of the fight. I was in the john, humming along with the Rude Astronauts' rendition of "Sea Cruise" while relieving myself of the burden of a half-pitcher of Budweiser—as the old saw goes, you don't buy beer, you only rent it—when there was a godawful thump-crash-bang from the front room. My eyes jerked up from my meditations as the music ground to a halt and, amid the cacophony, I heard someone describing someone else as a goddamn sumbitch asshole, or similar words to the effect. I couldn't be certain, because it was drowned out by more demolition work which sounded only slightly less painful than root canal surgery.

A wise man would have stayed put in the men's room. The Rude Astronauts were not, by definition, the only obnoxious space types out there tonight. Pack a few dozen ornery drunks into a bar, that's one thing; pack a few dozen of the Cape's blue-collar workforce into Diamondback Jack's on a sticky-hot Saturday night in July, and that's quite another. Cross one of 'em and there's gonna be trouble: "Hey, pal, you gotta nice house? Huh? You gotta nice wife? You got nice kids? You gotta nice cat? Don't fuck with me, or I'll drop a dead satellite on 'em." But I'm a journalist by trade and lifestyle, which by definition makes me a dummy; reporters go where angels fear to tread. I zipped up my fly and cautiously ventured out front into the barroom, figuring that I would probably see the result of some guy getting too personal with another man's wife or girlfriend on the dance floor.

I came through the door just in time to see Jack Baker sprinting from behind the bar, his trusty Louisville slugger clenched in his right hand. That was a surprise in itself. Jack's got a gut the size of a medicine ball—have you ever met a skinny bar-owner?—but he moved like Ricky Brock stealing second for the Indians. "Make a hole!" I heard him shout, and as the roomful of regulars veered out of his way, Jack hurled himself toward the epicenter of the melee, which was not on the tiny dance-floor in front of the stage where I expected, but toward the left rear end of the barroom.

Five men were on the floor, wrestling with each other in a bath of blood and beer. The three on top looked like regulars—denims, sneakers, cowboy shirts, a couple of Skycorp caps—but the moment I glimpsed the two guys who were pinned down, I knew they didn't belong in this place. Not that I recognized them personally; like the other three, they were complete strangers, but judging by the way they were duded out, I recognized their type.

They were company men. Any company; pick one, they all look alike. Skycorp, Uchu-Hiko, or Galileo if you choose the privates, or maybe NASA, FBI, CIA, NSA, NSC, FAA, FDA, DEA, IRS or any of the rest of the alphabet soup one normally associates with the government bureaucracy which haunts the Cape. However, Diamondback Jack's was one of the few places which was tacitly verboten to suits. If you're not a working-class spacer who does more at the Kennedy Space Center than carry around a clipboard and a nametag, you should have had better sense than to walk into the joint. These guys—with their off-the-rack sport coats, nylon golf shirts, flat-top haircuts and matching used-car-dealer mustaches—stuck out in a dive like this. Someone should tell these bozos that just putting on a pair of Levis and Monkey Ward topsiders doesn't do the trick; even New York City subway cops have a better sense of camouflage. These yahoos had narc written all over them; I wondered how they had gotten through the door in the first place.

Jack was already pushing back one of the regulars with his baseball bat; the other two were backing off, suddenly mindful of the mess they had created. The two suits on the bottom were beginning to pick themselves off the floor; one of them, a guy with thinning blond hair, had a large rip down the back of his plaid sport coat and one eye which was half closed from a bruise he had taken from a punch. He looked as if he were in bad shape; I instinctively went forward to give the guy a hand off the floor. People are people, right?

"Hey, hey..." I said as I knelt down to grab the suit from under his armpits, intending to help him to his feet. "Don't...let's take a look at..."

"Fuck you," he snarled. And then the jerk, still sitting on his ass, whipped around with his right fist and nailed me square in the nose.

So much for my application to the Good Samaritan Hall of Fame.

Things became a bit confused for awhile after that, and I didn't catch everything that happened. My getting decked touched off a free-for-all of punching and harsh language. Not that anyone was standing up for me, because I didn't mean shit to most people in the bar; it's just that the only thing Florida barcrawlers enjoy more on a humid summer night than drinking, dancing, or looking to get laid is fighting. From my dazed perspective, it resembled a feeding frenzy in the water hazard of a miniature golf course, right after you toss some popcorn into the midst of a bunch of bored catfish. Fight? Good! Let's punch someone!

Jack gave up on the baseball bat and grabbed the fire extinguisher instead; a few loud shots of carbon dioxide at the ceiling above the crowd cleared the bar in a hurry. He didn't have to go to that extreme, though; anyone with any sense was getting the hell out of there. The Rude Astronauts had already packed up their instruments and sound equipment and quietly loaded them into their van as fast as possible; they were hired to play, not brawl, and Jack didn't have chicken-wire erected in front of his stage. In the main ring, the suits had long since lost; they were thrown out the door and although a couple of members of the original fight went out into the parking lot to discuss proper public etiquette with them, I do not believe Miss Manners would have approved of their form of instruction.

Meanwhile, out in the bleacher-seats of Hell, I was slumped in one of the booths—half-stunned, holding a wad of paper napkins against my snoot, tasting blood running down the back of my mouth. Funny thing about a nosebleed: it's more embarrassing than painful. I've got a glass nose and I'm no stranger to having my face hit. All those teenage years of getting beat up in the schoolyard for being a smartass instead of a jock taught me a few things about controlling nosebleeds, so previous experience told me that all I had to do was sit still, lean my head back, keep something absorbent pressed against my face and breathe through my mouth. It didn't do anything for all the blood on my shirt, but at least it would save me from getting hosed by Jack's fire extinguisher.

The next time I remembered anything clearly, it was when things were calm again. The mob had been cleared from the bar, the place was empty, and somebody had placed a Budweiser tallneck on the table in front of me.

"Here," said a voice. "Rinse your mouth out with this."

As I looked up, my benefactor settled in the seat on the other side of the booth. It was one of the guys who had originally been in the brawl, although you could barely tell it; he didn't have a mark on him except for some beer splattered across the front of his cowboy shirt. Not surprising; he was a big guy with a linebacker's build, the type of person who doesn't start fights but always finishes them.

He also looked a bit old to be mixed up in this sort of shit: mid-fifties, with crow's-feet around his alert blue eyes, close-cropped grey hair, country-style long sideburns framing a square jaw. A pro. An old-time spacer. Hang around the Cape long enough and you can always tell the type.

Yet he also looked vaguely familiar...

Fuck it. "Thanks," I said as I picked up the bottle, took a long drink and swirled beer around inside my mouth. I glanced around; Jack was looking the other way for the moment, so I spit it out onto the bloody, booze-drenched floor. The place was a mess already, and it got the clotted-blood taste out of my mouth. The guy on the other side of the table smiled, but didn't make a federal case out of my slobbish behavior. He had seen worse.

"Just wanted to tell you I'm sorry that you got hurt," he said. His voice had a soft, southern gentleman's lilt to it: Colonel Mississippi Cornpone crossed with Deke Slayton. "I know it wasn't your fight and that you were trying to break things up."

He shrugged, his face becoming more serious. "Wasn't my fight either...at least I didn't start it. I'm just sorry that you had to get in the way."

I was about to reply when there was a screech of car tires peeling out of the parking lot. A few seconds later, the door banged open and two men entered from the lot. I immediately recognized them as the two other regulars who had been in the fight. One of them glanced our way. "They're outta here, Sugar," he said.

At first, I thought there was a woman sitting behind us, but the adjacent booth was vacant. "Sugar" isn't the sort of nickname one normally associates with a fellow who looks tough enough to pound nails with his fists, but my friend didn't seem to mind. "Okay, Mike," he said, solemnly nodding his head. "I think we've seen the last of 'em for awhile. You and Doug go grab yourselves a cold one and take it easy."

Jack already had a couple of tallnecks waiting for them on the bar; it was a funny way for Baker to be treating guys who had just wrecked his place, chased out his customers and his band, and caused him to close down early on a Saturday night. But instead he quietly grabbed a broom and dustpan and went to work sweeping up the debris while the two men picked up their beers.

Pretty weird shit, all things considered. If the suits weren't on their way to the county hospital emergency room, then they were headed straight for the Merritt Island cop shop. Yet if either one of Sugar's friends seemed to give a damn, they didn't show it. There's a certain untouchable look about men who've just beaten the crap out of someone who deserved it, but Mike and Doug weren't northern Florida yee-haw rednecks looking for a brawl. The way they carried themselves told me that they, like Sugar, were pros...

Sugar.

There was something familiar about the nickname, matched with that face, which tickled the back of my mind. My head was stuffed with clotted blood; I couldn't think straight. "So what was this all about, anyway?" I asked, and Sugar looked back toward me. "I mean, I got into the show late, so why did you get into a fight with these guys?"

Sugar shrugged off-handedly. "Well, y'know how it is. We just came over to have a couple of beers and they were on our case again, doing the usual surveillance routine. They kept watching us and Doug got pissed, so he went over to get them to leave and they..."

"Shut up!"

The shout came from Jack. He was kneeling on the floor next to the broken juke-box, gathering the scratched CDs which had been thrown from its shattered case. He stared at Sugar with anger in his eyes; Sugar instantly went quiet.

"Al's a regular here," Baker went on, more quietly now, "but he's not a pro. He's a reporter." He glanced at me, sour annoyance in his face. "I let him in because he doesn't talk too much...but he's still with the press, so watch your mouth, okay? He's not one of us."

Not one of us. Christ. I sighed, wiping my nose again and dropping the paper wad on the table. My old outsider-insider status with Diamondback Jack's had once again returned to haunt me.

Outsider, because I was a stringer for the *Times* and journalists are traditionally unwelcome among the pros at the Cape. Conventional wisdom says that since we ask dumb questions at press conferences and never get the facts straight, stick our noses (bloody or otherwise) into places where they don't belong, always blab secrets better left untold, and are generally pains in everyone's collective ass, we are untrustworthy as a collective whole. Journalists rank with sand fleas at the Cape; barely tolerated, never welcome. Insider, because I was a regular at Diamondback Jack's. I normally went there to drink, not to play reporter. My notebook and recorder stayed in the car where they belonged; if someone told me a story, it was with everyone's explicit permission...and under no circumstances would it appear in my paper (okay, so I cheated a little by writing the stories I heard as thinly-disguised fiction). Most of the time, the gossip and rumors never left the walls of the bar.

It was a hard-fought status, being the token blabbermouth in good old boy territory; for this reason alone, though, my presence was tolerated. Jack Baker was one of the very few people who was aware of my profession, and it was only because I had demonstrated the ability to keep secrets that I was allowed in his bar in the first place. I was always careful never to toe the line.

This time, though, it looked as if I had stepped over it. Mike and Doug put down their beers and were studying me with expressions which suggested that I was the next person to make a visit to the parking lot. For a few moments I wondered if Jack Baker would be tacking my hide to the wall alongside that of the rattlesnake he had allegedly killed during a fishing trip in the Everglades. There was— as purveyors of purple prose are permanently predestined to pontificate —a pregnant silence, and I thought I was going to have a baby.

"Reporter. Well now..." Sugar folded his hands together on the tabletop and gazed at me with speculative amusement. "You're not trying to wrangle a story out of this, now are you?"

I quickly shook my head and started to say that it had only been a curious question, but Sugar nodded his head. "No," he continued, "I don't think so. But if ol' Jack here says you can be trusted, then I'll believe you."

He looked toward his companions, who had eased off a little but still hadn't relaxed their guard. "In fact, perhaps we should take our case to the press. They keep trying to pick a fight with us, so maybe it's time we fought back. What do you say, gentlemen?"

Doug looked suspicious, but he slowly nodded his head. "I dunno," Mike murmured. "They're pissed at us enough already. If we go spilling our guts..."

"What are they going to do that they haven't done already?" Sugar spread open his hands. "We're grounded, we're broke, we're unemployed, our names are dirt in the industry. They call us on the phone in the middle of the night, they follow our wives and kids all the time...hell, we even can't step out for a beer without having a couple of them tagging along. Maybe we should have gone public eleven months ago." He gestured toward me. "I don't know this guy, but he's press and he's already seen part of it. Perhaps we should just go ahead and come clean. How can it get much worse than it is already?"

I already didn't like the sound of this. Contrary to popular myth, most journalists don't go looking for trouble; it finds them, whether they invite it or not. Many years ago, when I had been a staff writer on a muckraking weekly paper, I had done a story about a junkyard which was using its lot as an illegal hazardous-waste disposal site, taking toxic chemicals from local manufacturers and burying them in the back acre. Nearby community residents had tipped me off, and the story which I wrote caused the state's environmental agency to investigate and finally shut the place down. The junkyard owner was pissed off at me; for several weeks, thugs made frequent visits to the newspaper office in search of yours truly until the circuit court passed verdict on the junkyard and the chap in charge was sent off to prison.

Even then, it had been several months before I stopped checking over my shoulder whenever I walked the streets.

It was beginning to look like a replay of that incident. I started measuring the distance to the door. Then my friend stuck out his hand. "Name's Ted Saltzman," he said. "My friends call me Sugar."

Sugar Saltzman. All at once, the connection became clear. I felt stupid for having missing it before.

Yes, I had heard of him. Everyone at the Cape had heard of Sugar Saltzman. And at the moment I finally linked the face to the name, I knew I wasn't going to leave the bar until I had heard his story.

✳ ✳ ✳

If you haven't heard of Sugar Saltzman, you don't read newspapers or watch TV. He was not only a legend in the space industry, but one of very few spacers whose name ever became known outside the insular community of the Cape. He was the last of the old-school astronauts, and his rise to fame was matched in velocity only by his descent into infamy.

Before Saltzman joined NASA, he had been an Air Force fighter-pilot. When he was still in his twenties, he had flown F-117's out of Saudi Arabia for sorties over Baghdad during Gulf War I. Not long after the war, he quit the USAF to enlist in the NASA astronaut corps. He flew numerous orbital missions on the second-generation shuttles before NASA was reorganized into a regulatory agency and space industrialization was privatized. He was Skycorp's first-draft pick among the old NASA shuttle jockeys; the story goes that Rock Chapman himself had recruited Saltzman, on the basis of a brief exchange the two old flyboys had at a burger joint on Route A1A. "Why do they call you Sugar?" Rock had asked, and Sugar had replied, "Because everything I do comes out sweet."

Indeed. Sugar Saltzman was an ace among aces and a pro among pros, a genuine hot-shit shuttle jockey; even the best of old-guard NASA astronauts from the last century couldn't match his record. While working for Skycorp, he amassed more flight-hours than any other pilot in history, sometimes under conditions which pushed the proverbial envelope. When his shuttle lost power to its APUs just prior to re-entry, he suited up and went EVA to fix a shorted-out conduit in the aft engine section, relying on talk-through from the ground and his own memory of the complex wiring system; another pilot might have curled into a rescue ball and waited for someone else to save his ass, but Saltzman had taken care of the situation himself, and brought his vessel and crew safely home. And when Phoenix Station had suffered an electrical fire and lost life-support, giving its crew less than two days of oxygen before they asphyxiated, Sugar had taken a rescue team into low-orbit even as a killer hurricane was bearing down on the Cape from the Bahamas.

If there was any pilot who typified the mysterious, grace-under-pressure quality which Tom Wolfe had once called the "Right Stuff," it was Sugar Saltzman. Skycorp had been only too happy to capitalize on his local fame; they needed a 21st-century hero to match the Scott Crossfields and Chuck Yeagers of the past, if only to enhance their corporate self-image. The public was tired of actors and politicians and self-made celebrities; they wanted someone they could genuinely admire, that larger-than-life person whom every man could emulate. Sugar Saltzman fit the bill and Skycorp was only too willing to oblige. Since Saltzman regularly flew one particular shuttle—then called the *John Young*, itself named after one of NASA's legendary astronauts—Skycorp rechristened it, allowing Sugar to choose the new name. The pilot picked the name of an old RAF Lancaster which had flown bombing missions over Germany during World War II; an artist had repainted the Lanc's topless Vargas girl on the shuttle's forward port fuselage, along with the shared name of the two craft. The *John Young* thereby became known as *Sugar's Blues*.

Sugar did talk-shows and interviews, modeled T-shirts and did cola commercials and all the rest, but he never stopped flying; he remained on Skycorp's active-duty roster and didn't sell out to become a full-time celebrity, and more so for the better. For the next few years, both the shuttle and its commander were legends in their own time. Skycorp allowed him to select his own regular crew; his picks were Mike Green as his co-pilot and Doug McPherson as his cargo specialist, both of whom were already seasoned shuttle honchos. The heavy-breathing magazine writers who profiled Skycorp's star team inevitably referred to them as the "Blues Brothers."

For a brief time, they were the ace kids on the block. Nobody could touch 'em, either for real flying skill or artificial hubris. But it didn't last for very long.

Shortly after Saltzman's twenty-fourth orbital mission, the pilot and his crewmates were accused of being "habitual drug offenders"...junkies, once you get away from mediaspeak.

When the hammer came down, I wasn't around to be part of the public trashing. The *Times* had dispatched me to Sydney to cover an international space-tech conference, so I wasn't in town when Sugar Saltzman and his crew were busted. I'm glad I wasn't involved; it was an ugly situation.

In short, Saltzman, Green and McPherson had been at the Cape for a pre-flight mission briefing when a security officer from NASA's Law Enforcement Division requested that they open their ready-room lockers for what seemed to be a routine inspection. It happened all the time—NASA had firm rules against alcohol being allowed within KSC, and everyone was used to spot-checks—so the Blues Brothers had complied with the request, yet when the lockers were searched, each man were found to be in possession of various drugs. A shaving kit in Saltzman's locker contained a quarter-ounce of marijuana and a small vial of cocaine; Green's jumpsuit pocket held a few joints, and a tinfoil packet concealed in one of McPherson's boots contained a couple of grams of hashish, plus a small pipe which had been recently smoked.

All three men claimed innocence, and even the NASA cop who had made the bust later claimed to be skeptical despite the hard evidence; he had been following up an anonymous tip which had been posted in his computer's e-mail, and he had only made the search because of departmental policy to investigate all such allegations. Yet, within a few hours of the bust, an over-eager NASA press spokesman went public with the charges against the men, and the unskeptical space-beat reporters at the Cape eagerly aped the official line; before the end of the day, the Blues Brothers were being called the Space Junkies.

The crew of *Sugar's Blues* immediately protested that they had been framed; they volunteered for urine and hair-root testing, but if they had hoped that the lab analyses would confirm their innocence, they were wrong. All three tests came back positive, showing that the spacers had been using pot, coke, and hash for a period of at least several months.

By the time I got back from my Australian junket, it was all over; NASA had permanently grounded Sugar Saltzman and his mates, and Skycorp had almost instantly fired them. Although the court later threw out the subsequent federal lawsuit because of legal technicalities, their careers were finished. The editorialists and media commentators vented their usual bathos, pathos, phony shock and rehearsed outrage; meanwhile, the public suffered its own private heartbreak before it forgot the whole thing.

For their own part, Sugar and his men refused to speak to the press. They went to ground, rarely seen around the Cape. As usual, the story was a ten-day sensation. By the time Skycorp shame-facedly re-rechristened *Sugar's Blues* as the *John Young*—its voluptuous Vargas girl painted over, never to be seen on the flight-line again—Saltzman, Green, and McPherson had quickly faded from the public mindset. Bunny Chaykin-Schnienkovitch had once again flashed her boobs on TV; in the face of such monumental artistic achievement, who could remember what's-their-names, the pothead astronauts?

And now, here they were. Up from the underground and ready to talk.

Jack cocked a finger at me, motioning for me to follow him into the tiny office behind the bar. Once you were back there, he half-closed the door. "Look, Al..." he began.

"Look, I swear it wasn't my idea," I said before he could go on. "But if they've got something on their minds that they want to tell me..."

"Okay, okay, I understand. It's your job and all that." He thrust a finger in my face. "But you understand me. Nothing about my place gets into anything you write. You got me straight on that? I've let you get away with it twice before because nobody around here reads that rag you moonlight for..."

"I'll let my editor know that. He'll be so touched..."

"...but this time I really mean it. You guys haven't been within a hundred miles of here, I swear to God, 'cause if you do..."

"Okay, okay. Ease down." I put up my hands defensively. "I promise you, if I write a story, I won't mention where it came from. I promise."

Baker stared me straight in the eye, then slowly nodded his head. I could understand that he wasn't crazy about having his bar used as a confessional, but I intuitively realized that there was much more to it than that. Jack knew something — bartenders run second-place only to God for knowing everything, because if you don't do church you probably speak to your bartender instead—and it frightened him so much that he didn't want to have anything to do with it. The only reason why he was going along with this was because of his obvious respect for Sugar Saltzman.

And Jack wasn't the only person who was being paranoid. Although Doug volunteered to be interviewed with Sugar, Mike opted to sit outside the bar and watch for a possible return of the suits. After I went out to my car to fetch my notebook and recorder, Jack locked the doors and switched off most of the lights, signaling that Diamondback Jack's was closed for the night. He then placed two pitchers of beer in front of us, and retired to the back office, allegedly to balance the books.

I switched on my recorder and opened my notebook as Sugar poured a beer for me. "The morning we made our last flight on the *Blues*..." he began.

"Let's get it straight for the man, Cap," Doug interrupted, pushing forward his own beer mug. "It was last April 12."

"April 12, 2023. Like I could forget." Sugar pushed the topped-off mug in front of me and reached for his former co-pilot's glass. I noted that he left dry his own mug. "Anyway, the *Blues* was already on the pad, because we had a milk run to Olympus Station scheduled the day after tomorrow. Mission 24 for us, and I didn't think it was going to be much different, except that after Mission 25 I was half-planning to tender my resignation to the company."

This surprised me. "You were about to retire anyway?" I asked, and Sugar sagely nodded his head. "Was it because of a medical problem or...?"

Sugar chuckled. "Yeah, you could say that, if you want to call getting old a medical problem. Hell, I'm pushing sixty. Counting the missions I did for NASA before I joined Skycorp, I would have gone up thirty times. That's enough. All I wanted to do was hand over the wheel to Sir Douglas here, buy me an old crop-duster or something and spend my golden years farting around Cocoa Beach."

He laughed again, but it sounded forced this time. "That was the plan, at any rate. But then, two days before we were supposed to go up, I get a call at three in the morning from Gene Antonio, the chief of Skycorp's astronaut office, telling me there's been a fire."

"A fire up there," McPherson added, cocking his thumb toward the ceiling. "Y'know what he means?"

I knew. In this context, "fire" was a code-word for a life-threatening emergency in orbit. NASA, Skycorp and the other space companies started using it groundside to mask serious situations, in order to obfuscate the press who might overhear cellular phone conversations. Just such a thing had happened during the Phoenix Station accident, when half of the Cape press corps learned that there was trouble in low-orbit because of an uncoded conversation between two NASA techs on their car-phones. Saying that's there been a garbage can fire is much more innocuous than saying that the life-support system of a spacecraft has gone kaput and that a rescue mission is necessary.

Green and McPherson were also awakened by the astronaut chief, but it wasn't until a half-hour later, when the Blues Brothers were convened in the green room of Skycorp's Operations and Checkout Building, that they learned the exact nature of the emergency. Attending the meeting were NASA flight director Joe Marx, Skycorp astronaut chief Eugene Antonio, and NASA press liaison Margaret Jacobi; also present, to their surprise, was a person named Edward Collier, who was introduced as being a corporate rep from a pharmaceutical firm called Space BioTech, itself a subsidiary of a much larger multinational biotech company, Spectrum-Mellencamp, Inc..

"We got the skinny while we were having our coffee and doughnuts," Sugar said. "Spectrum-Mellencamp owned a small spacelab in low-equatorial orbit, about three hundred miles up, called Bios One. They operated it as a microgravity R&D facility to whip up stuff like fertilizers, human growth hormones, junk like that. Collier told us that, for the past year or so, Space BioTech had been using it to develop a new pharmaceutical."

"That sounds rather vague."

"Yeah, it was," McPherson said, "and he was real elusive about it. I tried to ask him exactly what he meant, but he said that he couldn't tell us much more because of the firm's proprietary interests." He sipped his beer. "That's when I first got a bad feeling about the whole deal."

"Yeah," Sugar agreed. "So did I, but there was too much else going on, so we didn't push him on it. Since there were three lives on the line, I didn't feel like we needed to know everything."

At 0100, an unmanned orbital transfer vehicle, which had been launched by a Big Dummy from the Cape the previous evening, had attempted to dock in the garage module of Bios One. It was a routine bi-weekly resupply mission, but in the last few seconds of the manoeuvre, something had gone seriously wrong; the OTV's main engine had misfired while the spacecraft was under remote control from Bios One. The exact cause of the misfire was still unknown, although NASA troubleshooters suspected human error by the controller on the little space station. Whatever the reason, the OTV had rammed the garage. The crash had punctured the cargo craft's LOX tank and the vehicle had exploded.

Details were fuzzy after that. Debris from the explosion had punctured the hull of the spacelab's command/lab module, one of the station's two major cylinders. Ned Hersh, Bios One's general manager who had been on duty in the command module at the time of the accident, had managed to transmit a Mayday before radio contact was lost; he said that there was a blowout in Module One, but no other information was relayed before the downlink was severed at the source. If the garage module was destroyed and Module One was crippled, then it was assumed that communications had been lost when the nearby telemetry mast, mounted on the portside solar wing, was totalled by the explosion.

In fact, everything else was based upon assumption. If there were any survivors, they had to be in Module Two, the habitation cylinder mounted above Module One. And if the portside solar wing had also been damaged, then fifty percent of the spacelab's power supply was nullified; given the proximity of the outboard oxygen tanks to the garage, it could also be assumed that much of Bios One's life-support capability had also been nixed.

There was one further problem. According to ground tracking by the USAF Space Command in Colorado Springs, it seemed as if Bios One's orbit had radically shifted. It appeared that the explosion's force had managed to nudge the spacelab out of its orbit; since there was an apparent loss of control from the station itself, Bios One's orbit was decaying and it was being gradually hauled down the gravity well. Within a week, at the very least, the space station would begin to enter Earth's upper atmosphere, where it would be destroyed.

Phoenix Station, the major NASA space station which was also in equatorial orbit, had been notified of the emergency, but the crew couldn't do anything about it; its present position was on the other side of Earth, and they didn't have the capability to effect a long-range rescue mission since their transorbit shuttle, unluckily enough, was presently down for repairs. Mir 3, the Soviet space station, was in an entirely different orbit and inclination, all but completely out of reach; Olympus Station, Skycorp's powersat construction station, was located in geosynchronous orbit almost twenty-two thousand miles away, and therefore useless for something like this.

But von Braun-class shuttles were designed for quick-turnaround and launch, and since weather patterns around the Cape were forecast to remain stable for the next twelve to twenty-four hours, it was entirely possible that a rescue mission could be launched from the ground. "*Sugar's Blues* was already on the pad, ready to go," Sugar went on. "In fact, NASA had already called for fueling and a fast-cycle launch by the time Antonio had given us the call."

I shook my head. "I don't understand. If they were asking you to perform a rescue operation..."

"Ain't no asking about it," Sugar interrupted. "There's this sub-paragraph in the federal regs, the SOS clause, which says that if an American-registered manned spacecraft is in trouble while in orbit, then NASA can use right of eminent domain to commandeer whatever resources are available to rescue the crew members. So we were drafted from the git-go."

"Not that we were about to refuse," Doug said. "I mean, even if those guys were employed by someone else and had dumbfucked something easy like an OTV rendezvous, they were still spacers. You help out whenever you can. No one had to wave the rule book at us." He shrugged. "Besides, we were the Blues Brothers. Skycorp's all-star team, the danger boys. You think we were going to back down from something like this? I lived for this kind of action."

"At first sight, it looked pretty much a cut-and-dried mission," Sugar said. "We would launch at 1800 hours, ascend to orbit, and link-up with Bios One. We'd find the survivors if there were any, load 'em into the shuttle, and bring 'em home. It was all pretty much by the book. No problem."

He picked up the pitcher, pushed his neglected mug beneath it, and began to pour himself a drink. "Then this Collier character opens his pie-hole. 'No, no, no,' he says. 'Spectrum-Mellencamp has considerable dollar investment in Bios One, Space BioTech has an important logistics module linked to it, we can't just rescue the crew and let everything burn up.' Yackety-yack and don't talk back. As it turns out, he wants us to uncouple the log-mod on the station, haul it into *Blues'* cargo bay, and bring it home with us."

"The same logistics module which is manufacturing something he wouldn't tell us about," McPherson said. "The way he came across made it sound as if he really didn't give a shit for the poor bastards on his station. He wanted that fucking module brought back, first and foremost."

Sugar grimaced at the memory. "I told the NASA guys that he had to be pulling my dick. I mean, making rendezvous with a station in a decaying orbit is one thing, performing a rescue operation is quite another. Okay, we can swing that. But disengaging a five-ton logistics module from the superstructure, hauling it into the *Blues'* cargo bay with the RWM, and bringing it back home...I mean, didn't they have their priorities a little bit confused here?"

He topped off his beer and put the pitcher down, yet he didn't pick up the mug. "But, no, they sided with Collier. Retrieving the log-mod was just as essential as rescuing the personnel. No compromise. Even Gene, who usually had more sense than that since he was once a pilot, went along with it."

"Mike and I pitched a bitch," McPherson said. "Y'know, we knew what was ahead of us. We make it sound easy, but handling a fire is really a bitch, especially when your target is incommunicado and in a decaying orbit, and you've got to land heavy. All that seemed to fly right over Collier's head, though. He seemed to think we were truck drivers or something. Pick up some stuff at Point A, bring it back to Point B...no goddamn idea what he was talking about."

"Did you accept the mission then?" I asked.

They simultaneously nodded their heads. "Yeah, we accepted," Sugar said. "Like we had a choice?" Then he picked up his beer and, tipping it toward me, gave me a sly wink. "But I still knew that, given a choice between rescuing the survivors and bringing home their precious log-mod, there was only one way I'd go."

I stopped the recorder for a few minutes while Doug visited the john; meanwhile, Sugar stepped outside for a second to ask Mike if he had seen anything. The car which the two suits had driven away from Diamondback Jack's had not returned, but Mike didn't want to come back inside. I was holding open the door while Sugar spoke to his former co-pilot; it was difficult to tell in the darkness, but it looked as if Green had Jack's baseball bat with him.

"The launch and orbital insertion was right by the numbers," Sugar went on, once we had all returned to the booth. "Our communications was a closed-channel downlink with Huntsville SOC, which in turn had us patched in with KSC. Since we were using a military frequency, no one could eavesdrop on us. A press blackout was in force, but people knew something was going on..."

"I remember," I said. "I was at the press center when they finally told us about the fire."

Sugar nodded his head. "Yeah, and you probably bought the party line, didn't you?" I winced and started to say something, but he just smiled. "No hard feelings, pal. At the time, I didn't want you know the truth either."

The official explanation for the early launch of *Sugar's Blues* had been that an unidentified manned spacecraft was having unspecified problems and that the shuttle had been launched to give assistance, but the NASA public affairs office had refused to release any details. Although no one outside Skycorp's Operations Center in Hunstville and Firing Room Two at the Cape knew what was going on in Earth orbit, the crew of *Sugar's Blues* was only too aware of the extent of the crisis. Within an hour of its launch from Pad Five-B, the shuttle rendezvoused with Bios One.

As they made the primary approach, they could see that the spacelab was a wreck. The garage module was almost completely demolished, blown apart from the inside by the collision of the OTV. The port solar wing had been completely sheered away from the explosion—taking with it the high-gain antenna, as anticipated—and there were long rents in the gold Mylar which covered the outer fuselage of the adjacent command/laboratory module. However, the station's navigational lights were still shining, indicating that Bios One had not lost all of its internal power, and Module Two looked reasonably intact. Two elongated lateral nodes connected the habitat modules; attached to Node One, just above the habitation module, was the beer-can shaped Space BioTech logistics module, apparently unscratched.

McPherson focused a 35mm camera through the dorsal observation window and shot a full disk of film while the two pilots gently manoeuvred *Sugar's Blues* toward the crippled station. The main docking collar, located at the bottom of Node One next to the garage, was obstructed by wreckage, but once they had wrenched open the cargo bay doors, Sugar and Mike managed to hard-dock with the undamaged auxiliary docking adapter, located on top of Node Two directly across from the logistics module. Through the flight deck windows, they could partly see through the cupola windows at end of Module Two; although the windows were dimly illuminated by a weak amber glow from within, they could see no apparent motion. The windows of Module One's cupola were completely dark. Altogether, Bios One appeared lifeless.

"We couldn't raise anyone on the comlink, but that wasn't surprising since the communications center was located in Module One," Sugar said. "I decided to go down and take a look-see. The airlock indicator told me that there was pressure within the node, but I didn't want to take any chances with a shortout in the sensor circuits, so I suited up before I went into the airlock."

"Mike stayed on the flight deck," McPherson said, "while I went back to the mid-deck to power-up the RWM and get ready to bring the log-mod aboard." He smiled a little as he picked up his beer. "The boss here, as always, wanted to hog all the glory."

"Yeah," Sugar replied, "like I really had to arm wrestle you for the privilege." Doug grinned, but there seemed to be little humor within his expression. "Anyway, so there I went...through the airlock and down the access tunnel 'til I reached the Module Two hatch. The pressure light was green, so I undogged it and pushed myself inside."

Up until now his delivery had been methodical and concise, an almost monotonous just-the-facts-mister retelling of the key points of the mission. Now Sugar's voice dropped slightly as he clasped his hands together and gazed down at them.

"It was so weird," he murmured. "Remember what it was like when you were a kid and you snuck into some old house that everyone said was haunted? It was like that. Only the emergency lights were on, so everything was colored red. Nothing and nobody was moving. The galley table was folded down and there was a food tray attached to it, but nobody was sitting there eating. Through my helmet, though, I could hear someone talking..."

"The monkeys," McPherson prodded. "Tell him about the monkeys."

Saltzman quickly nodded his head. "Yeah, right. The monkeys." He took a deep breath, still staring at his hands. "Next to the hatch there were two little cages in the wall, and in each one a Rhesus monkey was floating around. Now, y'know, caged animals usually go berserk when someone gets near 'em, but these little guys hardly noticed me, even when the light from my helmet lamp touched 'em. At first I couldn't figure it out...they were alive, because I could see them move and there was steam coming from their noses..."

"It was cold in the station?" I asked.

"Yeah, it was cold," Sugar said impatiently. "The heat was turned down. It was cold..." He paused to collect his thoughts again.

"Anyway, so I look in and I see that each of the monkeys has its own little computer terminal in there. Little screen, big oversized keys, a little food-pellet dispenser rigged up next to the computer. Typical stimulus-response experiment...whenever they gave some right answer, another pellet would be shot down the tube to the monkey. But since the tube was transparent, I could see it was empty."

He rubbed a hand across his forehead. "I peer into the cages, and I can see that the monkeys are tapping the same keys over and over again, and the same equation keeps appearing on the screens. Two plus two minus one equals three...two plus two minus one equals three...same thing, over and over. And each time that happens, I saw a blue light appear on the screens and I could hear a little beep from the computers, and the food slots would open but nothing would come out. But the monkeys didn't care. They weren't even looking at the tubes. They were completely transfixed by the screens. All response, no stimulus."

He let out his breath. "No one had cleaned their cages for awhile, so the poor little bastards had monkey shit floating all around them. They were practically swimming in their own crap. It was plastered to their fur, but they didn't care. All they could do was enter the same first-grade equation into that stupid computer, again and again and..."

Sugar picked up his beer and took a long drink. Talking about the Rhesus monkeys had hit a nerve. I had seen it before; people get upset when they see cruelty to animals. It's a little bizarre, sometimes, the priorities we can make. This was a man who had once dropped bombs on a densely-populated Iraqi city, possibly killing scores of helpless civilians, and he was unsettled by the memory of two monkeys who had been...

Hypnotized? Brainwashed? I didn't think it was possible to mesmerize a simian. I shot a look at McPherson. He was silent, his arms folded across his chest.

"What about the crew?" I asked softly.

Sugar had been taking it easy on the liquor until now. He paused to go to the bar, pour himself a shot of George Dickel, and pump it back before he returned to the booth. "I had just managed to get off my helmet," he said, "when the curtain of one of the sleep niches slid open and this guy pushes himself out. I found out later that he was one of the scientists, name of Robillard. George Robillard."

He picked up the beer pitcher and poured a chaser into his mug. "But by then, I could hear this voice speaking from the other end of the module. I had been hearing it through my helmet when I had first come into the station, but now I could make it out distinctly. At first I thought someone was reciting a poem, but then I realized that someone was reading aloud. At least, that was what I thought it was."

He shrugged. "Then out comes this George Robillard, who tells me he was asleep when the *Blues* docked and didn't know I was there. Then he tells me that he and another guy, named Eric Schwinn, are the only two left alive. Ned Hersh, the team leader, had been down in Module Two when the accident had happened. There had been a blowout, but he stayed in there to transmit a Mayday before the emergency hatches had autosealed and locked him inside."

"Hersh was dead?" I asked.

Stupid question, but I had to be sure. Sugar didn't notice. "As a doornail. Robillard and Schwinn had been holding out for a rescue attempt. He was kinda surprised that it was from the Cape, though, 'cause he thought someone from Phoenix Station would be on their way."

Doug cleared his throat and Sugar looked toward him. "Mike and I had been monitoring all this through the comlink," McPherson said, "but Mike had shut down the feed to the Cape and Huntsville as soon as the boss had started talking about the monkeys. He dicked around with the radio and caused some fuzz before he told CapCom that we were losing our telemetry with the comsats, but it was really because we were beginning to smell a rat. So the boys back home didn't hear everything that was going on up there."

"Right," Sugar said. "Anyway, so I say to Robillard, 'Well, the cab's here and we've got the meter running, so you can get your friend Eric to stop reading aloud to pass the time.' It was supposed to be a joke, but he doesn't see it that way. 'Maybe you ought to see this,' he says to me, then he leads me down the passageway to another niche, where the voice is coming from. He pushes back the curtain and..."

Sugar paused. He clenched his hands together again, not looking at me as he continued. "Jesus Christ," he whispered, almost too inaudibly for my recorder to pick up, "I'll never forget that moment."

I waited until he was ready to speak again. When Sugar returned from the depths of his memory, his voice was hollow and flat. "Schwinn was zipped into his sleep restraint, all the way up to his neck," he said. "The only light in the niche came from a little reading lamp above his head and there was a paperback book floating in midair nearby, but he wasn't reading it. The book was <u>The Snows of Kilimanjaro</u> by Ernest Hemingway, but it wasn't in his hands and he wasn't reading from it. He was..."

His voice trailed off again. "What was he doing?" I asked.

"He was reciting it," Sugar said. "Aloud. Every line, as perfect as if he had spent months memorizing the whole blamed thing. And the look on his face, it was..."

He sucked in his breath, visibly trying to steady himself. "He looked like the monkeys in the cages, but worse. His eyes were glazed, his head was lolling forward. His face was completely dead. Just staring straight ahead like a zombie, there were these words coming out of his mouth. He didn't notice me or the other guy, not even when I clapped my hands and shouted his name. I pushed myself right in front of him and stuck a penlight in his eyes, and though the pupils contracted normally, he barely responded. It was as if he had been lobotomized or something."

He picked up his beer and took a sip. I noticed that his hands were trembling ever so slightly. "So I turn around to Robillard and I say, 'What's going on with this guy? Is he on drugs or something? Make him stop talking, for God's sake.' And that's when Robillard breaks down and tells me...tells us, since Mike and Doug can hear us through the comlink...the whole thing."

Sugar put down his beer and looked at me. "That's when we first heard about Project Flashback."

While Saltzman and Robillard unzipped Schwinn from his cocoon and began to haul the scientist toward the node hatch, Robillard explained what had happened to Schwinn and Hersh.

For the past several years, Space BioTech had been developing a drug which would enhance short-term memory. The principal objective had been to produce a pharmaceutical substance which would provide a clinical antidote for Alzheimer's Disease, but there was also hope within the biotech firm and its parent company that they could spin off a non-prescription derivative—already called Flashback—which would be an over-the-counter recreational drug. Although the clinical-issue drug would be more beneficial to medical science, Spectrum-Mellencamp believed that the real money would come from Flashback, and the project had swung in that direction.

The essential idea was that, since the mind tends to remember tactile pain but forget short-term pleasure experiences, Flashback would crosswire the cerebral circuitry and perform the exact inverse function: it would allow the user to store away the sensory nuances of any given pleasurable act. After ingesting Flashback, a person could have a good meal, read a great novel, have sex or whatever while under its influence. The immediate, real-time perception of the given experience would be subtly heightened, yet that would not be the immediate payoff; much later, after the drug had worn off, the memory of the experience would remain firmly engraved, able to be recalled precisely as it had happened. In theory, one would remember the best tastes of a meal enjoyed at a four-star restaurant, recall favorite passages once read from a novel or short story, or relive the most orgasmic heights of lovemaking with one's partner. It would be similar to the flashbacks experienced by habitual LSD users, yet voluntary and without any of the nasty side-effects.

It was a risky proposition. The drug had to be completely perfect, safe, and non-habit-forming, or the FDA would never give approval. However, market analysts predicted that the company could potentially reap billions of dollars in worldwide sales, both in its clinical and recreational forms. After three years of top-secret research, Space BioTech had indeed theoretically developed the drug; as anticipated, though, its molecular composition was so complex and fragile that it could not be assembled within Earth-normal gravity. The final phases of R&D, therefore, would have to be in orbit, in the microgravity confines of Bios One, with the specially-designed logistics laboratory performing the final synthesis. If everything worked according to plan, Bios One would become the new space-based source of Flashback; the company's market analysts had even predicted that Flashback's mystique of having been produced in outer space would help to push sales.

This had been the plan, yet the final R&D phase had taken much longer than expected. The spacelab's log-mod was a sophisticated machine, worth almost as much as the rest of the space station itself, but it couldn't perform miracles. The wildly complex chemical matrix had stubbornly resisted molecular bonding; more tinkering had been required. Instead of two months, the space-based R&D of Flashback had stretched into a year. Six different three-person crews had to be shuttled up to Bios One over the past twelve months; the resultant cost-overruns were staggering.

Spectrum-Mellencamp had already lost tons of money in a blood-serum anticoagulant which had failed in the marketplace, and its board of directors was beginning to suspiciously reassess the millions of dollars which had already been spent on Project Flashback. And then there was the industry rumor that a rival German biotech company was on the verge of developing their own version of Flashback. If it went on much longer, the parent company might be forced not only to dump Flashback, but Space BioTech as well.

Pressure came from the top down, extending from the executive boardroom of Spectrum-Mellencamp to the basic research labs of Space BioTech. While they were in space, Robillard, Schwinn and Hersh suddenly found their careers on the line. If Team Six didn't come home with something useful, then the whole thing was kaput; Spectrum-Mellencamp would dump Space Biotech, and since there was a recession currently in progress, there was little chance that the little company—with no orbital facilities of its own, since Bios One belonged to Spectrum-Mellencamp—would be repurchased by any other space company. Team Six had to produce or perish. And then, two days before the accident, the message was received from the powers-that-be that they were expected to board a Galileo, Inc. spaceplane which was scheduled to be launched from the Cape in less than a week to collect them from Bios One...with or without satisfactory results.

It was time to shit or get off the pot. Fish or cut bait. The three scientists were now under an extraordinary deadline; their jobs would be forfeit if they came back from orbit with little or nothing to show for it. However, the latest batch of Flashback produced by the log-mod had looked particularly promising. They had tried it out on the spacelab's Rhesus monkeys, and although the apes had trouble responding to external stimuli while under its influence, at least they were able to reproduce the arithmetic test which had been established to judge the drug's effectiveness.

Yet this still wasn't sufficient proof. They needed stronger evidence that Flashback worked. Ned Hersh, as station manager and team leader, decided to take the ultimate risk: he would try the drug himself. Robillard had argued against it, but Schwinn had been more pragmatic. At this juncture, they were damned if they did and damned if they didn't. It was Jekyll-and-Hyde territory, completely unethical if not reckless, yet it seemed the only way to go. Team Six didn't have the luxury of safe, protracted experimentation; if they didn't come home with something worth showing to Spectrum-Mellencamp's directors, they wouldn't have a laboratory in which to experiment anyway.

So Hersh had ingested a low concentration of the new batch, then sat back and began to read a computer maintenance manual, the most boring literature aboard the station he could find. After a few hours, Hersh reported no problems; even after he closed the book, though, he could recite from it line by line, with perfect clarity and total recall.

So far, so good, but Schwinn had not been satisfied. He insisted upon trying a slightly higher concentration. Again, Robillard had argued against it—the Rhesus monkeys, the first test-group, had still not come out of their trance—but Schwinn impatiently believed that a real acid-test was needed. So he dosed himself with Flashback, then picked up more complex—and more interesting—reading material, the Hemingway paperback with which he had been entertaining himself over the past few months. Robillard remained undosed, as much out of revulsion of becoming a guinea pig as from the necessity of being the experiment's control subject.

The dual experiments had occurred at 1800 and 2000 respectively, the day before the accident. By 2300, Robillard had sensed trouble. Although Hersh had finished reading the manual, he had difficulty in concentrating on anything else; Schwinn had whipped through The Snows of Kilimanjaro and even insisted upon re-reading it, refusing to be distracted by anything else. By 0030, Schwinn was in an almost hypnotic state; he was beginning to repeat Hemingway's prose verbatim. However, Hersh had seemed at least basically functional, although his thought processes were muddled. An OTV was scheduled for docking in only a short time; since Robillard was not trained to handle the teleoperational docking maneuver, Hersh insisted that he was capable of handling it from the command module. While Robillard confined Schwinn to his niche and stood watch over him, the station manager had gone below to bring in the cargo vessel.

But Hersh had been too distracted by his out-of-control flashbacks of a simple computer manual to handle the complex docking procedure. In the final phases of the maneuver, while he was in direct teleoperational control of the OTV, he had lost his bearings. Helplessly stoned on Flashback, he entered the wrong set of commands into the computer guidance program, causing the OTV's main engine to misfire.

Robillard believed that Hersh's distress signal had been the last cogitant thing the man had done. It was possible that, even as the module's atmosphere was being sucked out by explosive decompression, Hersh had been unable to remember where the exit hatch was located. The elegant beauty of schematic diagrams had been too much for him; Robillard had not even heard him scream.

The door opened just then and Mike Green stuck his head inside. "Car just cruised by twice on the highway," he said softly as we looked up. "Went up the road, turned around, and came back again. Couldn't see who was inside, but it looked like the one our pals were driving."

Sugar calmly picked up his beer. "Probably them. Think they saw you?" Mike shook his head, and Sugar shrugged nonchalantly. "Well, even if they didn't, they must have seen our cars. Unless they're really stupid, they know we're in here." He took a sip. "Time to finish up, gang. It's last call."

Mike shut the door, returning to his sentry post. Sugar chugged the last of his beer as indifferently as if we had been discussing Miami's chances of going to the National League playoffs. Doug closed his eyes and lay his head back against the seat; he looked as if he were ready to doze off in the booth. Perhaps the Blues Brothers had become used to being shadowed by thugs in cheap suits, but just being with them was making me nervous. My house was almost ten miles away in Cocoa Beach; I had an ancient car which could barely get up to forty and a tape recorder filled with one of the most incriminating interviews I had ever done. Sugar and his crewmates could handle a pair of goons, but I was only too aware that it was a moonless night and that, in the wee hours of Sunday morning, Route 3 becomes one hell of a dark, lonesome highway.

"So, anyway, we bundled Robillard, Schwinn and the two monkeys into *Blues'* mid-deck," Sugar continued, "then I put on my helmet and repressurized my suit and went down to Module One to retrieve Hersh's body." His face went grim as he spoke. "I've seen my share of death, son, but what happened to that man was the ugliest thing I've ever seen..."

I quickly nodded my head and held up my hand. I knew all about the effects of sudden decompression upon the human body. More than once drunken beamjacks and moondogs had entertained me with their favorite real-life horror stories, and I didn't need to hear one more detailed account of exploded entrails and frozen blood. There are journalists who thrive on that sort of thing, but I've never been one to rush to gruesome traffic accidents or weird murder scenes. I sleep better that way.

Thankfully, Sugar noticed the expression on my face and spared me the gory part. "Well, once I got Hersh into a body bag and Sir Douglas loaded him into a locker in the mid-deck, it was time for me to EVA."

Doug cleared his throat and half-opened his eyes. "We were hearing from the Cape again," he murmured. "Mike couldn't keep up the come-in-Tokyo shit any longer by then. Ed Collier sounded so genuinely relieved that we had managed to rescue two of his people, he almost forgot to tell us for the fiftieth time that they wanted the log-mod brought home." He closed his eyes again. "Fucking asshole."

"We had done this sort of thing on the RWM before," Sugar said, "so Doug and I didn't need a rehearsal. Once I got outside the station, I got on the cherry-picker, he raised me up and swung me around until I was above and behind the logistics module. It took me only a half-hour to unbolt the sucker from its node...after that, I would hang onto it while Doug hauled us both back into *Blues'* cargo bay, where I would tuck it down in the payload cradle for the ride home. Easy job. We've done it a dozen times."

"We were on an open comlink again," Doug said, "so we couldn't talk freely, and CapCom had insisted that I switch on the cargo bay TV camera and turn it toward the boss so they could see what he was doing out there."

Sugar barely paid attention to him. His eyes wandered toward the ceiling as he spoke, as if he were again gazing into an abyss which only a relative handful of men and women have seen. "But thirty minutes is a long time, y'know, when you're out there by your lonesome. Lot of time for a man to start wondering about things. While I was unbolting the module, I kept looking down at fat ol' mother Earth, and I started thinking..."

He sighed. "Well, about people. Nobody in particular, just people in general. Kids, mainly. I've got one myself...Ted Jr., a freshman in college now. And I thought, y'know, one of these days something like Flashback might be out there on the streets. I mean, acid was first made in a lab with all the best intentions, and look what happened there. And then there was crack and ecstasy and bizarro and all that other shit that has fucked people up. How long would it be before Flashback squirmed out of this company's labs? Even if it didn't become legal, how long would it be before it got out there? Who would be the first dumb kid to buy a hit on a basketball court? Hell, what if Ted gets hold of something like this? Is he going to become another basket case like poor Schwinn?"

Sugar looked down from the ceiling, his gaze returning to me. "Well, there I was, hanging onto a big tin can filled with this evil shit. All there is in the world, right there in my hands. Everything they needed to know about how to make more was in the thing. The basic data had been in the Module One computers, but even if it had been fried during the accident, we hadn't downloaded any of it. Bios One was going to burn up in the atmosphere in just a few days, anyway. No wonder Collier was so hot on getting this thing brought home. Since Robillard had told me Spectrum-Mellencamp had taken a beating from developing Flashback in the first place, they weren't likely to finance another expensive round of R&D. Everything they needed was right there in my hands..."

I could already tell what was coming next. "What about your career?" I asked.

Sugar shrugged his shoulders. "If they knew about what had happened, sure, I was in trouble...but I had the module between me and the TV camera, so they couldn't see exactly what I was doing, right?"

He lifted his arms above his head. "So, as soon as I had it unbolted and I had told Doug here to bring me in, I held onto it for a few seconds longer..."

Sugar grinned, then thrust his arms straight up. "Then I pushed the fucker away as hard as I could."

McPherson burped and nodded his head. "God bless you, Sir Isaac Newton."

That should have been the end of the story. The logistics module, propelled away from the spacelab's already-unstable orbit, tumbled down Earth's gravity well, picking up velocity with each passing minute. Retrieval by the *Sugar's Blues* was impossible; by the time Saltzman came back aboard and the shuttle undocked from Bios One, the log-mod was already beyond reach. Although Collier was screaming bloody murder at the apparent snafu, the ground controllers at KSC agreed that pursuing the falling module couldn't be done without considerable risk to the spacecraft and its crew and passengers.

And besides, hadn't the most important part of the rescue mission been accomplished? By the time *Sugar's Blues* made the deorbit burn for the return to the Cape, the module had entered the upper atmosphere above New Zealand and had been destroyed.

That should have been the end of the story, but it wasn't.

"When we had landed back at the Cape, there was an ambulance waiting to take Robillard and Schwinn away," Sugar said. "That was the last I ever saw of either of them. I saw some guys from Space BioTech unloading the cages with the monkeys, but when I asked about them later, I was told that the apes had died of natural causes shortly after landing. Cardiovascular stress or something like that. But by then, we already knew we were in trouble."

McPherson picked up the pitcher and poured the last of the warm beer into his mug. "Spectrum-Mellencamp smelled a rat and Collier demanded a NASA review board hearing," he said, "but there was nothing anyone could prove. Losing the log-mod was an unfortunate accident and the boss got an official reprimand." He grinned and reached over to slap the back of Sugar's wrist. "Shame on you! Losing a precious module like that! You've been a bad boy! Bad, bad, bad!"

Sugar smiled slightly, but otherwise his face remained serious. "Spectrum-Mellencamp's lawyers produced transcripts of our flight-recorder logs to show that there had been an unexplained comlink blackout during the mission, along with the film of the pictures Doug had taken during our primary approach to the station, but they couldn't prove anything. They didn't come right out and say it, but they tried to claim that we had conspired to destroy the logistics module."

"Well, they were right, weren't they?" I asked.

Sugar pursed his lips and shook his head. "No, not really. Mike and Doug weren't in on it until I told them while we were on the flight deck during the LOS." LOS meant loss-of-signal; spacecraft always experience it during re-entry through Earth's ionosphere. Nature has its convenient moments. "It was my decision to chuck the log-mod, but it was their option whether to come clean or to support my story that the module had slipped out of my hands while the cherry-picker was in motion."

He folded his arms across his chest. "They stuck with me, though, and we kept our stories straight during the hearing. Nobody could pin anything on us. Even though Spectrum-Mellencamp knew we had a bogus cover-story, they couldn't come right out and say why we would have wanted to get rid of a valuable log-mod.

That would have meant admitting the existence of Flashback."

"But what did Robillard have to say?" I asked. "And what happened to Schwinn?"

If there was any trace of smugness about Sugar Saltzman, it vanished immediately. He looked down at the table, his mouth tightening.

"So far as anyone knows, Schwinn is still in a mental institute," McPherson said quietly. "The company line was that he had suffered a complete nervous breakdown when Hersh had been killed. Bullshit about how they had been gay lovers up there and so forth. There was written testimony from Robillard supporting that claim, but he never appeared himself during the hearing." He raised an eyebrow. "About a week later, he suffered a massive stroke and died. Kind of coincidental, right?"

I felt myself getting cold.

"Of course, we couldn't tell anyone the truth about Flashback, either," Sugar said. He looked back up at me, propping his elbows his elbows on the table and clasping his hands together in an almost prayer-like gesture. "If we had, then we would have been admitting our own guilt. Disregarding NASA regs, deliberately destroying valuable hardware..." He shrugged and lightly clapped his hands. "And since Spectrum-Mellencamp claimed that their scientists had been working on a new form of blood anticoagulant, it was our word against theirs that Flashback even existed, or that it was a dangerous drug that had to be destroyed."

"And you know what a lawyer would ask," Doug muttered. "Define 'dangerous.' Define 'drug'..."

"Define existence. Define responsibility." Sugar sighed and shook his head. "So there it was. Neither of us was willing to come out and tell the truth, so it was kind of a stalemate. We were willing to let it go at that. I was just happy that we had managed to get rid of the shit before the company figured out where they had gone wrong and tried to refine the stuff. Bios One burned up in the atmosphere, so all the current data on Project Flashback was lost when it went down for the count. That should have been the end of things."

"Then you guys were busted..." I said.

"And we were grounded and lost our jobs." Saltzman slowly nodded his head. "Yeah, it was a frame-up. The dope in the lockers, the phony drug test report, the whole schmeer." He stretched back his arms, laying them across the back of his seat. "They must have had help on the inside to do all that, so my guess is that people within Skycorp and NASA were paid off. Again, there was nothing we could prove."

McPherson drank from his mug. "At first, we thought they were just trying to get revenge," he said, "but then we started getting the phone calls. Sounded sort of like Collier, but we could never be sure. Just this voice, warning us to keep our mouths shut or things would get worse."

"And then we started getting followed." Sugar picked up the pitcher, saw that it was empty, and put it back on the table with mild disappointment. "Guys in cars following our wives and kids, guys in cars parked outside our houses. That's been going on for about the last year or so. And now tonight..."

Doug hissed and slammed his mug down on the table. "I had had enough of these watchdogs," he hissed angrily. "Yeah, I was a little drunk, but when I see some dudes sitting right next to me, watching me while I'm trying to have a good time...well, I got a little pissed. So I stood up and asked them to leave, and one of 'em gives me this shit-eating grin and asks me why..."

"And you decked him," I finished.

McPherson smiled and belched into his hand. "No apologies on that score. It felt real fucking good."

"And now you know everything," Sugar said. He clapped his hand on McPherson's shoulder and gave his former cargo jockey a shake. "So what do you think?" he asked, looking at me. "Is this a good story for your paper or what?"

It was a damn good story.

We left Diamondback Jack's right after that. Jack Baker came out of his office locked up behind us, never saying a word to any of us. By unspoken agreement, the Blues Brothers left the parking lot before me; they piled into an old Dodge pickup truck with Sugar behind the wheel. He revved the engine and spun gravel as he tore out of the parking lot, making as much noise as possible, while I hung back in the shadows of the bar. Almost as soon as he had ripped down the Route 3, a pair of headlights appeared on the road and a late-model Ford screamed down the highway behind them. I waited until the night was still and quiet again, then I got in my car, tucked my recorder and notebook beneath the seat, and took a different route home. I scared shitless until I pulled into my driveway,

Sunday was spent transcribing the interview tape and collating my notes; by Monday morning I was on the phone, attempting to confirm the allegations. I spent the next four days bird-dogging the story. Sugar Saltzman and Doug McPherson were on the record, but I wasn't surprised that no one else spoke with equal candor.

Edward Collier at Space BioTech consistently remained unavailable for comment; he was always in a meeting and he never returned my calls. Spokespersons at Space BioTech and Spectrum-Mellencamp gave bland, PR-robot responses to my questions; they had never heard of Project Flashback and had never been involved in memory enhancement experiments. Some of them claimed never to have heard of Bios One. Attempting to contact higher officials in the company was futile, except when I got an executive vice president from Spectrum-Mellencamp who hogged a solid twenty minutes of tape telling me about his company's fine accomplishments in agriculture and famine relief, then hung up before I asked my first solid question. Skycorp told me that it didn't discuss the records of its current and former employees. NASA, as usual, lived up to the rep which long ago had earned the press corps interpretation of its initials: Never A Straight Answer.

Eventually, though, I learned three things.

First, a lab analyst for the small Tampa-based biotech firm which had handled the drug tests which had been given to the Blues Brothers admitted—on the record, but without attribution—that it was possible that the results of the hair and urine samples which had been submitted by Saltzman, Green, and McPherson could have been doctored. The lab wasn't completely secure and the vials could have been switched, or someone could have tampered with the computer analysis of the valid tests. It had been done before in that selfsame lab; indeed, all that would have been necessary to get the most damning evidence would have been the switching of labels on a few test tubes.

Second, a biotechnology market analyst from a Wall Street brokerage told me that one of the hottest targets for the biotech industry was the development of a memory enhancement drug, and that Spectrum-Mellencamp was indeed a contender in the race. She also said it was conceivable that such a pharmaceutical, if it were ever manufactured, could eventually lead to the marketing of a street-legal recreational drug; the FDA could be cowed if the clinicals turned out correctly. The notion unsettled her as much as it did me.

Third, after contacting a leading aerospace contractor, I found that Spectrum-Mellencamp was spending several hundred million dollars for the construction of Bios Two, the replacement of the spacelab they had lost. One of the principal components of the new station was to be a logistics module, dedicated to the space-based refinement of pharmaceuticals. Skycorp had been subcontracted by Spectrum-Mellencamp to place the new station in orbit sometime within the next two fiscal years.

By Friday, I had enough solid info to use in the story. It would be one hot-shit work of investigative journalism: the secret development of a dangerous drug, the resultant deaths of two scientists who had been directly involved in the project, the insanity of another, the cover-up which had annihilated the careers of a living legend and his crew. All the denials and greed and lies. The sort of story a working journalist spends his life dreaming about, the stuff from which Pulitzers are made. In a breathless plunge, I spent the full day writing the final draft and faxed it straight to the paper. A senior editor immediately called to play Twenty Questions; satisfied, he hung up after telling me that I had just made his day.

Everything I knew went into the article...including its principal source, Diamondback Jack's.

In my headlong rush to double-check everything, I had completely forgotten my vow to Jack Baker. In the third and fifth paragraphs of the story, I mentioned that the interviews with Sugar Saltzman and Doug McPherson had taken place in the bar, following a violent fight with a couple of corporate henchmen who had been shadowing them for the past year. I called Diamondback Jack's by its name, even mentioned its exact location on Merritt Island.

Substantiation of fact is the operative term in the news business. Breaking a promise is what they call it in real life.

My article appeared on the front page of the Sunday edition of the *Times,* in a center box above the fold. I didn't go down to the bar that night; when I saw the article and realized what I had done, I swore to myself that, sometime in the next week, I would drop by and try to make my peace with Jack Baker. That, or give him a chance to give me his best swing with that Louisville Slugger he kept beneath the counter. Sometime in the next week, or the next month, after the heat had blown over.

But the heat didn't blow over; I had shed light, so naturally there was combustion to go with it.

They didn't retaliate against me. Only amateurs and religious fanatics try to take revenge upon reporters, because you have to kill 'em to make sure that they won't write about you again...and even then, there's no guarantee that the guy at the next desk won't be assigned to pick up where the first one left off. And they couldn't try any more shit with the Blues Brothers; after the story was published, if Sugar had even stubbed his toe, it would have been blamed on Spectrum-Mellencamp. No, when they decided to strike back, they had to pick another target.

The night my article was published in the *Times,* in the early Monday morning hours shortly after Jack had chased out the last of the drunks out of his bar and went home, someone broke into his bar and torched the joint. The combined force of old timber, alcohol, grease and vile rumors caused the place to burn to the foundations before the first trucks arrived on the scene. The county fire marshall later confirmed that it was arson; with three separate points of origin, it sure as hell wasn't caused by a cigarette.

I can't honestly say that I miss the place. It was one of the seediest low-rent dives I've ever hung out in. Nonetheless, it was a part of the Cape's history, a place where both the best and the worst of the high frontier found common ground, if only in complaining about the foul bathrooms and the seldom-swept floors. Its demise is symbolic of the passing of an era; we're entering a dangerous new age in this so-called conquest of space, and even the old familiar hangouts of washed-up astronauts and deadbeat reporters are possible targets.

Bios Two will not be built; Spectrum-Mellencamp and Space BioTech are now under criminal investigation by a federal grand jury, and it's possible that some people will go to prison. Sugar Saltzman's good name has been restored: although he's in retirement, I've lately heard that Green's and McPherson's flight status has been reinstated by NASA. Sometimes the good guys win, after all.

But no one ever tells me secrets anymore. I still go to the press conferences, pick up the news releases and rewrite them as news stories for the *Times,* but my usefulness as a reporter has been shot. When a journalist fucks over his sources, his career is effectively over. He's untrustworthy, a bad risk, and everyone knows it. And that's why I now drink alone.

But, like I said, truth is a dangerous business. The public has a right to know. Right?

LIVE FROM THE MARS HOTEL

Rachel Keaton; program director, WBXL-FM, Boston:

I first heard the Mars Hotel while I was working as a jock at KMCY in St. Louis. At the time 'MCY—"Mighty Mickey, the rock sound of St. Louis"—had a progressive contemporary format, and the playlist represented much of the progressive music that was coming out at the time: the experimental groups from the Far East, the latest British invasion, and of course the acoustic revival. This was the early '20s, y'know, and there was some interesting stuff coming out even before the Mars Hotel appeared, so the timing was right for their first single.

Looking back on it, I think I was one of the first jocks in the country to play it, and that was a matter of being in the right place at the right time. About six months earlier the DJ who handled the Sunday afternoon acoustic show, Ben Grady, had left 'MCY to become music director at a Los Angeles AOR station. The acoustic revival was just getting started and I had developed a taste for it, the work that was coming out of Nashville and Austin and Muscle Shoals, so I managed to bug Heidi Schlossberg, who was the program director at the time, into letting me take over Ben's show.

It was a lot of fun, because many of these artists were recording on obscure labels, so finding stuff to play was a little like, y'know, exploring new territory. But I kept discovering guys who had skipped back forty, fifty years and were reviving David Bromberg or Johnny Cash or the Earl Scruggs Revue. It was a neat time to be in the music business, since it was finally dredging itself out of the glitzy Hollywood punk scene where it had been stuck for...

I'm sorry (*Laughs.*) I'm getting off the subject. Where was I?

Right. Well, I got Ben's old show and renamed it "The Wireless Hour," and one Sunday afternoon in—I guess it was '22, maybe '23

—Heidi walked into the air studio with a single in her hand. She had been in that day doing some extra work left over from last week, which included opening all those boxes of records that radio stations get swamped with all week. Well, she had this one single she had just taken out of a box, and the moment I spotted it in her hand, I knew it had to be two things. One, because it wasn't a CD and was pressed on old-fashioned vinyl instead, it had to be from some small, destitute label. Second, it had to be good, because she had obviously listened to it in Studio B and thought it was so hot that she had not bothered to master it onto a cart yet.

"Put this on," she says, handing me the disc. "You'll love it!"

I took it out of her hand, saw that it was on a label I had seen a couple of times before, Centennial Park Records, a little Nashville company which had started up a couple of years earlier and hadn't put out anything special. The 'A' side was an old Bob Dylan, "Knockin' on Heaven's Door." The 'B' side was "Sea Cruise", the Leiber and Stoller classic. The band was something called the Mars Hotel.

I gave Heidi this look, y'know, that Hiroshima was God's gift to pop music. 'Trust me,' she says. 'You'll eat it up.' So I cued up the Dylan song and segued it in after the next couple of ad spots. I didn't expect anything special, right?

I dunno. What can I say that hasn't been said before? It was fantastic. I could tell that the band, whoever they were, were only three guys: a vocalist on guitar, a bass player, and somebody on synth doing piano, percussion, and pedal steel. There's been a million bands like that and a million people have done Dylan, most of them badly. But these guys made "Knockin' on Heaven's Door" sound like they had just written it. Very fresh, stripped-down. Unpretentious. They played like they meant it, you know what I mean?

So I look up and say, "Who are these guys?" Heidi just grins at me and asks, "Where do you think they're from?" I glanced at the label again and say, "Well, they're obviously from Nashville."

She just shook here head. "No, they're from Mars."

Alan Gass; former station supervisor, Skycorp/Ucho-Hiko Arsia Base, Mars:

Well, it's no secret that life at Arsia Base was rough. Always will be rough, or at least until someone gets around to terraforming Mars, which is wild-eyed fantasy if you ask me. But even if you disregard the sandstorms and scarcity of water, the extremes of heat and cold and...well, just the utter barrenness of that world, it's still a hell of a place to live for any extended period of time.

I guess the worst part was the isolation. When I was station manager we had about fifty men and women living in close quarters in a cluster of fifteen habitats modules, buried just under the ground. Most of these folks either worked for Skycorp or the Japanese firm Uchu-Hiko, manufacturing propellant from Martian hydrocarbons in the soil which was later boosted up to the Deimos fuel depot, or were conducting basic research for NASA or NASDA. The minority of us were support personnel, like myself, keeping the place operational.

A lot of us had signed on for Mars work for the chance to explore another planet, but once you got there you found yourself spending most of your time doing stuff that was not much different than if you had volunteered to live underground in Death Valley for two years. For the men working the electrolysis plant, it was a particularly hard, dirty job—working ten or twelve hour shifts, coming back to the base to eat and collapse, then getting up to do it all over again. The researchers didn't have it much easier because their sponsoring companies or governments had gone to considerable expense to send them to Mars and they had to produce a lifetime's worth of work during their two years or risk losing their jobs and reputations.

The base was located in a visually stunning area, the Tharsis region, just south of the equator near the western flank of Arsia Mons. When you went outside there was this giant, dead volcano looming over you, and on a clear day you could just make out the summit of Olympus Mons way off to the northeast. But after a few weeks the novelty would wear off. You'd become used to red rocks and pink skies, and after that what would you have? There was never any time for sightseeing. After awhile you started looking forward to the next big sandstorm, just to watch this giant swirling red curtain coming toward you like the wrath of God. (*Laughs.*) You wouldn't spend much time watching because the wind could shred your suit in a minute, but at least it was exciting.

Anyway, one night I had just come off my shift in the command module and I was walking back to my bunkhouse through the connecting tunnel, which was called Broadway. I was beat, and I didn't feel like going to the wardroom because I wasn't hungry—not that the food was particularly appetizing anyway—but the way to Module Five took me past the wardroom, Module Three, which we called the Mars Hotel. I had just walked past Three when I heard a guitar being played and someone singing.

I really didn't notice it at first, because I figured it was coming from a tape, but then I heard another guitar joining in and someone else beginning to sing, and then there was an electronic piano chiming in. But the second guy couldn't sing and the piano was a little off-key, and suddenly I realized that I wasn't hearing a tape.

That stopped me in my tracks. I don't know if I can describe that feeling of puzzlement and wonder. It was like a rare bird had just flown down Broadway. I mean, which was stranger? Seeing a rare species, or just seeing a bird in the first place? I backed up a couple of steps, wondering if I was hallucinating, and looked through the open hatch.

Partial transcript of an interview with the Mars Hotel, originally broadcast on NBC's The Today Show, *July 27, 2022 (Note: this interview was taped and edited in advance in order to contract the time differential during Earth-Mars transmissions).*

Judith King, host: "So how did you come up with the name for your group?"

Tiny Pronzini, lead guitarist: "Um...which of us are you asking?"

King: "Any one of you."

Joe Mama, synthesizer player: "During that last nineteen minute delay we thought it over and decided that we wouldn't tell you that we used to be called the Mars House of Ill Repute, but the record company made us change it because it was too long to fit on the label."

Gary Smith, bass guitarist: "You shouldn't ask Joe straight questions like that, I'll warn you right now."

Mama (to Pronzini): "I told you we should have used a different name. Now we're going to have to answer that question for the rest of our lives."

Pronzini: "Look who's talking. No, it's...(*Laughter.*) See, there's two reasons. One, the wardroom here is called the Mars Hotel. It was once called the Mars Hilton, but somehow it got shortened. Second, there's an old album by the Grateful Dead, whom we all admire, called *From the Mars Hotel*. The wardroom is the place where we've always rehearsed, and we've all been influenced one way or another by the Dead, so it sort of came natural."

Smith: "After we started jamming together and people here at the base started coming to listen to us during their off-shifts, they tried to stick us with names."

Mama: "Things like, y'know, the Tharks, the Mike Mars Blues Trio, John Carter and His Bare-Ass Barsoominans..."

Smith: "Worse things, when we sounded bad, like Dryheaving Sandworms..."

Prozini: "Eventually the name that stuck was the Mars Hotel Band, which sort of made us sound like a Ramada Inn lounge act that plays bar mitzvahs. (*Laughter.*) Before long the last part of the name was dropped and we became just, y'know, the Mars Hotel."

King: "I see. And when did you start playing together?"

Mama: "When we got sick of Monopoly."

Prozini: "Please forgive him. The steel plate in his head..."

Smith: "Tiny got us started, though he won't admit it."

Prozini: "Oh, I'll admit it! I just didn't want to take all the credit."

Mama: "Don't worry. You won't.

Smith: "Oh, hell. If nobody will give you a straight answer, I will! (*Laughter.*) Tiny and I were shooting the breeze one night in Module Six, our bunkhouse, about the things we missed out here, and one of the things was live music. We're both from New England—he's from Massachusetts, I'm from New Hampshire—and as we talked it turned out that we had both gone to the same places where you could hear live, acoustical music. Bluegrass, blues, folk, rockabilly..."

Prozini: "I'm telling the story, so get lost. (*Laughter.*) And it further turned out that both of us know how to play guitar. Well, I knew Joe here had a portable Yamaha synthesizer that he had smuggled out here and was hiding in his geology lab..."

Mama: "Hey! I told you not to say anything about that!"

Prozini: "Don't worry about it. You're famous now. Anyway, I managed to pull some contacts on the Cape and get a couple of guitars shipped to us on the next Mars-bound ship, and once we roped Joe into the combo, we started playing together in the Mars Hotel. And it was just like that."

King: "I see. From what your audience here on Earth has heard so far, you principally cover songs other people have written. Some of them quite old, in fact. Why aren't you writing songs of your own, about Mars?"

Prozini: "Well, uh..."

Smith: "We're lazy." (*Laughter.*)

Mama: "Actually, I'm working on composing an epic twenty-hour opera inspired by old *Lost in Space* episodes. It's tentatively entitled 'Dr. Smith Unbound.'"

Prozini: "You're a sick man, Joe."

Gary Smith; former lead guitarist, Mars Hotel:

That was a pretty ridiculous interview, as I recall it. We had just heard that "Knockin' on Heaven's Door" had cracked the Top Forty in the US and Canada, which we had never dreamed would happen, when we got a request from Skycorp's PR office that we do an interview for *The Today Show*. We didn't take it seriously because, really, we didn't take any of it seriously. "We're music stars? They've got to be kidding!" That sort of thing.

But, deep down inside, when we actually got around to doing the interview, the question that we dreaded the most—although none of us really discussed it—was the one we got about why we weren't writing our own songs. When you watch the tape you can see how we avoided answering that completely, with Joe'e remark about *Lost In Space* being the closest we came to giving a reply. But we had answers for that.

One, of course, was that we liked playing the old stuff. It was what made us feel good, what took our minds off the hellhole conditions out there and so forth. That's really how the Mars Hotel got started in the first place. None of us aspired to be professional musicians. We didn't even care if we had an audience or not, although we didn't mind when base personnel started gathering in the ward room during our sessions. An audience was something that was thrust upon us, just as fame on Earth was thrust upon us by circumstances beyond our control. It just started with the three of us sitting in the Mars Hotel, trying out things like "Kansas City" or "Police Dog Blues" or "Willie and the Hand Jive"—we were out to entertain ourselves, period.

But secondly—and this was what we didn't want to admit—none of us could write songs worth a damn. Not that we didn't try. At one time or another each of us said, "Hey, I'm going to write a song about Mars," and that person would disappear for awhile, think think think, y'know, and come back to the other guys with something. "Here's a song, let's try it." And it would always turn out as some hackneyed, pretentious bullshit. Metaphorical nonsense about raging sandstorms and watching Phobos and Deimos rising and how I miss you, my love, now that we're worlds apart. Boring shit, not at all the kind of thing any of us wanted to play.

After awhile we just gave up, saying to ourselves and each other, "Screw it, I'd rather do 'Johnny B. Goode' any old day." But our failure to produce anything original that said something about the human condition out there really gnawed on us, though I kept thinking that there had to be a good song somewhere about watching the sun rise over Arsia Mons. But it really bugged Tiny, who was probably the most creative of the three of us, who worshipped Woody Guthrie and Bob Dylan and Robert Hunter. I know for a fact, because one of the guys who shared his bunkhouse told me, that he secretly kept attempting to write songs, late at night when he thought no one was watching. I kinda felt sorry for him. It was like masturbation—an ultimately futile attempt to scratch an unscratchable itch.

Alan Gass:

After Tiny and Gary got those guitars—I think they bribed Billy DeWolfe, who was one of the regular pilots for the Earth-Mars supply runs, into smuggling them aboard the *Shinseiki*—and they put together the band with Joe, I had to keep after the three of them constantly to do their jobs. Tiny and Gary were both miners—"the Slaves of Mars", we called them—and Joe was a soil analyst in the geology lab, so they all had important industrial functions to fulfill, and it was my job to make sure that Skycorp got its money's worth from them.

As a band, they were pretty funny to watch. Gary looked normal enough, since he would just stand there wearing his bass. But you've seen the pictures of Tiny. He was literally a giant. Six-foot-four, three hundred pounds, almost all of it muscle. Sometimes he wouldn't even bother to sit in a chair, but would lie on the floor with his guitar resting on his huge chest, playing along with his eyes closed.

Joe was the strangest of the bunch. He looked a lot better in the pictures you've seen, if you can believe that. (*Laughs*). His Japanese and American bloodlines had crossed to produce one freakish-looking individual: narrow, squinty eyes, jug ears, too tall and skinny with his hair cropped so short that he was almost bald. "Joe Mama" wasn't his real name, but I don't think anyone knew his real name. He would put his mini-synth in his lap and as he'd play—looking like he was typing, the way he held his hands—his eyes would narrow even more and his mouth would hang open and his head bob back and forth as if his neck was made of rubber. If you didn't know better, know that he was an MIT graduate with a near-genius level IQ, you would have sworn he was an idiot.

The funniest thing, though, was how they sounded when they were rehearsing in the Mars Hotel. It was a big, steel cylinder, you've got to remember—very bare, hardly any furniture except for some tables and chairs and a couple of data screens suspended from the ceiling. As far as acoustics go, it sounded like they were playing in a tin can. The sound would reverberate off the walls and make them sound louder than they really were, and you could hear them all over the base. At first a few people minded, but once they got good— believe me, they were just awful at first—people stopped complaining and started coming by to listen. After awhile, I stopped being strict with them about keeping their hours on the clock. Their music was like a little piece of Earth. God knows they were good for morale.

Salvador "Sal" Minella; chief dietician, Arsia Station :

I think their best moment was on Christmas night in '21, when they played for the beer bust we held in the Mars Hotel. Everyone knows what they sounded like that night, because that was the performance that Billy DeWolfe taped and brought back to Earth.

You know that DeWolfe was the one who smuggled Gary's and Tiny's guitars out there, right? Well, DeWolfe was a pipeline for all sorts of things. You sent him a message asking for something and arranged a cash transfer from your bank account back home to his, and unless NASA or Skycorp caught him he would make sure that it was loaded into the cargo lander of either the *Enterprise* or the *Shinseiki* when it left Earth the next time. You might have to wait nine months or more, but if Billy could get it for you, he'd do so, with only a slight markup.

We had long since arranged for eight cases of Budweiser to make it aboard the *Enterprise* in '21, because the timing was that the ship would arrive, just in time for Christmas. Al Gass had already arranged with Skycorp for some freeze-dried turkey to be sent out, but Billy and I had figured that the crew would appreciate some suds more than the turkey. Christmas dinner and the party afterward would be held in the ward room, and I managed to twist Tiny's arm into getting his band to play after dinner.

To make a long story short...well, you've heard it already. It was a damn good show. We drank beer, we danced, we had a good time. We forgot about Mars for awhile. You can hear a little bit of that in the background on the tape, but a lot of the stuff was edited out, like Joe playing a weird version of "White Christmas" and that sort of thing.

About halfway through the evening, I spotted Billy DeWolfe standing near the stage, which we had made out of a collapsed cargo pallet, with a cassette recorder in his hand. I don't think the band noticed what he was doing—and if they did, they wouldn't have cared—but I wandered over to him and said, "Hey, you trying to steal the show or something?"

Billy, just grinned and said, "I'm only getting something to show the folks back home what they're missing." I remember getting a kick out of that. Never stopped to consider if the son of a bitch was serious.

Billy DeWolfe; former Skycorp/NASA deep-space pilot:

It wasn't my idea at first to record the Mars Hotel so I could take the tape to a record company. It's just that the trip back to Earth is as long as the trip out, and since the command crew doesn't get to ride in the zombie tanks like the passengers, you have to find things to entertain you during that long haul. I made the tape so I would have something to listen to while I was standing watch, that's all, so it pisses me off when people say that I was trying to rip off the band.

I didn't consider taking the tape to a record producer until much later. I had been listening to it over and over, and at some point it occurred to me that it was too bad that people on Earth couldn't hear the Mars Hotel. Then, the more I listened to it, I realized that it was a really good tape. There was hardly any background noise, and what there was sounded just like the audience sounds you hear from any recorded live performance. I thought it was as good as any CD or tape I had ever heard. By the time the *Enterprise* rendezvoused in LEO with Columbus Station, I had decided to contact a cousin who lived in Nashville to see if he could provide me with any leads to the record companies there.

Why didn't I ask permission from the band? (*Shrugs.*) I was embarrassed. I knew none of those guys were into this for the money, or even to be heard beyond Arsia Base. They wouldn't have given themselves the chance to make it big. But I wanted to do them a favor by trying to give them that chance. Hey, if doing somebody a favor is criminal, I plead guilty.

Gary Smith:

Did we mind what Billy did? Of course we minded! (*Laughs.*) We bitched about it all the way to the bank!

Excerpt from "Martians Invade Earth!" by Barry O'Connor; from <u>Rolling Stone</u>, June 21, 2023:

DeWolfe was turned down by every major record company on Nashville's "Music Row" before he approached Centennial Park Records with his tape of the Mars Hotel. Indeed, company president and producer Saundra Lewis nearly ejected the space pilot from her office as well when she heard that DeWolfe had not been authorized by the group to represent them. She also did not believe that the tape had been recorded on Mars. "My first thought was that it had been recorded in a basement in Birmingham, not in the wardroom of the Mars base," Lewis recalls.

She was impressed by the tape, however, and after extensive double-checking with Skycorp, she established that Tiny Prozini, Gary Smith, and Joe Mama were, in fact, active personnel at Arsia Base. Even though the Mars Hotel had no track record, Lewis decided to take a gamble. Centennial Park Records, while it had gained some respect among connoisseurs of acoustic bluegrass, blues, and rockabilly, was close to bankruptcy. "Since a virtually finished product was already in our hands, I felt like we had little to lose to cleaning it up and releasing it," she says. With DeWolfe acting as the group's agent, the company got permission from the Mars Hotel to release an edited version of the tape as an album, entitled *Red Planet Days.*

"We were surprised that a tape of one of our sessions had made its way to Nashville," says Tiny Prozini, "and for a little while we wanted to strangle Billy. But we figured, 'What the hell, maybe it will even sell a few copies,' so we gave in and signed a contract." Prozini leaned back in his chair and shrugged. "But we had zero expectations about it. I even said that we'd find copies in the cutout bins by the time we got home."

Yet when *Red Planet Days* was released and the single was sent to rock and country stations in the U.S. and Canada, there occurred one of those unanticipated surprises which happen in the music industry once every few years. In hindsight, it can be explained why the album took off like a bullet; it was released at the time when the public was beginning to rediscover the acoustic grass roots sound. This was particularly the case on college campuses where students, sick of several generations of formula hard rock, were once again listening to dusty LPs recorded in their grandparents' time by Jerry Jeff Walker, Howlin' Wolf, and the Nitty Gritty Dirt Band. A new band which had that old sound filled the gap. Yet there was also the fact that this was an album which had been recorded on Mars, by a group that was still on Mars.

"It added a certain mystique, no doubt about it," says Lewis, "and I'll admit that we marketed that aspect for all it was worth."

Within two weeks of its release, "Knockin' on Heaven's Door" was added to the heavy rotation playlists of every major market radio station in the country, and *Red Planet Days* was flying off the shelves in the record stores. By the end of the month, Centennial Park Records went back to press for a second printing on the disc, the first time the company had ever done so with one of its releases.

"It's the damndest thing I ever saw," says WNHT Program Director Ben Weiss, who is credited with being the first New York City radio manager to add the Mars Hotel to his station's playlist. "No one even knew what these guys looked like. Not one concert appearance."

Which was precisely the problem for Centennial Park Records. The company, which only months before had been on the verge of filing under Chapter Eleven, now had a runaway hit. Unfortunately, neither a follow-up album nor a concert tour was possible, for the band was thirty-five million miles away. It was a record producer's nightmare.

"Naturally, we had to bring the mountain to Mohammad," says Lewis...

LIVE FROM THE MARS HOTEL

Gary Smith:

I can't say that we were overwhelmed by the news that the disc had become a hit. In fact, we were sort of underwhelmed. For one thing, it seemed like a distant event, and not just because of the miles involved—none of us even had a copy of the CD, because it hadn't been pressed by the time the last supply ship had left Earth. During a transmission from SOC someone had held a copy up to the camera for us to see, but that was about it. We had never heard it played on the radio, of course. In fact, we barely remembered what we had played that night. So it was no big deal. It was almost as if we hadn't made the tape.

We were going back to being space jocks by then. The novelty of playing together was beginning to wear thin, and there was a lot of work that had to be done at the base before summer, which is sandstorm season there. But I also think we were unconsciously defending ourselves against this celebrity status which had been thrust upon us. Not that it wasn't fun to play music, but somehow people had started pointing fingers at us, saying, "Ooooh, superstars!" We hated that shit, and we wanted to get away from it.

But, y'know...(*Shrugs*). That wasn't the way it worked out. About a month before the next cycle ship, the *Shinseiki*, arrived in Mars orbit, we received a priority message from Skycorp, signed by the CEO himself. It told us that our contracts had been terminated and that we were to return to Earth aboard the *Shinseiki*. It turned out Skycorp had struck a deal with Saundra Lewis and a Los Angeles concert promoter. Skycorp was scratching our contracts so we could come to L.A. to cut another album and then do a concert tour.

Alan Gass:

I'm not sure that they wanted to stay, but I don't think they wanted to go, either. Mars gets under your skin like that. It seems like a terrible place while you're there, when you're working in spacesuits that smell like week-old socks, and living in tin cans, but secretly you come to love Mars. I've been back for several years now, and there isn't a day when I don't think about the planet and wish I was back there.

I think Tiny especially realized that he was leaving something special behind. But no one gave them a choice. Skycorp, which had taken a beating from the press because of the cost overruns and fatalities incurred by the powersat project, had seen a chance at good publicity in the Mars Hotel. There's a clause in the fine print of everyone's contract that says the company reserves the right to terminate an employee's duty whenever it pleases, and Skycorp called in that clause when it made the deal with the record company. Joe, Tiny, and Gary weren't fired so much as they were, to use the old Army phrase, honorably discharged, but the deal still stank anyway.

The night before they left on the *Shinseiki* they played one last gig in the Mars Hotel. Everyone showed up, and everyone tried to put a good face on it, but it was different then before. It was definitely a goodbye show, and no one wanted to see them go. But more than that, there was this sense that the Mars Hotel, the band, didn't belong to Mars anymore. It was another resource which had been dug out of the rocky red soil and flung out into space for someone else to use.

The band was also very somber. They played as well as they always did, but they didn't seem to have their hearts in it and they didn't play for very long. After they did "Sea Cruise" they just put down their instruments and smiled uncomfortably at everyone—the place was very quiet then—and mumbled something about needing some sleep before the launch next morning, and then they sorta shuffled out of the wardroom. Just like that, it was over.

Saundra Lewis; producer, <u>Red Planet Days</u> and <u>Kings of the High Frontier</u>:

I don't know why it didn't work out...
(*Long pause.*) No, no. Scratch that. I know, or at least I think I know, why the Mars Hotel bombed after we got them back here. It's just hard for me to admit it, since I was part of it.

In the music business we tend to put talents into convenient little niches, thinking that if we can put a label on that which we can barely comprehend, we somehow control the magic. So the little niche that was carved for the Mars Hotel was "Oldies Band from Mars." Once we had made that label, we went about forcing them into the niche.

Once we got them back to Earth and into a studio in L.A., we got carried away with the realization that, unlike with *Red Planet Days*, here was a chance to tinker with the band's style. The euphemism is "finetuning", but in this case it was meddling. The unexpected success of the first album had made us overconfident; I, at least, as the producer, should have reined myself in.

But we hired backup singers and session musicians by the bus load, and added strings and horns and electric guitars and drums and choruses, thinking that we were improving the quality while, in fact, we were getting far away from that elegant, stripped-down sound that was on *Red Planet Days*. Joe's mini-synth was replaced by a monstrous, wrap-around console he could barely operate, for example. Nor did we listen to their ideas. Tiny wanted to do "John Wesley Harding", for instance, but we decided that we wanted to have a more country-oriented approach, so we forced them into doing Willie Nelson's "Whisky River" instead, saying that it was bad luck to do two Dylan songs in a row. (*Laughs*.)

The only bad luck was that there were two many cooks in the kitchen. *Kings of the High Frontier* was an overproduced catastrophe. In hindsight, I can see where the errors of judgement were made, where we had diluted the very qualities that made the band strong. But worse than that, we failed to recognize a major reason why people liked the Mars Hotel. But we were too busy fooling with the magic, and it wasn't until they went out on the road that the lesson was learned.

Gary Smith:

The promoter had booked us into medium-size concert halls all over the country. The tour started in California and worked west through the Southwest into the South and up the East Coast. It should have been just the three of us, and maybe doing small clubs instead, but the record company and the promoter, who were pulling all the strings, decided to send along the whole mob that had been in the studio doing the album.

We had no creative control. There was virtually nothing that we could veto. Each night, we were trying to do soulful, sincere versions of "Knockin' on Heaven's Door" on these huge amphi–theater stages with three backup singers, a couple of guitarists, a drummer, two horn players, and a piano, so there was this wall of sound that just hammered people back in their seats. And in the middle of this orchestra there were me and Tiny and Joe, wearing these silk silver jumpsuits that were some costume designer's idea of what we wore on Mars, while overhead spun a giant holographic image of Mars.

So it was all slick Hollywood-Nashville bullshit, the exact opposite of everything we wanted our music to be, manufactured by twits and nerds with a cynical outlook on what people wanted. (*Shakes his head.*) Well, you can't sell people what they don't want. Even though the concerts were almost all sell-outs, from up on the stage we could see people wincing, frowning, leaving their seats and not coming back. I stopped reading the reviews after awhile, they were so grim. And *Kings of the High Frontier* was DOA in the record stores, of course.

It ended in Baton Rouge at the tail-end of the tour. It had been another hideous show, and afterwards, while all the session players were drinking and screwing around in the hotel, the three of us slipped out and caught a cab to an all-night diner somewhere on the edge of town. At first all we wanted was to get an early morning breakfast and to escape from the Nashville bozos for a little while, but we ended up staying there until dawn, talking about everything that had happened over the past few months, talking about what had happened to us.

We knew that we were sick of it all—the stardom, making crap records, touring—so there was practically no argument over whether we should break it up the band. We didn't even try to think of ways to salvage something from the wreckage all we wanted to do was to give the Mars Hotel a mercy killing before it became more embarrassing.

No, what we discussed was why things had turned so sour so quickly, and somehow in the wee hours of the morning, drinking coffee in the Louisiana countryside near the interstate, we came to the conclusion that we had been doomed from the moment we had left Mars.

It wasn't just the way *Kings of the High Frontier* had been made, or that we were doing George Jones instead of David Bromberg or Willie Nelson instead of Bob Dylan because someone decided that we should have the Nashville sound, whatever that is. No, it was the fact that we had been playing music that had been born on Earth, but we were doing it on Earth. What had made the Mars Hotel different many months before had been the fact that we were playing Earth music...on Mars.

It was a strange notion, but it made more sense the longer we considered it. We had taken a bit of human culture to Mars, and then exported it back. It was the same culture, we hadn't changed the songs, but what was different was that it had been performed by people living on another world. Back here, we were just another band doing a cover of "Sea Cruise". People take culture with them wherever they go, but what makes a frontier a home is when they start generating a culture of their own. We had been proving, without really realizing what we were doing, that it was possible to do something else on Mars than make rocket fuel and take pictures of dead volcanos.

It was then that Tiny surprised Joe and me. He pulled out of his jacket pocket a small notebook and opened it. I had seen him, now and then during the tour, sitting by himself and writing in it, but I had never really paid attention. Now he showed us what he had been doing—writing songs.

They weren't bad. In fact, they were pretty good. There was one called "Olympus Mons Blues", and another piece that hadn't yet been titled, about running from a sandstorm. Not sappy or stilted, but gritty, raw stuff. Great Mars Hotel material.

"But this isn't for us," he said when I commented that we should try playing them before we ended the tour. `At least this isn't anything that can be played here. I've got to go back there for this stuff to make sense, or if I'm going to write anything else about it."

It was ironic. While we had been on Mars, Tiny hadn't been able to write a thing about the place. It took coming back to Earth for the words to finally come out. But his memories were beginning to dry up, the images were beginning to fade. Tiny knew that he had to go back if he was going to produce any more Mars songs. Nor would anyone appreciate them if they were sung from any place else but Mars.

He had the notion to apply for another duty-tour with Uchu-Eiko, since Skycorp obviously would be displeased if he tried to get his old job back from them. Joe was also up for it, but I wasn't. I liked breathing fresh air again, seeing plants that weren't growing out of a hydroponics tank. They didn't hold that against me, so we decided that, once we had fulfilled our contract obligations by finishing this tour, we would formally dissolve the band.

Afterwards, I moved back up to New Hampshire and started a small restaurant in North Conway with the money I had made. On weekends I play bass with a small bluegrass jug-band on the weekends, but otherwise I lay low. I got postcards for a while from Tiny and Joe, telling me that they were now working for the Japanese and were being trained at the Cape for another job at Arsia Station.

A month before they left for Mars on the Enterprise—by coincidence, the pilot was to be Billy DeWolfe, who had gotten us into this mess in the first place—I got a final card from Tiny: "We still need a bass player. Please reconsider. C'mon down and we'll make room for you."

I didn't write back, figuring that he was just being cute. The shuttle up to Columbus Station and the *Enterprise* launched from the Cape a few days later, and Joe and Tiny were on their way back...

(*Long pause.*) Funny. I almost said, "On their way back home." I guess it was. I guess it always will be now.

Billy DeWolfe:

When Tiny and Joe climbed through the hatch into the manned lander, I never thought for an instant that I would be the last person to see them alive. I would have been piloting the lander down myself, if it weren't that I had to close down the *Enterprise* and bring the cargo lander down. I suppose I should consider myself lucky.

There weren't any great last words from either of them that I can recall, only Joe grinning and saying, "See you later," just before I shut and dogged the airlock hatch. I remember both of them being happy as hell to be back, though. During the two days since they had come out of the zombie tanks, while we were on our final approach and Mars was getting bigger and bigger, they had been talking about music, working on a song together—and they had been talking about making music, not just playing the oldies. (*Laughs.*) They said that when they were ready, they would give me a new tape to take back to Earth with me, as long as I didn't take it to Nashville.

And y'know...suddenly, they were gone. I was on the command deck safeing everything for the return flight when Arsia Control came over the comlink saying that they had lost telemetry with the lander.

LIVE FROM THE MARS HOTEL

Alan Gass:

We buried them where we found them at the crash site, northeast of the Tharsis Montes range just above the equator. We wrapped Joe and Tiny, along with the three other people who had been in the lander, in the parachutes that had tangled after aerobraking, and buried their bodies under piles of rocks. I went back a few weeks later to place markers we had made from pieces of the wreckage. The floor of the desert shifts around a lot, so I don't know if the graves are even visible anymore.

Billy found their instruments in the cargo lander, and they're now in the Mars Hotel, hanging on the walls. Some country music museum wanted us to ship them back, so we could put Tiny's guitar and Joe's mini-synth on display, but we refused. It's more appropriate that they stay on Mars...

It's funny that you ask. A few days ago I got a letter from a friend who's still stationed there, telling me that somebody's been playing Tiny's guitar. Guy from Florida, who wanted to try it out and thought it was okay to take it down from the hooks. I don't think anyone minded very much. Besides, my friend says he's pretty good.

PART TWO
ALTERNATE SPACE

ON THE ROAD: PAKACHOAG HILL

The first flight with a rocket using liquid propellants was yesterday at Aunt Effie's farm in Auburn...Even though the release was pulled, the rocket did not rise at first, but the flame came out, and there was a steady roar. After a number of seconds it rose, slowly, until it cleared the frame, then at express-train speed...It looked almost magical as it rose without any appreciable greater noise or flame, as if it said, "I've been here long enough; I think I'll be going somewhere else, if you don't mind."

— Diary of Robert H. Goddard
March 17, 1926

The first major step toward the conquest of space occurred with that rocket launch from the top of Pakachoag Hill. The rocket, a barely streamlined apparatus of pressure chambers and tubes, weighed about ten and one-half pounds loaded with its fuel of liquid oxygen and gasoline. It only rose forty-one feet and traveled one hundred eighty-four feet before crashing back into the snow-covered hillside; the flight lasted about two and one-half seconds. Yet in retrospect, it was as significant an achievement in the history of flight as the Wright brothers' first flight on the sands of Kitty Hawk in North Carolina.

There's now a monument on the site of that launch, erected in 1960 by the American Rocket Society. Asa and Effie Ward's farm is long gone from the hilltop; although the farmhouse remains, it has been replaced by the Pakachoag Park golf course. An historical marker near the road directs one to a small white granite obelisk, four feet tall, which stands between the first hole tee and the ninth hole fairway.

The obelisk is nicked on the top and sides from the impacts of stray balls. On one side are the carved the words:

ON THE ROAD: PAKACHOAG HILL

SITE OF THE LAUNCHING OF WORLD'S FIRST LIQUID PROPELLANT ROCKET BY DR. ROBERT H. GODDARD 16 MARCH 1926.

If you look at old pictures of that historic day, you can see that, except for the golf course, the site has changed remarkably little. The rolling hills in the background are still there, of course, but so is the gnarled old willow tree fifty feet away and the low rock wall which runs alongside the ninth hole fairway.

As the first rocket launch site, Pakachoag Hill is not terribly impressive. It pales in comparison to the high-tech spaceport on Merritt Island at Cape Canaveral, Florida. As an historical site, it is not as impressive as the monument at Kitty Hawk to the Wright brothers' first flight; that monument is many times larger, and on a clear evening it can be seen for miles on Cape Hattaras by its spotlights. You could break your kneecap on the Goddard monument while searching for it in the golf course on a dark night. Like the man himself, one can only appreciate Goddard's contribution in an intellectual rather than physical context.

Many people thought he was crazy, the thin, balding physics professor from Clark University. Six years earlier, his sponsor for the early rocket experiments, the Smithsonian Institution, had published one of Goddard's monographs, "A Method of Reaching Extreme Altitudes," in which he had proclaimed the feasibility of sending a rocket to the Moon. For making this speculation he was hooted at by the press and by some of his fellow faculty members at Clark. Thus, even though his wife Esther recorded the preliminary stages of the launch on a motion picture camera (unfortunately, she ran out of film before the flight itself), newspapermen were not invited to Pakachoag Hill. No one remembers the names of the cynical newspaper columnists and the Clark professors who used to condescendingly ask him about his "moon-going rocket."

The reconstructed remains of that first successful liquid-fuel rocket and its test stand are displayed today in the main lobby of the Smithsonian's National Air and Space Museum in Washington, DC, near the Apollo, Gemini and Mercury space capsules, next to a mock-up of the Viking Mars lander which touched down on Mars fifty years after Goddard's launch. There are few spacecraft among those on exhibit which do not owe something directly to Goddard's achievement.

One might say that, in view of the lasting affects of Goddard's accomplishment, there should be a taller monument on Pakachoag Hill. Goddard was a quiet man, however; if he were alive, such a monument would probably embarrass him. Besides, there's a certain irony to having a golf course on the site of the beginning of the space age. After all, it was astronaut Alan Shepard, the first American in space, who smuggled a golf club and a ball onto the Apollo 14 spacecraft, and played golf on the grey sands of the Moon.

GODDARD'S PEOPLE

A morning in wartime: May 26, 1944, 5:15 a.m. PST. Day is barely breaking over the California coastline; for the crew of the B-24 Liberator *Hollywood Babe,* it's the fifth hour of their mission. The bomber has been holding a stationary position since midnight over the ocean southeast of the Baja Peninsula, flying in narrow circles at 25,000 feet. Its classified mission has been simple: watch the skies. The vigil is about to end.

Gazing through the cockpit windows, the captain notices a thin white vapor trail zipping across the dark purple sky. Many miles above and due west of his plane's position, the streak is hopelessly out of the *Hollywood Babe's* range, even if the bomber were ordered to intercept the incoming object. Becoming alert, he glances over his shoulder at the civilian in the jump seat behind him.

"Sir, is that what you're looking for?" the captain asks.

The civilian, an agent of the Office of Strategic Services, quickly leans forward and stares at the streak. "Son of a bitch," he murmurs under his breath. For a moment he can't believe what he's seeing. Only yesterday he had been telling someone that MI-6 must be getting shell-shocked, because now they were sending science fiction yarns to the OSS. But, incredible or not, this was exactly what the OSS man had been told to watch for.

He turns to the radio man in the narrow compartment behind the cockpit. "Sergeant, alert White Sands now!" he yells over the throb of the B-24's engines. "It's on its way!"

Many miles away, warning klaxons howl at a top-secret US Army facility in the New Mexico desert. Around a spotlighted launch pad, technicians and engineers scurry away from the single-stage, 75-foot winged silver rocket poised on the pad. Cold white oxygen fumes venting from the base of the rocket billow around the steel launch tower. The gantry is towed back along railroad tracks by a locomotive, and fuel trucks race away to a safe distance where the ground crew and several soldiers wait, their eyes fixed on the pad.

In a concrete blockhouse four hundred yards away, more than a dozen men are monitoring the launch. Among them, nine civilian scientists are hunched over control panels, anxiously watching hundreds of dials and meters as they murmur instructions to each other. In the middle of the blockhouse a frail, scholarly man peers through a periscope at the launch pad as the countdown reaches the final sixty seconds.

For more than two years, these ten men have worked toward this moment; now, in the last minute, most of them are scared half to death. If the launch is unsuccessful, there will be no second chance. If the rocket blows up, as so many other rockets have before it, the Navy pilot inside the machine will die. But far worse than that, New York City, thousands of miles to the east, will suffer a devastating attack. An 80-ton incendiary bomb will drop into the middle of Manhattan, and there will be nothing in heaven or on earth to stop it. If the launch is successful, it will be the crowning achievement of American technology; if it fails, it may be the beginning of the end for free society. The stakes are that high.

"Ten...nine...eight..." an Army officer recites tonelessly. Staring through the periscope, Robert Hutchings Goddard absently wipes his sweaty palms against the rubber grips and silently begins to pray...

Forty-seven years ago, in the early morning hours of a summer day in World War II, a huge rocket called the A-9—the *Amerika Bomber*—hurtled down a horizontal track in Germany and climbed to the highest altitude ever achieved, 156 miles above the earth. Horst Reinhart, a young Luftwaffe lieutenant, became the first man in space. One hour and thirty-six minutes later, the rocket christened the *Lucky Linda* blasted off from New Mexico, and US Navy pilot Rudy "Skid" Sloman's triumphant howl was picked up by ham radio operators across the continent as the United States became the world's second spacefaring nation.

This is much is well-known; what has been largely lost to history, though, is the leading role played by a mild, stoop-shouldered physics professor from Worcester. Not because of neglect—Robert H. Goddard's place in the annals of spaceflight as the father of American rocketry has been assured—but because of enduring cold war suspicions. In the years since his death in 1945, facts about his private life, particularly during the Second World War, have remained hidden, mainly because of national security interests. Goddard was known to have had a vague "consultant" role in Project Blue Horizon, but little more has been discovered by Goddard's biographers. The official record shows that Goddard spent the war teaching at Clark University in Worcester, Massachusetts: not much else is in the public record.

Yet if that part of Robert Goddard's biography is opaque, even less known is about the top-secret research group which was once codenamed Team 390. Each year, on the anniversary of the *Lucky Linda's* flight, the seven survivors of the American rocket team gather at a sportsmen's lodge in New Hampshire, on the shore of Lake Monomonac. Once again, in the lodge's den, the secret tale is told. As the seven old men speak, more than a few times their eyes wander to the framed photo of Goddard which hangs above the mantle.

They are all that remains of Team 390, but they rarely call themselves by that name. Now, as then, they are known among themselves simply as Goddard's People.

The affair began on the morning of January 19, 1942, when OSS agent William J. Casey (later to become the Director of the Central Intelligence Agency during the Reagan Administration) arrived in Washington, DC, from London on a US Army DC-3. An attache case handcuffed to his wrist contained a top secret Nazi document which British MI-6 agents had discovered at Peenemünde. By noon, the document—codenamed Black Umbrella, unofficially known as the "Sanger Report"—was on the desk of President Franklin D. Roosevelt.

The United States had been directly involved in World War II for only six weeks when the Sanger Report was unearthed. Isolationism had crumbled after the Japanese attack on Pearl Harbor, and fear was running high in the country that North America itself was the next target of the Axis powers; in Washington, anti-aircraft guns and air raid sirens were already being erected on city rooftops. Black Umbrella could not have arrived at a better time to have been taken seriously.

Peenemünde is a seldom-visited fishing village on Germany's Baltic Coast. During the war the village had become the base for secret Nazi rocket research for the German Army. Germans had been vigorously developing liquid-fuel rockets even before Adolf Hitler had become Chancellor, and the Nazis had incorporated rocket research into their war plans, recruiting a team of civilian rocket scientists, with Wernher von Braun as their chief scientist. British Intelligence had known that Peenemünde was the site of secret rocket experiments; a large missile called the A-4 was alleged to be in the final phases of R&D. "Silver and Gold", two MI-6 agents working undercover on Peenemünde as janitors, had been monitoring the continuing development of the A-4 rocket, later to be known by the Allies as the V-2.

In recent months, however, more puzzling things had been happening in Peenemünde. Something new was being developed in a warehouse which was kept locked and guarded at all times; rumors around the base had it that an even more ambitious weapon than the A-4 was being built by von Braun's rocket team. High Command officers such as Hermann Göring, Rudolf Hess, and Heinrich Himmler had been regularly visiting Peenemünde, spending long hours in the warehouse, yet Silver and Gold had no idea of what was going on.

Finally, the two agents had a stroke of luck. In a few precious, unguarded moments, a 400-page document, stamped "State Secret" had been carelessly left out on von Braun's desk by his personal secretary. Without reading the report, Silver had used a miniature camera to photograph as many pages as possible. The team then managed to smuggle the microfilm out of Germany, not knowing what information it contained except that it was part of a report which should have been kept under lock and key. The microfilm made its way to Whitehall in London, where MI-6 intelligence analysts had translated the contents. Horrified by what was found in the report, they rushed the transcript to Washington.

Black Umbrella was a detailed proposal by Dr. Eugen Sanger, an Austrian rocket scientist employed at the Hermann Göring Institute, the Luftwaffe's research center. Sanger had proposed the construction of a one-man, winged rocket-plane, an "antipodal bomber" capable not only of orbital flight but also of flying around the world to attack the United States. The rocket-plane—nicknamed the *Amerika Bomber* by Sanger—was to be almost a hundred feet long, weigh one hundred tons, and be propelled by a liquid-fuel rocket engine. Carrying an 80-ton bomb load, it was to be launched on a rocket-propelled sled which would race down a two-mile track to a sharp incline. The rocket-plane would disengage from the sled at the end of the track and, now accelerating 1,640 feet per second, would climb under its own power to suborbital altitude.

Using the Earth's rotation for a "slingshot" effect, the *Amerika Bomber* would make a series of dives and climbs along the top of the atmosphere as it orbited the earth, skipping like a rock on the surface of a pond. The skips would not only help preserve fuel, but also keep the rocket-plane far above the range of conventional aircraft. In this way, the bomber could fly over Europe, Asia, and the Pacific Ocean to the United States. Two of its atmospheric skips could carry it across the continent and, after diving to an altitude of 40 miles above the East Coast, the ship could drop an 80-ton bomb on New York City. The *Amerika Bomber* then could fly across the Atlantic back to Germany, landing like a airplane on a conventional airstrip.

It would obviously be a tremendous effort by the Nazis to develop and successfully launch the Sanger bomber; New York was not a military target, either. But the sheer terror of the scheme—the vision of a Nazi rocket-plane diving from space to drop an 80-ton incendiary bomb on Times Square—would be worth its value in propaganda alone. And if a squadron of antipodal bombers were built, as Sanger suggested, Germany would be in control of the highest of high grounds: outer space.

There was little doubt in the White House that the Nazis could pull off Black Umbrella. According to British intelligence, German civilians had been actively engaged in sophisticated rocket research since the 1920's under the aegis of the Verein für Raumschiffahrt. Almost immediately after Adolf Hitler became Chancellor, the Gestapo had seized all journals and records of the German Rocket Society, and the German Army had scooped up almost all members of the VfR, including Hermann Oberth, von Braun's mentor. It was also known that the German Army was diverting enormous amounts of men and material to Peenemünde, although it was also suspected that the Nazis had another, more secret missile base located somewhere else deep within the German borders.

According to declassified White House minutes of the meeting, President Roosevelt turned to OSS Director William "Wild Bill" Donovan after hearing the report on the Sanger project. "So, Bill, who's in charge of our rocket program?" he asked.

"We don't have a rocket program, Mr. President," Donovan replied.

"All right," Roosevelt said calmly. "Then who is the leading rocket expert in America?"

"I don't know if there is one," Donovan said.

"Yes, there is," answered the President. "Somewhere out there, there's got to be someone who knows as much about these things as von Braun. Find him. He's now the most important man in the country."

The man they found was Robert H. Goddard, and he didn't feel like the most important man in the country. He was only a brilliant scientist who had long since become fed up with being called a crackpot.

Goddard had been obsessed with rockets since reading H.G. Wells' The War of the Worlds as a youngster. Born in Worcester, Massachusetts, in 1882, Goddard had pursued his obsession throughout his life; he earned his bachelor's degree in engineering from Worcester Polytechnic Institute and shortly thereafter became a professor of physics at Clark University. Goddard's secret dream as to build a rocket capable of landing men on Mars. It was a wild idea which would drive the scientist throughout his life, and also earn him as much trouble as encountered by predecessors like Galileo Galilei and Percival Lowell.

In January, 1920, the Smithsonian Institution, one of Goddard's sources of funding for his early rocket research, published a 69-page monograph written by Goddard. The monograph, titled "A Method of Reaching Extreme Altitudes", mainly described how liquid-fuel rockets (themselves still only a theoretical possibility) could replace sounding balloons for exploring the upper atmosphere. The paper was mostly comprised of equations and tables, and thus would have escaped the notice of the general public had it not been for brief speculation at its end of how such rockets, perhaps someday in the future, could be used to reach the Moon. Goddard wrote that a rocket could crash land on Earth's satellite and explode a load of magnesium powder which would be visible to astronomers on Earth.

Compared to Goddard's real objectives of manned space exploration, this was a rather modest proposal, but the press didn't see it that way. Newspapers reported Goddard's speculation with little accuracy and less respect. He was either scoffed at from such pinnacles as *The New York Times* (which claimed that rocket propulsion was impossible in outer space because there was no air for rockets to push against) or treated as wild-eyed fantasy by papers such as the local *Worcester Telegram* (whose headlines speculated that passenger rockets carrying tourists into space would be possible within a decade). Few newspapers took Goddard seriously; for the most part, he was regarded as a crazy college egghead.

Goddard, a shy and softspoken person, was appalled by the press attention and embarrassed by the ridicule. He henceforth took his research underground, particularly his experiments with rocket design and his efforts to launch a liquid-fuel rocket. Although he continued to devise means of sending rockets into space—including his own design for a rocket-plane—he carefully hid his notebooks in his laboratory file cabinet, in a folder ironically marked "Gunpowder Experiments." There were no reporters present in the hilltop farm field in nearby Auburn, Massachusetts, on the cold morning of March 16, 1926, when Goddard successfully fired the world's first liquid-fuel rocket.

By 1942, though, Robert Goddard was no longer in Worcester. Following the explosion of one of his rockets, the Auburn town council outlawed all types of "fireworks" within city limits. Following a brief series of experiments at the US Army's Camp Devens in nearby Ashby, Goddard went on sabbatical from Clark University in 1931 and moved his residence and rockets to Roswell, New Mexico. There were a couple of contributing reasons for the move besides the unacceptability of rocketry in Massachusetts. The professor had battled tuberculosis throughout his life, which the damp New England climate scarcely helped, and the arid Southwestern desert also was a better site for rocket tests. In this sense, rural New Mexico was a fair trade for urban Massachusetts. He broke the sound barrier with a rocket in 1936, and by 1942 Goddard rockets were reaching record altitudes and achieving greater sophistication. Although largely unpublicized, his rocket experiments were on a par with the A-series rockets being developed in Nazi Germany. Few people knew about the feats which Goddard rockets were performing over the New Mexico high desert.

Yet Goddard's fortunes had also suffered, largely because of the bad press he had already endured. Although he continued to receive grants from the Guggenheim Foundation and from one of his admirers, Charles A. Lindbergh, the Smithsonian Institution had stopped funding his research. And though he had already developed solid-fuel ordnance such as the bazooka for the US Army, the War

Department had expressed no interest in his liquid-fuel rocket research. Obscurity had become a double-edged sword for Goddard: he had found the solitude he craved, yet he was struggling to finance his experiments.

All that changed on the morning of January 29, 1942, when two civilians from the OSS and an officer from the US Army General Staff, Col. Omar Bliss, found Robert Goddard in the assembly shed at Goddard's ranch with an assistant, working on another high-altitude rocket. The rocket scientist greeted his unexpected visitors with courteous surprise; he dismissed his assistant and sat down on a bench outside the shed to hear what they had to say.

Bliss, now living in retirement on Sanibel Island, Florida, remembers the meeting he had with Goddard. "He was completely shocked, horrified," Bliss says. "He told us that he had kept up with German research during the '30s and knew that they were making progress with their rockets, but he had no idea that their work had come this far. We asked if Sanger's plan was possible and he thought about it a minute, then told us that if they had the resources and a little luck, yes, they could make it work. He knew that von Braun and Oberth were working for the Nazis, and he had no doubts that they and others had the knowledge to develop the *Amerika Bomber*."

The men from Washington asked Goddard if he had any ideas how to prevent New York from being blitzed from space; Goddard indicated that he had a few notions. "Then we asked him if he would help us," Bliss recalls. "I was afraid that he would refuse. People had treated him so unfairly before, after all. But he at once nodded his head, yes, he would do whatever was necessary to stop the Nazis."

The space race had begun.

Robert Goddard's role in what would become known as Project Blue Horizon, however, was not played in New Mexico. For various reasons, the War Department returned the professor to his home town. Although the *Lucky Linda* would be launched from the White Sands Test Range less than 100 miles from Goddard's ranch, Washington decided that the best place for Blue Horizon's brain trust was in Massachusetts.

The Department of War wanted to keep Goddard within arm's reach, and Massachusetts is closer to Washington, DC, than New Mexico. Yet it was also decided not to take unnecessary risks. Goddard was reputed to personally tinker with his rockets while they were on the launch pad. This fact was known by Dr. Vannevar Bush, President Roosevelt's science advisor, who gave orders for "the Professor" to be kept away from the rockets themselves. In hindsight, this was good logic. There were many spectacular explosions in White Sands over the next two years of the crash program, one of which claimed the lives of two technicians. It would have been disastrous if Goddard himself had been killed during one of these accidents.

There was some resistance by the War Department to having Project Blue Horizon located in Worcester because another top-secret military R&D program was already underway in Massachusetts: the radar defense project being developed in Cambridge at MIT's so-called "radiation laboratory." It was felt by many in the Pentagon that having two secret projects working so near to each other would be risky. Goddard was not eager to return to Worcester, either. It had become difficult for him to endure the New England climate, and he especially chaffed at not being able to witness each rocket test. Bush argued, however, that neither Clark University nor MIT were high-profile enough (at the time) to attract Nazi spies; having Blue Horizon camouflaged by a college campus, like MIT's "Rad Lab," made perfect sense.

The White House won out over the Pentagon, and Goddard went along with his relocation orders. Esther Goddard, always protective of her husband's health, naturally returned to Worcester with Robert. They moved back into their former residence, where Goddard had been born, and readjusted to life in New England's second-largest city.

To build the security cover for Blue Horizon, the FBI coerced Clark University's directors into reinstating Goddard's status as an active faculty member. It was arranged that Goddard's only real academic workload was to teach a freshman class in introductory physics. In the university's academic calendar for the semesters from 1942 through 1943, though, there was a listing for an advanced-level class, "Physics 390", whose instructor was "to be announced." But even senior physics students at Clark found it impossible to enroll in the class; it was always filled at registration time.

Goddard's "graduate students" in Physics 390 were a group of nine young men enlisted from the American Rocket Society, unrepentant rocket buffs and far-sighted engineers with whom Goddard had corresponded over the years. Goddard had quickly hand-picked his group from memory; the War Department and the FBI had contacted each person individually, requesting their volunteer help. None refused, though the Selective Service Administration had to issue draft deferrals for four members. The FBI moved them all to Worcester and managed to get them quietly isolated in a triple-decker on Birch Street near the campus.

Team 390 (as they were codenamed by the FBI) were strangers even among themselves. Almost all were from different parts of the country. Only two members, Lloyd Kapman and Harry Bell, both from St. Louis, had met before, and although Taylor Brickell and Henry Morse were known to each other from the letters page of *Astounding Science Fiction*, of which they were both devoted readers, they had never met face to face. The youngest, Roy Cahill, had just passed his eighteenth birthday; the oldest, Hamilton "Ham" Ballou, was in his mid-thirties, and was forced to shave off his mustache to make him appear younger.

And there were other problems. J. Jackson Jackson was the only black member of the team, which tended to make him stand out on the mostly white Clark University campus (his odd name earned him the nickname "Jack Cube"). Michael Ferris had briefly been a member of the American Communist Party during his undergraduate days, which meant that he had undergone intensive scrutiny by the FBI and nearly been refused on the grounds of his past political activity before he had agreed to sign a binding pledge of loyalty to the United States. And Gerard "Gerry" Mander had to be sprung from a county workhouse in Roanoke, Virginia: a rocket he had been developing had misfired, spun out across two miles of tobacco field and crashed into a Baptist preacher's house.

Once they were together, though, Blue Horizon's R&D task force immediately hit it off. "We spoke the same language," recalls Gerry Mander, who now lives in Boston and who was then the team's "wildcat" engineer. "Rockets were our specialty, and putting something above the atmosphere was a dream we all shared. I mean, I was a young snot from backwoods Virginia, so sharing a room with a colored man like Jack Cube, at least at the time, seemed more unlikely than putting a guy in orbit. But Jack talked engineering, so we had that much in common, and in a couple of days I didn't even care."

"We were all a bunch of rocket-buffs," says Mike Ferris, the team's chemistry expert, "and the War Department had given us carte blanche to put a man in space." He laughs. "Man, we were like little kids thrown the key to the toy store!"

Team 390 had little doubt about what was needed. The only device capable of intercepting the Sanger bomber was another spacecraft, and the only reliable navigation system was a human pilot. Since the '20s, Robert Goddard had drawn, in his "gunpowder experiments" notebooks, rough designs for a rocket-plane, along with notes for gyroscopic guidance systems and other plans which turned out to be useful for the team. Studies at the California Institute of Technology had also suggested that a single-stage rocket-plane could be sent into space on a suborbital trajectory, with the ship gliding back through the atmosphere like a sailplane.

The team postulated that a spaceplane, launched by a liquid-fuel engine and ascending at a forty-five degree angle, could function as one-man space fighter capable of intercepting the *Amerika Bomber*. Upon studying the Sanger Report, Team 390 further realized that the bomber would be most vulnerable during the ascent phases of its flight. At these points, the ship was slowest and least maneuverable, a sitting duck for another spacecraft's ordnance. So if the US ship were launched from New Mexico just as the German ship flew over the Pacific coast, it could intercept the *Amerika Bomber* before it reached New York City and shoot it down with ordinary solid-fuel rockets.

"We came up with it in one night over beer and pretzels in the Bancroft Hotel bar," says Henry Morse, the team's electrical engineer who now lives in Winchester, New Hampshire. "Bob wasn't with us that night, but we had gone through his notebooks and read all that stuff he had thought up, so it was mainly a matter of putting it together. We knew we didn't need a very sophisticated ship, nothing like a space shuttle today. Of course, we didn't have time to make anything like a space shuttle. Just something quick and dirty."

"Quick and dirty" soon became buzzwords for Goddard's People. The team took the plan to Goddard the following morning, during their "class" in Goddard's lab at the university. By the end of the day, following many hours of arguing, scribbling notes on the chalkboard, and flooding the trashcan with wadded-up notes, Team 390 and Goddard settled on the plan. The professor was amused that his "grad students" had come up with the scheme in a barroom. "If Mrs. Goddard will let me out of the house, I'd like to be in on the next session," he told Morse.

The FBI, though, was not amused when it discovered that Team 390 had been discussing rockets in a downtown Worcester bar. There was always the chance of Nazi spies. The FBI was especially sensitive given the proximity to the MIT Rad Lab only forty miles away. Team 390 was ordered to stay out of the Bancroft, and J. Edgar Hoover assigned special escorts for Goddard and his team. The team thought the FBI was over-reacting.

"It was a pain, of course," Roy Cahill recalls. "We couldn't visit the men's room without having a G-man escorting us. They were also parked all night outside Bob's house and our place on Birch Street. Esther couldn't stand it at first, but she changed her mind after the City Hall thing."

By early 1943, the V-2 missiles were perfected and the first rockets launched against targets in Great Britain. The Allies had been flying air raids upon V-2 launch sites in occupied northern France, and finally against Peenemünde itself. During one of the early reconnaissance missions over France, Ham Ballou—temporarily brought over to England for the purpose of gathering much-needed intelligence on the V-2 rockets—flew over the Normandy coastline in the back seat of a P-38J Lightning, snapping pictures as the pilot dodged anti-aircraft flack. Ballou returned to Worcester with little which was immediately useful to Team 390, but for a while he was able to claim that he was the only person among Goddard's people who had come under enemy fire—until Goddard himself almost caught a bullet.

Following a devastating Allied air raid on Peenemünde, the German High Command covertly transferred the principal R&D of the *Amerika Bomber* 250 miles inland to Nordhausen, where the base of a mountain had been hollowed out into vast caverns by prisoners from the nearby Dora concentration camp. This was the secret Nazi rocket facility which MI-6 had been unable to locate. Many of the same European Jews who built the Nordhausen site were later sacrificed in grotesque experiments, over the objections of von Braun and Oberth, which tested human endurance to high-altitude conditions.

Little of this mattered to Reichsführer Heinrich Himmler, whose Luftwaffe had now taken over the A-9 project from the German Army. He was more concerned with the fact, surmised through briefings with von Braun, that the German rocket team's work had been largely inspired by Goddard's research; he suspected that the United States might be embarked on a secret rocket program of its own. Although Gestapo agents in America had not found any evidence of a US space initiative, Himmler decided not to take chances. In March, 1943, he ordered the assassination of the only known American rocketry expert: Robert Hutchings Goddard.

For all of his brilliance, Goddard was also absentminded about the mundane tasks of life; he could forget to fold his umbrella when he walked in from the rain. On March 30, 1943, the Worcester City Clerk's office sent the professor a letter informing him that he had not filed his city taxes. Goddard received the letter while working in his lab. Both irritated and alarmed, he put on his coat and immediately bustled out to catch the Main South trolley downtown. He left so quickly that his FBI escort, who was relieving himself in the men's room, missed the professor's departure.

But the Nazi Gestapo agent who had been watching Goddard for a week, waiting for such a break, didn't miss the opportunity. Following Goddard from his post on the Clark campus, the assassin also took the downtown trolley, getting off at the same stop in front of City Hall. As Goddard marched into the building, the Nazi slipped his silenced Luger Parabellum from his trenchcoat pocket and followed the scientist inside.

At the same moment, Worcester police officer Clay Reilly was walking downstairs from the second floor of City Hall when he spotted a trenchcoated man, carrying a gun, closing in on another man, who was walking toward the tax assessor's office. The second man was unaware that he was being pursued, but Reilly immediately sized up the situation.

"I didn't think twice," Reilly, now retired from the force, says in retrospect. "I pulled my pistol and shouted for the guy to freeze. He decided to mess with me instead."

Reilly was a crack shot on the WPD firing range; his skill didn't fail him then. The Gestapo agent turned and aimed at Reilly, and the officer nailed the assassin with one shot to the heart before the Nazi could squeeze his trigger. Goddard himself fled from City Hall, where he was spirited away by his FBI escort, who had just arrived in his car.

No identification was found on the body of the man Patrolman Reilly had shot. The *Worcester Telegram* reported the story the next day under the front page headline, "Mystery Killer Shot in City Hall". No one knew that he had been trying to kill Goddard; Reilly didn't recognize the scientist and Goddard had not remained at the scene. Clay Reilly was promoted to sergeant's rank for his quick thinking, but it wasn't until long after the war that the policeman was informed of the identity of the man he had shot or the person whose life he had saved, or the fact that J. Edgar Hoover himself had insisted upon his promotion.

✳ ✳ ✳

"Everything changed for us after that," says Henry Morse. "I guess we were sort of looking at Blue Horizon like it was a kid's adventure. Y'know, the Rocket Boys go to the Moon. But Bob's close call sobered us up."

The incident also sobered up the White House. Upon the insistence of Vannevar Bush, the FBI hastily sought a new base of operations in New England for Team 390. Within a week of the attempted assassination, a new locale for Project Blue Horizon was found: the Monomonac Gun & Rod Club, which had been closed since the beginning of the war. The lodge was located in the tiny farm community of Rindge, due north of Worcester just across the New Hampshire state line, close enough to Worcester to allow the rocket team to quickly relocate there. Because the club was accessible only by a single, unmarked dirt road, it had the isolation which the FBI believed was necessary to keep Team 390 hidden from the world.

The FBI purchased the property, and in the dead of night on April 6, 1943, all the rocket team's files and models were loaded into a truck. As far as Clark University's collegiate community was concerned, Dr. Goddard had taken an abrupt leave of absence due to health reasons, and nobody on campus seemed to notice the sudden departure of the small, insular group of grad students from Physics 390.

The Monomonac Gun & Rod Club was set in seven acres of New Hampshire forest on the northwestern side of Lake Monomonac. The club consisted mainly of a two-story whitewashed lodge which dated back to the turn of the century; it had a handsome front porch which overlooked the serene main channel of the lake, a couple of spartan rooms on the upper floor which contained a dozen old-style iron beds, and a single outhouse beyond the back door. Mail from relatives was still sent to Worcester and forwarded once a week to New Hampshire; except for Esther Goddard, none of the families of the rocket team were made aware of the fact that their sons and husbands were now in New Hampshire.

The former sportsmen's club was a far cry from the comforts of Clark University; most of the rocket team were unused to roughing it in the woods. Mice had taken up occupancy in the kitchen next to the long dining room, and the only sources of heat were a fireplace in the den and a pot-bellied stove on the second floor. One of the first orders of business was to knock down the hornet nests in the upper bedrooms and under the porch eaves. "The first week we were there, we almost went on strike," laughs Gerry Mander. "If it hadn't been for the fact that we were in a race against time, we might have told Bush and Hoover and all the rest to stick it until they found us some decent accommodations. As it was, though, we knew we had little choice."

Yet there was another major problem in the relocation. In New Mexico, the engineering team at White Sands was building unmanned prototype rockets based on the plans sent by Goddard's team, firing the rockets as soon as they could be made. The major hurdle was in producing a reliable engine for the spaceplane, now dubbed the "X-1". It had to be capable of lifting 65,500 pounds to orbit, yet most of the prototypes exploded, sometimes on the launch pad. For each small success, there were dozens of setbacks. There had been several pad explosions already, and in the latest failure a couple of technicians had been killed when the liquid-hydrogen tank ruptured during pressurization.

"Part of the problem was that the team wasn't in New Mexico to oversee the final stages of each test," Morse says. "We were expected to build rockets without getting our hands dirty, and you simply can't compartmentalize a project like that. What it came down to, finally, was that we had to have a test-bed in New Hampshire, whether Van Bush liked it or not."

It took Robert Goddard several weeks of lobbying to convince Vannevar Bush that some of the hands-on research had to be done by his people. Once Bush finally caved in, though, the next task was to locate an appropriate location for the construction of the new prototype. A giant rocket engine is difficult to conceal; it simply could not be constructed on a workbench in a sportsmen's club.

One of the prime military contractors in Massachusetts was the Wyman-Gordon Company, which was making aircraft forgings for the Army in its Worcester factory. Upon meeting with Wyman-

Gordon's president in Washington, DC, Vannevar Bush managed to finagle the company into renting out a vacant warehouse on the factory grounds. Final assembly of Team 390's new prototype engine—referred to as "Big Bertha"—would be made in Warehouse Seven, from parts made across the country and secretly shipped to Wyman-Gordon. Big Bertha's aluminum outer casing was cast there as well, although only a few select people at Wyman-Gordon knew exactly what it was.

Secrecy was paramount. Only a handful of Wyman-Gordon workers were involved in the construction of Big Bertha; all had survived extensive background checks by the FBI, and what they were told was on a strict "need-to-know" basis. The FBI put counterspies to work in the factory to guard against Nazi infiltrators, and work on Big Bertha was done only after midnight, when the least number of people were at the plant. When necessary, the Team 390 members were brought down from New Hampshire to the plant to supervise the engine's construction, making at least three transfers to different vehicles en route, with the final vehicle usually being a phony Coca-Cola delivery van owned by the FBI.

It was a little more difficult to find a suitable site for test-firing Big Bertha; Wyman-Gordon's plant was located in the middle of a residential neighborhood. This time, though, the rocket team didn't leave it to the FBI; Henry Morse and Roy Cahill borrowed Esther Goddard's car and spent several days driving around southern New Hampshire trying to find a place for the test-firing. After only a few days, they finally located a dairy farm in nearby Jaffrey, New Hampshire.

Jaffrey had a freight line which ran straight up from Worcester, and the farm was located only two miles from the siding. Its owner, Marion Hartnell, was a World War I veteran who just had lost his only son in the fighting in France. He had no love for the Nazis, and once he was approached by Goddard himself, he eagerly volunteered to let the team use his barn for the test-firing of Big Bertha. "We told Mr. Hartnell that there was a possibility that our rocket might blow up and take his barn with it," Cahill recalls. "The old duffer didn't bat an eyelash. 'So long as you can promise me you'll shoot that rocket of yours right up Hitler's wazoo,' that was his response. He even turned down our offer of rent."

In the night of November 26, 1943—Thanksgiving eve, exactly six months before the launch of the *Lucky Linda*—Big Bertha was loaded onto a flatcar at the Wyman-Gordon rail siding. A special freight train took it due north across the state line to Jaffrey, where after twelve a.m. on Thanksgiving Day the massive rocket engine was carefully off-loaded onto a flatbed truck, which in turn drove it to the Hartnell farm. An Army Corps of Engineers from Fort Devens in Ashby, Massachusetts spent the rest of the morning anchoring the prototype engine onto the concrete horizontal test-bed which had been built in the barn. Shortly before noon, Goddard and his scientists began making their preparations for the test while the townspeople of Jaffrey unwittingly enjoyed their Thanksgiving meals. Team 390 waited until exactly 10 p.m., then Robert Goddard threw the ignition switch on the control board outside the barn.

"I think everybody was standing a hundred feet away from the barn door when we lit the candle," Mander recalls. "When it went, I almost wet my pants. I thought we were going to blow up the whole damn farm."

Big Bertha didn't explode, though; the engine produced 60 tons of thrust for the requisite ninety seconds. "When it was over," Morse says, "Bob turned to us, let out his breath, and said, 'Gentlemen, we've got a success. Now let's go have that Thanksgiving dinner.' I swear, the old man was ready to cry."

The next night, Big Bertha was taken back to the Jaffrey rail head, loaded onto another flatcar, and started on its long journey across America to New Mexico. The first big hurdle of Blue Horizon had been jumped. Yet, despite the place he had earned in history, farmer Hartnell never told anyone about the Thanksgiving rocket test which had been made on his farm. He died in 1957 still maintaining secrecy, leaving the new owners of his farm puzzled at the strange concrete cradle which rested inside his barn.

The final months of Project Blue Horizon were a race against time. MI-6 and the OSS knew that the Nazis were in the final stages of building the *Amerika Bomber*, but the location of work was still unknown and the Nazis' rate of progress was uncertain. Silver and Gold had long since been pulled out of Peenemünde, so the Allies were now blind as to what the Nazis were doing. Reconnaissance flights by the Allies over Germany had failed to locate the two-mile launch track which Sanger had specified in the Black Umbrella document. Unknown to MI-6, it had been built near Nordhausen by the Dora concentration camp prisoners and camouflaged with nets; the Luftwaffe's scientists were coming steadily closer to fulfilling their primary objective; within the secret caverns of Nordhausen, the sleek antipodal rocket-plane was gradually taking shape and form.

Nonetheless, there was talk within the White House and the Pentagon that the Black Umbrella report had been a red herring. There had already been one similar instance, earlier in the war, when the Nazis had been suspected of developing an atomic weapon. In response, the War Department had begun a crash program to develop its own atomic bomb. This program, based in rural Tennessee and codenamed the Manhattan Project, had been unsuccessfully struggling to develop an atomic bomb when a Danish physicist, Niels Bohr, managed to escape to the West with the reliable news that the Nazis were nowhere close to attaining controlled nuclear fission, let alone perfecting an atomic bomb.

Although minimal atomic research was secretly continued at the Brookhaven National Laboratory on Long Island, the Manhattan Project had been scrapped, mainly to fund Project Blue Horizon. Now, however, some people within the Pentagon were saying that Sanger's antipodal bomber was another chimera and that vital American resources were being wasted. On their side in the White House was Vice President Harry S Truman, who had begun referring to the American rocket program as "Project Buck Rogers." Yet Vannevar Bush persisted; unlike the atomic bomb scare, there was no proof that the Nazis were *not* developing the *Amerika Bomber*. Roosevelt pragmatically followed his advice, and Project Blue Horizon was not cancelled.

"Not knowing what the Germans were doing was the scary part," Roy Cahill recalls, "so all we could do was work like bastards. We stopped thinking about it in terms of the glory of putting the first American in space. Now we only wanted to get someone up there without killing him."

Through the early part of 1944, Team 390 rarely left its makeshift laboratory at the sportsmen's club. The ten scientists were constantly in the lodge's dining room, pulling twenty-hour days in their efforts to design the rest of the X-1. The FBI bodyguards had taken to cooking their meals for them, and the long table in the middle of the room was buried beneath books, slide rules, and teetering mounds of paper. Big Bertha had only been one component which had to be designed from scratch; life-support, avionics, telemetry and guidance systems, even the pilot's vacuum suit still had to be developed. As the long New Hampshire winter set in, the days became shorter and the nights colder; tempers became frayed. More than once, members of the team went outside to settle their disputes with their fists. The only instance of relaxation any of the team's survivors remember was the December morning after a nor'easter dropped seven inches of snow on them; they dropped work and had a spontaneous snowball fight on Lake Monomonac's frozen surface.

"Bob was the one who really suffered," Henry Morse remembers. "His health had never been good, and the overwork, plus the hard winter we had that year, started to gang up on him. Esther used to come up from Worcester to make sure that he didn't overexert himself, that he rested once a day, but he started ignoring her advice after awhile. None of us was sleeping or eating well. We were frightened to death that the very next day we would hear that the *Amerika Bomber* had firebombed New York. It was that much of a race."

Piece by piece, the X-1 was assembled in New Mexico from the specifications laid down by Team 390. Unlike Big Bertha, some vital components such as the inertial guidance system were installed virtually without testing. There was simply not enough time to run everything through the wringer. The White Sands engineers knew that they were working from sheer faith. If Goddard's People were crucially wrong in any one of thousands of areas, the spacecraft they were building would become a deathtrap for its pilot.

"How in the hell did we get a man into space?" After many years, Morse shakes his head. "Because we were scared of what would happen if we failed."

In the end, it was a photo finish. Both the *Amerika Bomber* and the X-1 were finished and brought to their respective launch pads in the same week. Goddard and his team left New Hampshire for White Sands on May 15 to oversee the final launch, whenever it occurred. It was now a matter of waiting for the Germans to launch the *Amerika Bomber*.

The denouement is well recorded in the history books. The vigil at White Sands ended early on the morning of May 26, 1944, when high-altitude recon planes and ground-based radar spotted the *Amerika Bomber* over the Pacific Ocean. Within twenty minutes the X-1—christened the *Lucky Linda* by its pilot after his wife—was successfully launched. Skid Sloman piloted the X-1 through a harrowing ascent and intercepted the A-9 in space above the Gulf of Mexico—during its final ascent skip before the dive which would have taken it over New York. High above the American heartland, Sloman destroyed the *Amerika Bomber* with a solid-fuel missile launched from the X-1's port wing. Sloman then successfully guided his ship through atmospheric re-entry to touchdown in Lakehurst, New Jersey.

With the landing of the *Lucky Linda*, Project Blue Horizon was no longer top secret. Once the X-1's mission was announced to the American public by Edward R. Murrow on CBS radio, it became one of the most celebrated events of World War II. The destruction of the *Amerika Bomber* was also one of the final nails in the Nazi coffin. So many resources had been poured into the project that the rest of the German war machine suffered. Sanger's squadron of antipodal bombers was never built, and within a year, Germany surrendered to the Allies. The *Lucky Linda* flew again in August, 1945, modified to drop a massive incendiary bomb on Hiroshima, Japan. Japan surrendered a few days later, and World War II ended with the dawn of the Space Age.

Yet the story doesn't end there.

Because the technology which had produced the *Lucky Linda* was considered vital to national security, the OSS clamped the lid on the history of the spaceplane's development. The story which was fed to the press was that the ship had been entirely designed and built in New Mexico. The OSS felt that it was necessary to hide the role that Robert Goddard and Team 390 had played.

In the long run, the OSS was correct. When the Third Reich fell, the Russian White Army rolled into Germany and took Nordhausen, capturing many of the German rocket scientists. Josef Stalin was interested in the *Amerika Bomber* and sought the expertise which had produced the spaceplane. Unknown to either the Americans or the Germans, the Soviet Union's Gas Dynamics Laboratory had been secretly working on its own rockets under the leadership of Fridrikh Tsander and Sergei Korolov. The Soviet rocket program had stalled during Russia's Great Patriotic War, however, and Stalin wanted to regain the lead in astronautics. But von Braun, Oberth and other German rocket scientists escaped the Russians and surrendered to American forces; eventually they came to the United States under "Operation Paperclip" and became the core of the American space program.

The lead was short-lived; in March, 1949, the USSR put its own manned spacecraft into orbit. Shortly thereafter, Brookhaven physicists announced the sustenance of nuclear fission, demonstrated by the explosion of an atomic bomb in the Nevada desert. This was followed, in less than a year, by the detonation of a Soviet atomic bomb in Siberia. The new cold war between the two superpowers moved into the heavens; for the next twenty-six years, until the passage of the United Nations Space Treaty in 1974 which outlawed nukesats, no person on Earth could ever feel safe again.

Richard Feynman, the Nobel laureate, accurately assayed the situation in his memoirs, <u>Get Serious, Mr. Feynman:</u> "It was bad enough that the US and USSR shared the capability to launch satellites into orbit; now they both had atomic bombs to put in the satellites. In a more sane world, it would have been bombs without rockets, or rockets without bombs—but, God help us, not both at once!"

Because the United States was now competing with Russia for dominance in space, the American rocket team lived under oaths of secrecy for more than forty years, forbidden to discuss publicly what they had done in Worcester and Rindge. Robert Goddard himself died on August 10, 1945, the day after the firebombing of Hiroshima. Esther Goddard remained silent about her husband's involvement with Blue Horizon until her death in 1982.

Other members of Team 390 passed away over the years with their lips sealed, yet almost all remained involved in the American space program. J. Jackson Jackson became the presidential science advisor during Robert Kennedy's administration, and Hamilton Ballou was the chief administrator of NASA during the time of the first lunar landing. Ham and Jack Cube are both dead now, but each May 26, the seven remaining members of Team 390 make their way to Rindge. Sometimes they are accompanied by children or grandchildren; in the last forty-seven years, seldom has any of the former teammates missed this anniversary. The Monomonac Gun & Rod Club belongs to them now, a gift from their grateful country.

They spend the day getting the club in shape for the summer—or, rather, telling the kids what to do, now that the youngest founding member is in his mid-sixties. The old men sit together in rocking chairs on the front porch, drinking beer, kidding each other that FBI agents are watching them from the woods. When the chores are done, they and their families have dinner together, sitting alongside each other on benches at the long oak table in the lodge's dining room where they once scrawled notes and bickered. This is always a festive occasion, punctuated by laughter and dirty jokes. Another tradition is seeing who can get raunchiest, within certain unspoken limits. Their wives roll their eyes in disgust and the kids make faces, and none of the seven men give a rotten damn what they think.

After dinner, as the wives and young people tend to the clean-up, the old men retire to the lodge's main room; Henry and Roy and Mike, Lloyd and Harry, Gerry and Taylor settle into chairs around the fieldstone fireplace, cigars and drinks in hand, their feet warmed by the fire. After a while, they begin to talk. As the wives and children and grandchildren gradually filter into the room, while the sun sets beyond the lake and the crickets and bullfrogs strike up the nocturnal orchestra, seven friends once again tell their secret tale.

On occasion, they look at the framed photo of Robert Goddard which hangs above the mantle. At other times, though, their eyes wander to another, smaller picture which hangs beside it, a shot which is familiar to nearly every person in the civilized world: the spacesuited figure of Neil Armstrong, the first American to set foot on Mars during the joint US-USSR expedition in 1976, opening an urn and scattering Goddard's cremated ashes across the landing site at Utopia Planitia.

JOHN HARPER WILSON

John Harper Wilson, the first American to set foot on the Moon, lives today in peaceful obscurity in a log cabin in Rindge, New Hampshire. There's no mailbox on the narrow dirt road leading to his house, and the clerks at the post office in town are among the small handful of townspeople who are aware of the famous resident. Wilson visits the post office two or three times a week to check his rented box, which is seldom full. Although John Harper Wilson's names is in the history books, the man himself has almost been forgotten.

Inside the cabin, surrounded by birch and pine trees near the shore of Lake Monomonac, there is little to show that its occupant was once an astronaut. Wilson's wife Leanne, who was photographed nearly twenty years ago tearfully watching her husband on TV as he descended the ladder of Eagle One, has decorated the log walls with Tibetan carpets. Wilson himself—his brown hair now turned grey, his once athletic build now slightly paunchy—has become an amateur expert on Buddhist culture and Tibetan history. It is only in Wilson's small office, in a guest room adjacent to the living room, that one finds memorabilia from the Luna One expedition: a model of a moonship, a bit of grey rook suspended in an acrylic cube, a framed photo of the twenty members of Luna One, posed in their heavy space armor on the surface of the Moon, surrounding the American flag that was planted there.

Wilson, the mission commander, is the astronaut in the center of the group. Next to him is his second-in-command, Captain Neil Holliday. Their helmets almost entirely cover their faces, except for a narrow eye slit, so it is impossible to read their expressions. Wilson says that he was smiling when the picture was taken.

"Bloody wonder, right?" he asks. "Neil wasn't smiling. I couldn't see his face, but I know that he wasn't smiling. I think he wanted to murder me right then."

Wilson pauses, gazing at the group photo. "Pretty remarkable that they let a traitor stand in the middle of the picture, isn't it?" he wonders aloud.

It has taken nineteen years for the true events concerning Luna One to become public. For almost two decades the US Air Force, the Federal Bureau of Investigation and the White House had successfully prevented historians and the press, along with the greater public at large, from finding out what occurred on the Sea of Tranquility on July 20, 1969.

For all those years, the four-and-a-half minute communications blackout from Tranquility Base has officially been described as a "technical failure." And since the mission's return to Earth six weeks after the landing, John Harper Wilson has virtually disappeared from the public eye. When Congress awarded Medals of Honor to the members of Luna One, all but Major Wilson attended the ceremony on Capitol Hill. Wilson was said to be too sick to attend, and Neil Holliday accepted the medal for his friend. Wilson says he never received the medal from Holliday.

After nineteen years, Wilson has finally broken his silence, at risk of persecution by the Department of Justice. Sitting on an overstuffed couch in his living room, absentmindedly juggling the acrylic cube with its bits of moonrock from hand to hand, the retired Air Force officer spoke about Luna One and the events leading up to those four minutes and thirty seconds of missing history.

"I changed my mind on the way to the Moon," he began.

A manned expedition to the Moon had been an Air Force objective since the early 1950s, during the postwar Space Age that followed the Blue Horizon Project, the secret race to beat Nazi Germany into space which saw the first suborbital flight of Robert H. Goddard's spaceplane in 1944. Spurred by the victory of the *Lucky Linda* over Germany's *Amerika Bomber*, the Pentagon became convinced that the key to strategic military superiority was the control of outer space. General Omar Bliss, the Army's chief of the Blue Horizon Project, summed it up during testimony to the House Committee on Science and Technology in 1949: "Gentlemen, military advantage has always rested on taking the high ground, and space is the new high ground. America must take this hill, or risk losing its freedom."

Congress and the Truman and Eisenhower Administrations agreed, and the new US Air Force was given virtual carte blanche to establish a permanent American presence in space. With the aid of former German scientists from the Nazis' Peenemünde rocket base, the *Lucky Linda* was superseded by the 265-foot, three-stage Atlas-class spaceships, the first of which was launched on April 10, 1956, from the Air Force Proving Grounds at Cape Canaveral, Florida. Subsequently, the Air Force space effort was retitled the US Space Force, and the base was redesignated the US Space Force Canaveral Launch Center, more commonly called "the Cape."

Propelled by almost limitless budgeting, the American space effort continued at a breakneck speed. By 1963, Space Station One, the 250-foot "Space Wheel", had been completed in orbit five hundred miles above the equator, and the United States was firmly established as the world's first spacefaring nation. The imagination of the American public was captured. *Collier's* and *Life* breathlessly reported each new success to millions of readers; CBS anchorman Walter Cronkhite became the first journalist to report from space during a three-part series filmed aboard the Wheel; and *Star Trek*, a somewhat melodramatic TV series produced by Irwin Allen, was the second-highest rated network program for years, surpassed in the Neilsens only by *I Love Lucy*.

Yet the distinctly military flavor of the American space program disturbed many on Capitol Hill. In 1959, a move was made by members of the Senate to bring the program under civilian control. The "Space Act", proposed by two Democratic leaders in the Senate, John F. Kennedy of Massachusetts and Lyndon B. Johnson of Texas, would have created a civilian space agency, the National Aeronautics and Space Administration, or NASA.

Naturally, the bill was vigorously opposed by the Pentagon, which claimed that a civilian agency could not possibly put a man on the Moon before 1970. But the Space Act didn't need Pentagon hostility to kill it, only the loss of its primary sponsors. Kennedy, the Democratic presidential nominee in 1960, lost the election to Richard M. Nixon; Johnson also lost his seat in the Senate in the same election year.

With Kennedy and Johnson both suddenly out of office, NASA died along with the Space Act; the bill was killed in the Ways and Means Committee. Under the conservative Nixon Administration, the space program remained under military control. Since Nixon was an ardent supporter of the military space effort, the Space Force formally proposed, shortly after the election, a manned expedition to the Moon, Luna One.

The justification for this enormous effort—initially budgeted at $4 billion, although by the time John Harper Wilson set foot on the Moon almost $9 billion had been spent—was that if the United States didn't lay claim to the Moon, the Soviet Union soon would. This was a tenuous argument. The Soviet space program had been handicapped by a string of accidents, including the spectacular explosion of an unmanned Vostok spacecraft in 1957, and it was not until 1959 that the USSR managed to put its first cosmonaut, Yuri Gagarin, into orbit. Yet the Pentagon managed to convince the White House and Congress that the Soviets were embarked upon a crash program to establish a military base on the Moon and were on the verge of catching up with the American space program. With Nixon and Senator Phyllis Schlafly (R-NY) leading the charge, Congress approved a ten-year program to put an American base on the Moon by 1970.

Which is where John Harper Wilson enters the picture.

Wilson had been under scrutiny by the Space Force as a possible commander for a lunar expedition since 1958, the year he first piloted an Atlas into orbit. The misfire of a starboard maneuvering rocket had sent the third stage into an end-over-end tumble which threatened to send the winged spacecraft into a lethal orbital decay. Wilson demonstrated extraordinary grace under pressure by firing other MRs in exactly the right order, thus pulling the ship out of its tumble and saving its cargo and the lives of its crew. This rescue made Wilson a hero, and the Space Force started to keep an eye on the young former test pilot from Concord, New Hampshire.

Past and active Space Force personnel, who have asked to remain anonymous, remember Wilson as an easygoing, unpretentious family man when he was based at the Cape. Married to his college sweetheart and with a young son, John Wilson, Jr., he was a career officer, loyal to the Space Force even though he managed to take things with a few grains of salt. "Johnny was no hotshot, and this was when we had plenty of hotshot space cadets at the Cape," recalls one former USSF officer. "He never pulled brass on anyone. You could get along with the guy. He knew he was good, but he used to joke about how when all this was over he would go manage a trailer park somewhere. Other guys kept saying how they were going to be the first man on the Moon."

On Saturday nights Johnny Wilson could be found in the officers' club with his best friend, Captain Neil Holliday. Wilson and Holliday had met when they were jockeying jets at Edwards Air Force Base, and both had managed to be transferred to Cape Canaveral at the same time. In the club, Johnny and Neil would guzzle beer and watch *Star Trek,* laughing uproariously at the less-than-plausible adventures of space hero Captain Jim Kirk and his wisecracking scientist buddy Arnold Spock. Afterwards would come the all-night poker games, and more than a few times the MPs would have to drive Johnny and Neil back to their homes.

Holliday was even less reverent towards the Space Force than Wilson was. Wilson, years later, recalls the practical jokes Holliday often played, like slipping lemonade into his weekly urine test or slipping a *Playboy* centerfold into another pilot's map case, so that when the space cadet unrolled it during a mission briefing, out would fall Miss April.

"Neil probably shot himself in the foot with some of those gags, and that's probably why he never made Major," says Wilson. "But underneath all the wiseguy stuff was a loyal USSF officer. He never made a spectacle of it, but he was really hard when it came to space."

Wilson and Holliday flew orbital missions through the early '60s, and in 1963 both spent six months aboard the Wheel as senior officers. By this time, construction of the three moonships—passenger ships *Eagle One* and *Eagle Two*, and cargo ship *Eagle Three*—had commenced. Sometimes the two officers would take a space car from the Wheel out to the orbiting construction zone where the skeletons of the massive Luna One ships were slowly being assembled.

"We kept saying to each other, 'When we go to the Moon, when we walk on the Moon,'" Wilson recalls. "There was no if about it. There was no doubt in our minds that we were being groomed for Luna One, even if the Space Force hadn't officially announced who the crew would be. There were other guys in the running, of course, like Pete Conrad and Al Shepard and Buzz Aldrin, and at one point the odds-on favorite was Neil Armstrong for the command spot. But I knew it was going to be my mission, and Holliday knew that he was going to be riding shotgun. I mean, who the hell else was there?"

Wilson's intuition proved correct. On February 19, 1966, he was summoned to the office of the Cape's base commander, USSF General Jeffrey Marco, where Wilson was informed that he would lead Luna One to the Moon. The target date for the landing would be July 4, 1969; his second-in-command would be *Eagle One's* pilot, Neil Holliday.

✳ ✳ ✳

Yet by 1966, America was having second thoughts about its destiny in space. President Nixon, in his second term in office, had further escalated the war in Viet Nam, and many thousands of young men had been killed in what was increasingly being perceived as a war without an objective. As draft-dodging increased and college activists began publicly burning their draft cards, disenchantment towards the military spread to the space program.

Norman Mailer published a blistering attack on the program, Why Are We Going to the Moon?, which prompted Democratic senators William Proxmire of Wisconsin and Walter Mondale of Minnesota to revive the Kennedy-Johnson Space Act. Democratic presidential candidate Robert Kennedy made the military space program a central issue in his criticism of the Nixon White House. Radicals Abbie Hoffman and Jerry Rubin led two hundred students in a sit-in in front of the gates of the Cape, and actress–activist Jane Fonda confronted Buzz Aldrin in an angry chance encounter at LaGuardia Airport in New York. *Star Trek* was cancelled following a fast plummet to the bottom of the Neilsen ratings.

The shift in the country's attitude toward space was not unnoticed by Major Wilson. "I was confused," Wilson remembers. "One day I was a national hero who couldn't go to the movies without being hounded for autographs. The next day I was being stopped on the street by the same kids who once idolized me and who were now asking why I wanted to blow up the world.

"I didn't want to blow up the world," he continues. "But it started to make me wonder what the Space Force wanted to do, because I knew a top secret objective of the Force was to place nuclear missiles on the Moon Base once it was established. I had never really thought about that before, but now...well, I started to think about it a little bit."

Another former Space Force officer stationed at the Cape at the time says that Wilson's attitude began to change. "He became more serious, less happy-go-lucky about things," he recalls. "We all but stopped seeing him in the officers' club, for one thing. We thought it was, y'know, nerves, being under pressure about Luna One. It never occurred to us that he was having doubts about the program as a whole."

The real turning point for Wilson, however, didn't come until Christmas Eve, 1968. As was traditional with the Wilson family, John Jr. received one of his presents that night; this year he was given his first railroad set. Leanne Wilson remembers how the miniature tracks wound around the Christmas tree and under chairs and the coffee table, and how their five-year-old son couldn't be pried away from his tiny passenger train even to watch the TV as the spaceship *Columbus* made the first manned flyby of the Moon.

The *Columbus* mission was technically little more than a dry run for Luna One, scheduled for seven months later, but the Space Force needed something to impress the public in this new era of doubt about the space program. Thus a TV camera was mounted on the outside of the ship's superstructure. On Christmas Eve, at 8:35 pm EST, an audience of thirty million Americans watched on TV as the camera caught the unforgettable sight of Earth rising above the limb of the Moon.

This was soundtracked by a tape of the "Air Force Flight Song," but as John Wilson watched the earthrise on TV, he had a more profound thought. He recalled the opening verses of the Book of Genesis. After turning down the volume on his set, he quoted them from memory to his wife and son: "In the beginning God created the heavens and the Earth. The Earth was without form and void, and darkness was upon the face of the deep; and the Spirit of God was moving over the face of the waters. And God said, 'Let there be light'; and there was light..."

"This was a moment of epiphany for me," Wilson says years later. "I suddenly realized that, from the Moon, you see the whole planet, not just the United States of America. For the first time in my life I really saw that the USA was not the center of the universe, that my country, much as I loved her, was not the biggest thing on the planet. So why should America take sole claim to the Moon?"

Wilson leaned back in his chair, staring at the bit of moonrock in his hands. "It was a simple notion, really, but it was something that had never occurred to me before. And it kinda shook me up, because here I was, the man who in seven months was supposed to claim the Moon as territory of the United States. But how could I do this, knowing and believing as I now did?"

Later that evening, still trying to cope with his uneasiness, Wilson slipped out to the officers' club. The club was nearly empty that night—most of the base personnel were either on duty or enjoying Christmas Eve with their families at home—but he found at the bar his old friend, Neil Holliday. The two men grabbed a bottle of Scotch and hunkered down at a corner table to share some Christmas spirit, but what happened would further change Wilson's life.

Johnny Wilson had been careful not to express his recent misgivings about Luna One, knowing that such musings would find their way to Space Force security officers, but that night his brain was on fire and, soon, his caution was numbed by the Scotch. Before they had worked their way to the bottom of the bottle, Wilson had slurred his revelation to Holliday, who sat silently on the other side of the table, listening and occasionally pouring his friend another shot.

"I got drunk," Wilson says. "I got plastered, and I opened my heart to my best friend in the world. Now, people can do that all the time, but not necessarily in the Space Force. I don't recall exactly what I said, but I let it all hang out."

He paused, and shook his head. "And what do you know? The son of a bitch stabbed me in the back. Neil Holliday went straight to the brass with everything I had said."

Indeed. The day after Christmas, Capt. Neil Holliday went to the base hospital where he conferred privately with staff psychiatrists on the Moon operation, telling them about Major Wilson's revelations. Concerned, the psychiatrists immediately summoned members of the Space Force upper echelon and the intelligence staff. In an off-record, closed-door meeting at the hospital, Holliday blew the whistle on Wilson. Sources say that Holliday claimed Wilson was "losing his edge", that Wilson had told Holliday that he had received a message from God, that the Almighty didn't want the Space Force on the Moon, that the United States didn't have any right to claim the Moon for itself.

The sources say this put the Space Force general staff into a quandary. Luna One was only a few months away, and the crew was in the midst of intensive training. There was simply no way that Wilson, who had been preparing for the mission for the last two years, could now be yanked from the command seat and replaced. Nor could the flight be postponed; everyone was frightened that the Russians were preparing their own lunar mission, and the common perception was that the US was locked into a race against time to beat the Soviets to the Moon. Yet at the same time, they didn't want an unstable man to lead nineteen men and three ships to the Sea of Tranquility. Especially if that man thought he was under orders from God to keep the US from claiming the Moon, as Holliday had led them to believe.

But the staff psychiatrists didn't see it that way. "They pointed out that the major had been ripped when he had said these things to Holliday," one source recalls. "They asked, somewhat rhetorically, whether Wilson wasn't entitled to get blitzed and make some strange comments, considering the enormous pressure he was under. The shrinks weren't worried. 'Just keep an eye on him and keep your options open,' that was their advice, and the brass accepted it."

So the men at the meeting made an on-the-spot decision: Wilson would remain in command of Luna One, but Holliday was to closely monitor the major's mental condition. "The word was, if Wilson looked like he was going to crack, they were going to yank him from the top gun slot at once, even if he was standing on the Moon when it happened," the source says.

And why did Holliday snitch on Wilson? Wilson believes that his friend was merely looking out for the best interests of the mission. But the source, who was at the meeting, remembers that Holliday appeared very satisfied when he was told that, if Wilson were taken off Luna One, Holliday himself would have the command. "There's no question in my mind that Neil Holliday wanted to be the first man to walk on the Moon," he says.

It's now midafternoon and the conversation had moved into John Wilson's office in the cabin's guest room. Leanne Wilson brought a teakwood tray laden with Syrian bread, English chutney and hot coffee into the office, then retired to the living room to write a letter to John Jr., now a graduate student in physics at the University of Colorado in Boulder. Through the window a neighbor's cat can be seen, stalking mice and spiders in the backyard.

"Of course I knew I was being watched," John Wilson says as he spread chutney onto a slice of bread with a butter knife. "I figured out, from the way he was acting, the questions he was asking—have I been going to church, that sort of thing—that Neil was spying on me and regularly reporting to the shrinks and the top brass. So I kept my mouth closed, acted like nothing was different from before."

He smiles. "But, yes, I was making my own plans for the mission. But I said nothing to anyone, not even Leanne, and I wrote nothing in my journal. This was strictly between me and my conscience."

Sources say Holliday's reports to the Space Force high command revealed nothing unusual in Wilson's behavior prior to the mission; he wasn't talking about Genesis or mankind's right to claim the Moon, he hadn't been reading the Mailer book, he hadn't voted for Bobby Kennedy in the last election. The Luna One training team reported that Wilson's test scores had remained high and that his performance during flight simulations was superior. There was no hint that he was going to crash *Eagle One* into the Moon or attempt to blow out the pressure in the crew compartment.

After awhile, Wilson's Christmas Eve ramblings were written off by most of the brass as whisky talk.

By now, the Space Force had other problems. Bobby Kennedy had promised a civilian space program during his presidential campaign. Now, having defeated Ronald Reagan in November, the new liberal president was apparently intent on making good his promise. The Proxmire-Mondale bill to form NASA was gathering momentum on the Hill, and if Congress passed the bill there was little doubt that Kennedy would sign it into law. Thus, the Space Force would be dismantled and NASA would take over the space program as a civilian activity. Luna One was to continue as planned even if the Space Act were signed by the end of July—by now the landing had been pushed back two weeks due to a ruptured seal on a fuel tank on *Eagle Three*—but it would be the last hurrah for the all-military space effort.

In an effort to head off political disaster, the Pentagon was trying to recast Luna One as a peaceful venture. It downplayed the military significance of the lunar base and attempted to portray the mission as being in the spirit of human exploration. The hope was that this last minute PR effort would make the Space Act seen unnecessary and turn around the votes on Capitol Hill.

Yet while the Secretary of the Air Force was in front of Congressional committee claiming that the USSF should be renamed the "United States Peace Force," the talk on the Cape was of bitter resentment against the Commander-in-Chief. "Everyone knew that the civilians would blow it if they were given charge of the space program," Wilson says. "The Space Force was determined to keep control of the program, and the logic was that, if Luna One claims ownership of the Moon for the US, the public would force Congress to vote down the Space Act.

"I didn't like that idea," he continues. "More than ever, I didn't want the US to outright own the Moon...because it wouldn't be the people of the United States, but the Pentagon having sole right to the Moon. That was scary. Really, very scary."

Two weeks before the beginning of the mission, the day before the expedition members were launched to the Wheel for final preparations for Luna One, John Harper Wilson was given the text of the first words he would say upon setting foot on the Moon. The text, which had been carefully written by the Space Force, was classified Top Secret.

It read: "I, John Harper Wilson, do claim the Moon as sovereign territory of the United States of America. That's one small step for an American, one giant leap for America."

Wilson dutifully memorized the speech in case anyone asked for a rehearsal. Someone did. A few days before the launch of the three Luna One ships from Earth orbit, while relaxing in the space station's rec room, Neil Holliday innocuously asked Wilson what he would say when he stepped onto the Moon. Since Holliday was cleared for Top Secret, Wilson repeated the words for his friend.

"He just nodded and looked away," Wilson says, "but I don't think he was just wasting his time with that question."

On July 20, under the harsh glare of the early lunar afternoon, *Eagle One* descended like a steel monolith riding a blowtorch to the surface of the Moon. Its touchdown in the Sea of Tranquility was followed shortly by the arrival of *Eagle Two* and *Eagle Three,* the engines of each blackening the grey lunar dust beneath their landing struts. Several hours later, as planned, Major John Harper Wilson undogged the airlock hatch and began his long solo climb down the ladder to the Moon's surface.

"I wasn't thinking of history or how I would figure in it, or even about where I was," Wilson recalls. "I was thinking about my career while I was climbing down. 'They're going to court-martial me after I do this,' that was my main thought. I guess I wasn't sure that what I was going to do was right."

A TV camera outside the ship televised the final steps of Wilson's descent, and its images, along with Wilson's voice, were transmitted to 50 million people watching throughout the world, in their homes and on storefront sets and on giant screens set up in Times Square and Picadilly Circus. Those millions of viewers were witnesses when Wilson, obeying a higher call than nationalism or loyalty to the US Space Force, changed the script.

Wilson stepped off the landing pad, planted his booted feet solidly in the lunar dust, and spoke the words he had concocted weeks before. "That's one small step for man," he said slowly. "One giant leap for mankind."

There was a long pause from Mission Control at the Cape, longer than was obligated by the 2.6 second delay. "*Eagle One,* this is CapCom," the Cape's spacecraft communicator responded after almost a minute. "We didn't quite copy that, over."

Wilson spoke again, his voice steady. "I, John Harper Wilson, claim the Moon in the name of humanity, not as the property of any one nation, but as the common heritage of all the peoples of Earth."

He paused, then added, "We've come in peace for all mankind."

Senator Eugene "Rocky" Costello (D-MA) was in the Oval Office with President Kennedy when Wilson stepped onto the Moon. With them was Air Force Secretary General Malcolm Danforth. "When John Wilson said that, the President was sort of surprised," Costello says today. "He turned to General Danforth and said, 'I didn't know the Pentagon had it in them to be so generous.'"

The general didn't say much. He simply said, 'Yes sir, Mr. President' and then he excused himself, saying that he had to make a phone call. I started to say something about how nice it was for the Space Force to give us NASA when Bobby, the President, looked back at the TV and said, 'Hey, what happened to the picture?'"

Wilson had gone on to describe the soil he was standing on and the condition of *Eagle One*. but by then—according to the Space Force's explanation—there was a temporary communications failure. TV screens went black, and Wilson's voice was lost, and the communication link between Earth and the Moon was lost for four and a half minutes. The networks were informed by the Space Force that there had been a satellite snafu, but what had really happened was that the Cape pulled the plug on Wilson.

An anonymous Space Force source has recently leaked a classified partial transcript of the communications between CapCom, *Eagle One,* and Wilson during that brief black-out.

CAPCOM: "*Eagle One,* this is CapCom. Do you want to repeat what you have said? Over."

WILSON: "CapCom, *Eagle One.* I said that the soil is fine and powdery and that I can pick it up with my toe, and it adheres to my..."

CAPCOM: "*Eagle One,* you seem to have deviated from your mission profile. Please acknowledge, over."

WILSON: "CapCom, this is *Eagle One.* That's affirmative, over."

CAPCOM: "*Eagle One,* CapCom. Is this a deliberate change? Over."

WILSON: "That's affirmative, CapCom, over."

CAPCOM: "*Eagle One,* this is CapCom. Captain Holliday, do you copy? Over."

HOLIDAY: "CapCom, this is *Eagle One.* Holliday. We copy, over."

CAPCOM: "Holliday, Mission Command affirms that you are now in command on Luna One until further notice. Major Wilson has been relieved of his command. Do you copy? Over."

HOLLIDAY: "CapCom, this is *Eagle One,* Holliday. We copy, over."

WILSON: "I copy, CapCom. Thank you, over."

CAPCOM: "*Eagle One,* this is CapCom. Commander Holliday, you will descend from the craft and continue the mission profile. We are now in communications blackout and will continue on your mark. Major Wilson, you will place yourself under military arrest, and Mission Command orders you to desist from any communications until you are back inside the ship. Do you copy? Over."

WILSON: "We copy, CapCom. Wilson out."

HOLLIDAY: "We copy, and we are preparing to leave the ship. *Eagle One,* over."

After spending the better part of the six weeks confined to *Eagle One* and the immediate Tranquility base encampment—Neil Holliday led the expedition to Julius Caesar crater—Wilson returned to Earth with the rest of the Space Force team, and promptly vanished from the public eye. "I wasn't exactly brought back in manacles, but there was some loose talk before we lifted off of whether I should be left behind to monitor the automatic instruments," Wilson says half-jokingly.

There was not much the Space Force could do to Wilson, though. A court martial could not have been done in secret, and would have raised too many questions. So Wilson "retired" from the Space Force, under strict orders from the Pentagon that he never reveal what had happened on the Moon.

It was impossible for the Space Force to retract Wilson's statement. After all, millions of people had heard the major bequeath the Moon to humanity; Neil Holliday couldn't simply say, "No, we take that back, the Moon belongs to the United States." It would have caused international embarrassment for the United States in general and for the Space Force in particular. By the time Luna One returned to Earth, the Moon had become recognized as belonging to everyone and no one, and the United Nations was hammering out an agreement which would formalize these conditions.

Within three months of the first lunar landing, the Space Act was passed by Congress and signed into law by President Kennedy. NASA became an official government agency on January 1, 1970, and control of the US space program passed into civilian hands. While former Space Force officers continue today to work for NASA, they take their orders from the Administration, not from the Pentagon. Shortly after Kennedy's assassination, the US Space Force Canaveral Launch Center was renamed the NASA Robert Kennedy Space Center, and it became the springboard for future lunar expeditions and the continuing exploration of the solar system.

John Harper Wilson never talked to Neil Holliday again after Luna One came home; three years later, Holliday's T-38 jet trainer crashed at the Cape while he was practicing soft-landing maneuvers, killing Holliday and his co-pilot instantly. Despite the rift which opened between them during Luna One, Wilson bears no grudge against his former friend. "Neil thought he was doing what was right," he says. "I can't blame him for that."

Today, nearly two decades after Luna One, the United States has a self-sufficient, non-military base on the Moon. Instead of competing with each other, the US and the Soviet Union are embarked on a joint manned expedition to Mars, to be launched within the next two years. Civilians regularly travel into space, and the Hilton hotel chain has announced plans to build an orbital hotel in the 1990s. Yet Wilson denies that he was the catalyst in changing the direction of space exploration towards a more peaceful course. "Somebody else would have said something sooner or later" is all he says about his role in events.

So why has he decided to go public after all these years? The former astronaut shrugs and looks out the window as the early autumn sun begins to set behind the trees. "History gave me the chance to walk on the Moon," he says after some reflection. "I just wanted to give history back four and a half minutes that it was missing."

PART THREE
CONTEMPORARY SPACE

SCIENCE FACT: LGM

We live in the Milky Way galaxy: approximately 200 billion stars spread out among 100,000 light-years. Our solar system, located about 27,000 light-years from the galactic core near the edge of a spiral arm, is in the boondocks of the Milky Way. Out of nine planets and a sun, plus assorted comets, moons and asteroids, only our world is presently known to support life.

Where is everyone else?

On a cool, sunny autumn afternoon, Joe Caruso walks out the front door of the fieldstone cottage he inhabits with his wife and saunters down the hilltop roadway to begin his evening work. Later on, after an early dinner, he will go to the Harvard-Smithsonian Astrophysical Observatory to continue his observations of the planet Mars through its sixty-inch optical telescope; now, however, Caruso walks the opposite way, heading for the eighty-four foot radiotelescope perched on the ridge at the end of the road. It's time to look for aliens again.

The middle-aged former college instructor from Ohio pauses outside the concrete instrument shack adjacent to the massive silver dish, peering fondly at a large yellow garden spider which has strung her net in a corner next to the door. Most people, upon finding the arachnid, would have been repulsed and destroyed the spider, but Joe has practically adopted the creature as a pet. The spider is leisurely devouring an insect wrapped in a silk cocoon, and after taking a few moments to admire her handiwork, Joe unlocks the metal door and walks inside.

Within an small room inside the shack, pampered by air conditioning and protected by an alarm system, is a large, complicated computer system. Inside a transparent case are lined dozens of computer chip breadboards, each one containing the memory capacity of a high-end home computer. The computer is capable of scanning and analyzing 8.4 million different radio channels in the 400 kilohertz radio spectrum. It was hand-built by students from Harvard University and various volunteers; its components were purchased with a $100,000 private grant from movie director Steven Spielberg. Indeed, with its blinking red status lights, CRT screens, and tape reels, the Multichannel Spectrum Analyzer looks like a leftover prop from *Close Encounters of the Third Kind*.

Caruso is the watchman for this lonely outpost. After going to the telescope's control panel to routinely shift the antenna's lateral alignment by one-tenth of a degree—as he does every afternoon—Joe sits down behind the keyboard and types in commands which allow him to check what the radiotelescope has picked up. Interesting patterns are logged and saved in memory by the computer. They rarely happen. Today, there is nothing: the CRT screen shows a line of random spikes, the oscilloscope displays a fuzzy white bar, and from the audio speaker, a loud hiss. The music of the spheres is electromagnetic white noise, no more interesting than between-channel static on a car radio.

However, if and when the day comes that Project META's full-sky search of the Milky Way galaxy bears fruit, the computer screen may display a different pattern, like a regular series of sharply-defined, box-like lines. At 4:11 pm on August 28, 1986, just such a pattern was picked up by META, prompting it to be logged in the computer, along with a serial number, with the letters "WOW". A subsequent search of the sky, though, could not repeat the discovery, so the origin of the signal remains mysterious.

One day, there may be another such signal received here, one that can be tracked and confirmed by this and other radiotelescopes: a message from deep space, a collect call from another world— "Hello. We are here. Can you hear us?"

The search for extraterrestrial intelligence—SETI for short—is perhaps the most existential of modern scientific pursuits. It makes assumptions for which there is no hard evidence: first, that intelligent life exists in the galaxy, and second, that it is trying to make contact with other civilizations. As Joe Caruso points out, it has only recently been proven that planets exist in other star systems, such as the giant planet discovered by the Harvard observatory to be orbiting HD 114762, 90 light-years from Earth.

Allen Steele

(1993 UPDATE: this finding was later to be proven false, or at least unconfirmed).

SETI is also one of the most recent, if not underfunded, scientific enterprises. Although experiments such as Project Ozma, Project Sentinel, and Suitcase SETI have been conducted off and on over the last three decades, at this time only Ohio State University's SETI telescope and Project META are scanning space for LGMs — "Little Green Men", in the slang of the field. NASA research at the Ames Research Center in California has been slowed by budget cutbacks to little more than part-time work, and no one seems to know what SETI research the Soviet Union is doing these days.

Since Ohio State has been recently "off the air" due to technical difficulties, Project META (short for Megachannel Extraterrestrial Assay) may now be the only full-time monitor for ETs. The project is funded exclusively through private donations, mainly from the Planetary Society, the public space group co-founded by author-scientist Carl Sagan. With an annual budget of only about $25,000, META is a shoestring operation. The radiotelescope is a hand-me-down ex-NASA rig bought from Harvard University by the Planetary Society, while the nearby optical telescope is run by the Smithsonian Institution.

If SETI is existential science, then it's only appropriate that Project META's director, Paul Horowitz, is a professor of physics at Harvard University, the home of classic American existentialism. In his late 30s, occupying a hopelessly cluttered office near Harvard Yard, Horowitz is one of the generation of young research scientists who came bursting out of college campuses during the '60s. He first became interested in SETI during his student days at Harvard, when his roommate took a course taught by Sagan when he was lecturing at the university.

Horowitz's graduate work in astrophysics was paralleled by SETI research at the giant Arecibo radiotelescope in Puerto Rico and at Ames. As a professor of physics at Harvard, he helped start Project META, along with Sagan, under the auspices of the Planetary Society. If a legitimate radio signal from an extraterrestrial civilization is detected within our lifetime, it may possibly be Paul Horowitz who accomplishes the feat.

"I think it's become a completely legitimate branch of science these days," Horowitz says. "I think what has happened is that things have changed over the years. Things that people thought twenty-five years ago are no longer what people think, in terms of the evolution of planetary systems and the beginnings of life."

Astrophysicists now have a better grasp of how planets are formed and how life begins in primordial conditions, Horowitz notes; this in turn has increased their understanding of the potential for intelligent life in the universe. Another major change in SETI research has been the microelectronics revolution, making a search like Project META possible. "Progress there has been so rapid and astounding that it is now possible to analyze millions of channels simultaneously and really look for needles in haystacks, which really would have been far-fetched a generation ago," Horowitz explains.

Indeed, public acceptance of SETI is remarkably high. "I think that, in terms of grassroots support, this is a project that can't fail," Horowitz says. "People love it. It doesn't require special training in science to understand SETI.

"First of all, people understand that there could be other intelligent things out there," he continues. "It's in science fiction, in the culture, it's been there for a long time. Everybody looks at the night sky and wonders what the heck's going on. So what is it that's so hard to explain? Just the details, like the frequency of the carrier wave or why we look at certain kinds of stars. The technical details are new to them."

On the other hand, there are a number of popular misconceptions among the public about extraterrestrial intelligence. Horowitz has a small collection of supermarket tabloid headlines taped to his office wall, such as "Space Aliens Make Woman, 86, Pregnant." Both he and Caruso note ruefully that Project META has attracted its share of the lunatic fringe, such as visits or phone calls from people who claim to be in telepathic contact with aliens. "If you really did a random sample of people in this country or anywhere and asked how many thought we had already made contact with extraterrestrials, I bet you'd get a pretty high percentage," Horowitz says. "I bet twenty percent of the people in this country think that."

Project META has its technical drawbacks as well. Its location is in a place with a rapidly increasing population, and as the population rises, so does the potential for radio interference from even household sources. Interference is particularly high when the telescope is pointed towards the southern horizon, for instance. Sometimes the telescope intercepts regular, repeating signals which turn out to be from manmade sources.

"It's either equipment malfunction or interference in one form or another, and we've had a little bit of everything," Horowitz says. "And every now and then you get something that looks just right, but it doesn't repeat. Y'know, I can't say anything about that, except that it looks right and it doesn't repeat. You hope that any one of them is going to be the one that does repeat, but so far..."

It's intriguing to speculate what would happen if a genuine, real McCoy LGM were intercepted by Project META. Joe Caruso would probably be the first person to know, finding the signal during his daily inspection of the computer. If an interesting signal were detected, he would notify Horowitz, who in turn would probably have the telescope kept at that declination for another day to see if the signal repeated. If the LGM did repeat for several days, Caruso and Horowitz would unpin the telescope and track it across the sky, following Earth's rotation. If the signal were still there, Horowitz would notify another observatory elsewhere in the world and have its astronomers attempt to confirm the discovery, "because maybe it's just those MIT boys out there in the woods with their little transmitter," he laughs.

Although the event would be kept quiet until it was confirmed, Horowitz admits that the discovery would probably be leaked to the news media before a formal announcement could be made. "Although we wouldn't be very good at keeping a lid on it, even less good would be a national observatory with a staff of 100, and these guys are telling their wives and their kids and their dogs and everybody knows about it, and it just leaks out. A kid makes a comment to a friend at school whose father is a journalist and that's how the world will know of the First Contact."

The major problem after initial detection will be in translating the message. It would probably not be in Morse code, English, or Mr. Spock's Vulcan tongue, so decoding and deciphering the signal will take a very long time. Even then, Horowitz warns, pieces of the message may never be understood. All language is culturally based, and thus understanding the language of a completely alien culture will be difficult, if not impossible.

"Then you ask a more interesting question, 'What effect does this have on the whole world?'" Horowitz says. "Do we immediately convert our swords into plowshares and grow wheat because now we realize that there's a true religion and that the way to eternal nirvana and peace is there and will be explained in due course by these folks?"

He pauses and shrugs again. "You can believe that if you like...but if you want my opinion, it will have both short-term and long-term effects, but neither will be quite what we think. Short-term effect will be, 'Wow, great news! Even better than last week's great news!' It's on the front page of everything, and this will probably last longer than your average thing. Y'know, the radon scare lasted about three days, so this will last about a week, then it will degenerate to the fifth page of *The New York Times.*

"I think what will happen in the long term will be very interesting," Horowitz continues. "I think it will soak into your consciousness...that things are forever different, that we've lost our unique position, that we know the answer to whether there's other life, that we know the answer as to whether life can survive technology...You just don't feel the same about your place in the universe, and the way you do your silly little things on Earth is affected by that."

If Paul Horowitz is the avatar of Project META, then Joe Caruso is the sentry. How he came to be in the unique position of possibly being, one day, the first human to look at an alien signal, is a story of how a hobby turned into a profession.

Caruso had little more than a passing interest in astronomy until ten years ago, when he bought a little 60mm refractor telescope for fifty dollars at a flea market in his town in upstate New York. With no prior experience in star gazing and only a Golden Guide to astronomy to light his way, the junior college history teacher began looking at stars in his backyard at night. "I didn't know right ascension, declination, nothing," he says. "I just started finding my way around."

Hooked on his new hobby, he joined amateur astronomer groups and participated in organized "watches" of stellar phenomena. As he continued his night work, he became aware of how little people knew about astronomy. "I would be out in my backyard with my little telescope, and people who were college educated would come up to me and say things to me like, 'Y'know, I always wondered, like, what the differences between planets and stars are.' It got me to wondering why people don't know this. People who are college educated who don't know the basic geography of the heavens."

After instructing a course in astronomy at a small college and teaching history at the University of Hartford, Caruso went to Wesleyan College and earned a graduate degree in astronomy. Eventually he was hired by Paul Horowitz to be the curator of Project META. He couples this job with his observations at the Oak Ridge optical telescope down the road, and spends several days a week lecturing to the general public about astronomy and SETI. Although he works in a professional environment, Caruso still considers himself to be an amateur astronomer. He also still has the itch to teach and plans to eventually return to it.

"I'm really a telescope operator," he says. "But there's a need for this sort of thing. There's a lot of unemployed astronomers. People say that this is the age of science, [but] there's 20,000 astrologers in America and fewer than 2,000 astronomers...but there's a lot of technical jobs in astronomy. Computer operators and programmers and telescope drivers and things like that, there's quite a need for [them] in astronomy."

Like Horowitz, Caruso finds that people are generally open-minded about the subject of extraterrestrial intelligence. "What I find is that most people have a need to believe that it's there, just on a gut level," he says. "But it is kind of a strange job. It's kind of hard, when you're talking to people on the phone, to say, 'Oh, yeah, I gotta get off the phone, I have to go see if the aliens have contacted us.'"

Joe Caruso is also an avid reader of science fiction. His favorite authors are the hard SF writers like Larry Niven who make plausible extrapolations about alien life. However, he believes that the chances of radio contact with an alien intelligence to be slim, at best. For one thing, Earth has been radio-visible—that is, detectable from deep space by humankind's radio transmissions—for only about fifty years. Since radio waves travel at the speed of light, this means an alien civilization looking for us would have to be within about fifty light-years of Earth, which is not a great distance on the galactic scale.

And that's not the only thing which weighs the chances against first contact any time soon. "There is a basic assumption that SETI makes which is untestable," Caruso says, "and we won't know until it happens or doesn't happen, and that is whether there is the need to try to communicate among other beings that we feel. Now, most people think this would be a good thing, or at least an interesting thing. We don't know if aliens would feel like that. They may be brighter than us, but they don't have that need to communicate with other beings. It would never occur to them to do that."

On the other hand, Caruso recognizes that the implications of First Contact would be enormous. "It would be one of the greatest discoveries of all time, and that's why it's worth doing. People are always asking me, 'What do you think the chances really are of this happening? And I tell them, 'I think they're very, very small...but I know what the chance is if you don't look at all. It's zero.'"

HAPGOOD'S HOAX

HAPGOOD, H. L. (Harold LaPierre), Jr.—1911-1966; American pulp SF writer of the 1930s and 1940s. Although most of his short fiction is obscure today, Hapgood is best known (as Dr. H. LaPierre Hapgood) as the author of several allegedly non-fictional works on UFO contact, including <u>Abducted to Space</u> (1950) and <u>UFO!</u> (1952). These works were based on Hapgood's claim that he was seized by aliens from space in 1948, which is widely regarded as a hoax.

— <u>The Encyclopedia of Science Fiction and Fantasy</u>
Ursula May, editor (1981)

Lawrence R. Bolger; Professor of English, Minnesota State University, and science fiction historian:

Harry Hapgood. (*Sighs.*) It would figure that someone would want to interview me about Harry Hapgood, especially since the new collection of his work just came out. The field may not be able to get rid of him until someone digs up his coffin and hammers a stake in his heart...

Okay, since you've come all this way, I'll tell you about H.L. Hapgood, Jr. But, to tell the truth, I'd just as soon leave the bastard in his literary grave.

There were pulp writers from the '30s who managed to survive the times and outlast the pulps, to make the transition from pulp fiction to whatever passes as literature in this genre. Jack Williamson, Clifford Simak, Ray Bradbury...those are some of the ones whose work eventually broke out of the pulp mold. They're regarded as the great writers of the field and we still read their stories. They still find their audience. Their publishers keep their classics, like <u>City</u> and <u>The Humanoids</u> and <u>The Martian Chronicles</u> in print.

Those are the success stories. Yet for every Bradbury or Williamson, there's a hundred other writers—some of them big names back then, you need to remember—who didn't make it out of the pulp era. For one reason or another, their careers faded when the pulps died at the end of the '40s. H. Bedford-Jones, Arthur K. Barnes, S.P. Meek...all obscure authors now. Just like H.L. Hapgood, Jr.

Not that they were necessarily bad writers, either. I mean, some of their stories are no more crap than a lot of the stuff that gets into print today. But when the field started to grow up, when John Campbell began to demand that his *Astounding* contributors deliver realistic SF or else...well, Harry was one of those writers who fell into the 'or else' category.

But before that, he had been extraordinarily successful, especially when you consider the times. The Depression nearly killed a lot of writers, but those years were kind to him. He had a nonstop imagination and fast fingers, and for a penny a word, Harry Hapgood cranked out stories by the bushel. I was reading all the SF pulps at the time — I was in high school in Ohio then — so I can tell you with personal authority that there was rarely a month that went by without H.L. Hapgood's byline appearing somewhere. If not in *Amazing* or *Thrilling Wonder,* then in *Captain Future* or the pre-Campbell era *Astounding* or someplace else. "The Sky Pirates of Centaurus", "Attack of the Giant Robots", "Mars or Bust!" — those were some of his more memorable stories. Rock-jawed space captains fighting Venusian tiger-men while mad scientists with Z-ray machines menaced ladies in bondage. Greasy kid stuff, sure, but a hell of a lot of fun when you were fourteen years old. Harry was the master of the space opera. Not even Ed Hamilton or Doc Smith could tell 'em like he could.

You can still find some of his older work in huckster rooms at SF conventions, if you look through the raggy old pulps some people have on the tables. That's about the only place you can find Harry Hapgood's pulp stories anymore. I think his last published story, at least in his lifetime, was in *Amazing* in '45 or '46. The last time any of his early work was reprinted was when somebody put together a pulp anthology about ten years ago. When he died in '66, his career in science fiction had been long since over.

That's the main reason why he's been obscure all these years. But there was also the New Hampshire hoax. He died a rich man because of that stunt, but he also blackened his name in the field. I don't think anyone wanted to remember Hapgood because of that. At least, not until recently...

✳ ✳ ✳

Startled and dazzled by the sudden burst of light, I looked up and saw a monstrous disk-shaped vehicle descending towards me. Rocket fighters raced from the sky to combat the weird machine, but as they got close, scarlet rays flashed from portals along the side of the spaceship. The rockets exploded!

"Dirk, oh Dirk!" Catherine screamed from the bunker next to me, fearful of the apparition. "What can it be?"

Before I could answer, Captain Black of the United Earth Space Force spoke up. "The Quongg death machine, Miss Jones," he said, his chin thrust out belligerently.

I reached for my blaster. "Oh, yeah?" I snarled. "Well, they'll never take us alive!"

Captain Black stared at me. "They'll take us alive, all right!" he snarled. "They want us as specimens!"

> — *"Kidnappers from the Stars"*
> *by H.L. Hapgood Jr.*
> *Space Tales, December, 1938*

Joe Mackey; retired electrical engineer:

If I remember correctly, I first met Harry Hapgood back in 1934 or 1935, when we both lived in the same triple-decker in Somerville, Massachusetts, just outside of Boston. I was about nineteen at the time and was working a day job in a deli on Newbury Street to put myself through MIT night school. So, y'know, when I wasn't making grinders or riding the trolley over to classes in Cambridge, I was at home hitting the books. I got maybe four hours of sleep in those days. The Depression was a bitch like that.

I met Harry because he lived right upstairs. His apartment was directly above mine and he used to bang on his typewriter late at night, usually when I was studying or trying to sleep. Every time he hit the carriage return, it sounded like something was being dropped on the floor. I had no idea what he was doing up there...practicing somersaults or something.

HAPGOOD'S HOAX

Anyway, one night I finally got fed up with the racket, so I marched upstairs and hammered on his door, planning on telling him to cut it out 'cause I was trying to catch a few winks. Well, he opened his door—very timidly—and I started to chew him out. Then I looked past him and saw all these science fiction magazines scattered all over the place. Piled on the coffee table, the couch, the kitchen table, the bed...*Amazing, Astonishing, Thrilling Wonder, Planet Stories, Startling Stories*. Heaps of them. My jaw just dropped open because, though I read all those magazines when I could afford to buy 'em, I thought I was the only person in Boston who read science fiction.

So I said something like, "Holy smoke! You've got the new issue of *Astounding!*" I remember that was lying open on the coffee table. Brand new issue. I was too broke to pick it up myself.

Harry just smiled, then he walked over and picked it up and brought it to me. "Here, you can borrow it if you want," he said. Then he added, very slyly, "Read the story by H.L. Hapgood. You might like it."

I nodded and said, "Yeah, I really like his stories." He just blushed and coughed into his fist and shuffled his feet, and then he told me who he was.

Well, I didn't say anything about his typing after that, but once he found out that I was taking night classes at MIT, he stopped typing late at night so I could get some sleep. He figured it out for himself. Harry was a good guy like that.

Margo Croft; literary agent; former assistant editor, <u>Rocket Adventures</u>:

I was the first-reader at *Rocket* back then, so I read Harry's stories when they came in through the mail, which was once every week or two. Seriously. In his prime, he was more prolific than Bob Silverberg or Isaac Asimov ever was. But the difference was, Silverberg and Asimov were good writers, even in their pulp days.

No, no, scratch that. At a certain level, Harry was good. He knew how to keep a story going. He was a master of pacing, for one thing. But it was all formula fiction, even if he didn't recognize the formula himself. Anyone who compares him to E.E. Smith or Edmond Hamilton is fooling you. His characters were one-dimensional, his dialogue was vintage movie serial. "Ah-ha, Dr. Zoko, I've got you now!", that sort of thing. His understanding of real science was nonexistent. In fact, he usually ignored science. When it was convenient, say, for a pocket of air to exist in a crater on the Moon, there it was.

But his stories were no worse than the other stuff we published, and he got his share of fan mail, so we sent him lots of checks. For a long time, he was in our stable of regular writers. Whenever we needed a 6,000 word story to fill a gap in the next issue, there was always an H.L. Hapgood yarn in the inventory. He was a fiction factory.

I finally met him at the first World Science Fiction Convention, in New York back in '39. I think it was Donald Wollheim who introduced us. I was twenty years old then, flat-chested and single, ready to throw myself at the first writer who came along, so I developed a crush on Harry at once. He might have been a hack, but he was a good-looking hack (*Laughs*).

He had fans all around him, though, because he was such a well-known writer. I spent the better part of Saturday following him around Caravan Hall, trying to get his attention. It was hard. Harry was shy when it came to one-on-one conversation, but he soaked up the glory when a mob was around.

Anyway, I finally managed to get him into a group that was going out to dinner that night. We found an Italian restaurant a few blocks away and took over a long table in the back room. There was a whole bunch of us—I think Ray Bradbury was in the group, though nobody knew who he was then—and I managed to get myself positioned across the table from Harry. Like I said, he was very shy when it came to one-on-one conversation, so I gave up on talking to him like a pretty girl and tried speaking to him like an editor. He began to notice me then.

His lack of—well, for lack of a better term, literary sophistication—was mind-boggling. He had barely heard of Ernest Hemingway, and he only recognized Steinbeck as the name of his neighborhood grocer. The only classics he had read were by H.G. Wells and Jules Verne. In fact, the only thing Harry seemed to have ever read was science fiction or *Popular Mechanics,* and that was all he wanted to talk about. I mean, there I was trying to show off my legs—maybe I had no chest back then, but my legs were Marlene Dietrich's—and Harry only wanted to discuss the collected work of Neil R. Jones.

So I lost a little interest in him during that talk, and after awhile I started paying attention to other people at the table. I do distinctly remember two things that Harry said that night. One was that his ambition was to get rich and famous. He was convinced that he would write for the pulps forever. "Science fiction will never change," he proclaimed.

The other was a comment which sounds routine today. Every other SF writer has said it at least once, but I recall Harry saying it first, at least as far as I can remember. Probably, because of what happened years later, it's why it sticks in my mind.

"If aliens ever came to Earth to capture people," he said offhandedly at one point, "they wouldn't have to hunt for me. I'd volunteer for the trip."

Joe Mackey:

Harry Hapgood was a hell of a good person back then. You can quote me on that. He put me up to a lot of meals when I was starving, and he always had a buck to spare even when his own rent was due. But the day I saw him begin to hurt was the day when John W. Campbell rejected one of his stories.

I had dropped by his place after work. It was in the middle of winter—1940, I think—and the MIT semester hadn't started yet, so I had some time to kill. The mail had just come, and when I came into Harry's apartment he was sitting at his kitchen table, bent over a manuscript which had just come back in the mail. It was a rejection from *Astounding*.

This almost never happened to him. Harry thought he was rejection-proof. After all, his stories usually sold on the first shot. That, and the fact that *Astounding* had always been one of his most reliable markets. But Harry's old editor, F. Orlin Tremaine, had left a couple of years earlier, and the new guy, John W. Campbell, was reshaping the magazine...and that meant getting rid of the zap-gun school of science fiction.

So here was Harry, looking at this story which had been bounced back, "Enslaved on Venus". Just staring at it, that's all. "What's going on?" I asked, and he told me that Campbell had just rejected this story. "Did he tell you why?" I said. Harry told me he had received a letter, but he wouldn't show it to me. I think it was in the trash. "Well, just send it out again to some other magazine," I said, because this is what he had always told me should be done when a story gets rejected.

But he just shook his head. "No," he said. "I don't think so."

Something John W. Campbell had written in that letter had really gotten to Harry—it had cut right to the bone. I don't think Campbell ever consciously tried to hurt writers whose work he rejected, but he was known to be tough...and now he had gotten tough on Harry.

Anyway, Harry told me that he wanted to be alone for awhile, so I left his place. I wasn't really worried. I had confidence that "Enslaved on Venus" would be published somewhere else. But I never saw that story make it into print, and Harry never mentioned it to me again. I think he trashed it along with Campbell's letter. It wasn't even found in his files.

Lawrence Bolger:

Harry Hapgood became a dinosaur. His literary career died because he couldn't adapt. The World War II paper shortage killed the pulps, so there went most of his regular markets, and the changes in the genre swept in by John Campbell, H.L. Gold, Frederik Pohl, and other editors made his kind of SF writing unpopular. Raymond Palmer continued to buy his stories for *Amazing* until Palmer, too, left the field in the late '40s. By then, science fiction had grown up.

But Hapgood didn't grow with the genre. His stories were pure romanticism. He paid no attention to scientific accuracy or character development. He persisted in trying to write Buck Rogers stuff. Other writers learned the new rules, changed their styles to fit the times, but Harry Hapgood wouldn't—probably couldn't—change chords. So while Robert Heinlein was creating his "Future History" series and Ted Sturgeon was writing classics like "Baby Makes Three", Harry was still trying to get away with space heroes and bug-eyed monsters. The more sophisticated SF mags wouldn't touch that stuff.

It was sad. He still went to science fiction conventions on the East Coast, but he was no longer surrounded by fans. They just didn't want to talk to him anymore. The magazine editors tried to tell him where he was going wrong, why they weren't buying his stories any more. I remember, at one SF convention in Philadelphia, over–hearing John W. Campbell patiently trying to explain to Harry that, as long as he persisted in writing stories which claimed that rockets could travel to another solar system in two days or that Jupiter had a surface, he simply could not accept any of Harry's work.

Harry never listened. He stubbornly wanted to play by his own rules. Gregory Benford once criticized science fiction which "plays with the net down", SF stories which ignore basic scientific principles like the theory of relativity. In Harry Hapgood's case, he was playing on a different court altogether. All he could write were stories in which lizard-men kidnapped beautiful women and the Space Navy always saved the day. But he was playing ping-pong among Wimbleton champs, and he wouldn't realize that he was in a new game."

Margo Croft:

After *Rocket Adventures* folded, I went down the street to work as an associate editor at Doubleday, helping to edit their mystery line. That was in '48. I had all but completely withdrawn from the science fiction scene by then, but I still had a few contacts in the field, people with whom I'd touch bases now and then.

Anyway...one of Doubleday's whodunnit writers lived in Boston and I occasionally took the train up there to meet with her. On one of those trips I had some time to kill before catching the train back to New York. I had my address book in my purse and Harry's number was written in it, so I called him up and told him I'd buy him lunch downtown. It was mainly for old time's sake, but also I wondered if he had recovered from the collapse of the pulp market. By then, I hadn't seen him in a few years.

Harry wasn't looking good. He had lost weight and he had started chain-smoking. He wore a suit which looked as if it had been new in 1939, and I knew it had to be his best suit. The last time he had made an SF magazine sale had been the year before. He wouldn't admit it, but I knew that he had been trying to pay the bills by writing articles for some furniture trade magazine. It was ironic. Harry, who had practically thrived during the Depression, was on the skids during the postwar boom. Ironic, but not funny.

It was a painful lunch. He didn't want to talk much. He knew I was paying, so he ordered the biggest item on the menu. It was probably the best meal he had eaten in months. I told him that I had married—my first husband, Phillip—and though he tried to take it well, I could see that he was disappointed. I suppose he had noticed that girlish crush I had on him ten years before, and was sorry now that he hadn't done anything about it then. (*Shakes her head.*) Poor man.

His personal life was a wreck, so I tried to talk to him about his writing. I told him that Doubleday was starting to publish science fiction and that they were looking for established authors; he should take a crack at it. He didn't say much, and I got the impression that he had lost interest in SF. Somehow that didn't make sense. Harry was a science fiction writer top to bottom. He should have jumped at the chance.

He had stopped at a newsstand before meeting me at the restaurant and he had picked up a handful of magazines. It was his usual reading matter—all the SF magazines—but in the stack was also the first issue of a new magazine which I had heard about through the grapevine. That was *Fate,* the UFO digest that Ray Palmer started publishing to take advantage of the flying saucer craze after he left *Amazing.*

Sure, it was the type of thing which Harry Hapgood would read. Nothing sinister about that. But I remember, over dessert, watching him absently pick it up and thumb through the pages. Then he casually asked me what it would take for him to write a bestseller.

"I'm talking about a science fiction novel," he said. "I mean, something that would sell like crazy."

Coming from Harry Hapgood, that would have been hysterical if it hadn't been so sad. I didn't really think he was capable of writing an SF novel that was even publishable — and it would be years before science fiction scratched the bestseller lists. But I told him that he had answered his own question.

"Write something that a lot of people will want to read," I said. The obvious answer, of course. Harry just nodded his head and kept flipping through *Fate.*

Joe Mackey:

I remember Harry's disappearance very well.

By then I was working as a draftsman for a refrigerator company in Boston, but I still lived downstairs from Harry, in that triple-decker in Somerville. I had gotten home from work and was settling down on the couch to read. Harry knocked on my door, stuck his head in, and said that he was going out for ice cream. Did I want to come along? I told him, no, thanks anyway, and so he left. I heard the front door downstairs open and close...and that was it. That was the last time I heard from him for five days.

Next morning I went up to his place for coffee before going to work—something I did every morning—and found his door unlocked. His lights were still on, but he was missing. I was a little worried, but I figured, what the hell. I turned off the lights and went to my job. But when I got home that evening and found that he still hadn't returned, I called the police.

Nothing was missing. His suitcase was still in the closet, his toothbrush was still next to the sink in the bathroom, there was even a half-finished furniture article in his typewriter. He had just walked out to get ice cream and...phhtt! Vanished. The cops searched the neighborhood, thinking he had been mugged, maybe killed and left in an alley somewhere, but there was no trace of him. He hadn't checked into any hospitals and the cab drivers didn't report picking him up anywhere. The newspapers reported his disappearance the next day, as a minor item buried in the back pages. Nobody seemed to be really concerned, though. Except me. I was worried sick about the whole thing. Y'know, maybe Harry was going to be found floating in the Charles River or something.

Then...well, you know what happened next. He turned up in the boonies of New Hampshire, saying that he had been kidnapped by a flying saucer.

A lone pedestrian, found on Route 202 in Hillsboro, was brought to Hillsboro Police Station Tuesday night, after he wandered out of the woods and flagged down a driver. The man, identified as a Somerville, Massachusetts, writer, has been sought by Massachusetts police as a missing person since last week.

Harold LaPierre Hapgood, Jr., 38, of 19 Waterhouse St., Somerville, was found on the roadside near the Antrim town line by the Rev. Lucius Colby, minister of the First Episcopal Church in Henniker. According to Hillsboro Police Chief Cyril G. Slater, Mr. Hapgood stumbled out into the highway in front of the Rev. Colby's automobile, waving his arms and forcing the driver to halt. The Rev. Colby then drove Mr. Hapgood to the Hillsboro Police Station.

> *Chief Slater says that Mr. Hapgood, a magazine writer, has been sought by the Somerville, Boston, and Massachusetts state police departments since Friday, May 7, when he apparently vanished after leaving his residence in Somerville. Chief Slater says that although Mr. Hapgood appears to be in good health, he was delirious when brought to his office. Mr. Hapgood claims that he was kidnapped by a space ship piloted by creatures from another planet...*

> — *Hillsboro News-Register*
> *Hillsboro, NH*
> *Thursday, May 13, 1948*

Lawrence Bolger:

Did Harry Hapgood really get kidnapped by a UFO? Not a chance. If he got kidnapped by anything, it was the Trailways bus he caught at the station in Boston.

When a reporter from one of the Boston papers retraced Hapgood's trail, he found that the driver remembered someone who looked like Harry getting on in Boston and getting off in Keene, New Hampshire. He used false names when he bought the ticket and when he checked into a hotel in Keene for four days, but his description was matched by the bus driver, the hotel clerk and chambermaids, even the waitress at the diner where he ate breakfast and dinner. The only thing which wasn't established was how he got from Keene to Hillsboro, so one can only assume that he hitched a ride...and it sure as hell wasn't in a flying saucer.

It wasn't an ironclad story at all. Hell, it was a blatant fraud. He didn't have a shred of evidence to support his claim that he had been teleported off the street in Somerville, taken into space in a UFO, and examined by strange little men for four days.

On the other hand, he didn't need any proof. The country was in the midst of its first big flying saucer flap, started by Kenneth Arnold's sighting of UFOs over Mt. Rainer the year before. There were a lot of true believers like the Fortean Society, and whenever newspapers or the Air Force debunked a sighting or a kidnap story, these people would claim that it was part of a government conspiracy to cover-up the UFO "invasion" or whatever.

HAPGOOD'S HOAX

Harry Hapgood knew what he was doing. First, he sold a first-hand account of his experience to Ray Palmer at *Fate*. After that story was printed and enough newspapers had written about his "ordeal", he wrote his book and sold it to a minor hardback publisher, changing his byline to H. LaPierre Hapgood so that he wouldn't get confused with H.L. Hapgood, Jr., the pulp writer.

(*Laughs.*) No one noticed the name change, because no one paid any attention to science fiction in those days. The only people who really knew that H. LaPierre Hapgood had started his career as a science fiction hack were SF fans. Since they were considered to be even further out on the fringe than the UFO cultists, no one paid any attention to them.

And what do you know? It became a runaway bestseller...

Margo Croft:

The odd thing about Harry's first book is, if you take it as science fiction, it's a pretty good yarn. His narrative skills, developed from all those years of grinding out stories for the pulps, really lent themselves to this sort of thing. It has an almost-convincing sense of realism. I mean, if you checked your skepticism at the door, you could have ended up believing him. And a lot of people did.

If Harry had applied himself to writing science fiction, he could have re-emerged in the field as one of the major writers of the '50s. (*Shrugs.*) But maybe he was fed up with science fiction. I dunno. I guess he was more interested in making money, at that point.

One of the funnier stories about the hoax was that, after Abducted to Space was published and made it to the bestseller lists, he got invited to be the commencement speaker at graduation ceremonies at some small liberal arts college in Illinois. As academic tradition sometimes has it, for his services he was presented an honorary doctorate in astronomy from the school. It didn't mean a damn thing, but Harry and his publisher milked it for all it was worth. So Harry overnight became Dr. H. LaPierre Hapgood, the professional astronomer. (*Laughs.*) He didn't even graduate from high school!

✳ ✳ ✳

When I awoke, I found myself lying in a circular chamber. The walls rose around me as a hemispherical dome, white and featureless except for a pulsing red orb suspended from the apex of the ceiling.

The room seemed to hum, just above the range of audibility. I was lying on a raised platform which seemed to be made out of metal, except that it was soft where I lay. I attempted to move my arms, then my legs, but discovered to my alarm that I was completely paralyzed. Yet there were no visible restraints on my arms or legs.

Then, directly in front of me, a section of the wall faded and became a screen. I saw the black expanse of outer space. In the center of the screen hung Earth, and I realized that I was thousands of miles out in space. I was terrified. How did I get here? What would be done to me? Most importantly, would I ever be released?

A few moments later, a low section of the wall to my right slid upwards, and the first of the Aliens slowly walked into the chamber ...

—H. LaPierre Hapgood
<u>Abducted To Space</u>

Joe Mackey:

Harry moved out of the place in Somerville as soon as he got the advance money for <u>Abducted to Space</u>, but by then he and I weren't on speaking terms. I was pretty upset with him by that time. I thought we were friends, but he had used me to establish credibility for that cock-and-bull story of his. Hell, when the reporters starting showing up to interview him about his experience, he would send them downstairs to interview me as a "reliable source". Of course, they never printed my opinion that he was making the whole thing up. Just the part about how I found his place empty one morning.

So I didn't really mind when he moved out to one of the ritzier parts of Chestnut Hill, but I did keep up with him, from a distance. I'm sure you know a lot of this already, right? After he and his publisher made a mint from <u>Abducted to Space</u>, he did <u>UFO!</u>, which was just a rehash of the first book, except that he embellished the story a little. Seems he "remembered" a lot of details in his dreams, which he claimed were buried in his subconscious by the aliens. That's a lot of horseshit—excuse my French—because I could see he was just recycling stuff from his old pulp stories. Probably had his copies of *Thrilling Wonder* and *Amazing* right there on his desk when he was writing the thing.

It was after he put out <u>Odd Visitors</u>, the third book, that he really went for the nugget. He started that UFO cult of his—whachacallit, the International Center for Extraterrestrial Studies—and soon had every dingbat in the country sending him donations. Ten dollars got you a mimeographed newsletter every couple of months, and a hundred bucks put you on a list of "honorary contactees".

The money was supposedly going for the construction of a "UFO spaceport" on some land he had purchased out in the western part of the state. The line was that, when the space arks arrived, they would land at the spaceport and take aboard human passengers for a voyage to another planet, which Harry called Nirvanos. Complete crap—but, y'know, there's a lot of mixed-up people out there who'll buy into just that sort of thing.

My wife and I drove out there one Sunday to check it out. Found a three-acre plot in Leicester, off a dirt road in the middle of nowhere. Just a big cleared cow pasture, surrounded by a barbed wire fence with an empty shack in the middle and a big billboard at the end. It had some weird symbols painted on it and was strung with Christmas lights, which some local kid was hired to switch on each night. And that was his spaceport.

I bet Harry spent no more than five hundred dollars on the thing...and he probably took a million to the bank, in donations from a lot of sick, gullible folks.

I can't tell you how much I despised the son of a bitch.

Margo Croft:

Harry dropped out of sight for about a dozen years, and while he did the UFO craze of the '50s ran its course. By the time Alan Shepard went up in space, flying saucers were a joke. The company which put out Harry's three UFO books went under—I think the publisher went to jail for tax fraud—and no respectable house would touch the ravings of Dr. H. LaPierre Hapgood. He kept his UFO cult going for a little while longer, after he moved it to Mexico to escape the IRS, but eventually it ran out of steam. On occasion I heard scuttlebutt about some millionaire American expatriate who had made his money writing UFO books, now living in a mansion-compound just outside of Mexico City, never seen by outsiders. I knew who he was, and I didn't give a damn.

Then it was 1965, and I had left Doubleday and was starting my own literary agency. I wanted to take on some science fiction writers as clients, so I started hitting the major SF conventions, trying to find the next Robert Heinlein or Isaac Asimov. I found myself at an SF convention in the Chicago area, in a private party filled with the hot young writers of the day—Roger Zelazny, Harlan Ellison, Larry Niven, some others I can't recall. The hotel room was crowded and smoke-filled so I went in search of a quiet corner of the room. And when I got there, I found Harry Hapgood.

He was old, old before his time. I was only a few years younger than him, but he seemed (*long pause*) so wasted. Used up, like something had been sucking blood out of him for fifteen years. If he were a millionaire, it didn't show. His clothes looked like they had been bought off the rack at Woolworth's, and he was so thin, so pale...I might not have recognized him if it hadn't been for his nametag.

"H.L. Hapgood, Jr.", it read. He had gone back to his old byline, but if anyone had recognized his name, they didn't come to meet him. "Hapgood" was a foul name to conjure in SF circles. Science fiction writers and fans had long been misassociated by the general public with the UFO crazies, just as they're now lumped in with the New Age crystal freaks. H.L. Hapgood was the name of one of their own, a writer who had turned Quisling and sold out to the lunatic fringe. In a crowded party, he was all alone. I couldn't believe that he had dared to show his face at an SF convention.

He recognized me at once. He might have even been waiting for me. I wanted to turn and walk away. But then he said my name, and I stayed. I sat down on the windowsill next to his chair, and listened to a dying old man.

He said...

(*Sighs*). I'm sorry. I can't go on. Will you turn off the recorder now, please?

✳ ✳ ✳

I've been asked, "Why did you try, when you knew ninety-nine percent of the people wouldn't believe you?" My reply, when it wasn't self-incriminating to answer the question, was simple. "You're missing the point," I said. "It doesn't matter if ninety-nine percent of the people won't believe you. It only takes the remaining one percent to make you a rich man."

I have done many terrible things to become rich, and I won't apologize for all of them. The New Hampshire hoax was only the first of many. I have deceived and manipulated countless people. I have no regrets about bilking total strangers for their money. If they were silly enough to send me money for the privilege of hearing more of my lies, then they deserved what they received. You get what you pay for.

Yet, for those whose friendship I betrayed, I feel a vast, unspeakable shame. The wealth I reaped is a poor substitute for the friends I have lost. The debt I owe them can never be repaid, even by the division of my estate.

The greater part of my estate, though, I bequeath to Minnesota State University, for the continuance of its English department's science fiction research program. My actions have tarnished the genre. Perhaps this will help to make amends. However, there is no reason why the program should be blackened by the name of a liar, which is why this donation will be made anonymously.

As for my three UFO books, I commend them to death. I have appointed Margo Croft to be my literary executer, and she has been instructed to make sure that they are never again reprinted. They will follow me into the grave, never again to rot anyone's mind.

As for my remaining work...Margo, you may do with them as you please.

> — Harold L. Hapgood, Jr.
> Last Will and Testament
> (Recorded July 28, 1966)

Lawrence Bolger:

Shortly after Harry Hapgood's funeral, the University sent a couple of graduate researchers from the SF program down to Mexico, to visit Hapgood's mansion. They went along with Margo Croft, who had yet to set foot in Harry's house, even though the two of them had reached sort of a reconciliation just before he died. Both our students and Margo were interested in the same thing, the vague reference to "remaining work" Hapgood had alluded to in his will.

Outside the high walls of the compound, a few of Harry's remaining followers were still holding vigil—wild-haired old ladies clutching frayed copies of <u>Abducted to Space</u>, intense young men with madness lurking behind their eyes, a smiling married couple wearing aluminum foil spacesuits, waiting for Harry's space ark to arrive and carry them to the promised land in the sky. Within the mansion, men were packing in crates his furniture and belongings — jade and porcelain vases, Spanish iron sculptures, Elizabethan tapestries—in preparation for Sotheby's auction of the estate. As Hapgood had directed, the house itself and its grounds would be donated to Mexico for a mental institute. Perhaps this was a final, wry joke on his part.

Margo and the researchers found Harry's office virtually untouched. Only the lawyers had been in there, to retrieve the file cabinets containing Harry's financial records. There was another file cabinet in the office, though, and a desk; in the drawers, they found the last literary work of H.L. Hapgood, Jr.

They counted sixty-four short stories and three novels: meticulously typed, almost all completed, and none previously published. All had been written since the early 1950's, most in the last few years of his life, when Harry was fighting his cancer. All science fiction...not a UFO book in the whole bunch. Enough writing to fill a career.

Yet there were no rejection slips in the files, nor were there copies of cover letters. No indication that Harry had ever submitted any of these stories to magazine or book publishers. It was as if he would write a story, then simply stash it away and start another one. Hapgood had lived alone; there had been no one to read his work.

Why? (*Shrugs.*) Who knows? Maybe he couldn't face rejection...he didn't want to see any of those stories come back in the mail. But they were good stories, nonetheless. Hapgood had obviously learned something about writing in the intervening years.

You know the rest, of course. Margo brought the manuscripts back to New York, and one of her clients culled the best short stories from the stack, edited them into a posthumous collection, and managed to get it published. The damn thing's been selling like crazy ever since. (*Laughs.*) Perhaps Harry's legion of UFO cultists is still out there, loyally buying multiple copies from the bookstores. That's the only explanation I have for the new book getting on the *New York Times* bestseller list last week. And now the same publisher is going to issue his novels in a uniform edition. They'll probably become bestsellers, too. So go figure...

So who got the last laugh? Maybe this is Harry's final revenge. His place in the genre's history has been revised, and hardly anyone out there remembers the New Hampshire hoax. That's the conventional wisdom. But, y'know, he didn't survive to see his new acceptance in the field. Literary success doesn't do you much good if you're dead, right?

Look at it this way. Harry always said that the UFOs were coming back to get him. And he was right. The flying saucers got him in the end.

ON THE ROAD: WAITING FOR THE END OF THE WORLD

(NOTE: In this 1993 reprint, the first names of the sources have been changed, and their last names were never used. They are, however, real people—AMS.)

"You can have peace. Or you can have freedom. Don't ever count on having both at once."

— *Robert A. Heinlein*

Sam and Regina are a young couple living in a middle-class section of Worcester. Sam's the supervisor of a machine shop; Regina works as a shipping clerk. They share a small apartment with a couple of cats, one of which is a not completely housebroken kitten. Regina likes Stephen King's novels and they've got all the film versions on videotape to play on their VCR. Both are amiable: Regina is the more soft-spoken of the two, and Sam has a good sense of humor and likes to laugh. They are, all in all, among the nicer married couples one could expect to meet in the city. You would never worry if they moved in upstairs from you.

They keep a large supply of canned goods and both are adept at first aid. They're learning how to preserve and can foods as well as the fundamentals of home gardening. They have studied numerous combat manuals, information packets from Civil Defense, and books on survival after nuclear war.

They are also well-armed. When they were married, Sam gave Regina a gold-plated Colt .22 revolver in a trophy box and Regina gave Sam an Uzi semi-automatic submachine gun. In a large closet, along with a large assortment of camping equipment, are two 30.06 hunting rifles with telescopic sights, four compound bows, a large crossbow with a telescopic sight and razor-tipped bolts, a hand-size crossbow, a Chinese AKS semi-automatic carbine with a folding stock, an AR-15 semi-auto carbine (the civilian version of the U.S. Army's standard combat weapon), two 20-gauge shotguns and enough ammunition to get them through the next World War. They also keep a loaded pistol beneath their bed.

Sam and Regina are survivalists, two of a number of people in the country who have decided that the future may be a dangerous place in which to live, and they have taken measures to prepare themselves for the worst.

"It was one of those things where you wake up one day and you start realizing that everything's not the way it should be, and you can more or less see things going downhill," Sam says, sitting on the couch in their apartment, holding Regina's hand with one with hand and scratching behind the Siamese kitten's ear with the other. "You get flashbacks from the stuff you learned in history class and everything's pointing to the decline of civilization."

While Sam believes that global nuclear war is the most immediate threat, he also thinks that it's possible that the United States and the Soviet Union may resolve their differences. Social collapse in the United States is a future he sees as happening right now, with the government losing touch with the citizens and the police being unable to prevent crime or protect the public.

"There's a lot of [scenarios] which could happen," he says, "anywhere from nuclear warfare to economic decline to governmental breakdown, where even the police are saying, 'Every man for himself.' Hopefully it will never happen. The thing with survivalism is that it could happen anytime, that nobody wants it to happen, not even the hardcore survivalists."

At the same time, Sam considers himself to be more realistic about survivalism than the types he calls "closet mercenaries," those just looking for an excuse to play out a fantasy role, who "want to go out and load that gun up and run out into the street—'There's the enemy, shoot!'" He says that at one time he stockpiled food relentlessly and had weapons all over the house. He had also been a member of a survivalist group in Westborough, but had quit when he realized that most of the group were simply venting personal frustration by indulging in war games in the woods. His extremism had leveled off when he realized that "it's not going to happen all at once."

"I had heard of it before I met Sam," Regina says, "and when I first started going out with him I thought he was a nut." Sam laughs. "I mean, he's got cupboards loaded with canned vegetables, all dated on the bottom with the month, day, and year, and I went, 'Whoa!'"

But then she started getting interested in staying alive if the worst were to happen. Sam has since trained her in the use of firearms and in hand-to-hand combat, and she has trained herself to handle first aid and outdoor skills. "I'm hoping nothing does happen," she says earnestly, "but if something were to happen and he were to get killed, I would have to learn to take care of myself."

The most visible factor, which most people focus upon when thinking about survivalism, is defense. Sam acknowledges that survivalism has attracted its share of gun nuts and paranoids, but at the same time he believes firearms are necessary. "If something ever did happen," he says, "the first major priority would be defense. It'll be a matter of supply and demand. If you have it, everyone else is going to want it, and if you want it bad enough to keep it you're going to have to defend it."

Sam says that even though his beliefs don't faze his friends, "My mother thinks I'm psychotic. She really thinks, 'If I'm going to die, I'm going to die.' I have a totally opposite opinion. I figure that, if you are given the idea to survive, you've got a fighting instinct to stay alive. Some people would just rather give up. They say, 'If the bombs drop, I'd rather be dead.'"

He believes that preparing for social collapse or nuclear war is essentially like taking along a first aid kit on a road trip—but a step further. "A lot of people are survivalists and just don't realize it," he says. "If they can see far enough into the future to see that a problem could happen and they prepare for it, then they're survivalists."

Regina takes an upbeat view toward their preparations for an uncertain future. "Some people look at a survivalist as being someone who is waiting for the worst to happen, someone who has a pessimistic view of the future," she says. "But if you look at it the other way around, it's more of an optimistic view of the future, because we're at least preparing to survive, and we have a better view of the future in saying that, 'Okay, we're prepared to live in what's going to happen in the future, and we're strong enough to do this.'"

WINTER SCENES OF THE COLD WAR

"Are you comfortable, Mr. Shaw?"

"Umm...yeah, I guess."

"Good. We'll try not to take very long with this, but we need to find out exactly what happened up there."

"Is this my debriefing?"

"Not in a formal sense, no. We just need to find out some details for the final report to the Director."

"Oh. Okay."

"I've heard it was rough."

"You could say that, yes."

The wind was picking up now, making the black, greasy cable over his head sing. The ski lift creaked as each sudden gust caused his chair to violently sway. Shaw, huddled on the wooden seat, looked down between his legs and watched the snow-covered mountainside passing by fifty feet below him. He clutched his skis, the poles, and the long Mylar bag containing his rifle closer to him. It was nearly impossible, but he briefly imagined the wind picking the chair off its runners, hurling it down, dashing him on the ice and rocks below.

"Tango Station to Frosty One, come in, please." He heard Brim's voice in the two-way radio headset he wore underneath his wool cap. "Come in please, Frosty One, over."

Frosty the Snowman. You're cute, Brim. "Frosty One, Tango Station," he replied between chattering teeth into the tiny mike dangling in front of his mouth. "We copy, over."

"How are you doing there? Over."

He was cold as hell, but that was nothing he was going to admit to Brim. "We're copacetic, Tango. What's the word? Over."

"No news, Frosty One. Big Bird report on Geronimo is negatory. Repeat, negatory. We're still green-for-go with your run. Do you copy? Over."

Shaw gazed through his yellow-tinted goggles at the line of empty chairs preceding him up Wachusett Mountain. He was almost at the summit now; it was visible as an opaque blur, barely discernable through the snow which sheeted around him. "Big Bird" was the Bell AB47G which had made a couple of fast, low-level passes over the slopes before the nor'easter had forced the helicopter away from the mountain, where the unpredictable wind patterns made flying especially dangerous. He was not surprised that the chopper had not spotted Geronimo. Even if the snow were not so thick, Weyler would have the sense to hide if he spotted the helicopter.

"We copy, Tango," he said to his headset mike. "Green-for-go. Frosty One over and out."

The chair dipped lower to the ground, passed a line of trees, and suddenly Shaw was at the summit, passing the lift station on his left. He spotted the red-jacketed lift operator through the window. He swung up the metal safety bar and jumped off, his boots crunching through several inches of new snow before resting on the packed ice beneath. He floundered out of the way of the chairs, dropped his equipment on the ground, and knelt to stick his booted feet into the snap-down bindings of the Rossignol telemark skis. The lift operator ran out to help him.

"I'm okay," he shouted to the kid, waving him away. "I'm fine." The lift operator — a college boy with an eager, innocent face — stopped and stared at him. Look, it's James Bond arriving to save the world. "Clear out!" Shaw yelled over the howling wind.

The kid backed away, then hurried to catch the next chair going down the mountain. Down to the base lodge, where there was a warm fire, Irish coffee, dry socks and perhaps a comely ski bunny with whom to cuddle. From up here, Shaw could not even see the foot of the mountain.

Shaw locked the heels of his boots down against the long, slender skis; now he had the leverage to make good turns on the sharp, steep curves just ahead. He stuck the tips of his poles deep into the packed snow—the wind buffeted against them, but didn't send them sailing—and unzipped the cover of his weapon: a Heckler and Koch G-11 sniper rifle, complete with an integrated Starlight scope, looking like something from a science fiction movie. Good FBI equipment.

He checked the fifty-round clip, then slung it by its strap over his left shoulder and under his right arm. Standing up, yanking his poles out of his snow, Shaw paused to check his bearings. To his left, at the edge of the treeline, was the top of Summit Loop, leading around the mountaintop to the Administration Road trail which, in turn, led to the North Road cut-off trail connecting to Balance Rock Road. Somewhere along those steep, winding trails was Charles Weyler.

"Okay, Charlie," he muttered. "Let's go skiing."

"Tell me about Charles A. Weyler."

"You mean it isn't in your files?"

"I want to hear what you have to say about him, please. For the record."

"Okay. Charlie Weyler was a Soviet sleeper, employed by the GRU. Your typical Harvard MBA yuppie type, except that he decided on an original approach to making himself a millionaire before age thirty. We first found out about him when he paid a discreet visit to the Soviet consulate in Boston in May, 1984, where he apparently made an offer to sell his services to the Russians. They checked him out, found that he wasn't doubling for us, and decided to take him up on his offer. They were interested in some work that a company called Biocybe Resources was doing, and they managed to...."

"Back up a step, please. What is Biocybe Resources and what has it been doing?"

"Hey, I know this is in your files already."

"Please answer the question, Mr. Shaw."

"Jeez...all right. Biocybe is a small company based at the Worcester Biotech Research Park which has been working in nanotechnology. Essentially, they've been developing a biochip...."

"I don't understand."

"Sort of an organic computer chip. That is, a microchip which isn't manufactured like a printed circuit, but grown in an organic culture, so that it resembles a human brain cell. Very advanced stuff. The point is, if something like this could be perfected and mass-produced, it would make computers smaller, faster, and cheaper to produce, and leave everything that we now call 'state of the art' in the dust."

"Okay. Go on."

"Well, Biocybe managed to produce a prototype of a biochip which it dubbed Ozymandias 88-F, or the Oz Chip for short. Since the Soviets have been lagging behind the West in computer technology for decades now, this is something they could really use. Charlie Weyler was its point man. He had been planted in the company as its marketing director and, when everyone was sure that the Oz Chip had been perfected to a certain point, they directed Weyler to steal the prototype and the plans."

"And you were there to stop him."

"I had been waiting for Weyler to make his move, yes."

"As the field agent handling the case."

"Yes. Of course."

✳ ✳ ✳

Shaw had been sitting in his Ford Escort just long enough to start getting bored when he spotted Charles Weyler leaving through the side exit of One Biotech Park and begin walking through the near-empty garage. The problem was, when Shaw got bored during stakeouts, he started to smoke again. Usually it didn't matter, but this time it was a serious mistake.

He had found some stale Merits squirreled away in the glovebox and was fumbling with the lighter—again wondering how GM could put a microprocessor in the ignition system and still fail to make a dependable, half-decent cigarette lighter—when he glanced up and saw Weyler heading for the silver BMW CSi parked a few slots away. The BMW was virtually the only other car in the lot this Saturday afternoon; it had cross-country skis and poles fitted into the roof rack and an old Bush/Quayle sticker on the rear bumper. At that moment, as Shaw was looking up from behind the wheel with his stupid cigarette hanging out of his stupid mouth, Charlie Weyler turned his head and looked directly at him.

Weyler quickly looked away. He walked a few more steps, then abruptly he broke stride and bolted for his car.

"Aw, shit!" Shaw yelled. The unlit cigarette fell into his mouth as he scrambled to unbuckle his seat belt and throw open his door. By the time he was out of his car, Weyler had revved the BMW's engine and was peeling out of his slot, sliding briefly on a patch of ice as he ripped out of the garage, heading for the industrial park's exit and, beyond, the safety of the weekend traffic on Route 9.

Shaw ducked back into his Ford, wrenched the key forward in the ignition and slammed his foot down on the gas pedal to hot-start the engine, and grabbed the radio mike from under the dashboard. "Station Baker to all units!" he shouted into the mike. "Geronimo is on warpath niner! Repeat, Geronimo is on warpath nine!"

✳ ✳ ✳

"And then you lost him. How did that happen?"

"The net we put up wasn't right for the situation. There was a lot of weekend traffic on Route 9...Spag's traffic, we call it here...and the two units were in the wrong places. Tango, the car across the highway from One Biotech in a convenience store parking lot, couldn't get across the four lanes in time. The other car, Delta, was in the breakdown lane up the street from the park. It was in the right place, but the timing was all wrong. Weyler spotted 'em, I guess, and swerved over into the passing lane. When those guys tried to cut him off, they got in a collision with a civilian who came barreling up the right lane. So Weyler managed to dry clean us and get away."

"I guess you weren't pleased."

"Hell, no, I wasn't pleased. If he hadn't spotted me in the garage, we could have nailed him before he made the highway."

"Then you admit fault for his escape?"

"That's what it sounds like, doesn't it? He pegged me. I could have had a bumper sticker which read, 'FBI Special Agent' and it wouldn't have been more obvious."

"Take it easy, Mr. Shaw. This isn't a formal case review. What made you think he was heading for Wachusett Mountain?"

"Well, it was a process of elimination. Weyler must have known that his cover had been blown. He was smart enough to know that we must have covered his drop zone at the Galleria, where he was to meet his handler that afternoon, and his condo in Holden..."

"You were trying to outguess him."

"Uh-huh. I figured that he needed to somehow get rid of the Oz Chip prototype which he had swiped from the Biocybe lab. We didn't know it then, but he also had copied onto a computer diskette the project notes for Ozymandias 88-F. He had to dump that stuff somewhere, which meant that he had to arrange an alternate drop with his handler. We knew also that he had a cellular telephone in his car, so he could get in touch with his handler."

"Go on."

"It was sort of dumb luck. I had spotted his cross-country skis on the roof-rack of his car. His dossier had already established that he was an expert skier, and we already knew that he had gone cross-country skiing in Rutland State Park that morning. What better way to drop the Oz Chip than to arrange a zone that he could reach by skiing to it? Some place his handler could reach as well, where they could make the hand-off with only a few people around? Well, there was only one place that he could get to in a hurry which met that description...."

"Wachusett Mountain."

"That's right. Right off I-290, which he could reach from Route 9 and I-190."

"Not a bad guess."

"It didn't suck, no."

"But you didn't take the weather into consideration, did you?"

"To tell you the truth, I didn't even notice that it had started to snow."

The young woman behind the counter of the ticket booth stared at the photograph of Charles Weyler for a moment, absently adjusting her wire-rimmed glasses. "Yes, I've seen him. He was here...um, about an hour ago."

"Where did he go?" Shaw asked impatiently, his hands shoved in the pockets of his parka. "Did he buy a lift pass?"

"Yeah...wait a minute, no." She thought it over. "No, I sold him a trail pass."

"A trail pass? For the cross-country trails?"

"Yes, sir. I remember because he was carrying his own skis and poles." Her eyes squinted as she sought to recall the memory. "And a blue gym bag, too. He looked like he was in a hurry. He went that way." Leaning over the counter, she pointed to the beginning of the cross-country trail, just beyond the rental shop. "About an hour ago," she repeated. "I'm not in any trouble, am I?"

"No, ma'am. Thanks for your help." Shaw took the photo back and slipped it into his pocket, then turned and hurried back to the parking lot of the ski area. A cold wind snapped snow into his face, and icy slush was filling his shoes. He muttered obscenities under his breath and zipped his jacket up to his neck.

Brim, the Boston field office agent who had been in the Tango car which had been hung up in traffic during the botched interception on Route 9, was standing next to Weyler's BMW, talking to one of the state police officers from the Holden barracks who had arrived at the scene. Two more FBI agents were working over the sleeper's car: the doors, the trunk hatch, the hood, and even the gas tank cover were wide open as the cleaning crew methodically searched the vehicle. Under normal circumstances the BMW would have been hauled to the Springfield field office to be torn apart, with every loose piece of lint inspected and cataloged, but there simply wasn't time for such painstaking work.

Men and women in multicolored ski tights and carrying downhill equipment sauntered past the BMW, transfixed by the activity until they were each shooed away by another state trooper. Brim saw Shaw trudging towards them, excused himself from the trooper, and shuffled over past the police cruiser parked behind Weyler's car. "Good hunch, buddy. You got a cigarette?"

"Naw, I just quit." Shaw stamped his feet in the snow to keep warm. "We're still in a mess. The girl at the ticket booth..."

"Hey, Shaw! C'mere!" One of the cleaning crew, Kadrey, was crawling out of the BMW as they turned around. As Shaw hurried over, Kadrey held out a small plastic bag over the roof of the car. Shaw took the bag from his hand and peered inside. Within the bag was a bullet.

"Under the front passenger seat," Kadrey said. "Forty-five. There's some little scrapes on the sides that say it was loaded into a loose clip."

Shaw gazed at the round. There were a number of different firearms which used clip-loaded .45 caliber ammo, from Saturday night specials to submachine guns, but the absence of a gun in the presence of a bullet meant one thing for certain. Charlie Weyler was armed.

"Things just got tougher," Brim murmured, looking at the bullet. "Weyler must have gone to the summit. Either he's up there, or he's gone by now."

Shaw gave back the baggie to Kadrey, turned around and walked off, Brim following him. "No. He got here about an hour ago and bought a trail pass," he said, thinking aloud. "Maybe...perhaps Charlie was going to meet his GRU contact at the summit for the drop."

Brim looked at him. "Then if Charlie's on the trails..." He stopped and grinned. "That's a big mountain. He couldn't have gotten to the summit in an hour. And if no one is being let on the lifts, then we've got him. He can't meet his handler, right?"

Shaw had stopped and was gazing up at the mountain. The light snowfall which had started when he was in Worcester was rapidly turning into a nor'easter. The last radio weather forecast he had heard had stated that massive storm fronts from both the Great Lakes and the Atlantic seaboard were converging over New England; already the storm was being predicted as being the worst since the blizzard of '78. Low, sullen grey clouds were scudding across the sky, and already the summit was beginning to white out. Although the ski lifts were still running, to keep the cables from freezing solid and snapping, the runs were being closed. The ascending chairs were empty, and the red-jacketed ski patrollers were herding the last downhillers off the mountain.

""Uh-huh," Shaw said. "But we're still in trouble. If Weyler gets to the summit and doesn't find his contact, he'll dead-drop the Oz Chip. Find a tree knoll or a rock to stash it under, then find another way out. Someone else will come back and retrieve the chip later." He shook his head. "There's no two ways around it. We're going to have to get Weyler on the mountain."

Brim glanced up at the mountainside. "Great. How the hell are we going to do that?"

Shaw shrugged. "Only one way, bub."

"We weren't aware that you knew how to ski cross-country, Mr. Shaw."

"I picked it up when I worked for the Denver field office, my first job for the Bureau. It's a hobby. I never thought I would have to use it for an assignment."

"Had you ever skied Wachusett Mountain before?"

"No. This was the first time for me."

"That's funny. How could you have known that there was a cross-country trail there, if that was the case? Wachusett is mainly known for its downhill runs."

"Well...um, I had always meant to try out Wachusett. I just never got the chance, until this instance. Not that it really mattered, though. When I bought my gear in the ski shop, I got a good map of the mountain. That's when I saw that one could reach the cross-country trails from the summit. That was a break, since otherwise I would have been trying to catch up with Weyler from the bottom of the mountain. Since he had a long head start, that would have been almost impossible. This way, all I had to do was head down the mountain and intercept him on his way up."

"I see. Of course, you were able to equip yourself for the mission from your car trunk."

"Uh-huh. Headset radios, the Heckler and Koch...they were in the trunk. All I had to get were the skis and the warm clothing. I had to buy that, since they didn't have telemark cross-country skis in the rental shop. Um...I put it on my Treasury card, but if the Bureau wants me to reimburse it for the expense..."

"Don't worry about it now. I'm curious about your radio trouble, though. Tango Station lost contact with you at one point. Why did that happen?"

"I dunno. I think I went out of range or something."

When he had reached the intersection of the Summit Loop and the Administration Road trail, in the densest part of the forest about one-third of the way down the mountain, he stopped, impaled his poles in a drift and unlatched his heels from the skis. It was a relatively level slope from here on; now he needed to use Nordic techniques, rather than alpine.

The wind was broken by the trees, but he could still hear it whining through the snow-fleeced timber, softly creaking against the branches, sending heavy falls of snow plummeting to the ground from on high. Somewhere not far away in the forest something splintered and crashed. The woods were silent, if only for a moment, until the wind picked up again and the trees recommenced their death-rattle protests.

Shaw unzipped his parka, took off his right hand glove and reached into the warm cavity next to his stomach. He found the tiny radio unit strapped near his waist. He raised his left hand and put it on the headset mike, and gently rubbed his forefinger against the padded mike pickup. "Tango, this is Frosty, do you copy?" he murmured, caressing the mike with his finger.

"Frosty...Skkhh...Tango, we...shhkk...please give your..." he heard through the headphones.

"Tango, this is Frosty, do you copy?" Shaw repeated. He listened to a few more garbled words, then he calmly switched off the radio, pulled the headset out from under his cap and lay it around the base of his neck. He pulled his poles out of the snow, pushed his right foot ahead, planted his right poles next to it, pulled forward as he pushed off with his left foot and pole, and continued his journey down the trail.

Shaw skied around a shallow curve in the snowed-over roadway and found himself at the top of a sharp rise. Far below was the top of a scenic overlook. Just beyond that, to the left, was the intersection of the North Road cut-off trail, leading to Balance Rock Road. He stopped here and scanned both sides of the trail before finding what he was looking for: a large boulder just off the right side of the trail, a perfect natural blind. He skied off the path to the boulder and checked its position. Perfect. He could see straight down the rise, but was himself concealed by the boulder.

He unlocked the toes of his skis, pulled his boots loose from the bindings, and carefully lay the skis and the poles against the side of the boulder. Then, kneeling behind the huge granite rock, he unshouldered the Heckler and Koch and assumed a sniper's crouch, resting his right elbow on his knee, his right hand supporting the rifle's plastic stock.

He switched on the built-in Starlight scope and peered through the eyepiece. An early twilight was falling on the mountainside, but the scope magnified the available sunlight filtering through the storm clouds, rendering the trail as clear as if it were noontime on an uncloudy day. Shaw spent a few minutes fine tuning the sight, aligning the electronic crosshairs on a distant tree stump, then he switched the fire-control lever to single-shot and settled down to wait. The snow hissed around him. Except for the moaning wind, the silence was almost complete.

His timing had been good; he did not have to wait longer than fifteen minutes before Weyler made his appearance. It had taken him about this long to make his way uphill, from the first cut-offs on the lower trails at the base of the mountain to Balance Rock Road, then up the snow-packed roadway to the more difficult grade of the North Road trail. As Shaw watched, a lone skier emerged from the forest.

Charlie Weyler paused at the overlook, perhaps to catch his breath, then began to struggle up the sharp rise. Leaning forward, laboriously planting his poles in front of him as he herringboned his skis one step at a time, he forced his way up the trail. The wind rippled the loose red fabric of his ski parka and tossed the absurd orange pommel on the top of his cap. There was something dangling on a strap under his right armpit. Shaw could not clearly see what it was, but he had little trouble making a good guess.

Shaw waited until Weyler was about fifty yards from his position, studying him through the cross-hairs of his scope, before he decided that it was time.

"Weyler!" he shouted.

Weyler's response was automatic. He dropped his poles, simultaneously kicked his racing boots out of his bindings, and hurled himself to the right, heading for the trees. Right move, maybe, but definitely in the wrong direction. Shaw let Weyler get a few feet, then he carefully swung his rifle to the right and squeezed the trigger twice. There was barely any recoil, little more noise than two loud grunts, but two caseless Dynamit Nobel rounds slammed into the trunk of a birch about three feet from Weyler.

Weyler stopped and whirled around, swinging up the Ingram MAC-10 submachine gun Shaw had figured he would be packing. Crouching low, Weyler swung the Ingram in an arch from left to right. The compact gun snarled and .45 calibre bullets chopped through the trees. A couple of shells ricocheted off the boulder in front of Shaw, but the FBI agent only ducked back a little. Weyler was firing blind.

"Are you through yet, Charlie?" Shaw shouted.

Weyler held his crouch, defensively moving his gun back and forth, but not firing. "Is that you, Shaw?" he shouted back.

"I want the chip and the disk, Charlie," Shaw called back. "Drop 'em on the path and you get to live."

Weyler was nervously glancing in Shaw's general direction. "That was you in the garage, wasn't it?" he said loudly. "What's the matter, don't you guys trust me?"

"You sold out to the Chinese, pal," Shaw answered. "That was really stupid. I'm making sure you keep your first deal. Dump the chip and the disc in front of you, then you can take the trail down the other side to Harrington Farm. Your other car's still down there, I checked for you this morning."

Weyler was still hesitating, but now he was looking straight at Shaw's boulder. He had focused in on the sound of Shaw's voice. "Don't be a jerk, Charlie," Shaw said. "Do it now or you're screwed."

Shaw carefully flipped the fire-control lever over to full-auto. He watched through his scope as Weyler, keeping his right hand on his gun, carefully reached his left hand around to his right pocket. Ripping open the Velcro flap, he reached inside and first pulled out a small grey capsule. He slowly pulled it out and stuck one end into the snow, then he withdrew a 3.5-inch plastic computer diskette and dropped it on the ground next to the capsule containing the Oz Chip prototype.

"As I understand, we have yet to locate the Oz Chip or the diskette."

"That's correct. My guess is that Weyler managed to conceal them somewhere on the mountain before I found him."

"Hmmm. Why do you think he did that?"

"Well, he probably figured that, with the nor'easter coming in, his handler wouldn't be able to make it to the summit. So he must have dead-dropped them somewhere on Wachusett for another agent to retrieve later. Like I said, in a tree knoll or under a rock...God knows where they are now. They weren't found on his body."

✳ ✳ ✳

Then, as Shaw anticipated, Weyler suddenly lunged to his left, bringing up his Ingram to fire in the direction of Shaw's voice.

Shaw never gave him the chance to shoot. Keeping the crosshairs centered on Weyler as he moved, Shaw squeezed the trigger of his rifle. The Heckler and Koch growled and ten rounds slammed into Charlie Weyler's chest. Blood sprayed, and Charles A. Weyler, former director of marketing for Biocybe Resources and double-agent for the People's Republic of China, was hurled backwards. His dead body hit the trail and rolled downhill several feet, leaving a bloody streak along the virgin snow. The echo of the gunfire was lost in the woodland before his corpse came to rest.

"He fired first?"

"That's correct, yes."

"How did it happen?"

"I warned him to stop, but he was armed with an Ingram MAC–10 and he immediately commenced to fire. I managed to reach a boulder off the trail, and I fired back once I was able to get a clear shot. I'm sorry, but I was not able to take him alive."

"I see. You then searched his body and were not able to find the stolen items?"

"Yeah, that's right. I then followed his path down the mountain, trying to find where he might have hidden them, but by this time it was getting dark and the snow had buried his tracks. In fact, I consider myself lucky that I managed to get down to the lodge without getting lost up there."

"Yeah, that is lucky."

"Has anyone found the Oz Chip yet?"

"No. We still have a team searching the mountain, but like you said, it could be anywhere. Four feet of snow buried everything."

"Uh-huh. That's unfortunate. But since he's dead, the opposition can't find it either."

"That's the upshot, isn't it? Nobody gets the thing."

"That's right."

* * *

Shaw slung the rifle back over his shoulder, picked up his skis and poles, and tromped out of the woods to the trail. He stopped next to where Weyler had been shot, knelt and picked up the Oz Chip and the computer diskette. He opened his parka and slid them both into an inside pocket where they were well-hidden by the jacket's thick padding, then closed his parka and bent to put on his skis. It would take him only about an hour to return to the base of the mountain. By then it would be completely dark, and the snow was still coming down. His alibi would be perfect.

He latched down his heels, carefully stood and picked up his poles, then pushed off, gliding down the hill past Weyler's body. He barely glanced at the other GRU sleeper as he passed, but favored him with a final piece of advice.

"Don't mess around with Moscow, pal," he murmured.

✳ ✳ ✳

"I think that's all for my questions, Mr. Shaw. Thanks for your cooperation."

"My pleasure. I hope it's been helpful."

"It has been. Oh, and by the way, congratulations on your commendation. I understand you're flying to Washington tomorrow to receive it from the Director."

"Thanks. Yeah, it's quite an honor."

"Is there anything that goes along with it?"

"No pay raise, if that's what you're asking, but I am going to take a little vacation once I get through in DC I need to take a break."

"I'm sure you deserve it. Any place special?"

"Italy. I've always wanted to see Venice."

ON THE ROAD: CAN YOU COUNT THE ANGELS DANCING ON A PIN?

Occasionally, one stumbles across some fact about the natural world that boggles the mind, a fact which is not at all obscure, but still more overwhelmingly impressive than any manmade construct on the face of the earth. Suddenly, our own existence—which at times seems to fill the entire universe, distorting Galilean physics so that Sun, planets and stars revolve around the great Me—is put in its proper perspective.

An example of this is the distance between our planet and the nearest star besides the Sun, Alpha Centauri. The distance is 4.3 light-years, an easily graspable sum...until one realizes that this translates to approximately 25,800,000,000,000 miles. It means that even if a starship could travel at the speed of light (an impossibility according to the theory of relativity), it would take that ship more than four years to get to our solar system's neighbor. When one further finds that the Milky Way galaxy, which we inhabit in a remote region of one spiral arm, is 100,000 light years in diameter, and that this translates to approximately 600,000,000,000,000,000 miles...well, the ten trips that men have taken to the Moon, which is only about 240,000 miles away, no longer seem quite so impressive.

On the opposite end of the scale, there is the microscopic universe.

In the basement of one of the ten laboratory buildings at the Worcester Foundation for Experimental Biology is a means of seeing into the micro-universe, just as radio telescopes allow us to peer at the galaxy. This is a transmission electron telescope; it is used by the research scientists at the foundation to study a variety of organisms which exist on a range of size below that which normal optical telescopes can detect.

The electron microscope looks, and works, nothing like a normal microscope. It is a large cylinder, about a foot in diameter and about six feet in height, which is mounted above a wraparound console where the operator sits. Unlike an optical microscope, which focuses light onto a specimen, in an electron microscope a stream of electrons is shot from the top of the cylinder down through the specimen to be studied, which is mounted on a slide inserted in the middle of the scope. An image of the specimen is thus transmitted to a screen at the base of the microscope and can be studied through a magnifying eyepiece mounted in front of the screen. There is also a camera attached to the microscope so that photos may be taken of the specimen.

During a public tour of the foundation's facilities given one afternoon to a handful of visitors, a postdoctoral fellow in cellular biology, Dr. Harold Hoops, demonstrates the massive instrument. The object of the demonstration is a cross section of a sample of *Cilia flagella,* a microorganism which is, as Hoops puts it, "a plant which thinks it's an animal." *Cilia flagella* is grown in the labs at the foundation by scientists because its cellular makeup closely resembles human cells, yet it is far less expensive to whip up and study a batch of microflora than it is to obtain and study human cells. It also has a hair-like structure which is easy to observe, Hoops explains. A drawing of the microorganism resembles a grape with a long, skinny tale.

As Hoops explains the function of the electron microscope, he passes around the slide on which the specimen is placed. This is the visitor's first encounter with the dynamics of size associated with this kind of work. The specimen is mounted on a metal grid in the slide which is permeated with hundreds of holes. The diameter of the grid is almost exactly the diameter of the character "o" printed on this page; it has about three hundred holes per inch. The specimen placed on this grid appears as a barely perceptible mote of dust, so tiny that even when the slide is held up to the light it is practically invisible.

Hoops slips the slide with the grid and specimen into a slot halfway up the trunk of the microscope, then briefly works the pushbutton controls on the console until the image appears on the microscope's screen, a small oval surface behind a Plexiglass cover. He then adjusts the magnifier, which is much like a conventional microscope, until he is able to make out the *Cilia flagella*. Then he lets his visitors peer through the lens.

Now the dust mote has expanded to the apparent size of a small discus, magnified one-half million times by the microscope. What is seen is a roughly oval-shaped collection of cells: a single large, tan oval surrounded by a cluster of tiny, bubble-like cells. It almost looks like an alien creature brought back to Earth by an interstellar probe, not like something born on this planet.

The visitors step up, one at a time, to peer at the tiny critter, and someone finally asks how big it is. Hoops calmly says that the *Cilia flagella* measures about 200 nanometers in diameter; each bubble-like cell lining its epidermis measures about 25 nanometers.

Now, one has to stop and realize just how big a nanometer is: one billionth of a meter. Compared to the size of an atom, of course, something 25 nanometers in diameter is roughly comparable to the diameter of Earth compared to the diameter of the solar system. The most powerful electron microscope in existence has only recently photographed the shadowy outlines of an atom. So, in comparison to an atom, an object 25 nanometers in diameter is a big, fat bulls-eye.

But, on the other hand, to be able to see something about 25,000,000,000 times smaller than the length of a meterstick is nothing to sneeze at. It's a feat inversely equivalent to radio astronomers' recent accomplishment of being able to detect a planet orbiting a star some hundreds of light-years away. One stares down the lens at a specimen of *Cilia flagella* and wonders just how in the hell anything that small can possibly be alive.

A matter of scale, that's all. Sometimes we, as a race, are a bit too intellectually self-centered for our own good. Everything "real" is that which is at our eye-level or within our personal reach. "Big" is the height of the John Hancock Building. "Little" is something you have to get tweezers to pick up. "Far away" is, say, a drive from Worcester to a relative's house in New York; "very far away" is a plane trip to London. Therefore, distances such as light-years or sizes like nanometers are beyond our everyday perspective. The mind can hardly grasp the fact that vast universes exist just outside the safe confines of our own solar system...or in a speck on the tip of your fingernail.

This is, perhaps, what science is ultimately good for: putting things in their proper proportions, for stealing away from us our blind, self-aggrandizing delusions of our importance in the space of things. After all, little *Cilia flagella* doesn't know, or care, that vastly larger, more "important" creatures exist all around it, just as we are ignorant of its existence.

Kinda takes you down a notch, doesn't it?

TREMBLING EARTH

"OKEFENOKEE SWAMP, also spelled Okefinokee, primitive swamp and wildlife refuge in southeastern Georgia and northern Florida...The swamp's name probably is derived from the Seminole Indian word for 'trembling earth', so called because of the floating islands of the swamp."
— *Encyclopedia Britannica*

1. *The Mesozoic Express*

A high-pitched chop of helicopter rotors from somewhere high above the treetops, the faint invisible perception of drifting on still waters, hot sunlight on his face and cold water on his back. An amalgam of sensations awakened Steinberg, gradually pulling him from a black well. Awake, but not quite aware; he lay in the muddy bottom of the fiberglass canoe and squinted up at the sunlight passing through the moss-shrouded tree branches. His clothes were soaked through to the skin and even in the midday sun he was chilled, but somehow that didn't register. All that came through his numbed mind was the vague notion that the canoe was drifting downstream, bobbing like a dead log in the current of the...

Where was he? What was the name of this place? "Suwannee Canal," a voice from the fogged depths of his mind informed him. Yeah. Right. The Suwannee Canal. How could have he forgotten? "Up Shit Creek and no paddle," another voice said aloud. It took him a moment to realize that the voice was his own.

The helicopter seemed to be getting closer, but he couldn't see it yet. Well, if I'm drifting, maybe I need to find a paddle. Steinberg sat up on his elbows and his eyes roamed down the length of the canoe. Muddied backpacks, soaked and trampled sleeping bags, a rolled-up tent, a propane lantern with a broken shield, a black leather attache case which for some reason looked entirely appropriate for being here...but no paddle. Must have fallen out somewhere back there. Yes, Denny, you're definitely up Shit Creek...

"That's a joke, kid." The new voice in his head belonged to Joe Gerhardt. "Laugh when the man tells you a joke..."

No. Don't think about Joe. Don't think about Pete. He shook his head and instantly regretted it; it felt as if someone had pounded a railroad spike through his brain. He winced, gasping a little at the pain. Aspirin. Tiffany has the aspirin bottle...

Where's Tiffany? The thought came through in a rare instant of clarity. Where's Tiffany? She was right behind me when we were running, she was right behind when...

Something bumped the bottom of the canoe, behind his head. He slowly looked around, his gaze travelling across sun-dappled water the color of tea, and saw the long, leathery head of an alligator just below the gunnel of the canoe, slit-pupilled green eyes staring up at him. Startled, Denny jerked upward a little and the gator disappeared beneath the water without so much as a ripple. If his hand had been dangling in the water the gator could have chomped it off, yet somehow Denny wasn't frightened. Just Old Man Gator, coming by to visit his canoe without a paddle here on Shit Creek...

Where's Tiffany?

Now the sound of rotors was much louder. The exertion and the headache had drained him; feeling as if all life had been sucked from his bones, Steinberg sank back into the bottom of the canoe, the back of his throbbing head finding a cool puddle of water. Mosquitos purred around his ears and before his eyes, but he couldn't find the strength to swat them away. He stared back up at the blue sky and listlessly watched as the twin-prop Osprey hove into view above the treetops. I know that thing, he thought. I was in it just yesterday. Me...and Joe Gerhardt...and Pete Chambliss...

And now he really didn't want to think about them. Especially not about what happened to them, because if he did he might remember the sound of jaws tearing into flesh, of screams that go on and on and on...and if that happened he might just jump right out of the canoe and take his chances with Mister Old Man Alligator, because even if he didn't know what happened to Tiffany, he knew what happened to Gerhardt and the senator. And that's not a joke, kid. That's not funny at all...

He watched as the Osprey grew closer and found to his relief that there was a little mercy to be found in Shit Creek, because his eyes closed and he rediscovered the bliss of oblivion.

✳ ✳ ✳

Transcript of the Kaplan Commission Hearings on the Assassination of Senator Petrie R. Chambliss; Washington, DC, July, 2004. George Kaplan, former United States Attorney General, presiding. From the testimony of Daniel Steinberg, former legislative aide to Sen. Chambliss.

KAPLAN: Thank you for being here with us today, Mr. Steinberg. The Commission realizes that you're involved in serious litigation in regards to this incident, so we're especially appreciative of the effort you've taken to speak to us.

STEINBERG: Yes, sir. Thank you, sir.

KAPLAN: Many of the facts of this case are already known to us, Mr. Steinberg, both from public accounts and from the testimony of witnesses before you. However, there has been a great deal of confusion and...might I add for the benefit of the press pool reporters in the hearing room...obfuscation on the part of the media. There has also been some lack of corroboration among the testimonies of prior witnesses. It's important for this Commission to get the facts straight, so some questions we might ask you may seem redundant. So I hope you don't mind if...well, please bear with us if we seem to be beating the same ground that's been beaten before.

STEINBERG: Not at all, sir...I mean, yes, sir. I understand completely.

KAPLAN: Good. To start with, Mr. Steinberg, can you tell us why you and the late Senator Chambliss went to the Okefenokee National Wildlife Reserve last April?

STEINBERG: Well, the senator felt as if he needed to take a vacation, sir. We...that's his staff and the senator, sir...I mean, his Washington staff, not the campaign committee...

KAPLAN: We understand that. Please, just relax and take your time.

STEINBERG: Uhh...yes sir. Anyway, Pete...that is, the senator...had just come back from Moscow, after his discussions with the new government regarding the unilateral nuclear disarmament treaty. Everyone had been burning the candle at both ends, both with the Moscow arms talks and the presidential campaign. The campaign for the Super Tuesday primaries was coming up and the Senate had gone into recess, so Pete...I'm sorry if I'm so informal, Mr. Kaplan...

KAPLAN: That's quite all right. We understand that you were on a first-name basis with the senator. Carry on.

STEINBERG: Anyway, Pete wanted to take some time off, do something just for fun. Well, he is...I'm sorry, he was...an avid outdoorsman, and he had taken an interest in the paleontological research being done at the Okefenokee Wildlife Refuge because of his position on the Senate Science Committee, so he decided that he wanted to take a canoe trip through the refuge and...

KAPLAN: Excuse me, Mr. Steinberg. The chair recognizes Dr. Williams.

FREDERICK WILLIAMS, Ph.D; Chancellor, Yale University: Mr. Steinberg, you say the senator wanted to visit the Okefenokee Swamp. I can understand that he might have wanted to take a break by taking a canoe trip, since I'm an aficionado of the sport myself, but I'm still not sure of his intent. Was it because he wanted to paddle where he had not paddled before, or was it because he wanted to see the dinosaurs?

STEINBERG: Well, it was both, sir. I mean, he could have taken a raft trip down the Colorado River, but he had done that a couple of times before already. And he did want to see the dinosaur project and it was going to be in a Super Tuesday state besides, so the exposure couldn't hurt...well, he just came to me and said, "Denny, what do you say to a little canoe trip down South?"

DR. WILLIAMS: And what did you say?

STEINBERG: I said, "Sounds great, Pete. Let's go."

DR. WILLIAMS: And you didn't consider this to be an unsafe venture?

STEINBERG: No, sir. Not at the time, at least. Why should I?

DR. WILLIAMS: I would think that you would want ask yourself that question, seeing as how you're facing a charge of second-degree murder...

✳ ✳ ✳

The Bell/Boeing V-22 Osprey which had carried them the last leg of the trip, from Moody Air Force Base in Valdosta to the Okefenokee National Wildlife Refuge, had barely settled on the landing pad when Pete Chambliss unsnapped his seat harness and stood up in the VTOL's passenger compartment. "Okay, boys, let's go!" he yelled over the throb of the rotors.

Before anyone could stop him, the senator had twisted up the starboard passenger door's locking lever and was shoving open the hatch. Denny Steinberg looked across the aisle at Joe Gerhardt. The Secret Service escort only shrugged as he unsnapped his own harness, then stepped to the rear cargo deck to pick up Chambliss's backpack. Gerhardt had barely lifted it from the deck when it was grabbed from his hands by Chambliss. Hefting it over his shouter, Chambliss turned around and pounded Denny's shoulder with his huge right hand.

"C'mon, Denny!" he boomed. "Let's go get that river!" Then Chambliss jumped out of the Osprey and was trotting out from beneath the swirling blades of the starboard nacelle. Two officials from the Deinonychus Observation Project, a man and a woman who had come out to the pad to greet their honored guest, seemed unprepared for the sight of Senator Petrie R. Chambliss—dressed in jeans, red flannel shirt, and hiking boots—suddenly appearing in their midst, grabbing their hands and pumping them so hard it seemed as if he were about to dislocate their elbows. Their expressions, to Steinberg's eye, matched that of the Soviet Foreign Minister's, the first time Kamenin had met Pete Chambliss in Moscow last week. The senator from Vermont was an awful lot to take in one dose.

The Osprey's pilot, who had watched everything through the door from his right-hand seat in the forward compartment, looked at Steinberg. "Is he always this enthusiastic?" he asked loudly, grinning at the young aide from beneath his mirrored aviator shades.

Steinberg nodded and the pilot shook his head and looked away. Just then the rear cargo raised open and a ground crewman pulled down the loading ramp. A handful of men and women tromped up the ramp and walked to the front of the aircraft. They pulled down the folding seats, barely taking notice of Gerhardt and Steinberg. One of them, a redneck with shoulder-length hair, glanced out through a porthole, then looked at Denny. "That the guy who's running for president?" he yelled. Denny nodded and the redneck nodded back. "Sheeit, I shoulda gotten an autograph. Hey, Jake, gimme a cigarette!"

The guy he called Jake, who had a greasy mustache and wore a John Deere cap, fumbled in his shirt pocket for a pack of Marlboros. "Buy some yourself sometime, Al. Hey, Greg! Take us outta here, willya? This place gives me the creeps!"

"Lemme get rid of the VIPs first, okay?" The co-pilot leaned around to look at Denny and jerk his thumb at the open passenger hatch. "Get going!" he yelled. "We gotta go up again! Time to take the part-timers home and come back for feeding time!"

Before Denny could ask what the co-pilot meant, Gerhardt had grabbed both of their packs and clambered out of the VTOL, holding his straw cowboy hat down on his head against the prop-wash. Steinberg picked up the attache case containing the senator's communications system and clumsily lowered himself from the hatch, then dashed out from under the rotors. As soon as he was clear, the engines roared to a higher pitch and the Osprey—Air Force surplus, dark grey with a scowling, cigar-chomping Albert Alligator from the Pogo comic strip stencil-painted on its fuselage above the words *"The Mesozoic Express"*—lofted into the air once again. Denny watched as the hybrid aircraft cleared the treetops, then the two engine nacelles swiveled forward on their stub wings to their horizontal cruise configuration and the Osprey roared away, heading east.

Steinberg turned around and scanned the compound in which he had just been deposited. Once, when the refuge had been open to the general public, this had been a big tourist attraction of southeastern Georgia: campgrounds, a picnic area, a visitor's center and museum, a concession stand and a boat ramp. Now it looked like the last outpost of civilization on the edge of the Early Cretaceous period. The visitor's center had been converted into a main lodge for the University of Colorado science team which presently used the place; the concession stand and picnic tables were gone, replaced by Quonset hut dorms, laboratories, generator shack and the chopper pad. Fresh stumps showed where trees had been felled throughout the compound, which was enclosed by a high fence topped with concertina barbed wire. Beyond the fence was the vast morass of the Okefenokee Swamp—and it didn't look like the sort of place where Pogo Possum and Albert Alligator were likely to be found.

Eying the phlegm-like strands of Spanish moss dangling from the cyprus trees on the other side of the fence, swatting away a bat-sized mosquito from his face, Denny Steinberg—legislative aide to Senator Petrie Chambliss, alumnus of George Washington University, owner of a two-bedroom condo in Georgetown and an antique apple-red '68 Corvette Stingray which he'd rather be polishing right now—had to ask himself: How the hell did I get talked into this trip?

Because he had mentioned to Pete that he was once a canoe instructor at a Boy Scout camp in Tennessee, that's how. And because the senator didn't forget anything. And because if the man goes to the White House next year, Denny Steinberg wanted a new office just down the hall and that meant buttering up the presidential frontrunner whenever possible. Even if that entailed going along on a canoe trip in a godforsaken hellhole like this.

Chambliss was still talking to the project officials, his arms folded across his broad chest; he wore a faintly bemused smile on his face as he listened to them, probably because—if prior experience were any indicator—someone was overexplaining things to Chambliss. There was a natural assumption people made that, because Pete Chambliss looked like a barroom armbreaker, he also had the mind of one. At six-foot-four, with the muscle-bound build of a former Notre Dame linebacker, Chambliss did have the appearance of a former bouncer. When he had first taken office, his political foes on the hill had tried to smear him with the label "Conan the Senator" until it quickly became apparent that Petrie Chambliss was no Green Mountains hillbilly. Thuggish looks notwithstanding, the Democratic chairman of the Senate Foreign Relations Committee was now regarded as one of the most intelligent legislators in Congress. It was only when Chambliss ventured beyond the Beltway that he ran into people who equated physical size with lack of intelligence. That was a handicap in this race; in his sound bites, the big lug came off as King Kong trying to sound like Thomas Jefferson. The staff was still working on him, for instance, to be careful to use "isn't" instead of his habitual "ain't." But so far, the polls hadn't shown this to be a major liability. Considering that the Republican incumbent sounded like a squeamish English teacher from a prep school for girls, perhaps the voters were ready for—as one *Washington Post* columnist put it— "the reincarnation of Teddy Roosevelt."

Joe Gerhardt was standing about a dozen feet away with their backpacks, casually gazing around the compound. As Steinberg watched, the Secret Service man reached into the pocket of his denim jacket, pulled out a pack of Camels, shook one loose and stuck it in his mouth. Steinberg sauntered over, and Gerhardt held out the pack to offer him a smoke.

"No, thanks." Denny cocked his head towards Chambliss. "Shouldn't you be with your man?"

The two of them had met only this morning when they had boarded the senator's chartered jet at Washington National. Instead of the normal business suit favored by the agency's dress-code, Gerhardt was wearing jeans, a T-shirt and denim jacket. Otherwise, he had the bland, unnoticeable features of a Secret Service bodyguard. He didn't look at Denny as he lit his cigarette with a butane lighter. "Nope," he replied drily. "Not unless he changes his mind."

"What's that supposed to mean?"

"Remember when we took a pee-break at the airport? Well, the senator told me that, considering that this is his vacation and that Secret Service protection was something that had been forced on him, he would prefer it if I didn't shadow him."

Gerhardt exhaled pale blue smoke. "'It's okay if you're nearby,' he said, 'But if you're close enough to be able to tell the color of my piss, then you're too close.'" He grinned and shrugged. "We aims to please."

"Maybe you should be a little less considerate." Steinberg lowered his voice. "In case nobody briefed you earlier, Pete's been in the thick of some crucial events lately. There's a lot of people who don't appreciate his role in the strategic arms talks and a few would like to see him dead before he becomes president. We've got the death threats to prove that somebody out there means business..."

"The New American Minutemen Enclave. Uh-huh." Gerhardt ashed his cigarette and cast a wary eye at the compound. "Yessir, this looks just like a NAME stronghold to me, all right."

"Cute. It would be appreciated if you were a little more observant, okay? Like, do your job? Pay a little attention?"

Gerhardt nonchalantly blew smoke through his nostrils and looked down at the muddy ground. "Looky here, son..."

With his left hand, he opened his jacket a couple of inches. The butt of a submachine pistol stuck out from the holster suspended under his left armpit. "That's a Ingram MAC-10," he softly drawled, "and I don't think I need to give you a lecture on its specs to show you I mean business, too. But if you don't believe me, there's a buzzard on top of that big cyprus behind me, on the other side of the fence." Gerhardt didn't look around. "If you want, I'll pick it off for you."

Denny peered in the direction Gerhardt had indicated. The tree was about a hundred yards away and the turkey vulture in it was nearly invisible against the sleet grey sky; Steinberg saw it only once as it lazily stretched one taloned foot up to scratch its long head.

"That's okay," Steinberg said. "I'll believe you."

"Good. Then stay off my case. I know what I'm doing." Gerhardt took another drag from his cigarette, dropped it on the ground and stomped on it with his boot before walking off. "The senator wants to start his vacation. I think I'll join him."

Chambliss was walking away with one of the officials. The other one, the woman, was walking towards them. Gerhardt politely touched the brim of his cowboy hat as she passed, then looked back over his shoulder at Steinberg. "Get the packs, won't you, son?" he called out. "The man needs his bodyguard."

Steinberg looked down at the three forty-pound nylon backpacks and the attache case piled on the landing pad. Gerhardt was through with playing porter; now it was his turn.

"Son of a bitch," Denny hissed. He managed to pick up two of the heavy North Face packs and was struggling to grab the top loop of the third pack between his forefingers when the young woman, whose blond hair was braided down her back and who had the longest legs this side of a Ford Agency model, recovered the third pack from his fingertips.

"Let me get that." Before he could object, she grabbed the third pack and effortlessly hoisted it over her shoulder. "Looks like your pal left you in the lurch."

"Umm...yeah. Something like that." Feeling vaguely emasculated, but nonetheless relieved to be free of the extra burden, Steinberg grasped the handle of the attache case. "I take it you're with the science team?"

"Uh-uh," she replied, starting off in the direction of the lodge. "I'm Tiffany Nixon, refuge naturalist. Team Colorado's out at the Chessier Island observation tower. Bernie Cooper's taking the senator and your friend out there now. We'll catch up with them after we dump this stuff at the lodge."

A few dozen yards away, Bernie Cooper—a thin, balding man in his early forties—was climbing into the driver's seat of an open-top Army surplus Hummer, with Pete Chambliss taking the shotgun seat and Joe Gerhardt climbing into the rear. Gerhardt glanced in their direction and gave him a sardonic wave, then the Hummer started off down the narrow paved roadway leading to the side gate. Denny suddenly didn't mind; he was trading one ride with an SS asshole for another with one of the most beautiful women he had met in a long time. Things were beginning to look up...

"Secret Service?" she asked.

"Hmm? Excuse me?"

"Your friend." She nodded towards the departing vehicle. "Is he the Secret Service escort or are you?"

"Him. I'm the senator's aide. He's the one packing a gun."

She frowned as they reached the lodge's front porch. A second Hummer was parked out front. "If he shoots at one of my gators," she said as she dropped the backpacks next to the pine railing, "I'm going to smack him upside the head with a paddle. C'mon inside and I'll give you a gronker. Bernie had the ones for the senator and the other guy in his jeep, but I was supposed to take care of you."

Tiffany opened the screen door and led him into the cathedral-ceilinged lodge. Ah, so, he thought as she walked down a short hallway past a couple of offices to a supply closet. This was the guide they were going to have for their canoe trip. "From what I hear, alligators aren't the worst things we have to worry about out there," Steinberg said nonchalantly, watching as she unlocked the door with a key. "If he shoots at any lizards, it's going to be one of the big ones."

To his surprise, Nixon gave a bitter laugh. "Okay by me. I didn't ask for those monsters to be put in here." The naturalist turned on the light, picked a couple of plastic yellow cartridges the size of cigarette packs off a shelf, and handed one to him. "Clip this on your belt and switch it on when I tell you. You know what it's for?"

Steinberg nodded. He had already been told about the reflex inhibitors. When the dinosaurs were still in their infant state, pain-inducers guided by Intel microchips had been surgically implanted in the pain centers of their brains. The tiny nanocomputers were powered by hemodynamic microgenerators which kept the batteries perpetually charged by the blood flow to the brain. The inhibitors— for some reason called "gronkers"—also held Intel nanochip boards, wired to short-range radio transmitters fixed to the same frequency as the receivers in the pain-inducers and, once switched on, were continuously transmitting a signal on that bandwidth.

If one of the dinosaurs came within a hundred yards of a person wearing an inhibitor, the aversion program hardwired into the microchip nestled deep within the dinosaur's cranium automatically sent a painful electric charge into the beast's nervous system...and if the big bastard didn't get the hint and kept coming, the charge continued at quickly increasing intensity until, at approximately one hundred feet, voltage sufficient to knock it cold was delivered into its brain.

The idea was to allow the researchers to get near enough to the deinonychi to observe them at close range without imperilling themselves. Steinberg knew the technology was proven and sound, but it still made him uneasy to trust his life to a plastic box. Idlely turning it over in his hand, he noticed a strip of white masking tape on the side; written on it was the name NIXON. "Hey, I think I got your...uh, gronker. Why do you call 'em that anyway?"

"Um? Oh, it doesn't matter." Tiffany was already clipping the other unit, marked STEINBERG, onto her belt. Once Denny had fastened his own inhibitor to his belt, she gave it a quick tug to make sure it was secure. "They all work the same," she added. "Don't worry about it. If the ni-cad battery dies, it'll beep three times before it goes down. If that happens, tell one of us and we'll get you out of there. Just don't lose it, okay?"

"Why do you...?" he repeated.

"Because when they get zapped, they go 'gronk' just before they fall down." She switched off the light, relocked the door and walked past him towards the front door. "Well, you guys came here to see some dinosaurs. So let's go meet Freddie and his playmates."

* * *

From the testimony of Bernard Cooper, Ph.D.; Professor of Paleontology, University of Colorado, and director of the Deinonychus Observation Project.

REP. PAT McCAFFREY, R-IA: I'm probably the least informed person on the Commission about the project, Dr. Cooper. If you don't mind, would you please tell in layman's terms how you and your colleagues managed to revive three dinosaurs from their fossil remains? Isn't that a bit like squeezing blood from a rock?

DR. COOPER: Well, it's a bit of a misunderstanding to typify all fossils as dead rock. Back in the 1980s, it was discovered from the Coleville River dig in Alaska that certain fossils contained what are known as biomarkers...infinitely small patterns of the amino acids which were contained in the original bones. Certain chemical processes are used to detect and isolate these amino acid patterns, and from them we were able to discover intact DNA sequences. The first attempts were made on the remains of duckbill dinosaurs found in the Coleville River dig, but the real success was made when the University located the remains of three deinonychi at an Amoco drill site on the Alaskan North Slope...

REP. McCAFFREY: That's...ah, Freddie, Jason, and Michael, correct?

DR. COOPER: Yes, ma'am, that's correct. We were quite excited to make this discovery, of course. Up until then, the only deinonychus remains to be found had been in the Morrison Formation in Colorado, so it was quite remarkable to find three more of this species in Alaska...although perhaps not quite so remarkable in hindsight, since the duckbill had been from the Late Cretaceous and deinonychus comes from the Early Cretaceous, so really they weren't so far removed in time, considering the tectonic dispersal of Northern Hemisphere landmasses following the breakup of the ancient Asiamerica supercontinent when...

REP. McCAFFREY: I appreciate your enthusiasm for the subject, Dr. Cooper, but would you please keep to the matter at hand? The revival of the, uh...how do you say that?

DR. COOPER: Deinonychi, ma'am. Sorry to digress. Well, to make the story short, we found that the three fossils each had remarkably intact biomarkers which allowed us to isolate their DNA patterns. Using bird DNA as the general mold, you might say, we were then able to genetically replicate the patterns found in the fossils. From there, it was relatively easy...although it really wasn't that easy...to clone living cells of each deinonychus we had found, and from those cells we were finally able to reconstruct their fetuses. It's...um, all detailed in the final report to the National Science Foundation which is part of this testimony. The project reached success in 2002 when Jason was born at the University of Colorado, shortly followed by the revitalizations of Freddie and Michael.

REP. McCAFFREY: I see...I'm curious, Dr. Cooper. Although it has no direct bearing on this matter, how did these three...um, dinosaurs...get to be named Freddie, Jason, and Michael?

DR. COOPER: Well, ah...(*Coughs*) One of the graduate researchers on the project was a fan of horror movies and...uh, given the rather bloodthirsty tendencies of the species, he dubbed them with the names. They seemed appropriate to most of us and so they stuck. It was humorous...um, at the time, that is.

REP. McCAFFREY: "Rather bloodthirsty tendencies". So you were aware from the beginning that we were reviving a dangerous breed of dinosaur. Is that correct?

DR. COOPER: Ummm...yes, ma'am, I have to say that's correct. But we were certain that we would be able to contain them from doing any real harm during the observation period.

REP. McCAFFREY: You were certain...(*Sighs*) God save us from fools and research scientists.

✳ ✳ ✳

There was a lockbox attached to the fence next to the gate, and above it was hung a large wooden sign. As Tiffany Nixon climbed out of the driver's seat of the Hummer and unlocked the box, Steinberg read the sign:

DANGER!

NO UNAUTHORIZED PERSONNEL
BEYOND THIS POINT!

Enter this area with EXTREME CAUTION! Stay on the roadways or the boardwalk at all times. Make no unnecessary noises. Do not smoke. Food is absolutely forbidden. Menstruating women and persons with untreated cuts or scratches should avoid this area.

Wear your inhibitor at ALL TIMES! In case of failure, proceed to this gate AT ONCE and LEAVE THE AREA IMMEDIATELY!

Log in when you enter the area and log out when you leave.

Failure to comply with any of these regulations may subject you to criminal prosecution under federal law, punishable by fines (up to $1,000) and/or jail sentence (up to 1 year).

On the bottom margin, someone had hand-written in pen: "Please do not feed or harass the dinosaurs." And someone else had scrawled below that: "Dinosaurs! Please do not eat or harass the humans!"

"You've got some funny people working here," Steinberg muttered.

"If you say so." Nixon signed them into the logbook within the box. "You can turn on your gronker now." Steinberg reached down, pushed a switch on the little unit, and watched as a green status light came on and the gronker beeped once. Nixon did the same, then she pulled a two-way headset radio out of the box and fitted it over her ears. She touched the lobe where the bone convection mike rested against her upper jaw, softly said something that Steinberg didn't catch, then locked the box and walked around in front of the cart to unlock the gate and swung it open. Steinberg obligingly drove the Hummer through the gate and Nixon shut the gate behind them and relocked it.

The roadway was getting more narrow now, invaded by dense vegetation which not been trimmed back in some time. They passed picnic sites which had been usurped by tall grass and weeds; a wooden sign with an arrow pointing to the Peckerwood Trail was almost completely overwhelmed by vines. Through the trees and underbrush he could see aluminum fencing and rows of coiled razorwire. The park which time forgot. "So tell me," Steinberg asked. "How did a nice girl like you...?"

"Get in a swamp like this?" Nixon cast him an amused glance. "I haven't heard a line like that since I quit going to health clubs." She swerved the Hummer around a pothole in the road. "Gotta fix that sometime," she observed. "I hope this isn't a pick-up scene, because it's too weird if it is."

"What? Me?" he protested. Yet that was his intent, whether he cared to admit it or not. Studying her out of the corners of his eyes, Denny couldn't help but to fantasize about a neat little sexual encounter over the next couple of days. A one-night stand in a tent, perhaps; the great outdoors already did things to his libido. Pete wouldn't mind—since his divorce two years ago the senator had made time with some of the more desirable women on the Hill, discretely out of view of the press—and the trip shouldn't be a total loss. But he was careful not to let on how close to the mark Tiffany had come. "This is probably much the same thing as a gym," he murmured, waving a hand at the jungle around them. "The reptiles here are only bigger, that's all."

"How true." She paused thoughtfully. "I was a lawyer before this. Contracts attorney with Meyers, Larousse & Sloane in Atlanta. I was your typical sixty-hour-a-week legal droid, working my butt off to become a full partner and unhappy as hell...all I really wanted to do was paddle a canoe around the Okefenokee on the weekends. I spent each week shuffling paperwork and waiting for Friday when I could load up my canoe and head down here." She shrugged. "So one day I decided to pull the plug. Turn life into one long weekend."

"And become a naturalist in a wildlife refuge? That's a switch."

"I know. The partners still haven't figured it out. Ask me if I care what they think. Anyway, I had been working here for about two years when the Interior Department decided to turn the refuge into a research center for the project. They canned most of the staff when they closed the place to the public, but as luck would have it they still needed a naturalist who knew the swamps, so they kept me around."

Denny nodded his head, but remembered something she had said earlier. "But I take it you're not happy about the dinosaurs."

"Take it any way you want," Tiffany said noncommittally. She slapped the steering wheel with her hands. "So here I am...and here we are."

The other Hummer was parked next to a trailhead; she steered their own vehicle off the road, switched off the engine, and climbed out. As Steinberg got out and joined her on the edge of the raised wooden boardwalk leading into the brushes, he heard the clatter of distant rotors. "C'mon," Tiffany said, heading down the boardwalk to a gate in the fence. "It's almost time for the main event."

"Hmm?" Denny shaded his eyes with his hand and peered up at the sky. Was that the Osprey coming back? The swamp seemed more dense now, as if the green maze were moving in around them like the fronds of a pitcher plant curling in around its prey. "What's that?"

"Feeding time," Tiffany said. "You'll love it." She opened the unlocked gate and looked over her shoulder at him. "Just like a budget hearing back in DC."

It was the second time that day he heard about feeding time, but she was already striding down the boardwalk before he could ask what she meant. He hurried to catch up with her.

From the testimony of Dr. Bernard Cooper:

KAPLAN: We realize that you're upset with Rep. McCaffrey's characterization of the project as reckless, in regards to the species of dinosaur which your team revived...

DR. COOPER: "Upset" isn't the word for how I feel, Mr. Kaplan...

KAPLAN: ...yet you have to realize that the burden of proof is upon you to convince this Commission that the project was not reckless, that you had taken adequate safeguards to protect visitors to the refuge...

DR. COOPER: Mr. Kaplan, the primary goal of Deinonychus Observation Project was not to establish a dinosaur petting zoo. When the Department of the Interior leased the Okefenokee refuge to the project, we did our best to make sure that the specimens would be isolated from the outside world and that the scientists conducting the observations would be thoroughly protected from the dinosaurs. Besides the fact that the Okefenokee Swamp was the most available site which approximately matched the natural environment of the Early Cretaceous era, it was also selected because of its isolation. Safety was a top priority and a considerable part of our NSF budget was spent on just that priority. The refuge was hemmed in with high fences with limited access to the swamp. Waterways such as Suwannee Canal were equipped with underwater fences to keep the dinosaurs from swimming out, even though this species isn't amphibious by nature. Roads were blocked to prevent vehicles from entering so that entrance to the refuge could only be made by aircraft. The specimens themselves were surgically implanted with the electronic inhibitors I described earlier. Every precaution imaginable was taken to prevent injury or death to anyone entering the refuge...

KAPLAN: And yet...

DR. COOPER: Please allow me to finish, sir. We anticipated that we might have some privileged visitors to the project, such as members of Congress who oversee the National Science Foundation, and we were thoroughly prepared to make certain that they were safe. However, I must point out to the Commission that we did not expect that a presidential candidate might decide to spent his vacation with us, let alone one who might be a target for assassination by a right-wing extremist group. We did not invite Senator Chambliss and his party to the refuge. To be quite blunt, Mr. Kaplan, if it had been within my power to do so, I would have refused to let him in.

KAPLAN: Then why did you allow the late senator to visit you?

DR. COOPER: Because the project is at the mercy of congressional funding, and we need all the friends on Capitol Hill we can get. You know the old saw about where an 800-pound gorilla wants to sit? Mr. Kaplan, with all due respect to the deceased, he was an 800-pound gorilla. He sat wherever he damned well pleased.

* * *

Under the rattle of the approaching aircraft, Steinberg heard the voices of the science team as he and Nixon arrived at the end of the boardwalk.

"Pack acquired at three-ten degrees northwest, downrange two–point–two miles..."

"Onboard telemetry good. We've got a clear fix. They're still in the trees..."

"Okay, bring in the Osprey for the drop..."

The observation platform looked like a giant pinewood treehouse, perched fifty feet above the ground on the big toe of the foot-shaped Chessier Island. A high steel fence and more razorwire surrounded the platform; Denny was suddenly made uncomfortably aware how exposed they had been while on the boardwalk. One of the men on the platform noticed Steinberg and Nixon and buzzed them through the boardwalk gate. Nixon led the way up the spiral stairway to the top of the platform.

The swamp opened up before him as a vast, primordial prairie. The plain of floating peat moss had been here for seemingly countless years, its mass having gradually bubbled up from the bottom of the swamp to form an almost-solid surface. The edges of the clearing were fringed with pine and cyprus trees draped with Spanish moss; the prairie was covered with high, yellow grass which rippled like ocean waves as a warm breeze wafted across it. The rippling grew more intense as the Osprey came in over the treetops and hovered above the plain. A covey of white sandhill cranes, startled by the VTOL's arrival, lifted off from the ground and flapped across the prairie straight towards the tower, irritably honking their distress, until they veered away from the tower and disappeared beyond the trees.

Under the canvas awning stretched above the platform, a couple of researchers were standing ready around their instruments: tripod-mounted Sony camcorders, Nikon cameras with humongous telephoto lenses, shotgun mikes, a dish antenna all pointed at the prairie. At a bench behind, a young man with a goatee beard and a ponytail was watching the screens of two Grid laptop computers on a bench, hardwired into a couple of CD-ROM datanets. The reels of a old-fashioned tape deck slowly turned, while a couple of monochrome TV monitors showed closeups of the swamp.

Chambliss and Gerhardt were standing with Cooper behind the

scientists, watching all that was happening before them. Like almost everyone else on the platform, they had high-power binoculars draped on straps around their necks. Stepping over the tangled cables on the floor of the deck, Steinberg walked over to them, hearing Cooper speak in a low voice: "...dropping them in just about..."

"Sorry I'm late, Pete," Denny interrupted. "I had to..."

Chambliss impatiently shushed him. Cooper irritably glanced at him, then continued. "The pack won't emerge until the Osprey's gone," he said quietly. "They're pretty shy about the chopper and they tend to hide from it, but once they come out they'll make pretty quick work of the bait. It's not much of a challenge for them. That's why the team has to record everything. Everything happens too fast to make many on-the-spot calls."

Denny watched as the Osprey settled down to within a few feet of the peat moss surface. Although its landing gear was lowered, the aircraft never actually landed on the swamp, undoubtedly because the floating surface of the swamp would never sustain its weight. The rear cargo hatch cranked open and he could dimly make out one of the crew members climbing out to pull down the tail ramp. Steinberg ducked beneath Chambliss's line of sight and scuttled over to Gerhardt. "What's going in?" he whispered.

"Feeding time at the OK Corral," the Secret Service agent murmured, still watching the swamp.

"I keep hearing that. What are they feeding 'em?"

Gerhardt looked at him and said, "Mooooo..."

Steinberg glanced down at one of the close-up monitors in time to see the bait being led down the Osprey's ramp by the crewmember: a full-grown cow, its bovine head twisting back and forth as it was dragged out of the hatch by a rope around its neck. "I don't fucking believe this," he murmured.

"There's a ranch in Folkston where they're kept," Tiffany supplied. He hadn't noticed that she had slid up beside him. She handed a spare pair of binoculars to him. "Did you know there's an overabundance of cattle in the country?" she asked softly. "This is how they get rid of the surplus. Feedstock for the dinosaurs." She smiled grimly. "They're not vegetarians and Purina doesn't make Dinosaur Chow, even if they would eat it. And they won't touch dead meat. They like their food fresh, if you know what I mean."

"Don't they get enough to eat out there?" Gerhardt asked.

"Are you kidding? They'd knock off every bear and deer in the refuge in a week if we let them forage and the ambient ecosystem would be shot to hell. Even the gators are too scared to take 'em on." She grimaced. "Not that the fuckers don't try," she added.

"Hmm? The gators?"

"The dinosaurs. They're eating the swamp alive. That cow's just subsistence rations for them." There was an expression in her face which was hard to interpret; there was something in her eyes which was hidden as she raised her binoculars to study the prairie.

Once the cow was on the ground, about two hundred yards from the platform, the crewman hastily pushed the tail ramp back into the Osprey and pulled himself into the hatch. He looked like he was in a hurry and Denny couldn't blame him one bit. The Osprey ascended, twin rotors counter-rotating like scimitars, and peeled away toward the distant compound. Abandoned in the middle of the prairie, the cow watched the aircraft depart. It lowed once, a lonely sound which the shotgun-mikes picked up, and it made a few tentative steps across the wobbly earth until its instincts took over and it began to graze on the tops of the high grass. The ASPCA would just love this, Steinberg thought as a chill swept between his shoulder blades.

"We've got movement at three-twelve degrees northwest," the Team Colorado researcher watching the computers said. "Downrange two-point-one miles and closing. They're coming in."

"Okay, it's lunchtime." Cooper absently twirled his index finger in the air. "Recorders on. Andy, logon DinoRAM. Look sharp, boys and girls."

As the researchers switched on the camcorders and focused in on the cow, the young man behind the computers tapped codes into one of the Grids which brought a new, map-like display onto one of the screens. Looking over his shoulder, Steinberg recognized the general geography of the Chessier Prairie, with tiny blinking spots denoting the locations of the heifer and the three monsters lurking just out of sight in the far treeline.

"It's called DinoRAM," Cooper quickly said to Chambliss. "It runs off the transceiver in their inhibitors. We use it to mimic the feeding habits of Jason, Michael and Freddie. In the collect mode Andy's running, we can instantly file new data from this day's feeding activity, then rerun it through the computer at our leisure, putting in different stimulae, weather variables and so forth to see what kinds of results emerge, sort of like a simulator. Nice little program."

Chambliss dubiously massaged his chin between his fingers. "Kind of hard on the cows, though, isn't it?" he asked, but Cooper didn't seem to hear him. Denny was about to add his own comeback when one of the researchers spoke up from the camera array.

"Movement on the treeline," she snapped, peering through binoculars at the far side of the clearing. "Three-thirteen degrees northeast and...okay, they're out of the trees."

"What type of approach?" Cooper asked, leaning on the back of Andy's chair to watch the computers.

"Walking," Andy replied. "They're bunched together, standard triangle formation." Three blue dots were diagrammed on DinoRAM's screen; he opened a window in the corner of the display and studied a graph. "Seventy-three-point-three percent probability that Freddie's in the lead. Lauren?"

The young woman who had made the sighting chuckled. "Good call. Freddie's still leader of the pack. Guess he won another argument with Jason."

Raising the binoculars to his eyes, Denny watched the prairie. At first he couldn't see the pack. Then they moved, and he could make out three sleek, man-sized shapes at the edge of the trees. "Damn, but they're small," he murmured aloud.

"You were expecting Godzilla?" Gerhardt whispered back. But he nodded in agreement. "Yeah. Cute little fuckers, aren't they?"

Suddenly, the three deinonychi began to sprint forward, running through the high grass towards the cow. "Here they come," Lauren said as the team members operating the camcorders tracked to follow them. "They're beginning to spread out..."

"Three-prong attack," Andy murmured, watching his screens. "Michael's heading southeast, Jason's cutting off the southwest, and Fred's going straight in for the kill."

Steinberg's mouth dropped open. "Jesus!" he said aloud. "You mean they're organized?"

"They're not dumb animals," Tiffany said quietly.

Suddenly the deinonychus to the far right changed course, veered in closer to the cow. "Hey!" Andy cried out. "Mikey's going for it! He's going to get that cow first!"

"Keep your voice down," Cooper said calmly. He studied the action through his own field glasses. "Jack, Jeff, keep a camera on Michael but make sure you follow Freddie and Jason. Don't let any of them out of your sight." The grad students behind the camcorders swiveled their instruments to keep all the dinosaurs in their viewfinders.

Now Steinberg could clearly see the deinonychus pack: each was about six feet tall, with light brown skin mottled with dark red tiger stripes, running erect on muscular hind legs, slender forearms tucked in close to their chests. They were somehow smaller than he had expected, but their very weirdness somehow made them look much larger, even from the distance. Although each had a total length of eleven feet, they only stood six feet high; the rest was a long, sinewy tail which lashed about high in the air. He had read that they didn't weigh very much, either: an average of 150 pounds, which accounted for their ability to stride across the floating ground without sinking.

In fact, they could have been mistaken as being harmless mini-dinosaurs—surely not as formidable as the ruling carnivorous dinosaurs of their time like the allosaurus or the albertosaurus—were it not for their heads. Long and wedge-shaped, with wide, wild eyes under bony ridges and massive jaws which seemed perpetually frozen in a demonic grin, exposing razor-sharp teeth. One look at that face, and all notions of cuteness disappeared: these were creatures which nature had designed to be killers.

Strangely, they somehow seemed more avian than reptilian. Of course they would, he reminded himself. They're ancestors to birds, aren't they? Yet knowledge of that clinical fact didn't help to shake his unease. They were too goddamn alien...

By now the pack was close enough that they could be seen without the aid of binoculars. The breeze shifted just then. It was either because of the wind shift, or because it heard the swift approach of its killers, that the cow looked up. Seeing Jason coming in from in front, the cow quickly turned and made a waddling effort to run in the opposite direction—only to find that route cut off by Michael and Freddie. Braying in terror, the heifer clumsily veered again and began to gallop toward the observation platform. "Oh shit, bossie, don't come this way!" one of the camcorder operators hissed.

"Forget about the bait, Jack. Keep your camera on Michael and Freddie." Cooper was intently watching the two deinonychi, who were practically running neck-and-neck now. "Well, now. Let's see if they'd rather fight or feed."

Freddie's massive head suddenly twisted about on its long neck and, in apparent mid-stride, it snapped savagely at Michael. The shotgun-mike picked up the rasping sound of its teeth gnashing together. Daunted, the other deinonychus slowed abruptly and peeled off as Freddie continued to careen forward at full charge.

"Looks like a little bit of both," Andy surmised.

"Did we get that?" Cooper asked Jack. The researcher, his eyes fixed on the viewfinder, gave him the OK sign with his thumb and forefinger. "Well, Freddie, first blood goes to you again," Cooper added softly. He sounded like a dog owner proudly watching his golden retriever bring down a rabbit. Denny looked around at Tiffany to say something, but the naturalist had turned around and was looking in the other direction, away from the killing ground.

Steinberg looked back just in time to see Freddie take down the cow. He almost wished he hadn't...

As it reached the fleeing cow, Freddie suddenly leaped into the air, vaulting the last few yards with its hindlegs stretched forward. The cow bellowed as Freddie's sharp, curved talons ripped into the soft hide along its belly and ribs; hot red blood jetted from its side as the disemboweled animal, its stomach muscles sliced open, toppled to the ground. Its death scream, hoarse and terrified, was cut short as Freddie's jaws closed around its neck and wrenched upwards to rip the cow's head from its neck. In a swift movement, the dinosaur hurled the head aside, an unwanted bloody morsel which landed near the base of the platform.

"Oh! It's a dunk shot for Fred!" Andy yelled.

"Sign the kid up for the Lakers," Jack replied, shaking his head. "Damn."

"Oh, my God," Chambliss whispered. He had been watching everything through his field glasses; the binoculars fell from his hand and dangled against his chest. The senator was pale; his hand was covering his mouth. Steinberg himself forced down the urge to puke. Like Nixon, he looked away. Gerhardt continued to watch, but even he seemed to be fighting down revulsion.

Cooper seemed unmoved. "Okay, ladies and gentlemen, that's a wrap," he said. As Jason and Michael moved in to wait their turns at the carcass, the researchers began unloading cartridges and discs from the recorders, jotting down notes on their pads, talking quietly among themselves. Steinberg watched Jack pull his wallet from his back pocket and hand a dollar bill to Andy; some sort of continuing wager was being settled for the day. Denny was sure that they had seen this kind of butchery dozens of times in past several months, yet he doubted that he himself could ever get used to it.

The project leader turned to Pete Chambliss. "Well, Senator, now you've gotten a taste of what we do out here," he said, once more assuming the aloof demeanor of a professional scientist. "Any questions?"

"No...no, not right now," Chambliss said quietly. The senator seemed to be recovering his poise, but Steinberg had never seen his boss more at a loss for words. Chambliss glanced over his shoulder at Steinberg and Gerhardt. "I think we'll be wanting to return to the base camp now, if you don't mind," he added stiffly. "We need to get ready for our trip tomorrow."

Cooper nodded. "Certainly. Tiffany will escort you back. I'll be seeing you around suppertime, all right?"

The three of them nodded their heads. Tiffany, still not looking at the grisly scene in the prairie, stepped past them to lead the way to the boardwalk steps. Denny fell into step behind Chambliss and Gerhardt—then stopped, feeling an eerie prickly sensation at his neck, as if someone were watching him.

He gazed back at the researchers. All were busy packing their gear, talking to each other, making notes. But beyond them, on the blood-drenched killing ground a hundred yards away at the edge of the safety zone, one of the dinosaurs was watching them leave. Jason's opaque black eyes were focused on the platform.

Denny took another few steps towards the stairway. Jason's huge head shifted to follow his progress. All at once, Steinberg realized that the deinonychus was watching him...

Watching him. Wondering how his blood tasted.

2. Off to See the Lizard

It was light that awoke him this time, a bright shaft of sunlight which hit his eyes as the passenger door of the Osprey was opened. When he awoke this time, he was lying on a stretcher which rested on the floor between the passenger seats. Someone—an older man with a balding forehead and wire-rim glasses—was holding his head steady between his hands, murmuring for him not to move, that he was suffering from a concussion. But he did move his head, just a little, and when he did he saw Tiffany being helped into the aircraft.

She was muddy and soaked; below her shorts her legs were torn with cuts and her hair was matted with dirt. She looked at him with astonishment as she was guided into a seat just in front of him. "Denny," she breathed. "You got out...thank God, you got out of there..."

He wanted to say something of the same kind, but instead his eyes drifted from her face to her waist. She was still wearing a gronker on her belt, a yellow plastic box just like his own...

His right hand moved, almost involuntarily, to his own belt, and there it was, the inhibitor which should have protected him, yet didn't. A vague memory stirred in his mind; he bent his neck a little to look down at the unit clasped within his hand. The red status light was still on. He wasn't looking for that. Something on the edge of his memory...

He turned the little box over in his hand. There, on the side of the case: a strip of white tape, marked with a name: NIXON.

"Don't move your head," the man sitting above him said soothingly. "Just take it easy. We'll get you back in a few minutes."

Someone shut the passenger door and told the pilot to take it up again. The Osprey's engines picked up speed; there was a weightless bobbing sensation as the VTOL began to ascend. He lay his head back down, feeling the darkness beginning to come once again—but an unformed thought nagged at him through the fog and the pain. His eyes wandered to Tiffany Nixon.

Someone else was peering at the cuts on her legs, but he could see over his shoulder the gronker on her belt. "Here, move a little to your left," she was told. She put her weight on her left thigh and moved so that a deep cut above her knee could be examined, and when she did, Denny saw the white strip of tape on her unit.

STEINBERG. Isn't that weird? She's got my gronker. I've got hers. STEINBERG...NIXON...STEINBERG...NIXON...

"Don't worry," he croaked. "They all work the same."

Tiffany looked down at him then. Her eyes moved first to his gronker, then to her own. Their eyes met and in that briefest of instants just before he passed out again, he realized what had happened down there...

From the testimony of Marie Weir; President, WTE Cybernetics Corp.

SEN. ANTHONY HOFFMANN, D-CA: As you're aware, the Commission would like to know of the details of the reflex inhibitors WTE designed for the project...that is, the so-called gronkers...

WEIR: Yes, Senator, I understand the importance of this Commission knowing these things. But on advice of our legal counsel, however, I need to inform you that this is proprietary information which, if made public, could be of great benefit to our competitors, so WTE's stance is that we're reluctant to divulge the...

KAPLAN: Ms. Weir, I appreciate your reluctance, but you have to remember that you're under federal subpoena to testify to this Commission. Failure to relinquish information which the Commission deems as useful for its investigation could be punishable by you and your company being cited for contempt.

WEIR: My attorney informs me that we can give you general information about our product in this hearing and divulge further information in executive session. I believe this is a fair compromise.

KAPLAN: The chair recognizes Senator Hoffmann.

SEN. HOFFMANN: Ma'am, the only compromise I'm interested in hearing about is whether the inhibitors you built could have compromised the lives of my late colleague and his party. If we have to put you under arrest to get that information, I'll gladly second the motion.

WEIR: Senator, I resent what you're implying. The inhibitors we built for the project were designed according to the University of Colorado research team's own specifications, no more and no less. They were subjected to rigorous field-testing before they were put into actual use, and once they were in operation we monitored their progress. Up until the incident of question, no failures were reported of our equipment. Not one. If you're searching for a smoking gun, I suggest you look elsewhere.

SEN. HOFFMANN: I've studied the report which WTE submitted to the Committee and on the face of it, at least, I have to agree. Under normal circumstances the inhibitors did perform according to the desired standard. I have no wish to start a fight with you on this point. The main question which I have, if your attorney doesn't mind, is whether the gronkers could have been tampered with in such a way to cause their failure.

WEIR: My attorney advises me...

SEN. HOFFMANN: The heck with your attorney, Ms. Weir. Just answer a simple damn question for me. Could have the inhibitors been sabotaged in advance? Yes or no?

WEIR: Yes. It's feasible that tampering could have occurred. The inhibitors can be opened with a set of precision screwdrivers.

SEN. HOFFMANN: Fine. I'm glad we're making progress here. Your attorney seems to be fidgeting, Ms. Weir. If he needs to visit the men's room, I think you can let him go now. I believe we can get some straight answers without his advice...

There had been three of them: a small pack although maybe much larger once, since the others had been killed by larger predators or simply died from disease or old age. They had been hunting together in a deep valley in a place which, one day, would be known as almost mythically as Asiamerica. It was twilight when the rainstorm had begun, but they were still hungry and there was still plenty of prey to be caught before the light vanished from the world. Perhaps they were in pursuit of a larger dinosaur like a lumbering tenontosaurus. Perhaps they had simply become lost on the way back to their den.

Whatever the reason, they had been caught unaware by the flash flood which had suddenly ripped down the valley. The rushing wall of water was on them before they could escape; the walls of the valley were too steep for them to climb, the current too fast for them to swim. Howling their anger at the dark sky, they were torn by branches and battered by stones. In their dying panic, they had clawed and bitten at each other. Finally, one by one, their heads went under the surface for the last time. Their lungs filled with cold water, the fire perished from their eyes, and they died.

Died, and were reborn almost seventy million years later, recalled to life in a sterile white lab by the descendents of the little rodent-like creatures they had once hunted...

Pete Chambliss's chair scooted back from the folding table where he had been working, interrupting Denny's reverie. He looked up as the senator picked up his empty beer can. "I'm going in for another one," Chambliss said. "Ready for another round?"

"Umm...no thanks, Pete. Still working on this one." He nodded toward the laptop computer on the folding table. "Did you remember to save?"

Chambliss glanced back at his temporary desk, made a self-disgusted grunt, and stepped back across the porch to type a command on the Toshiba's keyboard. Chambliss took the minicomputer with him on all his trips—tonight he was working on a speech for a National Press Club luncheon next week—but he was forever forgetting to save files in memory when he was working on computers. It was one of the little jobs of his aides to foresee this absentminded quirk. "Thanks," Chambliss said.

He walked across the porch and opened the screen door, then quickly stepped aside as Gerhardt came out. " 'Scuse me," the senator said as the two men sidestepped each other, then Gerhardt let the door slam shut behind Chambliss. Steinberg fixed his eyes on the darkness beyond the porch as he listened to Gerhardt walk onto the porch, pause, then slowly walk behind him. He heard the rocking chair beside him creak as the Secret Service man settled into it. Then, suddenly, a cold can of Budweiser was dropped in his lap.

Gerhardt laughed as Steinberg started, then popped the top on his own can. "Might as well enjoy yourself," he said. "Tomorrow night we're down to noodles and instant coffee." He took a long tug from his beer and indulged in a resonant belch. "God, I just love the great outdoors," he added sourly, propping his feet up on the rail.

Steinberg picked the can out of his lap and set it down on the floor next to his warm, half-empty beer. "I thought you guys were trained to endure hardship."

"Yeah," Gerhardt replied indifferently. "But I spent two years in the Marines lugging a gun across Central America. Every night down there I sacked out in some rainstorm promising myself that, if

I survived this shit, the nearest I would get to wilderness would be mowing the back yard on Sunday." He toasted the night with his beer. "And so what do I do? I join the Secret Service so I can escort some senator on a canoe trip through the Okefenokee. Same job, different swamp. Talk about justice, huh?"

"Maybe you should have been a lawn mower salesman."

"Maybe." Gerhardt took another long sip from his beer. "What's your problem, kid? Still upset because I made you carry the luggage this afternoon?"

"No." He took a deep breath. "I'm just upset because I'm stuck for a weekend with a raving asshole like you."

Gerhardt sighed and shook his head. "Jeez. Try to be nice, and look where it gets you." He looked straight at Steinberg. "Well, if it's any consolation," he said in a lowered voice, "I'd rather be somewhere else than with a brown-nosing little yuppie. I'm here because it's my work and you're here because you want to score points with the boss. Okay?"

Steinberg said nothing, but he felt his face grow hot. Like it or not, Gerhardt had scored a bull's-eye with that remark. He was saved from having to formulate a weak comeback by the screen door opening again and Chambliss swaggering out onto the porch. He held a beer in his right hand and his backpack was slung over his left shoulder. Just behind him was Tiffany Nixon, also carrying a backpack. "Let's go load the canoes, boys," the senator said heartily. "If we do that now, we can shove off a little earlier in the morning."

"Sounds like a right idea." Gerhardt drained his beer, crushed the empty can in his fist, and dropped his feet to the floor. Chambliss tromped across the porch and hopped down the steps. Tiffany threw Denny a quick smile as he stood up to follow, then Gerhardt grabbed his bicep and tugged him toward the stairs. "What's the matter, kid?" he murmured. "'Fraid you might get mud on those expensive designer boots of yours?"

"Fuck off." Steinberg twisted his arm out of Gerhardt's hand, then walked in front of him. Now more than ever, he wished he hadn't volunteered for Pete's spring vacation trip. But then he glanced at Tiffany Nixon's backside as she walked alongside the senator down to the dock and reconsidered. Maybe a little sweet seduction in the swamp would make it all worthwhile. After all, somebody had to share a tent with her tomorrow night, and since Gerhardt himself admitted that he had a job to do...

223

From far away, somewhere out in the moonless dark of the Okefenokee, there came a sound: a grruuuunngg from a reptilian throat older than time. Denny stopped on the porch steps as it faintly echoed across the wetlands, feeling an unseasonal chill. On the other hand, he thought, tomorrow night I may want to be sleeping with Gerhardt's MAC-10 instead.

✳ ✳ ✳

From the testimony of Harlan Lloyd Castle; superintendent, Okefenokee National Wildlife Refuge.

KAPLAN: Mr. Castle, can you tell us a little about the permanent staff of the wildlife refuge? That is, who works there and what do they do?

CASTLE: Well, sir, since the refuge was turned over to the University of Colorado team for their research, the staff was necessarily reduced in number, since we didn't have to maintain the campgrounds and visitors' center and so forth. In fact, we had to let go of most of our resident staff to make way for the team, so...

KAPLAN: Pardon me, sir. Your resident staff? What do you mean by that?

CASTLE: Those employees who stayed in the refuge on a full-time basis...the ones who lived there year-round. I was able to keep my own residence, of course, and our naturalist Ms. Nixon was able to keep her cabin, but our two full-time rangers and the chief groundskeeper were let go. Fortunately the Interior Department found them other positions within the national park system.

KAPLAN: So there was only Ms. Nixon and yourself living in the park besides the university team. Then who did the maintenance work? Mopping the floors, scrubbing the toilets, cooking for the research staff and so forth?

CASTLE: Well, the science team was responsible for its own cooking. When the changeover occurred, I told Mr. Yamato (*NOTE: Benjamin Yamato, Secretary of the Interior*) that I would be happy to have them in the refuge, but I'd be darned if I'd supply them with a concierge. (*Laughter*) Was that funny? Well at any rate, as for the day-to-day maintenance work, we had a number of part-time people who came in each day to do the groundskeeping and cleaning duties. And before you ask, they were brought in each day on the same aircraft which transported the...ah, livestock for the dinosaur herd.

KAPLAN: I see. And these part-timers...were they official employees of the refuge?

CASTLE: If you mean to ask if they were on the payroll, yes, but I wouldn't characterize them as civil service employees. Since it was rather menial work and part-time at that, we hired whoever we could find in the area who was willing to come in for four hours a day. Typically, we had high school kids, housecleaning staff from nearby motels, locals who wanted to moonlight for a few extra dollars a week...that sort of thing. Again, since we were no longer open to the public, we didn't need to have folks who had passed civil service examinations...just people who knew how to handle a broom or a toilet brush and who didn't get airsick when they flew in.

KAPLAN: I see. And was there much turnover for these jobs?

CASTLE: Typically, yes, sir, there was. People quit on us all the time. It was dirty work and it didn't pay all that well...in fact the Burger King in Folkston paid better wages than we did...so we hired who we could get. That's why it wasn't civil service work. There was so much paperwork involved with getting civil service employees that we managed to get an exemption from the Interior Department for these positions.

KAPLAN: Uh-huh. And did these part-timers have access to all the buildings? Including the storage closet in the main building where the reflex inhibitors were kept?

CASTLE: Out of necessity, yes, sir, Mr. Kaplan. Of course, the key rings were given to them when they clocked in at the beginning of the day and they turned them back in when they punched out on the time clock. But...ah, yes, they had access to all unrestricted areas of the main compound.

KAPLAN: And that includes the storage closet in the main building?

CASTLE: Yes, sir. There were some cleaning supplies which were kept in that closet, so necessarily they had to...

KAPLAN: I understand. One further question, Mr. Castle, and this goes back to what I was asking you about earlier. Just prior to Senator Chambliss's visit to the refuge, did you hire any new part-timers?

CASTLE: Ummm...why, yes. One of our cleaning staff, Mary Ann Shorter, suffered a collision with a hit-and-run driver on the highway. She was laid up in the hospital with neck and back injuries, so we had to find a new person to temporarily take her place. A young guy named Jake...um, Jacob Adderholt. He answered an ad we had placed in the Folkston newspaper and we hired him. As I recall, that was about a week before the senator came to the refuge.

KAPLAN: And did Mr. Adderholt come to work on the day that Senator Chambliss and his party arrive?

CASTLE: Yes, he did. In fact, he went out with the rest of the part-time staff on the same Osprey that...oh, good Lord, Mr. Kaplan, you're not implying...?

KAPLAN: Mr. Castle, did Jake Adderholt reappear for work at the park following Senator Chambliss's death?

CASTLE: Oh, my God...

KAPLAN: Mr. Castle, please, did Jake Adderholt come back to work after...?

CASTLE: No, he didn't, he...oh, my sweet Lord, how could have I known...?

His oar dipped again into the dark water. He pulled it straight back to his shoulder, raised it again and absently watched the cool water dribble off the end of the blade, then plunged it forward again into the river. The canal ran straight as a two-lane highway through the low, monotonous swampland; dredged by an industrial explorer in the 1890s in an attempt to form an intracoastal waterway before nature and lack of funds conquered his efforts, the Suwannee Canal was a liquid path through the Okefenokee. Further downstream it entered the deep bayou of the swamp, a long maze, before it ended at a manmade sill and the mouth of the Suwannee River. But that was a long way from here; they had only travelled the first five miles of the canal, and Denny was already tired.

He pulled the oar out of the water, rested across the gunnels behind the pointed bow of the Mad River canoe, tipped back his cap and wiped a thin sheen of sweat from his forehead. The early morning fog had long since been burned off by the rising sun; it was close to noon now and the day was getting warmer. An otter had been racing in front of them for a mile or so, occasionally sticking its furry brown head above the water to look back at them as if to say "Nyah nyah nyah, you slowpoke humans" before diving and racing forward again. The little animal had apparently lost interest in them, though, because Denny hadn't spotted him in the past half-hour.

"Out of shape?" Tiffany asked and he looked back over his shoulder at her. She was in the stern seat behind him; he watched as she effortlessly made a J-stroke to keep them in the middle of the narrow canal. "How long has it been since you paddled a canoe?"

"Longer than I care to remember," he admitted. About thirty feet behind them, the second canoe was moving down the river. Joe Gerhardt was doing the muscle work in the bow seat while Pete Chambliss steered from the stern. They had fallen behind because the senator had been constantly pausing to scan the area with his binoculars or to take snapshots of cranes, vultures, otters, and gators. If the Secret Service man had minded, though, he hadn't said anything; like Denny, he had taken off his jacket when the day had become hotter, and now they could all see the Ingram gun slung in the oversized holster under his left armpit. There was also a headset radio slung around his neck; every now and then he had paused to report in, radioing a status report to the compound.

"Catch your breath," Tiffany said. "We'll wait for 'em to catch up." She pulled up her own oar and lay it across the gunnels, then checked her wristwatch. "We'll be stopping on a little island just up ahead, so you'll get a chance to take a breather."

Denny shifted his butt on the lifejacket; they had long since taken them off and placed them on the hard metal seats. "Lunch?"

"Maybe," she said tersely. She was staring off across the grasslands to their right. Tiffany had been laconic all morning. When they had pushed off from the compound just after sunrise, she had done little more than to make sure everyone's gronker was switched on. Even though the temperature had continued to rise and all the men had stripped down to their undershirts, she hadn't pulled off her own shirt—which was too bad, since Denny would have liked to see what she looked like wearing only shorts and a tank-top. Their itinerary called for them to make camp on Bugaboo Island tonight— who the hell had come up with that name?—then to forge their way through the deep swamp tomorrow until they reached the end of the refuge and, just beyond that, Stephen C. Foster State Park, where they would be pulling out of the river for good.

If Denny still hoped to have an amorous adventure with her, it would have to be tonight on Bugaboo Island. Yet, somehow, he was beginning to have his doubts. Tiffany seemed aloof today; her refusal to take off her shirt was a bad omen. Maybe she had come to realize that she was one woman about to spend the night with three men and didn't want to do anything which would seem like a come-on to any of them. But he watched her check her watch again and wondered what sort of schedule she was trying to keep...

The second canoe was almost abreast of their own when Pete looked through his binoculars to his right and suddenly pointed. "Over there!" he whispered urgently. "There's the pack!"

Denny looked around. At first he didn't see them...then he did, and he involuntarily sucked in his breath. The three long necks of Jason, Freddie and Michael rose above the high yellow grass, about two hundred yards away. It didn't seem as if they had seen the canoeists as they slowly moved across the floating prairie. As Bernie Cooper had pointed out earlier, the dinosaurs seemed to have learned not to stick too closely together lest their combined weight cause them to sink through the peat moss. It was almost a pastoral scene: the bright clear sky, the noonday noon, the high grass wafting in the soft breeze, the distant figures of the dinosaurs. Like a landscape painted by an insane Winslow Homer.

As he watched, one of the deinonychi—Freddie, he reckoned, since it was in the lead—suddenly darted forward, its head snapping downward into the grass. A moment later Freddie reared up again, this time with a small animal caught in its jaws; a racoon maybe, or perhaps an otter which had not moved fast enough. Freddie's head arced back and they heard the wet leathery snap of its teeth as the unlucky creature was eaten alive. Then the dinosaur kept moving as Michael and Jason caught up with him, their heads slowly swiveling back and forth in search of more prey. The boys were out for a midday stroll. Don't mind us. Just looking for an appetizer or two before we go have a steer for lunch...

Denny was distracted by the sudden bump of the bow prodding against the shoreline; while he had been watching the pack, Tiffany had slowly paddled them to the shore. "Get out and pull us up," she said softly, pulling up her oar and carefully laying it in the canoe.

His eyes widened. "Are you kidding?" he protested. "The pack's right over there!"

"Get out and pull us up, Denny," she repeated. The scornful look in her eyes told him that she wasn't joking, and as the second canoe nosed into the shoreline next to them, Pete Chambliss was already loading a fresh disc into his Nikon. Joe Gerhardt half-stood in the bow, quickly scrambled forward with his hands on the gunnels to keep the canoe steady, and clambered off the front of the canoe onto the ground. He shot a look at Denny which relayed an unspoken admonition: "Kid, I'm not going to shepherd your camera-happy boss all by myself. Get moving."

"I hope you do know how to use that thing," Denny muttered back, meaning Gerhardt's MAC-10. Gerhardt said nothing, but fitted the radio over his head again and murmured something into the mike. Denny laid down his own paddle and carefully stood up to crawl out of the canoe. He managed to get out without tipping the canoe, then he grabbed the prow and hauled the front of the canoe onto the ground.

As Nixon began to crawl across the lashed-down camping gear in the middle of the canoe, Denny tentatively stood a few steps forward. The mossy ground squished and rolled under his feet as if he were walking on a feather mattress; it was no wonder that it was called trembling earth. Watching his feet, he took another few steps, then his right boot abruptly sank to his calf in the ground as it found a weak spot in the peat moss. He swore and pitched forward, throwing out his hands to catch himself; the sharp, serrated edges of some weeds cut against his palms, making him cuss and flounder some more before Tiffany grabbed him by the shoulders and hauled him erect.

"Cut it out, willya?" she hissed in his ear. "Test the ground with your foot before you put your weight on it...and keep your voice down."

"Not that it matters," Gerhardt said in a slightly louder voice. "They've spotted us."

Denny looked up again and felt his heart freeze. The pack had stopped moving and now they had each looked around, straight in their direction. As he watched, Freddie began to slowly move towards them, followed on either side by Michael and Jason. Triangle formation, just as Andy the researcher from Team Colorado had said yesterday.

"This is a really stupid idea," he said to no one in particular. "Let's get back in the canoes."

But Pete Chambliss was really stepping past him and Tiffany, holding his camera between his hands as he negotiated his way through the tall grass. Joe Gerhardt moved to his side, pulling the MAC-10 from his shoulder holster and cradling it in his hands. "It's all right," Tiffany said. "The gronkers will keep them at bay. Don't worry about them. Just try to relax."

"Sure. Right." Tiffany was already walking away, following the senator and the Secret Service escort. Steinberg looked back once at the canoes—an office in the White House couldn't be worth this crazy shit—but then he took a deep breath which did little to steady his nerves and stepped into the path made by the naturalist, as the four of them slowly approached the pack.

Five feet away from the canoes, ten feet, twenty...the three dinosaurs were still moving toward them, and although they seemed to be keeping their own distance, the gap between them had shrunk to only a few hundred feet. They gradually moved through the high grass like reptilian emissaries from a distant time. It was not at all like yesterday, when they had been separated from the pack by the tall platform and the security fence. This was to be a face-to-face encounter, and Denny was all too aware that Freddie was his own height; just tall enough to snap out and tear his head off. They were man-sized, but their relative lack of stature was not deceptive. These were not men, or even alien lizard-men out of some Hollywood space opera. They were born killers; in their own epoch, they had ganged-up on dinosaurs four times their size and ripped them to shreds.

But they'll stay back, he reminded himself. Tiffany's right. That's what the gronkers are for. Team Colorado's gotten closer than this without any problems. Don't worry about it. Yet he found that his feet refused to move any further, that he couldn't look away from the pack as it moved closer, closer...Transfixed despite himself by their awful beauty, he barely noticed that Tiffany had paused to let him pass her.

Five feet, ten feet, twenty... The three dinosaurs were still moving toward them, and although they seemed to be keeping their own distance, the gap between them had shrunk to only a few hundred feet. They gradually moved through the high grass like reptilian emissaries from a distant time, towering against a distant line of cyprus and pine.

Ahead of him, he heard the click and whirr of Pete's camera as the senator stopped to shoot more pictures. "Absolutely incredible," Chambliss said softly. "Just wonderful. It's like they're just posing for..."

Then, all at once, the pack charged.

3. The Smoking Gun

When he awoke again, it was to cool, crisp sheets against his naked skin, to the acrid smell of antiseptics mixed with the foreign yet unmistakable odor of dead flesh, to muffled voices and a strange pat-pat-pat of some liquid dripping onto a tiled floor.

"Oh, Christ, there's not much left."

"Do the best you can." He vaguely recognized Bernie Cooper's voice. "When the feds get here they'll want everything in situ that they can get for their..."

"Feds? Secret Service? Jesus, Bernie!"

"Secret Service, FBI, Interior, probably the Army and Navy and Air Force too for all I know...I've just been told to keep everyone in the refuge and let nobody leave. It can't be helped, Bob. The shit's hit the fan."

He opened his eyes to harsh fluorescent lights reflecting off formica and stainless steel. The light hurt his eyes and his head felt as if it were encased in taffy-soft cinderblocks; it was hard to think, but he gradually perceived that he was in the compound's clinic. Soft pressure across his forehead and the white edge of gauze just above his brow told him that his head had been treated as well. He moved his head to the right and saw that a screen had been moved into place across one half of the room; the voices came from the other side of the screen.

"If they want us to leave everything alone until they get here, then why are we...?"

"Because I don't want us to look entirely incompetent, that's why. It's going to be bad enough as it is without...look, I know they're in bad shape, but I want at least a preliminary autopsy performed before they get here, so just..."

"I can't do that, Bernie. You know I can't. I could lose my license." A slow intake of breath. The sound of a sheet being pulled back again. "God damn, just look at him. This is one fucking mess we're in. Did we get everything from the site?"

"Everything. Their personal effects are over there...the survivors, too, and we're not to touch them under any conditions. Especially not the gronkers, although we could only find the one belonging to the Secret Service guy."

"Where's the...no, don't tell me. I'd rather not know."

The slow pattering continued, just under the sound of the voices. He looked down, peering beneath the bottom of the screen. He could see two pairs of shoes on either side of the wheels of a gurney. Blood was pooled at their feet, seeping into the cracks of the white-and-tan tiled floor, dripping from the tabletop above.

"What about the other two? Nixon and...aw, what's his name, the senator's flunky?"

"Shaddup. He's right over there. They made it out okay. I thought the kid had a concussion, but it was just a bad cut and shock. She had to be stitched up some but otherwise she's fine. I saw her out in the corridor just a few minutes ago."

Tiffany. He had to tell someone what was going on. He opened his mouth to speak, but all he could manage was a dry, inaudible rasp. As he swallowed, trying to get his voice to work again, he heard the sound of a sheet being pulled forward again.

"Let's get out of here. I haven't seen anything like this since I interned in an emergency room. Where is everyone, anyway?"

"Down at the dock. We managed to get Freddie's body out of there before the animals got to it. I didn't want it on the landing pad, so that's the only place we can examine it."

"More attention being paid to that damn lizard than..."

He heard them walk across the room, then the sound of a door opening and swinging shut. Tiffany. He turned his head again, saw another gurney parked next to his own, but the covers were pushed aside and there was a warm dent in the sheets where she had once lain. She was gone...but he had little doubt that she would return. He had seen the look on her face in the Osprey.

He had to get up. Get up, get dressed, go tell someone what he knew before she came for him. Denny sat up, swung his legs over the side of the bed, and stumbled to the sink across the room. He cupped some water in his mouth and swallowed gratefully; his throat was no longer quite so parched, his head a little clearer. He was naked; second order of business to get on some clothes. Didn't the doctor say that his stuff was over there?

He walked across the cold floor to push aside the screen. Two bodies lay side-by-side on adjacent gurneys. He fought back the urge to vomit and was thankful for the sheets that covered them; he could tell that not much was left of either corpse.

There were four large plastic boxes on the counter under the medical cabinets; in them was the clothing he had worn, plus those belonging to the others. As he pawed through one of the boxes, groggily searching for his undershorts, he found the gronker he had been wearing. The one marked NIXON; he picked it up, stared bleerily at it, then placed it on the counter and reached into another box. Here, the one Tiffany had worn, marked STEINBERG. Good; he would need to show them to Cooper and the others to convince them of his story.

He placed her gronker back on top of her clothes, then returned his attention to his own clothing. He was about to step into his trousers when he heard the curtain slide back behind him. Denny began to turn around when the hard muzzle of a .22 Berreta was pressed against the side of his head and he heard Tiffany Nixon whisper, "Don't move."

He gasped involuntarily, but froze in place. "Tiffany," he murmured, not daring to even look back at her. "Figured you might be..."

"Shut up," she hissed. "Just get dressed."

The barrel of the revolver was removed from his skull and he heard her step away. He glanced across the counter, looking for something nice and lethal to throw at her. "Don't even think about it," Tiffany commanded, her voice raised a little more loudly now. "The building's empty, so no one will hear if I shoot you in the back. Just hurry up and get dressed. We're going for a little walk in the swamp, you and I."

Denny slowly nodded his head. He didn't turn around, but he heard a creak as she bumped against one of the gurneys. As he pulled up his pants, though, he happened to look at the reflective glass of the medical cabinets above the counter and found that he could see her clearly. Tiffany was still behind him, with the gun trained at his back, but with her free hand she had pried open the blinds of the far window and was peering out, undoubtedly watching the people who were gathered around the corpse of the dinosaur by the boat docks. Going for a walk in the swamp. Denny knew exactly what she was implying. "Tiffany," he continued, "you don't want to..."

Her face moved away from the window, and he quickly looked away from the medical cabinet. "I'm not kidding, Steinberg. Shut up and put your clothes on." Then she was looking out the window again. "And hurry up."

"Okay, all right." He slowly let out his breath as he zipped his fly. No way out of this. Christ, pal, she's got you dead in her sights. He reached for his shirt, and as he did he glanced down at the counter...and spotted the two gronkers he had just found.

Or was there a way out? Holding his breath, studying her reflection in the medical cabinet, Steinberg carefully reached for the gronker with his name written on it.

From the testimony of Alex J. Cardona; Director of Forensic Sciences, Federal Bureau of Investigation.

SEN. HOFFMANN: Mr. Cardona, I think I speak for the rest of the Commission members when I say that we appreciate the hard work the Bureau has done in this case. For the public record, can you summarize the findings of your lab?

CARDONA: Certainly, Senator. We...

KAPLAN: Excuse me, Mr. Cardona. I believe Dr. Williams has an important question to ask first before you go on. Fred?

DR. WILLIAMS: Mr. Cardona, the senator from California does not speak for us all, I'm sad to say. I've read your draft report to the Commission and I'm dissatisfied with one of your key findings. There is an unanswered question which interests every American.

CARDONA: I'm sorry to hear that, sir. How may I answer your question?

DR. WILLIAMS: Let me backtrack briefly, so bear with me. According to your draft report, the deaths of Senator Chambliss and his Secret Service escort were caused by tampering with the reflex inhibitors...the so-called gronkers...which they wore during the trip. It was found that someone...probably this Jacob Adderholt, if that was indeed his real name...had managed to substitute defective Intel 686 microchips into their units, ones which had been preconfigured to become inoperative at precisely 1200 hours on the day that the senator's party was scheduled to be in the refuge. It was because of the failure of the gronkers that the deinonychus pack was able to make the fatal attack on Senator Chambliss and Mr. Gerhardt...

CARDONA: That's correct, sir, although it should be pointed out that Mr. Gerhardt managed to open fire and fatally wound one of the pack before he was...

WILLIAMS: I understand, and Mr. Gerhardt will be receiving posthumous commendation for his bravery, but that's been pointed out before, so please don't distract me. Let me continue. Pending the outcome of the final investigation into Jake Adderholt's true identity, it can be safely assumed that he was a member of the New American Minutemen Enclave, considering that his fingerprints match that of a known NAME terrorist. At this point in your draft report, the FBI seems to imply that Adderholt was solely responsible for the deaths. Am I correct in inferring this from the report?

CARDONA: Sir, the FBI has not completed its investigation of the events in the Okefenokee National Wildlife Refuge. When it has done so, we will be issuing a final report which will clarify the findings of the draft report.

DR. WILLIAMS: Mr. Cardona, the director of the FBI has said that the final report will not be issued until at least a year from now. I'm losing patience with everyone involved in this investigation hedging their bets, and I think the public is, too. You found the smoking gun. What I want to know is, who pulled the trigger?

CARDONA: I beg your pardon, Dr. Williams, but it almost seems certain that Jake Adderholt was the person responsible for...

DR. WILLIAMS: I haven't made myself clear and I'm sorry for that. I'll rephrase it as a blunt question. Was Jake Adderholt acting alone, or did he have an accomplice? Was a second person directly involved in the assassination of Senator Petrie Chambliss? Specifically, was it an inside job?

CARDONA: I'm sorry, Dr. Williams, but the FBI isn't prepared to answer that question yet.

Denny stopped the Hummer at the end of the road and looked around over the rear of the vehicle. He could hear the distant aerial chop of a helicopter approaching; the noise grew louder until an olive drab Army Blackhawk helicopter abruptly soared over the treetops, heading for the compound behind them. He turned back around to see Tiffany Nixon climbing out of the front passenger seat, the gun in her hand still trained on him. "Looks like the feds have arrived," he said. "You know you're not going to get away with this, don't you?"

Tiffany winced in disgust. "Did you get that line from a James Bond movie or something?" She gently waved the gun toward the backpack in the back of the vehicle. "Sure I'm going to get anyway with it. Now pick it up and start walking. I'm going to be behind you...and don't even think about trying any 007 shit with me, okay? You've pissed me off enough already as it is."

He sighed as he carefully climbed out of the driver's seat and picked up the backpack—the same one, he noted, that she had in the canoe with them earlier in the day. "No need to knock James Bond, y'know," he grumbled as he put his right arm through the strap and tugged the pack over his shoulder like a rucksack. "Besides, I'm still curious...are you working for NAME, or is it someone else?"

"And you're expecting me to play Blofeld and spill the beans." Nixon was keeping her distance; even if he were stupid enough to try attacking her, she could still nail him before he made anything more than a dumb heroic attempt. "Just start walking. Right hand on the shoulder strap, left hand at your side. Now move."

Denny obediently began to march down the raised boardwalk, pushing aside the last gate and heading toward the observation tower in the Chessier Prairie where they had been only yesterday. He didn't have to look over his shoulder to know that Nixon was right behind him. She hadn't said much to him since she had captured him in the infirmary; once he had gotten dressed, she had escorted him out a back door of the lodge to the Hummer. No one had seen them leave the compound; even if the federal agents were looking for them now, it would still take a few minutes before they guessed that the two of them had gone this way—and even then, they might not immediately suspect foul play. As far as Denny knew, he was the only one who had seen through Tiffany Nixon's deception, that the killings of Pete Chambliss and Joe Gerhardt were not accidental.

He swatted aside some growth with his free hand as he strode down the boardwalk. Denny was surprised at how calm he felt, considering that he had little doubt that she intended to kill him. Would she shoot him, or maybe she was counting on the dinosaurs to do the work? Their gronkers were both switched on; she had taken the one she had found among his belongings in the infirmary, the one with STEINBERG written on the tape. If his suspicions had been correct, this fact was probably his only remaining hope for getting out of here alive...

"No, I'm not with NAME," she said suddenly.

"Excuse me?" He stopped and started to turn around, but Tiffany waved him forward again with the Beretta. "I thought you didn't want to talk to me."

"It's a long walk," she said tersely. "Might as well fill the time." The unspoken addendum was, "And since I plan to murder you anyway, what's the point in not letting you know?"

"But NAME is involved," Denny added, trying to keep his voice from shaking. "Am I right?"

A pause. "You're right," Tiffany said at last. "They sought me out because they needed a person on the inside...but I'm not with them. A bunch of fanatics, if you ask me."

"Uh-huh. I see." Keep her talking, he thought. The longer she talks, the less time she has to think...He remembered something she had said when they had first met yesterday. "Let me guess," he said, "You're doing this for all the gators and deer and rabbits in the..."

"Don't tempt me," she hissed angrily. Wrong words; he quickly shut up. They walked in silence for another few yards before she spoke again. "For the gators and the deer and the rabbits, right. They wanted Chambliss out of the way because he would negotiate away the nuclear deterrent if he became president, but that wasn't my objective. Having the pack kill Chambliss would help to ensure that the project would be ended. This ecosystem..."

She let out her breath; it came out as a nervous rattle. "The Okefenokee isn't meant to be a stomping ground for dinosaurs," she continued. "The Early Cretaceous should remain where it belongs, seventy million years dead and buried. No one should be trying to graft dinosaurs into this world. Nature can't cope with reincarnation, and if the pack survives the Okefenokee will die."

"But it's research," he argued, if only for the sake of arguing. "It's searching for answers, for..."

"For how many ways a new dominant species can destroy an ecological balance? Sorry, Denny, but I can't allow that to happen. I love this land too much. I've given up too much already to...don't stop, just keep walking."

"Hey, I love the balance of nature and all that," he babbled, "but this is kind of a drastic measure, don't you think?" She didn't reply. He licked his dry lips and forged on. "So you hoped that, if Pete were killed by a deinonychus, the public outcry would...?"

"Cancel the project," Tiffany finished. "They'd exterminate the pack and leave the Okefenokee alone."

"So you fucked with the gronkers to..."

"Not me," she said defensively. "There was another person involved who did that. Look, we're far enough along already, so I'll make it short and give you the rest. They told me that they wanted at least one survivor, someone who could go back and tell a story that would make it look like an accident. I was told that only my gronker would work when the time came, but the more I thought about it later, the more it figured that they were lying. After all, I was the only one who could incriminate NAME. It made sense that you would survive and that I had to die. I wasn't ready to make that sort of sacrifice, if you know what I mean."

They had reached the end of the boardwalk now. The platform was only fifty feet away, abandoned of personnel; the vast clearing of the prairie was spread out before them. "Stop here and put down the backpack," she said.

The gate to the enclosure around the platform was locked; he could tell that just by looking, but off in the distance there was something far more unsettling. Denny could see two now-familiar shapes moving in the distance. Jason and Michael, the surviving members of the pack.

"Hurry it up," Tiffany said. She must have spotted Michael and Jason as well. "Get the pack off, Denny."

He unshouldered the North Face pack and carefully lay it down on the boardwalk in front of him. "So you made sure our gronkers were switched," he said. "In fact, you did it yourself, to be certain I had the defective one and you had..."

"Right," she interrupted. "You can turn around now. Step over the pack first." Denny stepped over the backpack, then turned around to face her. He absently noticed that her hair was unbraided; the wind blew it around her shoulders and face, which now looked older for some reason. She was not a woman. he decided, who was accustomed to murder. "You got it," she continued. "The problem was, you managed to make it back to the canoe, and Michael and Jason can't swim. The minute I saw you in the Osprey, I knew I was screwed..."

"In a manner of speaking," he impulsively replied.

Tiffany smiled despite herself. "Yes, but not by you, my dear." Still keeping her eyes and the Beretta aimed at him, she quickly knelt to pick up the backpack. "I don't like doing this, y'know, but of all the guys on the trip you're the one I personally wanted to see become Dino Chow. I hate it when guys stare at me the way you did." She hoisted the pack and ducked her left arm into the strap. "And I really despise yuppies."

"But you like gators." Forced humor; the final weapon of the doomed. How many yards were they behind them now?

"They're better company than assholes like you." From not so far behind him, he could hear heavy footfalls across the floating marshland. Jason and Michael, the glimmer twins themselves, were coming in for the kill. Tiffany managed to shrug into the backpack without lowering the gun for more than a few moments. "Anyway, it's time to dust off the contingency plan," she went on. "I hike out of here and you get to be a late lunch. I'd shoot you first to put you out of your misery, but someone might dig the bullets out of your carcass and there's no sense in leaving behind any more evidence than I have to. Mikey and Jason are going to have to do the job for me. Sorry."

Denny wanted to make a smartass remark, but his mouth was too dry for him to speak. Tiffany backed up a couple of feet, still pointing the gun at him, then carefully stepped down from the boardwalk onto the mushy ground. The sound of the approaching dinosaurs was growing louder now. Denny could feel his pulse echoing in his ears like aboriginal drums. He glanced at her waist, saw the gronker with his name written on tape on its side, made himself look away. Don't guess, don't guess, please don't guess...

Tiffany was staring over his shoulder. "Gotta run," she said. "As they say in the movies, 'Goodbye, Mr. Bond'..." She stopped; for a moment there was a look of sympathy in her eyes. "I hope it's quick." Then she was off the boardwalk; turning around, she bolted for the treeline behind them, clumsily running across the trembling earth.

Denny glanced over his shoulder. The deinonychi were hurtling straight toward him; now they seemed to have grown, taking on the dimensions of the fabled tyrannosaurus rex. He saw cold, crazy eyes, dagger-jawed mouths agape and drooling ooze, powerful legs pummeling the peat moss ground like jackhammers, forelegs with razor-sharp claws outstretched to grab, tear—oh god oh god oh god what if I'm wrong—and threw himself flat onto the boardwalk, covering his head with his arms...

And howled with what he half-expected to be his last breath, "I SWITCHED THE GRONKERS!"

He kept his head down, even after Jason and Michael leaped across the far end of the boardwalk—completely ignoring him—and hurled themselves toward Tiffany. He shut his eyes and lay still as death even when he heard the futile low-caliber gunshots, her screams, the sound of ripping flesh...

From the testimony of Daniel Steinberg.

KAPLAN: In closing, Mr. Steinberg, I would like to extend the appreciation of this Commission for your cooperation. You've been most helpful in resolving some of the unanswered questions of this event.

STEINBERG: Yes, sir. Thank you, sir.

KAPLAN: We realize that you have personally suffered from your ordeal, both in terms of cost to your liberty and your reputation. I'm referring, of course, to the charges of second-degree murder which have been pressed against you by the federal circuit court in Georgia regarding the death of Tiffany Nixon. I cannot give you any guarantees, but I think your testimony here today may have some favorable bearing on your legal case. Frankly, considering the continuing FBI investigation of the matter, I would be rather surprised if the charges aren't dropped in their entirety. In fact, I expect that you will receive vindication for your role in this affair.

STEINBERG: I certainly hope so, sir, and I appreciate your support. Yet before I leave, may I make a final observation?

KAPLAN: Of course.

STEINBERG: I've noticed that, during these hearings, there has been some discussion of terminating the project...that, because the deinonychus pack caused the deaths of Pete Chambliss and Joe Gerhardt, the dinosaurs should be exterminated themselves. I believe this has also become a matter of public debate...

KAPLAN: We're aware that the public is interested in the fate of the dinosaurs. Since these hearings have started, this Commission has been deluged with letters defending their right to live, mainly from members of the scientific community and animal rights activists. On the other hand, I happened to catch a radio call-in talk show just last night in which the subject was addressed, and by a three-to-one margin the callers favored exterminating the pack...

STEINBERG: I caught that same discussion too, sir, but I'm not certain whether this is an issue which should be decided by the

Larry King Show. It makes about as much sense as the proposal to rename the refuge as the "Pete Chambliss Memorial Wetlands" (*Laughter*). I don't think Pete would have appreciated that...

KAPLAN: I tend to agree, Mr. Steinberg...

STEINBERG: The point is, Mr. Kaplan, that the dinosaurs were as much pawns in this...um, matter as I was. If the pack is exterminated and the research project is discontinued, then in the end Tiffany...that is, Ms. Nixon...would have succeeded in what she was trying to do. The Colorado project was begun in the name of scientific inquiry. It would be a waste to abandon it because someone tried to turn the dinosaurs into a murder weapon.

KAPLAN: But they did murder two men, Mr. Steinberg. Three people if you count Ms. Nixon. That's the undeniable fact.

STEINBERG: Only because killing is inherent to their nature. They can't help themselves...they came from a different world than ours. If the pack is exterminated and the project is discontinued, then the bitter irony is that Tiffany Nixon will have succeeded in the end. The dinosaurs will be lost to an act of terrorism.

KAPLAN: Mr. Steinberg, you may be correct. I can't fault your logic. Yet I'm afraid you're much too late in making your case for the dinosaurs.

STEINBERG: What?...I'm sorry, sir, but I don't understand what you're...

KAPLAN: This morning the Georgia state legislature decided that the two surviving members of the deinonychus pack should be treated the same way as wild or domesticated animals which have caused the death of a human being. We understand that...uh, Jason and Michael were both destroyed at nine o'clock this morning, about the time you began your testimony.

STEINBERG: I wasn't told...

KAPLAN: I'm sorry, Mr. Steinberg...and I believe Ms. McCaffrey would like to be recognized by the chair. Congresswoman?

McCAFFREY: I'm surprised by your last-minute plea for clemency for the dinosaurs, Mr. Steinberg. You witnessed the horrible deaths of Mr. Gerhardt and your friend and political mentor with your own eyes. If you had not turned the tables on Ms. Nixon, you would have met the same fate yourself. Perhaps you've had a change of mind in the meantime?

STEINBERG: Ummm...no, I don't think I've had a change of mind, Ms. McCaffrey. It's just that...well, I just don't believe science should be the victim of politics.

McCAFFREY: Mr. Steinberg, we'll have to forgive you for your innocence of youth. That is much too rash a statement. When has science ever been the victim of politics?

STEINBERG: Ma'am, I think you've got it wrong. The question should, when has science never been the victim of politics?

McCAFFREY: I see...Mr. Kaplan, I would like to make a motion for adjournment.

KAPLAN: The motion is seconded and passed. These hearings are adjourned until tomorrow.

About This Book

The display typeface is LiquidCrystal from the Corel font package; the text is Bembo, an Adobe Type Library Type One font. It was output on a Linotronic (L 330) printer at 1270 dpi by Spectrum Arts, Baltimore, Maryland. Princeton University Press, Princeton, New Jersey, prepared color separations and printed the interior pages on Springhill acid-free paper. Jesse Jones, Philadelphia, Pennsylvania, manufactured slipcases for the deluxe edition. It was prepared on a IBM 486sx using Aldus PageMaker 4.0 and CorelDraw 3.0 by John Boettinger-Lang, Medford, Massachusetts. David D. Leetham, Towson, Maryland, used WinFaxPro and Ami Pro for technical data conversions.